I0823289

HOW GIRLS ARE MADE

ALSO BY MINDY MCGINNIS

Under This Red Rock

A Long Stretch of Bad Days

The Initial Insult

The Last Laugh

Be Not Far from Me

Heroine

The Female of the Species

This Darkness Mine

A Madness So Discreet

Not a Drop to Drink

In a Handful of Dust

Given to the Sea

Given to the Earth

MINDY McGINNIS

HOW GIRLS ARE MADE

HARPER
An Imprint of HarperCollinsPublishers

HarperCollins Children's Books,
a division of HarperCollins Publishers,
195 Broadway, New York, NY 10007

HarperCollins Publishers,
Macken House, 39/40 Mayor Street Upper,
Dublin 1, D01 C9W8, Ireland

How Girls Are Made

harpercollins.com

Library of Congress Control Number: 2025936245
ISBN 978-0-06-337069-2
Typography by Laura Mock

25 26 27 28 29 LBC 5 4 3 2 1
First Edition

For Ashley, Holly, and Morgan—

Every night should be a girls' night.

AUTHOR'S NOTE

This book deals with topics many women of all ages struggle with in the modern world, including perfectionism, physical and emotional abuse, the profound negative impact of social media on mental health, and damaging societal beauty expectations, as well as sexual assault. If these subjects are difficult for you as a reader, please move forward with caution.

PART ONE

Spring begins with a funeral.

High heels sink into wet earth, dragging their owners closer to the dead. Men and boys scrape grass clippings from their dress shoes, flicking the remains into the light mist that has clung tightly to the small town for the past three days, leaving everything soggy. Headstones drip moisture, old names brought into stark relief.

The new one, freshly etched, leaks tears.

The air hangs heavy, grief weighing down tongues, the stillness of the cemetery settling on lips pulled sternly thin. Once the coffin is lowered, the spell will be broken, teeth and throats loosened. The clichés will come first—gone too soon; she's in a better place; God moves in mysterious ways. *Later, there will be real words.*

Later, there will be gossip cloaked in well-meaning questions.

Later, there will be long phone calls, searching for answers.

Later, there will be accusations and recriminations, waves of guilt, and surges of shame.

Later, someone will say—

You know what really happened, right?

CHAPTER ONE

Shelby

Up until last week, the only thing I'd ever lost was my virginity.

Then, I lost a fight, Ilsa Bunting dragging me to the mat and making me tap out for the first time in my career, a triangle choke sending black spots across my vision, chased by light, my brain losing blood, my carotid artery fluttering like a butterfly against her bicep.

Now, I've lost my shit and about a pint of blood, which is pouring out of my face, pooling onto the linoleum of the high school hallway. It's not the first time I've had a smashed nose, not the first time I've heard my own bones break, and certainly not the first time my blood has escaped my veins, flowing down my skin. I've been hit a hundred times by just as many people, taking my licks and delivering my own.

But I've never been punched by my boyfriend.

Rage wells up, a familiar burn that starts in my gut, a flash fire that gains oxygen when it hits my lungs, warms my muscles, and calls for me to get to my feet, face my opponent, hit back. But I'm not in the ring, and the person I'm fighting isn't a sparring partner—it's my actual partner, Jayden, the person who is supposed to cheer me on in fights, not throw his own punches. And it was a real one, a closed-fist roundhouse that has left me on my knees, clutching my face, blood seeping between my fingers.

I am stunned, a still animal, a wounded thing that cannot move. But my senses are flooding back, the ringing in my ears replaced by the shocked echo of my own thoughts, but in a male voice.

"What the fuck, man?"

The black edges of my vision recede, and Jayden hits the ground beside me, Rory Bledsoe on top of him, grinding his face into the floor. A forest of legs surrounds us, most of the senior class of Presnick High providing the backdrop for our breakup.

"Shelby, honey?" Cold hands tipped with a perfect French manicure grasp my shoulders. "Let's get you up. You need help."

Fallon Holloway has never touched me in her life, even though we've been through twelve years of public education together, in a class of sixty-five people. She's never touched me, and she's sure as hell never called me *honey*.

Actually, I'm pretty sure no one has.

I don't think anyone has ever told me I need help, either—because I don't. I'm Shelby fucking Black. I can deadlift three hundred pounds and leave boys twice my size dazed in the ring. My bedroom is decorated with championship belts and trophies depicting golden, plasticized girls frozen in fighting stances. What isn't in my room is the color pink, any hair ties that aren't black, or dresses—with the exception of one, in case of funerals.

And the next one I go to might be Jayden's, the way Rory is going after him.

I shrug Fallon away just as Mr. Wainwright breaks through the crowd, shoving aside bystanders. He pulls Rory off Jayden and screams at everyone to get to class, that the show is over.

But it's not. Phones are out; it's been captured from every angle and will likely be shared with the entire world in thirty seconds or less, each moment analyzed, every move dissected. My social media feed is about to blow up, my fans and followers are going to go after Jayden with pitchforks, and I'm going to have to sit down with my PR team to decide whether we're going to go with a fire-and-brimstone response, or wish Jayden the best, along with our thoughts and prayers and hopes that he gets the help he needs, while also condemning domestic violence in the strongest possible words.

That's what I'm thinking about as the crowd disperses, as I turn to Fallon to tell her to fuck off and never touch me again. I'm wearing my fighter face—grim, determined, stoic—when I lock eyes with Fallon, who isn't holding her phone, who has flecks of my blood sprayed across her cheeks.

Down the hall, a last, latent burst of anger erupts from Rory, as he slides out of Mr. Wainwright's grasp, punching a locker. Behind him, Jayden is being escorted by the freshman-math teacher, who has a paper towel in her hand but clearly can't decide if she should be seen tending to his wounds or not.

"Don't look at him," Fallon says, pulling an honest-to-God handkerchief out of her backpack. "Look at me." She dabs at my chin and lips, the sky-blue embroidery of her initials quickly overtaken by my blood.

"What happened?" Mrs. Dalford is a late arrival, her ignorance an invitation for Fallon to fill her in on the circus that was my former relationship and continue her climb on the ladder of adult approval. Instead, Fallon's attention remains on me.

"Let me see," Fallon says, pulling apart my lips, examining my teeth to make sure they're all still there, her voice calm and placating like the kindergarten teacher she'll probably become within the next five years.

"She's bleeding. You shouldn't be touching her," Mrs. Dalford says, no doubt imagining a river of STDs flowing from my body into Fallon's, infecting the student council president along with a dose of the testosterone that I'm always accused of using. Fallon's hands drop away from my face, automatically doing whatever an adult tells her.

"Run down to the office and call the squad," Dalford says to a sophomore who is standing nearby, staring at the blood pooled on the floor, a smear of someone's Asics pattern tracking through it.

"The squad?" I ask, hand going to my face. My nose is in the wrong place and oddly flat, the vision in my left eye fading as my eyelid swells shut.

"Oh . . . ," I say, suddenly realizing that I'm at school and not in the ring, surrounded by people who aren't used to flowing blood and smashed cartilage. Damage I've taken before, but never at the hands of someone whose bed I had been in, someone who had texted me just last night to tell me they loved me.

"Yeah, honey, the squad," Fallon says, putting both hands on my shoulders. Her eyes find mine—the one good one, anyway—and there must be something horrifying there, something that isn't my usual coldness and reserve, or the glimmer of a challenge. There must be something that's screaming to help me, to take care of me, to fix things and make them better, because Fallon Holloway defies a teacher and leans forward, her forehead touching mine. "You need medical attention."

I open my mouth to tell her not to call me honey, to get her face out of mine.

Instead, I begin to sob.

She folds me into her, standing on her tiptoes to take some of my weight as I fall forward, the bloody end of her handkerchief trailing down my back as she wraps her arms around me. She doesn't tell me it's going to be okay, doesn't say she understands and that I'll get through this.

She just holds me while I cry.

CHAPTER TWO

Fallon

"I'm just glad everyone is okay," Mom says, as she brings dessert to the table, a frozen strawberry cheesecake that has about five minutes of existence left on this earth.

"Everyone is *not* okay, Mom," I correct her. "Shelby's nose is broken."

Also, I'm pretty sure that Rory might have bruised Jayden's kidneys. But also, I know whose corner I'm in.

"What she means is, *we're* okay," Farrah says, already pulling the cheesecake dish toward her. "You and me. We're everyone."

"It's true," I deadpan, locking eyes with my little sister. "We are the only people that matter in Presnick."

"In all of Ohio," she trumps me.

"Possibly the country," I tell her.

"Maybe the world," she shoots back.

"The universe, even," I add.

"Alternate dimensions better prepare—"

"All right, you two," Mom says. "You know what I meant. You're my kids, my first priority. I care that Shelby's nose was broken, and I care a lot about the fact that her boyfriend is the one who broke it. But as a parent, when I get an all-call emergency statement from the school, it's you two I think about first."

"If you're about to tell me I'll understand when I'm older, you need to prepare for a dismissive gesture," I inform her. "An eye roll. Maybe a flick of the hand."

"Oh, this one is good, too," Farrah says, turning up her nose, and tossing her head, hair flying over one shoulder.

"I can't pull that off," Dad says, rubbing at his closely trimmed gray. "Also, that head movement was too fast. I'll get hurt."

"It's true," Mom says, sighing. "We're much too old for dismissive gestures."

"You're, like, forty-three," I tell her. "That's not old. You could still have more kids if you wanted to."

"Pass," my parents say in unison.

"Why ruin our perfect harmony?" Farrah agrees, nudging the cheesecake in my direction.

"Harmony that certainly doesn't exist in the school," Mom says. "This whole situation makes me question if it's a safe environment."

"This is still frozen in the middle," Farrah complains, bringing her fork down in an arc, stabbing her cheesecake. The fork stands upright, barely penetrating, a stream of red strawberry filling oozing down the side. My stomach lurches, remembering Shelby's fingers, parting a red river of blood. Her eyelid, bulging like a snail shell; the angle of her nose, pointing the wrong direction.

The truth is, I don't really know Shelby Black. I do, in the sense that everyone knows her. She's medium-grade famous in the youth fighting community, and while that's a pretty small circle, she's the biggest celebrity we've got in Presnick, if you don't count the guy that can slide his kneecap 360 degrees all the way around his leg and has a YouTube channel devoted to that fact. But he's a one-trick pony, and Shelby is a lot easier to look at.

And I mean, a lot.

She's casually beautiful in that clean, aggressive way that girls with heavy blond ponytails and washboard abs pull off effortlessly. She walks like she's about to fight or fuck somebody, and there are plenty of people lining up to do both, just so they can say they've touched her.

"What do you girls think?" Dad asks. "Do you feel safe at school?"

I think about Shelby's eyes, heavy lashes wet with tears, bewilderment flooding her irises. When she'd leaned into me, all of her strength was gone, her muscles simply weight hanging on bone, all of it asking my five-six frame to keep her upright.

"Thave?" Farrah repeats, her jaws sticking together with half-frozen cheesecake. "I dunno, there'th a lo' of raping in the bafrooms."

"There's a lot of *what*?" Mom shrieks, dropping her fork. It clatters off the rim of her plate, setting my teeth on edge.

"Thorry," Farrah says, waving Mom off as she rolls the cheesecake around in her mouth, finally thawing it enough to force down her throat. "Vaping. There's a lot of vaping in the bathrooms."

"I've never been so relieved to hear about a vaping epidemic in my life," Dad says, going for a joke. But his eyes are wary and focused on Mom, whose fork has smeared a strawberry stain on the tablecloth. Dad's hand creeps away from his plate, fingers nudging Mom's. She turns hers over, palm up, and he clasps it with his. The pulse in her neck is flickering, her heartbeat unsteady. Mom's having a panic attack at the dinner table in response to the mention of sexual assault, which has me feeling all kinds of emotions I'll have to sort out later. Right now, my job is to derail my sister, who is plowing ahead because she's never been adept at social skills, unless you include how to pass off your fart as someone else's.

"I mean, if people were getting raped in the bathroom—"

"Did you say you needed help studying for your environmental science test?" I jump in.

"What?" Farrah asks. "Sure, but it's not until—"

"It's never too early to make flash cards!" I announce, pushing back from the table and grabbing my sister by the wrist.

"Yeah, flash cards are always on point in your world," Farrah says, looking to see if Mom and Dad will agree that I'm a huge nerd.

"I'll clean up," Dad says quickly, waving a hand at the table. "You girls go ahead."

"Thanks, Dad," I say over my shoulder as I head for the stairs, Farrah in tow.

We get to her room, and I close the door behind us as she flops down on the bed, tossing her thick mane of curls out of her face.

"What?" she asks, eyes wide.

I look at my sister, whose face still holds a little bit of baby fat, thirteen years of life not melting it away yet. I'd seen her getting curious about shirtless boys at the public swimming pool this past summer, and if her official "talk" from Mom and Dad is anything like mine, it'll consist of them handing off an old romance novel and telling Farrah to let them know if she has any questions.

My own deep dive into Danielle Steel had cleared up quite a few details for me, but it had also left me woefully unprepared for reality, where locking eyes with boys across a room doesn't open up a pit of burning desire, and the only kiss that has ever left my lips tingling came when Brody Jackson forgot that I had a peanut allergy and pawed me after his PB&J on a biology field trip to the state park. Also, all the jokes about boys being better than girls at math? Patently untrue. At least, their measurement skills leave a lot to be desired.

I'm a tried-and-true geek; my superpower is research skills. I decided early on that I should treat sex like the SAT—prepare early, study hard, and be aware that the first time is probably going to be a disappointment. I got a 1500 on the SAT, and while I doubt that luck will hold when it's time to cash in my V-card, I will be walking into it with a wealth of information, if not experience.

My sister, on the other hand, treats life with a let's-see-what-happens-if mentality that extends to everything from switching over to organic deodorant to using duct tape to give herself a bikini wax. She's adventurous and not terribly concerned with personal safety, which makes for a fun friend, good times, and possibly dangerous situations.

"What?" Farrah asks again, clearly having missed Mom's reaction at the dinner table. It's not my job to fill her in. It might not even be my job to have this conversation with her . . . but I have a sneaking suspicion that no one else is going to.

"Vaping in the bathrooms—" I begin.

"Don't start," she says, crossing her arms. "It wasn't me."

"Okay." I wave her off. "But first you misspoke and said *raping*, so I thought maybe it's time someone talked to you—"

"Oh my God, are you teachable moment–ing me?"

"Yes," I snap. "Let's start at the beginning. Do you know what rape is?"

"This isn't . . . I can't . . . ," Farrah mutters, falling forward into a pillow.

"That's not an answer, and if you don't respond, I'll start explaining."

"It's when someone makes you have sex with them and you don't want to," she says, face still buried in the pillow.

"Yes," I tell her. "But what does that mean? Do you know what sex is?"

"Yeah," she says, pulling her face up and eyeing me over a corner of the pillow. "It's when a boy puts his penis inside your vagina?"

"Was that a statement or a question?" I ask. "Because—"

"It's when a boy puts his penis inside your vagina," Farrah repeats, sitting up this time, and enunciating. "I mean, if you're straight."

"All right," I concede, still holding Farrah's gaze. "But I just want to make sure you know that if anything ever happens to you, if anything ever goes wrong, you tell an adult. You tell Mom and Dad. You tell *me*."

"Okay," Farrah says, finally serious.

"I'll tell you what Mom and Dad told me," I go on, joining her on the bed.

"'No matter what happens, no matter where you are, or who you're with, you can *always* call us. We will come get you, no questions asked.'"

Afraid she might make use of that carte blanche in ways I never did, I add, "That doesn't mean there won't be consequences. But if you're ever in a bad situation, their priority will be to get you out of there and make sure you're safe."

"Okay," Farrah says. "Cool . . . thanks."

"And don't take a shower," I say, as an afterthought. "It's the first thing you'll want to do if you're assaulted, but it's important that you don't."

"Right." Farrah gives a quick nod, followed half a second later by a furrowed brow. "What does taking a shower have to do with anything?"

"The police will need to collect evidence—"

"Evidence?" Farrah asks. "Like fingerprints?"

"Noooo . . . ," I say, glancing at Farrah, suddenly aware that her quick comebacks might be a cover, her breeziness a way to gloss over embarrassment of her ignorance. "Not like fingerprints. Do you know what ejaculation is?"

"Uh, okay, so . . ." Farrah starts to redden, the creep of a blush climbing up her neck. "I googled it once, and I got this TikTok of a guy—"

"No," I say sharply, putting my hand up. "That's not the best way to learn about these things. If you have questions—"

"For sure," she says, suddenly leaning forward, the blush—and any hesitancy—gone. "So how does it even get in there? Because Kelsey and I tried to shove a deflated balloon into half a watermelon one time, and it just would *not* stay in. It kept falling back out, and we were both like, this is more work than we thought."

"Why would you use a deflated balloon?" I ask, completely baffled.

"Well, I mean, I've seen Dad when he forgets to take his pajama pants with him for a shower and he has to run back down the hall—"

I can't help it; I snort.

"Listen," I say. "Things . . . change when a man is alone with a woman—or another man, if that's what he's into—"

I break off, suddenly aware that I'm covering very basic things. "Didn't you have sex ed last year?"

"Yeah, we had sex ed," Farrah says, making quote marks around the last part of her statement. "There was a PowerPoint with kids smiling at each other, and a pie chart about STDs and some divorce statistics, and then the lady said that most high school relationships don't last, and she told the boys that if they have sex with their girlfriends now, that girl is probably going to be married to someone else someday, and they wouldn't want to have slept with someone else's wife, would they? Like, how would Evan feel if later he ended up married to Christian's girlfriend now, and Christian had sex with her, so Christian basically slept with Evan's wife, and doesn't that make him feel bad?"

My jaw has slowly been dropping while Farrah speaks, my eyebrows raising. My sister sees this and falls silent, suddenly wary.

"What?" she asks.

"So, she inferred that the boys would be committing some kind of betrayal of each other, by encroaching on their territory—that territory being their future wife's genitalia—who wasn't asked about her own thoughts and opinions in a class setting of her peers about theoretical sexual situations that she was a participant in?"

"Uh . . ." Farrah looks at me, then her eyes dart sideways.

"I'm not mad at you," I clarify. "I'm just trying to make sure I'm hearing you correctly. Your sex ed instructor was talking about sex as if the female involved has been somehow claimed by the first male she is with? Like we're hand-me-down sweaters at yard sales? Or cars that aren't exactly new but new to me? And also that we have no thoughts, or feelings about this ourselves, that we're just an object in a male-oriented transaction?"

"She was really nice about everything," Farrah says, the edges of her lips pulling down. "She just told us girls that we've got to be careful because boys only want one thing—"

It's a rare moment when I find myself stepping in to defend males; this is one of them.

"That's also not true," I tell her. "Some? Yes. All? No. Did they talk to you at all about birth control, prevention, condoms? Aunt

Rachel told me once that when she was in school, they practiced putting condoms on bananas—"

"Wait," Farrah interrupts, her eyes going wide. "A BANANA?"

"It's more like a plantain," I assure her, just as my phone goes off with a reminder that I've got a physics test tomorrow. I bite my lip as I balance my responsibilities.

"It's okay," Farrah says. "I'm good for tonight, and this isn't your job, anyway."

"No," I agree, not voicing my next thought.

Then whose is it?

CHAPTER THREE

Jobie

Scroll through any high school girl's feed and you'll see the same shot, same hair style, same white teeth and perfectly contrasting lip gloss. If you can't stand out, you bust your ass fitting in, and that's what I've been doing since I got my first phone in sixth grade, following the trend, maximizing the filter, and using the right hashtag. Every. Single. Time.

And I've got 2,461 followers to show for it. I guarantee three hundred of them are bots, and another hundred are just companies that gave me a follow after I tagged them—**Lavender infused hair shine from @Herbal!Girl is 10/10!**

I'm not funny, or clever. I'm not an expert at any one thing, and I don't have interesting hobbies. I'm allergic to dogs, and the only cat I have is just like me—boring, bland, and basic. Where I'm different from Princess Tinyhead—a name that she has grown out of and I regret giving her—is that she doesn't give a shit about her mediocrity. I care, I care a lot, and I've got weapons in my arsenal that can take me from a four to a seven, along with my determination.

Those weapons are things like good lighting, an understanding of posing, angles, filters, and eyelash extensions that set Mom back a couple hundred bucks every month. What I do takes a lot of time, a fair amount of work, and a big splash of cash. Mom funds the ongoing Jobie Personal Improvement Project as a monetary apology for the divorce, and Dad's love language is money. Or maybe it's guilt, but I don't care what his motivations are for filling up my checking account from across the country. I just text, **Thank you! You're the best! Love you!**, followed by a series of heart emojis once a month. My phone got wise and autofills it now, correctly identifying our only communication after I type just the first two letters.

Money can buy me boobs (I'm thinking about it), an ass (still have to convince Mom a BBL is worth the medical risks), and whatever mouth shape is cool in the moment (currently sporting a lip flip). Money can also change the color of my hair to the newest trend and buy me just the right outfit for wherever I'm going and whatever I'm doing. But I live in Presnick, Ohio, so where I'm going is likely the high school, and what I'm doing will probably be sitting at a football game, holding out my phone to get Fallon in the shot with me.

If I were so inclined, money could also buy me a following, but that's not the point. I want real people to actually be invested in me. I want genuine likes, heartfelt comments, and DMs from strangers asking me how I got that perfect bounce in my hair or what color my toenail polish is. And I'll tell them, and we'll confer, and suddenly I'll matter and will be sought after, my opinion carrying weight and maybe—*maybe*—the next thing I post will go viral.

That is currently not happening, and I'm kicking myself for it, because the other thing that money did buy me was scar removal, and right now what's trending is scars, and how you got them. A few minutes of scrolling tells me that I've got exactly the right kind of scar, in the perfect place, with a banger of a story.

At least, I *had* a scar.

My hand goes to my right eyebrow, where lasers have eradicated the pale white curl of a crescent moon. When Mom was pregnant with me, she swore I was going to be a guitarist when I got out of there. Apparently, I dragged my fingers across her ribs, tickle torturing her from the inside. At first it was cute, then it was annoying, and eventually became flat-out painful when I grew fingernails and kept strumming her rib cage like it was my personal Gibson.

But I wasn't just exploring the territory; I found my own face at one point in utero and latched on. I came into the world with a tiny, crescent moon mark at the edge of my right eyebrow. I was born scarred, which is a hell of a hashtag. But I can't cash in on it because I had that scar removed when everyone was going after mermaid skin.

"Shit," I say, tossing my phone aside, barely missing Princess Tinyhead, who doesn't react, because she cares so little about the outside world that even flying objects are boring. As soon as it leaves my hand, my phone vibrates and I dive after it, pushing aside throw pillows—mint green because that's what *@BedRedHead100* says is in, and she's accumulated six figures' worth of followers just from doing selfies while lying down—to find a text from Fallon.

Farrah doesn't know what an erection is.

That statement drives missing scars, lost opportunities, and follower growth out of my head for a moment as I stare at it, trying to figure out what autocorrect has done to my best friend. Farrah is in eighth grade and has an internet connection; she knows what an erection is. I experiment a couple of times before responding, just to see if I can figure it out, but my phone only offers up *eraser* and *error*, not even wanting to acknowledge that erections exist until I've finished typing out the whole word. Which is pretty funny, since an update last month finally allowed me to say *fucking*, without first suggesting that what I really meant was *ducking*.

I consider playing around to find out how quickly autofill can identify *vagina*, but I don't want my phone making a lot of assumptions the next time I text Dad, so that I end up saying **Thank you! You're the best! Love you! Fucking erection vagina.**

My phone vibrates with a follow-up text from Fallon.

And she didn't know that ejaculation was a thing.

Okay, so we're definitely talking about this.

But she's had a phone since forever, I text back. I flip over to my newest post—me, fulfilling the one trend I can right now, which is to share the strangest thing you have in your bedroom. The best I've seen so far is someone who had their glass eye sitting on their nightstand. My contribution was a squeaky toy of Michelangelo's *David* that I had bought for Princess Tinyhead. The post is doing okay—ninety-two likes, fourteen comments—but I can't compete with the girls who panned across to the other pillow and a boy they claimed was their stepbrother.

Apparently, Farrah really is only watching cat videos

Fallon's text flashes across the top of my screen, covering my follower count. Annoyed, I flick it away to find that I now have 2,457 followers. I've lost four in the past half hour, which is concerning. I'm about to open up my analytics app, which will tell me exactly who unfollowed me, as well as when, but Fallon wants to FaceTime. I tap, then quickly adjust my hair in the frame, turning my face for the right angle, so that the light from my bedside lamp is giving me a warm, soft glow.

Fallon, on the other hand, cannot be bothered. She's got a radiantly red pimple right in the middle of her forehead next to a patch of dry skin, and apparently no concerns that I could screen cap this and use it as an example of a combination skin type. Not that I would, of course, but Fallon's complete lack of concern about her physical appearance is something I'll never understand.

I pull away the single strand of hair that's become stuck in my lip gloss (**Autumn Apple Spice, welcome to my favorite season! @Lipsa^licious #lipglossgoals #lipglossboss #lipglosslife**). It leaves a silky trail on my cheek, marring the symmetry of my face. I wipe it away, aware that I just lost half my powdered blush.

"So Farrah doesn't know anything about sex," I say. "Is that really a bad thing? I mean, isn't it kind of nice that she's naive?"

"No," Fallon says firmly. "She'll be in high school next year. You know how some of the upperclassmen boys can be with freshman girls."

"Frosh meat," I say, remembering how Vince DiVotelli had taken a survey in biology when the sub had fallen asleep, tabulating the virgins and taking bets on how many would stay that way. I'd debated between which was the better answer, knowing full well that one would make me a goal, and the other an easy target. In the end, I'd gone with the truth.

"Wanna switch sides?" he'd asked, grinning at me as he added my name to the list of V-card holders on his phone.

I still had my days-of-the-week underwear—and generally made sure they were accurate—while Vince, a senior, had three-day stubble that was nearly a beard. I remember looking at it, wondering what that would feel like against my neck, or my—

"You're right," I say quickly, shaking my head to get rid of the imagery. "She's probably curious about boys . . . I mean, it's boys, right?"

"Yeah, she's into boys," Fallon confirms.

"And if she's in a situation where she thinks she's going to learn how to French-kiss but ends up with a dick in her face, that's going to be rough."

"Especially if it's not approximately the size of a deflated balloon," my friend agrees.

"Uh, what?"

Fallon explains about her little sister trying to plumb the depths of the sexual universe with an empty balloon and a watermelon, but I'm only half listening, still thinking about Vince DiVotelli, and his aggressive inquiry of my sexual status.

Funny, I never considered the option of just not answering.

"I mean, she'll have no idea . . . ," Fallon goes on, but my mind has wandered past Vince to that same year, and Derrick Allan, a sophomore who had matter-of-factly unzipped his pants and crawled on top of me about ninety seconds after our first kiss on Mom's sectional. He'd been completely flabbergasted that we weren't going to go at it like rabbits that've been fed a steady diet of porn and caffeine, while I'd been shocked that he simply assumed we *were*.

Even worse was the feeling after he left, when I wondered if I should have.

If another girl would have.

"And that's best-case scenario, with consent involved." Fallon is still talking. "God forbid if she were sexually assaulted, she wouldn't even have the right vocabulary to say what happened to her."

"Right," I say, my interest fading when I get an alert that I've got a DM.

"It's inexcusable," Fallon goes on. "She's had sex ed. Do you remember sex ed?"

"You mean when the gym teacher took the boys and the librarian took the girls and they told us that you *can* get pregnant the first time, so make sure your first time is after marriage?"

"I remember it that way, too," Fallon says, her mouth a flat line. "And the boys just came back pretending to jerk off."

I roll my eyes, "Like they'd just learned it."

"Did you learn anything from it?"

"From the boys pretending to jerk off?" I ask, pulling a long lock of strawberry-blond hair from behind my ear, and laying it across my chest. I hold the phone higher, scoot down in the bed a little bit so that I've got a sex bump in my hair. Everything I've got going on right now is *#cutegirlvibes* and I don't want to waste it.

"No. Hey, Jobie?" Fallon says. "Could you please look at me when I'm talking to you and not at your own face?"

"Huh?" I say, pulling my attention back to my best friend. I don't want to admit that I'd been about to slide her to the side and pull up my camera.

"Did you learn anything from sex ed?" Fallon pushes.

"Nope," I say, popping my lips. "I got it all from Mom's copy of *Outlander*."

"And how's that going?"

"Nothing has really measured up, so to speak," I tell her, sighing as I toss my head to the side, ruining the shot.

"Exactly," she agrees. "Most of us are either totally ignorant, or we've got unrealistic expectations."

"Well, yeah," I say. "But that's just like . . . the way it is, right?"

"It doesn't have to be," Fallon says, shaking her head, and I say the next words right along with her, having heard them every time she got irate about something over the past eighteen years.

"I've got an idea," we both say at the same time, and I erupt into giggles as Fallon's mouth draws even tighter.

"It's not funny," she says.

"Maybe, maybe not," I tell her, my thumbs flashing as I compose a text. "But you know what is?"

"What?"

"*Clitoris* autocorrects to *Clinton*."

CHAPTER FOUR

Shelby

"You're doing exactly the right thing," my publicist, Lee, says.

"Agreed," my agent chimes in, and Coach Faith nods alongside her, their three faces bobbing up and down in their respective squares on my phone.

"Going back to school immediately shows everyone how tough you are, shows the world that it takes a lot more than a sucker punch to keep you down," Coach Faith adds.

"But also, are you okay?" Lee asks.

"I'm fine," I say, even though the words are slurred, my puffy lips and the three stitches holding the top one together not allowing me to pronounce them quite correctly.

I'm sitting alone in the cafeteria, which isn't an entirely new experience for me. What I call confidence others call being a bitch. I've committed the sin of being talented, pretty, and not terribly friendly, which in a small town doesn't translate into people liking you. All the boys want to fuck me, and all the girls want to beat me up because of it, and the fact that neither of those things is going to happen has had everyone buzzing like a wasp nest that fell out of a tree since about sixth grade. Right now, the entire high school population of Presnick High is reduced to a hazy, colorful blur out of my one good eye. Even that blur isn't getting a lot of my attention, because my swollen nose is taking up most of my visual plane. It hadn't been easy to read the torrent of texts that came in from Jayden as soon as he had his phone—

I'm sorry.

I don't know what happened.

I lost control.

It won't happen again.

I'm so sorry, Shels.

I love you.

They were hard to read both because I was crying, and because my vision was shit for a solid twenty-four hours after the hit. I've had enough concussions in my life to know that my boyfriend—*ex-boyfriend*—had done damage to more than just my heart, but I also wasn't about to stay in the hospital for one more minute than I had to. It smelled like antiseptic and old people. Also, my sobs echoed . . . along with my stepmother's words.

What did you say?

Did you make him mad?

He wouldn't do something like that unless . . . ?

That last comment was delivered with a cocked head and an inquisitive look that clearly invited me to explain how I had provoked Jayden's knuckles into close contact with my nasal septum. Finally, Dad had said, "Jesus Christ, Taylor, go out in the hallway and shut up, would you?"

She'd gone, pouting, while I bit down on my already split lip, sucking on my own blood. The rest of the weekend had gone much the same way, the taste of blood in my mouth while Taylor got in her potshots about how if I wanted to act like a boy I shouldn't be surprised when I was treated like one, and Dad telling her to shut up, respecting one of us, while totally dismissing the other.

We're only half misogynistic in this household, I'd texted to Jayden, then deleted it, sending the message to Rory instead.

Half homophobes over here, he'd replied instantly.

Shit's confusing, I told him.

Fuck 'em all, Rory had concluded, to which I'd responded: **Unlikely. Between the two of us, we're just hitting the guys.**

What we didn't talk about was the fact that Rory is suspended for ten days and that I've got to make a decision about how aggressive I want to be when it comes to pressing charges. That discussion has been relegated to the adults in my life, and they simply won't stop.

"It's a personal matter," my Dad says now, having joined the call late.

"It happened in a public space, and everyone who didn't see it live has rolled the tape," my agent, Tara, pushes. "The state will automatically press criminal charges since he's a minor, but Shelby can also pursue—"

"No," I say, glancing back at my phone after glaring at a cluster of freshmen who had been staring at me over their green plastic lunch trays. "I just want this over with. No court shit."

"I understand that, Shelby," Lee says, her voice measured and careful. "But you have to consider how it will look to the public if—"

"She said no," Dad cuts in, and the group goes silent.

How it will look to the public is like I am okay with men hitting women. How it will look to the public is like I am a coward. How it will look to the public is like I'm beaten—and I was, first by Ilsa Bunting in the ring, then by taking a wallop from my boyfriend after we squared off about him sending a dick pic to Savannah Halden.

But how the public perceives what happened is out of my control and already decided, judging by the endless doomscrolling I did over the weekend. Part of the world thinks Jayden should be set on fire and the event live streamed. Another part is wondering how talented I actually am if I didn't see the punch coming. And the last part is dissecting an edit someone has put together of every available video source, weighing in on each second.

She wants to fight—0:22, when I come on camera, shouldering aside Cooper Malloy, my finger in Jayden's face.

Fucking dogging him—0:43, when Jayden shakes his head and tries to brush past me, but I follow.

Men can be assaulted too—1:05, when I grab his shoulder, turning him to face me.

Bitches be crazy—1:10, when my voice cracks as I shriek, "You fucking asshole!"

And finally . . .

Asked for it—1:12 when Jayden's fist connects with my face. And **No wonder she lost to Bunting, if she didn't see that coming.**

As I'm watching, a new comment pops up from *@in*my*digitalopinion2025*—**Men shouldn't hit women. Period. Dot. Full stop. There are no extenuating circumstances.**

"Not pressing charges is Shelby's decision," Coach Faith weighs in. "I understand why she just wants things to be over with."

Over with, like my relationship. Even if I'd wanted to fix things with Jayden, the restraining order that the State of Ohio automatically files in cases of partner violence means he can't contact me. I hadn't heard from him after the first flurry of texts, but I don't know if that's because he suddenly respects the law or a result of me blocking him on my phone and every app there is.

"What about the group therapy class?" Lee says. "If you're not going to press charges, it might be smart to let the public see you lean in to—"

I groan, my head falling forward. The other huge favor Ohio has done for me is requiring me to attend a victims of domestic violence class—which falls precisely during my evening training hours.

"It's bullshit," I'd yelled at Dad, throwing a wad of bloody cotton balls across the living room. "It's not like we're married. We broke up. I've got shit to do."

"Well, this shit is court ordered." Taylor had suddenly sprung to life, looking up from the bloody wad of cotton that marred her otherwise spotless floor. "You're finally going to learn that you don't get to do whatever you want all the time."

"I didn't *want* to get punched," I'd screamed at her, my split lip breaking open.

Now, my eyes slide back to my phone, the video paused on 0:22—me going after Jayden, not letting him walk away.

She wants to fight.

"And it wouldn't hurt to post about your experiences in therapy," Lee goes on. "What you've learned. How it's helpful. Takeaways for your followers."

"Like, I got beat up by my boyfriend so you don't have to?" I ask, and Lee purses her lips.

She's a perky go-getter; exactly the right kind of person to be a publicist. I'm sure she's earning her paycheck, trying to put a positive spin on assault.

"Sorry," I say. "My first class is this week. I'll . . . take notes, or something."

Lee nods as Coach Faith and Dad start to debate the options for making up my lost hours on the mats, and I flip away from the conversation, back to *@in*my*digitalopinion2025*'s comment. I've got some fanboys, dudes that will comment and like just about anything I throw up there, and that number triples if I've stripped down to my sports bra, but this person defending my honor is new to me, and I click on the profile.

I'm surprised to find out we've got five shared contacts, which means they must be someone I know. I flip through their posts but don't see anyone—or anything—familiar. I like their comment, and send them a DM, thanking them for standing up for me.

"We also need to discuss Rebel Outfitters," Tara says, and I flick back to my phone. "I couldn't even get a call back after the Bunting fight, but I got an email this morning saying they'd like to meet."

Rebel makes workout clothes for women, and we've been trying to land a contract with them for months. Losing to Ilsa Bunting had pretty much tanked that, but if they sign me now, it looks good for them—supporting a victim of domestic violence. I hate using the word *victim* to describe myself, but if they want to sit down, it could mean an endorsement, which could mean money, which is a very necessary thing, considering all my gym fees, training, and travel for competitions. I'm about to actually contribute to the conversation about my career for the first time, when a text slides across my screen.

Come sit with us! You don't have to be over there all by yourself!

It's followed by a series of blue hearts, and I'd roll my eyes if there was room in my swollen sockets. Fallon has decided that she is my new best friend, and bombarded me with texts all weekend. I know the bond that can form with adrenaline as a catalyst—I've hugged the girl I'd just been trying to pummel right after the bell, each of us grabbing the other by the back of the neck and screaming into each other's faces that they're amazing. Shit, I'm pretty sure I told Becca St. James that I loved her, right after I busted open her cauliflower ear.

You form a very real attachment to someone whose blood you've spilled, or someone who is wearing yours. Fallon's feeling that, and it isn't entirely evaporated for me, either. So while I don't think I've got much in common with the student liaison to the school board—or her best friend, Jobie, who always looks like she's waiting for an air horn to go off—I get up from my seat by the window and pick my way through a maze of chairs to their table. I nod, then point to my earbuds to tell them I'm on a call. Fallon gives me a thumbs-up, but Jobie's eyes go immediately to my screen, where the adults are still having an in-depth conversation about the brightness of my future, and how best to get me there. While she's watching, a notification pops up—*@in*my*digitalopinion2025* has responded to my message.

I glance at her, remembering that she was one of our mutual connections—although that means very little, since Jobie has friended everyone in Presnick High, including the staff, in hopes of a follow back. I mute my speaker and pop out an earbud.

"Do you know who this is?" I ask her, tilting my phone and pointing at the notification.

"Yeah, that's Baxter Latcha, the new kid?"

Jobie's voice goes up at the end of her sentence, like she's never said anything definitive in her life. I imagine using that approach in the ring, face-to-face with my competitor before the fight, yelling at her—*I'm going to fuck you up?*

"Baxter Latcha," I repeat, my gaze now roaming the cafeteria. I vaguely remember the new guy showing up a couple of weeks ago and all the girls making their assessments. It's rare in Presnick to get some new genes thrown into our pool. Most of the population is operating in the shallow end, where there's no diving, the water is suspiciously warm, and everyone is wearing floaties. There aren't a lot of winners to choose from, and when an attraction develops among us, we've got to do some quick DNA math to figure out if it's a good idea to investigate said attraction further—or a very, very bad one.

"He moved here from Illinois," Jobie continues, giving me the lowdown on the new kid in town while the adults ramble on in my other ear. "He doesn't have any siblings, his mom works at the Honda plant in Marysville, and he drives an electric car."

"Not for long, and not very far," I snort, wondering where the nearest charging station is. "Is he some kind of eco-junkie that is going to shame us for not using titanium straws?"

"Uh, I don't think so," Jobie says. "He's in my anatomy class. Kind of quiet. Cute though."

"Is he?" I ask. I remember passing him in the hallway when he first came here, my brain registering a new face, but not anything particularly interesting about it, and promptly dismissing him. Of course, I spend most of my time around chiseled bodies—girls and boys, men and women running around in booty shorts and man panties. It takes a lot for me to notice someone; my gym is basically live Instagram.

"He doesn't eat in the cafeteria," Jobie says, following my gaze as I make a last pass of the crowd. "He goes out to the Pee Pee Pine."

The Pee Pee Pine is a lone tree next to the boys' locker room that they all use as their outdoor bathroom.

"Did anyone tell him that might be a bad idea?" I ask.

"I tried," Jobie offers. "But he told me urine is sterile, so he's not worried about it."

"That's bullshit," I say. "Urine isn't sterile, and it dehydrates you."

Rory found that out the hard way after emulating his favorite boxer, who reportedly drinks his own urine after a workout to replenish his system. All Rory got out of that experiment was a liquid IV and a fresh wave of gay jokes.

"And it's February," I add, jerking my thumb toward the windows, where an inch of crusty snow rests on the ledge outside.

"He said he's from Chicago"—Jobie shrugs—"and that our wind isn't lake wind."

"He sounds like an idiot," I say.

"Would that work for you, Shelby?" Coach Faith asks in my ear, and I am pulled back into their conversation.

"What's that?"

"If we moved training to before group therapy?"

"Yes," I say quickly, noticing too late that Taylor has joined Dad's end of the call, her voice looming large.

"But what about schoolwork?" she pipes up. "It's like everyone forgets that you have to go to school just like a normal teenager."

It is like that, and I'm not a normal teenager. I've been training to fight since I could walk, popping in a mouthpiece when I was so young it was a choking hazard.

"My GPA is fine," I say.

It's not going to get me into premed or anything, but that doesn't interest me. College isn't on my radar, and grades don't matter in the ring.

"I've got to go," I say, jumping off my end of the call when the app reminds me that *@in*my*digitalopinion2025* has responded to my DM.

Sad that you've got to thank me for the support. It shouldn't be a question.

I appreciate Baxter's stance, but he doesn't know what it's like to walk around as a female 24/7—there's always going to be a question about what you should or should not be doing. And if some of my less-than-adoring public thinks I deserved Jayden's right hook, so be it. Being America's sweetheart was never the goal. I idly tap my fingers against the screen for a second, wondering how to respond, but he must have spotted that I'm active on the app.

How's your day today?

It's polite. It's kind. It's straightforward. It's exactly *not* what I'm used to. Guys at the gym that are taking their shot usually start by explaining to me what I'm doing wrong in my lift—typically they're the ones that are wrong, and I illustrate that slowly and purposefully, with visuals—and the boys from school mostly don't even try anymore. The ones that do attempt conversation usually start with a casual "What's up?" to which I respond, "Your dick, while you're creeping on my Instagram," and that kind of ends things.

The truth is that everyone from Presnick who is attractive or interesting has cycled through each other, and I'm aiming for greener pastures. Jayden and I have been on-again, off-again for the past four years, with his latest move landing us cleanly in the off-forever category. Over the weekend I'd decided that I need to just not have a boyfriend for a while. My completely smashed nose agreed. Except now, Baxter Latcha is asking me how my day is. I respond with the only thing currently on my mind.

Urine isn't sterile.

Jobie believed me, is the immediate response.

Jobie also believes that time zones are a form of time travel, I shoot back. This particular fact had been established when the French club went to Paris and she texted Fallon, asking what the future was like.

That story had made its way around the entire school, because nothing happens in Presnick, and when something does, there aren't that many people to tell it to.

You're funny, comes the reply.

I immediately give that a thumbs-up as a reaction, resisting the urge to use the heart instead. I *am* funny—at least, I think I'm funny. But it's not in the first tier of compliments lobbied at me. Most of them have to do with my tits, ass, or abs, in that order. I can't respond with much else. I have no idea if Baxter is funny, or cute, or anything other than . . . different. I consider flipping back to his posts to see if I recognize him in any of the shots, but first I scroll back through our conversation and realize I'm being rude.

My day is okay, I finally answer his initial question. I don't add that so far he's been the best part of it, since I've spent most of it hiding my busted nose and swollen eyes behind a curtain of blond hair, not letting others grab quick snaps for their own feeds.

Mostly I'm just trying to keep my head down and my face hidden.

I'd wish you luck, but I question your goals, Baxter shoots back immediately, causing my eyebrows to come together . . . or at least, as close as they can across the new territory that is my forehead. I don't like being questioned at all, and Baxter Latcha just lost a few points.

You've got a good face.

I pause for a second, wondering how to take that. He's not hitting on me, exactly. Lots of things can be good, including ugly pound dogs and just the right amount of support in a new pair of shoes. That doesn't mean they're sexy.

I particularly like the eyes to nose ratio.

2:1

Classic.

I snort, which is a bad idea, with my nose in its current state. Jobie glances over at me, clearly trying to read my screen. I tilt it away from her, and she takes the hint, reinvesting in her conversation with Fallon, which so far I have managed to filter out.

That ratio is a little more like 4:2 at the moment, if you take swelling into account.

A bubble with an ellipsis immediately appears, and I feel a little lift in my stomach, which I try to quell. My former relationship ended quite violently last week, the last thing I need right now is a crush. Especially on someone who I've talked with only online.

The base is still a 10/10, swelling is transitory.

One last statement and I'll let you go.

I answer with three question marks.

Screw that guy.

This gets a real smile, and a warmth fires in my gut. I can take care of myself both in and outside the ring, but Baxter's simple statement makes me feel oddly cared for. A boy who doesn't know me has an opinion about Jayden, and it's very similar to mine. I don't have a good response, but I don't need one, because Fallon's voice finally cuts through my focus, with an observation that can't be ignored.

"I just think that more girls need to be prepared for the reality of a penis."

CHAPTER FIVE

Fallon

"The reality of a penis?" Shelby echoes, her gaze lifting from her phone.

"Yes," I say, glad that she's distracted. Social media has been crucifying her, and that can't be good for her mental health after being assaulted by her boyfriend. I don't know Shelby that well, but I'm going to need her on my team for what I have planned, and I want to keep her talking. If my last comment was any indication, the way I do that is by keeping this dick-centric.

"When was the first time you saw a penis?" I ask her.

Shelby doesn't even hesitate. "Way early. I've got a bunch of boy cousins. We were camping together and skinny-dipping before we knew that what we had between our legs worked like a jigsaw puzzle."

"How about in a sexual situation?" I push.

She shrugs. "I've spent most of my life in a gym. You get real used to bodies, and lifting weights increases circulation. Dudes walk around at half-mast sometimes. Makes you realize how lucky we are that a lady libido can be on full blast, and nobody knows."

"They get . . ." Jobie blushes and lowers her voice, glancing around the room. "*That way* just from working out? Really?"

"Some of them," Shelby says, her voice still at regular-volume levels.

"And when they wrestle . . . I mean, friction is friction. It's not sexual."

"Wait," Jobie says, her voice growing louder now with disbelief. "Don't *you* wrestle with them sometimes? How is that not sexual? Or . . . awkward?"

"That's just how bodies work," Shelby says, completely unconcerned. "Had a new guy in our jiujitsu class one time; I got paired with him to roll. First thing he said to me was—I'm sorry if I get an erection, and I'm sorry if I don't."

"Smooth," Jobie says, nodding.

"It was, and he did," Shelby says.

Jobie leans toward Shelby, eyes alight. "So, what about when—"

"Let's save some of the questions for class," I stop Jobie.

"Class?" Shelby asks. "Did graduation requirements just change, like a shit ton? I definitely don't remember seeing any boy parts on my transcript."

"No," I say. "I've been thinking about how sex ed works here—"

"Or doesn't?" Shelby breaks in. "My cousin Alicia is in seventh grade; my aunt caught her sneaking out one night with a roll of toilet paper. She sat her down and told her that toilet papering might sound like fun, but if she gets caught, she could be charged with trespassing. Then she took Alicia's phone to see who she was supposed to be meeting, so she could call the other moms. Turns out she was sexting with another kid, and he'd made a list of all the things he wanted to do to her. One of them was, uh . . ."

For the first time, Shelby colors a little, a blush rising to meet the blue flesh circling her eyes.

"Defecate on her?" I supply.

"Yeah." Shelby nods. "And Alicia just thought that was a normal part of it."

Jobie is face down in her phone; I guarantee she just googled *defecate.*

"That is not a normal part of it. Thanks, Rock Bottom," I say.

"Yep," Shelby agrees. "But Alicia didn't know any better."

"Exactly," I say. "She didn't know any better."

"Oh, my holy hell," Jobie says, still looking at her phone.

"She googled *defecate,*" I explain to Shelby, who quickly hides a smile when Jobie turns to her.

"People do that?"

"People do that," she affirms. "But definitely not me, and certainly not everyone."

"So, here's the deal," I say. "Jobie and I were talking last night, and we both agree it would be a good idea to have sex ed that actually teaches girls about sex."

"Good luck getting that through the school board," Shelby says.

"We're not going to the board, or to anyone else," I tell Shelby, dropping my own voice low. "We're talking about off-campus meetings."

"Wait, like an extracurricular sex club?"

"We are definitely *not* calling it that," I tell her, now using a whisper.

Shelby's voice is at its normal conversational volume, which, perhaps due to her lifetime spent in a gym, is set at what most people would consider *raised* in the least, leaning more toward *confrontational* levels. There are definitely heads turning at the next table over, and I motion her to lean in so that I can continue.

"I looked into it," I tell her as Jobie scoots forward, the tips of her hair touching Shelby's light blond. "A group can register to utilize space at the rec center. An adult has to complete an application, but

Jobie and I are both eighteen, so we've got that covered. The only problem is that you need to have at least three people in your group in order to book a room in advance, and space is really hard to get."

"I get it," Shelby says. "You need me to be a third person on the paperwork, but you also need some kind of pull."

Pull is exactly the right word. When I'd called the rec center to inquire about available space, the guy on the other end had basically read the bullet points from their website back to me, until I mentioned it was for a self-defense class for teenage girls.

"Wait," he'd said. "Is Shelby Black going to be part of this? Is she coaching? Wait . . . are *you* Shelby Black?"

"No, I'm Fallon Holloway, which is how I introduced myself when we started this conversation," I'd said. "But Shelby Black might be interested in—"

I hadn't gotten any further than the possibility of Shelby being interested in order for him to clear a slot for us to use a room for three months in advance, letting me know what a great marketing angle it would be for them, just to have Shelby walk through the front door.

"Space at the rec center isn't the only problem," Jobie pipes up, correcting me. "The other thing is, Fallon and I are totally virgins."

"*Jobie*," I say though clenched teeth. I don't mind the fact being shared; I just know that particular word carries. Antennae probably went up at the varsity football table.

"I get it," Shelby says. "So you need me to get you through the door, but also to answer any questions about sex that might possibly come up at sex club. Because I've had sex, and I mean *a lot*," Shelby says, making me wince again. It's exactly that kind of flippancy that I don't want to headline our meetings, which I better clarify right away.

"I'm teaching the class," I say. "This isn't going to be a how-to. We'll be talking about things like birth control and—"

"But dicks will totally come up, am I right?" Shelby asks, one raised eyebrow letting me know the pun was totally intended, even if the effect is a little ruined by her black eyes. "I'm your girl. Where do I sign?"

"What are you talking about?"

My eyes go wide and lock with Jobie's, who looks like she's never going to get past the virgin stage of her life because she's about to have an aneurism. Shelby, on the other hand, seems completely unbothered, glancing over my shoulder at the person who has joined us.

"Hey, Mal," she says. "We're just talking about how most girls aren't prepared for the reality of a penis. Or, in your case, the reality of a pussy. Probably a little different for you, since you've got one and understand the ins and outs."

Shelby actually takes her index finger and rams it into a circle that she's made with her other hand. It's now my turn to be on the shortlist for underage aneurisms; Mal Targer is the only lesbian at Presnick—at least, the only one that's out. I've always done everything I can to project nonjudgmental, welcoming vibes when I pass her in the hall, but Mal isn't someone that actively seeks friendships. I don't know how hard it's been for her here, but I do remember that when she put her Thespian Club bumper sticker on her car that stated "Thespians Do It Onstage," someone took a Sharpie and changed the first two letters into an *L*. Of course, they weren't smart enough to change the *p* into a *b*, so it's now both defaced and inaccurate.

I don't know what Mal's life is like, but I do know it's probably lonely and more than a little frustrating. And now Shelby is making explicit hand gestures at her in the middle of the cafeteria, plunging one hand into the other like she's doing a science experiment about friction.

Shelby stops and seems to reconsider. "Or would it be more like—" She makes a V with her fingers and raises her hand to her face, but I grab her hand and slam it back down to the table before she can continue.

"I'm sorry," I say, turning to Mal, who is standing behind me, arms crossed. "She doesn't mean anything—"

"What, this one?" Mal asks, pulling out a chair and offering Shelby a fist bump. "I'm used to her. I think of Shelby Black like this—she might be an asshole, but she's *my* asshole."

"What's got two thumbs and is someone else's asshole? This girl," Shelby says, pointing back at herself. "And we're talking about creating an after-hours sex club."

"That is *not*—"

"Sold," Mal says. "But if you're the only members, I'm not spotting anybody with my shared interests."

"Nope," Shelby says. "I really like dicks."

"Me too," Jobie says, somewhat wistfully.

"Pause," I say, raising both my hands in the air. "To be clear, we are not creating a sex club. And we're also not just announcing it to everyone." I cut a look at Shelby, who shrugs.

"So, what *are* you doing?" Mal asks, draping her arm across an empty chair. "Because I heard the words *virgin*, *sex*, and *application*. The combination made me real curious."

"That last one really is just about paperwork," Jobie says.

"We're not happy with the current state of sex ed in the school," I say, trying to keep things on track.

"You mean, the heteronormative hour?" Mal asks, pulling out her phone. "My brother is in that class right now. He took a picture of one of the slides."

Mal enlarges the image on her phone, zooming in on the banner, and the logo for the sex ed program. The title—"We're All in It Together: WAIT"—makes my skin prickle, but it's easy to see what has Mal's back up. In front of the acronym is the outline of a family: mom in a skirt, dad standing next to her, smaller versions of themselves on either side. Behind them, there's an outline of a house, with a cat and a dog on either side of the front steps.

"Nuclear Stick-Figure Family 101," Mal says.

"Technically, those are pictograms," I say. "Like the bathroom signs."

"Technically, I don't give a shit," Mal snaps back. "All I see is one man, one woman, and one little replica of each of them. You know, a *real* family."

"Right," I say. "The icon for the entire program promotes straight pairings only."

"Uh-huh. And I find that way more offensive than anything that's ever come out of Workout Barbie over there," Mal says, tossing a thumb at Shelby.

I glance at Jobie, who's got her eyebrows—perfectly lined in, of course—up to her hairline. I might have thrown a correction at Mom when she used exclusionary terms with Farrah at dinner the other night, but I'd never thought about the fact that Rory, Mal, and anyone else in their camp is getting even less sex education than the straight kids.

"Would you want to be included?" I ask Mal, hoping that my years of practicing a smile that doesn't broadcast *I know you're a lesbian, and I swear it doesn't make me uncomfortable* will finally come to fruition.

"Sure," Mal says. "Are we watching porn?"

"No," I say firmly. "That is exactly the opposite of what I'm trying to do here."

"*The reality of a penis*, remember?" Shelby asks, putting air quotes around my words.

"Wait though," Mal says, eyeing me. "You said 'what I'm trying to do here.' What does that even mean? Why are you even doing this in the first place?"

"I . . ." All of my practiced phrases float away on a whiff of indecision.

"I just think nobody is preparing us for the real world," I say, hating the triteness of my own words. But something about it clicks, and all three of the other girls nod.

"No shit," Shelby says. "I'm a girl who grew up with an absent mother. Nobody ever said anything to me about menstruation, but I have to take tests about polynomials."

"How'd you figure it out?" Mal asks.

"I bled through my gi at the regional jiujitsu tournament in fifth grade. Another mom spotted it and took me into the bathroom, gave me a quick tutorial and a tampon. I had to fight in like five minutes, and let me tell you, that thing was *not* in right. I felt like I was rotating on an axis."

"Terrible visual," Mal says.

"Worse experience," Shelby shoots back.

"And you shouldn't have had to go through it," I say, turning to Mal. "Does that make sense? I don't want another little girl, alone in a bathroom stall, holding a tampon and having a stranger tell her what to do with it."

"It makes a ton of sense," Mal says. "But we're not, like, going to be bringing fifth graders in and doing hands-on activities with tampons, right? Because that's going to get us into a lot of trouble, real fast."

"No," I say. "Of course not. I think we keep it small at first—real small. Like, each of us brings one other person, and we just talk some things out, see how it goes. High schoolers only."

I look over to see that Jobie has pulled a Moleskin out of her backpack and is actually taking notes. "We've got the required three people," she says.

"Plus a gay," Mal chimes in.

"So what's next? You fill out the paperwork to use space at the center?" Jobie asks me.

"Yes," I say, looking around the group. "The guy I talked to said he could make the second-floor yoga room available."

"Perfect," Jobie says. "What do we need for the paperwork?"

"Signatures," I say, pulling the sheaf of papers out of my own backpack. "And . . ." I scan the top of the application, staring at the blank space that had left me racking my brain and coming up empty the night before.

"We need a name. *Not* Sex Club," I say quickly, when Shelby opens her mouth. She quickly pops it shut again.

"Hold on a second," Jobie says, her pen scratching across a blank page in her journal. "What if it's not sex club, exactly?"

"Kind of a Sex Club is also not a great name," Shelby says.

"No, but what about this?"

Down the left side of the page, Jobie has written the letters *S-H-A-F-T* as an acronym, with what each letter stands for written out next to it.

"Self-Help and Fitness Training," Mal reads, then bursts into laughter. "Oh my God, I love it."

"It's not a sex club," Jobie explains to me. "It's—"

"SHAFT Class, yeah I get it," I tell her. "Really not sure how I'm going to sell that to the rec board. And what's with the self-help part?"

"It's also a class for girls to express themselves," Jobie argues. "Walk in with a box full of googly eyes and pipe cleaners, maybe some finger paints. Tell them it's a great way for teens to unplug from their phones and be social face-to-face. Mental hygiene through group crafts. Adults like it when you say things like that."

"And what about the fact that I told the guy this was for a self-defense class?"

"Listen," Shelby says, all the confidence I pretend to have floating off her easily. "You've got my name attached. All the rec center wants is a shot of me walking in the front door, maybe some pics by the free weights. I guarantee they don't even look over this paperwork, let alone drop in on class to make sure it's following the mission statement."

"Adults also aren't as stupid as you think," I tell the group. "SHAFT Class?"

"Jobie's right," Mal says. "If it looks like a mental-health, self-care, me-time, crafting class, the staff isn't going to look too hard into it. They're just going to be glad that we're not under the bridge doing drugs."

I look dubiously at Jobie's handwriting, tapping my pen against my lips. "It is clever," I tell her.

"Clever and awesome," Shelby says, rolling up one sleeve and flexing her bicep. "Like, I'm getting a tattoo of it. Right here." She kisses her own muscle, leaving an unfortunate spot of blood behind, where her lip has split open again. She wipes it away without comment, but then lifts her phone, tilting it so that her one functioning eye has a good view while she inspects her reflection.

"I love the name, and I'm in." Jobie pulls the application away from me, filling in the group name herself, then signing at the bottom. She slides it back to me, and I glance it over.

"Not using the acronym is a lot less suspicious," I admit.

"I kind of like the full name anyway," Mal says. "Self-Help and Fitness Training."

"Yeah, self-help. I can self-help myself for days," Shelby says, setting aside her phone. She makes a circle with one hand, extending the other index finger. But I stop her, pushing one hand back down to the table.

"You and I are going to have a discussion about obscene hand gestures," I tell her.

"Anytime," she says, and flicks me off.

CHAPTER SIX

Jobie

My mom pulls men.

It's not a big secret my mom is hot. Guys at school have been telling me that since approximately fourth grade, which is about when the divorce happened and going to parent-teacher conferences became a gauntlet where I watched my teachers and my friends' dads flirt with her. It hasn't gotten better, mostly because dudes in my grade have been telling me to update her as soon as they turn eighteen, and because dating apps have opened her horizons beyond everything she's already tapped locally.

It's pretty typical for me to get screenshots of future prospects, asking me for an opinion on their bio and pic. When I was a kid it was kind of fun; like shopping for a dad. Later on, I figured out Mom wasn't looking for a husband, and even later it became depressing for a different reason—Mom has more options than I do.

Like, by a lot.

When I get home, she's got her work laptop open to all of her current real estate listings, one window displaying an email chain from a prospective buyer she's been greasing for three weeks, another on her Bumble account, where she's chatting with a match. She pops between the two, switching out professional with flirty easily.

"Hey." She glances up when I walk in. "How was school? Did you learn things?"

"Sure," I tell her, going to the fridge and pulling out the milk. "How's work? Did you sell things?"

"Eh," she says, tilting her hand from side to side. "I've just got a tease on the line here."

"Business or pleasure?" I ask, drinking directly from the jug.

"Real estate," she clarifies, turning back to her laptop. "I could land this fella on the dating app if I wanted."

"Do you?" I ask, coming to stand behind her as she pulls up her chat window.

"I don't know," she sighs, flipping over to his picture. "What do you think?"

"Same guy from last week?" I ask. Sometimes her dating options are a blur of chemically whitened teeth and homogenously handsome white dudes that haven't quite figured out their good side, or the best angle for a selfie. But I remember this one, mostly because he just used a group photo and circled himself for clarity.

"Yeah," she says, her voice purposefully flippant, the tone she usually adapts by the third or fourth date, a sure sign that she might actually like someone.

"He asked about dinner tonight, but I wanted to check with you first."

"I'm good," I tell her. "I've just got homework and then I'm . . ."

Not doing anything because I am irrelevant is how that sentence should end, but that sounds incredibly pathetic, so I finish with "just chilling."

"So, you'd be okay with me going out?" she asks, already typing a reply.

"And *staying* out?" I come back, looking at her over the milk carton as I take another swig.

"Women have needs," she says.

"I know," I tell her. It's our common dialogue when we skirt around the topic of her sex life, but this time my scripted response doesn't come out with the implied *ick* but rather with something close to wistfulness. Mom stops typing midsentence, and turns back to me.

"Is everything okay?"

"Yeah, I'm fine," I say automatically, but Mom doesn't accept my blow-off answer, instead following my gaze to her chat window, where her date has responded to her acceptance with a series of smiley faces and thumbs-up, along with—**I'm really looking forward to seeing you again**. The ellipsis bubble is still up, another compliment, unbridled enthusiasm, or just plain affection surely inbound.

Mom closes the laptop, eyeing me. "I can cancel."

"No, really," I tell her, shaking my head. "I'm just tired."

And that is most certainly true, but it's not the end of the sentence. The rest goes like this—tired of being less interesting than my friends, tired of being less attractive than my mother, tired of always being present but never accounted for, tired of being passed over, not noticed, or summarily dismissed. Tired of being the four in a flock of sevens, the dog at the pound that might get walked by a volunteer but nobody ever takes home.

"Jobie?" Mom asks, her eyes still on me. "I'm your mother. I can tell when you're lying."

"Didn't work so well on Dad, though, did it?" I snap, and Mom flinches.

"Sorry," I say automatically, my gut turning when I see the tears rising in her eyes. "I didn't mean . . . I'm just . . ."

"Well, you're not wrong, exactly," Mom says, sighing. "A bit rude, perhaps. You mind telling me where all this is coming from?"

"Nothing." I shake my head, and she narrows her eyes.

"Is this about boys?"

It's my turn to tear up and turn away, my jaw set hard as I take the milk back to the refrigerator, not responding.

"Jobie?" Mom pushes. "Is there something you need to tell me?"

A harsh laugh slips out, and I slam the fridge door, half-empty bottles of wine rattling against each other. "No, Mom, there's not something I need to tell you. There's nothing, that's the thing. I don't have boy problems, because I don't have a boy to cause them."

Mom is quiet for a second, legs crossed, assessing me. "They're not everything, you know."

"Easy enough to say when you've got your pick. I can't—" My voice cracks. I take a second, bracing myself against the fridge, staring down a picture of me and Fallon at prom last year, under the balloon arch, each of us trying to look like it was our plan to go together, not that nobody asked us. I try again, my voice weak, my words pathetic, hating the truth that I'm about to speak and the fact that it matters so much to me.

"I can't even get a boy's attention," I say.

"Getting it isn't all that hard," Mom says, her thumb rubbing against the empty spot on her ring finger where her wedding ring used to be.

"Keeping it is the trick."

Princess Tinyhead isn't doing anything interesting.

I am not doing anything interesting.

Shelby Black, apparently, is doing something very interesting.

Getting beat up by her boyfriend has only made her more popular, and the fact that she continued to post selfies with her mangled face has started a wave of dating-violence testimony reels that has *#hesaidhewassorry* trending locally. She gained a thousand followers over the weekend, and judging by the comments, half of them are offering to either beat up Jayden or fill the now-vacated position of being her boyfriend. The fact that she posted a workout video of herself hip-thrusting two hundred pounds did a great job of distracting from her bruises. She's got sympathy, sex appeal, and a loyal fan base to hit back at the haters on her behalf.

"Dammit, she's good at this," I tell Princess Tinyhead, switching back to my own account. Tonight, I've got 2,450 followers, and nothing to offer for the current trend—tattoos in memoriam. My feed is overloaded with dudes and *Mom* tats, with her birth and death year, and widows who will never forget the love of their life—mostly because they're very unlikely to land a new guy with the old one inked on forever. A new pic pops up, Shelby kissing her bicep where she's written, "Becca St. James's career" in black Sharpie. She posted literally seconds ago and already has fifty-two likes and five comments, one of which says—**STFU my girl Ilsa put you to sleep.**

I hop on fast.

Proud to be your friend!

She likes the comment immediately, responding **love you, rec life forever!**

I'm not Shelby's friend, and I know she doesn't love me. But it's the only way I'm going to get close to today's trend, and if any of the legions of Shelby's fans get curious about who this random friend that she loves is, I might gain a few followers.

I swipe back to my own account, where my last post is a picture of the peppermint spice latte I'd grabbed after school, my perfect French tips curled around the mug, my index finger draped across the lip to highlight the thin, silver band that I bought after *@Jadas!Jewels* let me know that gold is out and only white-toned metals matter right now. I'd spent time working on the caption, going for the perfect blend of not trying too hard while also hoping desperately to succeed.

Peppermint mocha time is the best time! #snowday #wintervibes #wintermood #cafemocha #coffeelover

I narrow my eyes, pulling my phone in closer to make sure I didn't mistype anything, like last fall when I'd accidentally used the hashtag *#pumpking* instead of *#pumpkin*, which can seriously skew your audience. I made sure to tag *@Neverending$Nails* in the hopes of a repost, since they get tens of thousands of likes, and I'd also thrown the Hail Mary of tagging Starbucks just in case they're super thankful that I let my scant followers know that peppermint mocha is on the menu. Presnick isn't big enough for a Starbucks, and I'd bought that particular latte at a local place called Grind the Bean—a name that Fallon had helpfully explained to me—but it's not *#shoplocal* month, so I'm hoping to catch some reflected light off the big corporations.

But it's not working.

That post has forty-five likes and two comments, both of which are from bots that follow those hashtags (**HARD DM!** *@beantweenteam400*, **Promote it on** *@CoffeeBrewCrewz99*!!!) I toss my phone aside, sighing.

"Why can't you be more interesting?" I ask Princess Tinyhead, who is marathon napping on my windowsill. She isn't even doing it cutely, with a perfect little tail curl or a sleepy-cat smile on her face. Instead, she's slouched against the glass, her nose leaving behind a snot smear. I grab my phone again, pulling up the camera and inspecting myself.

"Why can't *I* be more interesting?" I ask.

A notification pops up, letting me know that I've got comments on my selfie that I'd posted to the rb/HardLooksMaxxing group. I'd found the group after *@TopModelTip$$* had promoted it as a quick way to connect with other women who were looking to "improve, inspire, and uphold one another." They also offer honest ratings about exactly where you land on the beauty scale, which is what drew me in. Just being myself isn't exactly working out very well.

rb/HardLooksMaxxing is a sub-bottom on a site that Mom had initially blocked through her parental control app she put on all my devices when I was younger. Rock Bottom has been around since the internet got social and quickly gained a reputation as a forum that hosted incels, upvoted misogyny, and was generally populated by lonely twentysomething dudes living in their moms' basements. But most of that initial influx of users grew up, got jobs, landed partners, had kids, and formulated a different view on life. These days, Rock Bottom isn't any more deplorable than any other place on the internet. There's something for everyone—which means that you can see reels of people being dismembered by wild animals, watch ASMR videos of drains being cleared, or get gardening tips from a nice, silver-haired lady in a legit gardening getup, with a big floppy hat and a tool belt. You can also check out an extremely trim blonde mulching while totally nude, so it really is about what sub-bottoms you choose to join.

Mom's subscription to the parental control app must have expired at some point, which I discovered when I was allowed to join Rock Bottom in the first place, and became even more evident when I completely misunderstood how to find a sub-bottom at age twelve. I'd accidentally just searched for "sub-bottom," and learned a lot, real fast, about things that I didn't really want to know. Thanks a lot, auto play.

I keep my feed pretty clean as a rule. It's full of derpy animals, pimple-popping videos, makeup tutorials, and some bird feeder cams. *@TopModelTip$$* had led me to rb/SoftLooksMaxxing, which is only for women who are unapologetically interested in their own objective beauty and how to improve it through attainable actions like skin care, exercise, and facial massage. Women who want to elevate their game even further join rb/HardLooksMaxxing, where cosmetic surgery, fillers, and Botox are the first line of defense against aging. Or, in the case of younger members like me—against being average.

I'd posted a selfie this morning after being accepted into the group, by first swearing that I was female and also promising that I would blur out any pictures featuring nudity, or, if I chose not to, to understand that while the mods did their best to keep the sub members female only, there were surely a few guys posing as women, trolling around hoping to spot titties. Why they would bother hanging out here instead of just going to rb/titties, I don't know. I'd agreed to all these things, took a candid shot of my clean, makeup-free face, and thrown myself on the mercy of their well-meaning judgment, hoping for some ideas about what I can do to improve myself.

And they have ideas. A lot, actually.

@MuscleMommy!87—Depends on what kind of look you're going for, but rhinoplasty wouldn't hurt. Your nose is a little too snubbed for the shape of your face.

@White$wan_BlackHeart—Agreed with the above, but would suggest lengthening the nose, as the problem here isn't the shape of the face,

but the placement of your eyes. Too close together, imo.

@HollyGene'sBerry—Would consider ear pinning. You've got detached lobes, which can look good and can be complemented with the right earrings, but your pinnae is likely outside of what is considered an attractive head-to-ear ratio.

@Reverse*CowGirl69—I spot a lip flip! Let that shit fade. They're trending out.

@Fully/Vaxxed—An upper blepharoplasty is in order here. Your eyelids protrude a bit too much. If you went with it, I'd suggest a brow lift to complement. Your irises are pretty, work with what you've got.

@Karen*Is*MyActualName—All I see is forehead. Look into hairline advancement.

@JohnnyDepp(IfYou'reReadingThis)—Facial features in general need to be balanced, chin and cheek augmentation would do wonders for you.

@Bras-Are-Boob-Prisons—Kid, how old are you? What the actual fuck?

@Butterfly<In>TheSky—Jaw contouring wouldn't hurt, you need to feminize that line.

So my actual face is wrong. Neat.

My fingers hover, considering which invasive surgery to inquire about first, when someone else responds to the poster questioning my age.

@Bras-Are-Boob-Prisons—Kid, how old are you? What the actual fuck?

@Kat/Not/Cat—She's in rb/HardLooksMaxxing. She wants feedback on how to improve her looks through intense methods. That's the point of this sub. If you don't like it, you should leave.

@Bras-Are-Boob-Prisons—Right. And after reading this, what she walks away with is that she'd be better off going for full decapitation and getting a new head.

I consider that for a second, fully aware it's not possible, but also more attracted to the idea than I care to admit. I decide to stay out of the questionable morality discussion, and instead go for a straight answer of the actual question.

@Jobster{Lobster}—I'm eighteen.

I start googling some of the words I don't recognize from other posts that have popped up—*genioplasty*, *rhytidectomy*, and *blepharoplasty*—but *@Bras-Are-Boob-Prisons* is currently active on the sub, and is all over my admission of age.

@Bras-Are-Boob-Prisons—You haven't even grown into your looks yet. You're thinking about altering your bone structure before it's done changing. This is insane. Get off social media, stop looking at all those photoshopped and filtered faces, and start appreciating who you actually are.

@Kat/Not/Cat—Telling someone to appreciate who they actually are in a sub dedicated to plastic surgery is peak Boomer.

@Bras-Are-Boob-Prisons—I'm 45, shitface, and I've seen your selfies. There's less plastic in the ocean.

Great, I just got here and I've started a catfight.

A text message from Fallon slides across my screen, letting me know that she turned the paperwork in at the rec center and the lady at the front desk hadn't even blinked at the name.

SHAFT Class first contact scheduled for Wednesday at 7!

Does that sound bad, lol?

What happens in SHAFT Class stays in SHAFT Class.

I dismiss her messages and start reading about facial reconstruction surgery. I'm debating about whether I want to see operating room videos, when a DM comes in to my Rock Bottom account, something that only happened when I first joined and was hit by the usual onslaught of bots and guys asking gender, age, and location. You know, for data purposes.

@Bras-Are-Boob-Prisons wants to talk to me. I can see the first line of her message in the preview, which says—**just got banned from HardMaxx. Listen . . .**

"Oh no," I say, clicking over to our chat and accepting the message so I can read the whole thing.

@Bras-Are-Boob-Prisons—just got banned from HardMaxx. Listen, I know I sound like an old lady, but please don't do anything drastic to your face. You're too young and once you start it's hard to stop. Just look at @Kat/Not/Cat—she's cut to look good under the right kind of lighting, and she takes advantage of that. But I bet if she goes to the beach, kids run and scream.

It's not exactly nice, but just by browsing through the sub, it's clear that *@KatNotCat* and *@Bras-Are-Boob-Prisons* have a history. I didn't just break up the ultimate online friendship.

@Jobster{Lobster}—ha ha, lol. Yeah, I don't know about my face. It's not like I would just get surgery. I was just curious what other people thought of my looks.

@Bras-Are-Boob-Prisons—Rock Bottom can be a dangerous place for curious people. Just be careful out there, kid.

I tell *@Bras-Are-Boob-Prisons*, **thanks, I will be careful**. Just then another DM comes in on my Rock Bottom message inbox.

@!Cute!_Amy—Hey, saw your posts on HardMaxx, just wanted to say don't be so hard on yourself. I know what it's like to be cute but not hot. Hurts, but you need to learn to love yourself.

Ugh, loving myself is exactly the problem. I totally don't. And I've seen enough Pinterest inspiration boards with positive self-image quotes to last a lifetime. If those were going to make me feel better, they should have done the trick a while ago. Amy isn't wrong, though; being cute but not hot is exactly the problem. Shelby Black is hot, and she's got the workout videos to prove it. I'm the girl next door, but whose door you never actually knock on.

@Jobster{Lobster}—I know. I'm trying.

@!Cute!_Amy—There are plenty of guys out there who want cute.

@Jobster{Lobster}—send them my way, lol

I flip back over to rb/HardLooksMaxxing, where my unfiltered selfie has garnered more advice about what surgeries I should be considering.

@Walk(s)InTheRain53—Check out the app that New You just put out. It can give you some good ideas about what you want and don't want.

They provided a link, so I click through and download the app. I'm instructed to take a selfie of my clean face, in good lighting. I use the same pic I'd posted to HardLooksMaxxing, then scroll through the available options. The app can show me what I would look like after having various procedures and surgeries done. I click boxes, checking what the rb/HardLooksMaxxing posters had suggested. A scanner line passes over my selfie, and there's an endless spinner while I wait for my results.

When it loads, I lose my breath.

For once, for now, for this moment, I am beautiful.

My eyebrows are higher, my cheekbones more pronounced. My ears are smaller and my jawline is a straight, slicing plane. My lips are full and pouty, my nose perfectly shaped and positioned, my forehead no longer a broad eye-drawing mesa. Everything about me is heartbreakingly gorgeous. I save the pic to my phone, and the app prompts me by asking if I'd like to inquire about becoming a new me.

Yes, I would.

I punch in my email, and a couple of seconds later there's a notification in my Gmail. I click over to a welcome message from New You.

Hello, Jobie, and welcome to your journey toward perfection!

Here at New You, we believe that every woman should be able to move with confidence by putting their best face forward and allowing their true inner selves to shine through—nobody needs to know that the outer self had a tune-up!

Based on your choices while using our app, we believe that we can be a great partner to you. Below is a list of your chosen beauty adjustments, along with an estimate of your costs, as well as the contact information and address of our affiliate in your geographic area. Of course, actual costs may vary, and this email should only be used as a guideline to plan for your future as the best possible version of yourself—your new you.

I scroll down past the list of elective surgeries to find out how much it will cost to make me beautiful.

$75,000.

I huff and close out the email, well aware that no amount of surface texts to Dad, or late-date-night guilt from Mom is going to bring that amount of money in. I go into my photos, bring up the picture that the New You app had produced. I stare at this other version of myself, this smooth creature that a blade, some filler, and a lot of money can create. The phone slips in my hand, my thumb dragging across the screen and opening the camera app, snapping an accidental selfie. I go back to my photos, looking at this snub-nosed, huge-browed, realistic photo of myself, mouth hanging partially open, one eye half shut.

Then I look at the photo from the New You app.

And I start to cry.

CHAPTER SEVEN

Shelby

"Your face looks like shit," Rory says, popping out his mouthpiece.

I fake a jab and he slips it, moving easily for such a big dude.

"You should see the other guy's," I say, and he gives me a look. "Sorry, I couldn't come up with anything better. My head might still be ringing from that combo you threw."

"Then wear headgear," Coach Faith yells from the mats, where she is simultaneously training Tumbling for Toddlers while listening in on our sparring session.

I wave her off and lean against the ropes next to Rory, checking the south corner of the gym, where Dad is working as a personal trainer. His current client is a soccer mom who thought she was coming here to flirt and not lift; Dad has no patience for clients who are in it for anything other than personal improvement, and he's got her doing split squats with dumbbells while he stands five feet away, giving advice.

"I have seen the other guy's face," Rory tells me. "He definitely looks worse than you, but that's any given day."

"Ha," I say, tucking my own mouthpiece behind my ear. "How do I look, besides my face?"

"You're moving good," he says. "Couple days off didn't hurt you none. Ground game could use work, but you're throwing hands good as ever. You smooth, girl."

"Probably all the lube," I say. "Leaks out of your pores eventually."

"There she is, that's my disgusting friend," Rory says, showing me his glove for a bump.

I touch it, and he joins me on the ropes, trickles of sweat threading their way through his stubble. He's the only guy at Presnick High who has ever had the administration add rules for facial hair to the student handbook; I think it got added after a tech guy who came to fix the comm system walked right past Principal Scott in the cafeteria, mistaking Rory for the adult in the room.

"Seriously, though," Rory says. "You're doing good in the ring. How about up here?" He taps his own forehead, green eyes latched on to mine.

I sigh and look away, taking a moment to use the spit bucket in the corner before I answer.

"Okay, I guess," I tell him.

I can't lie to Rory. We've been dodging each other's punches since we could throw them, and when the day came that he could clean and jerk my body weight—we knew it was accurate, because he used my actual body—I'd celebrated with him, from about two feet above his head. Training partners get close, and Rory is the only person I've ever really let into my circle. Rory reaches over the ropes and pulls the cord on the boxing bell, sending the high-pitched *ding* across the gym.

"Round one," he says. "And I'm calling you out for timidity, that's a legal foul. Now answer my question for real."

I sigh and flop down to the mats, where he joins me, both of us dripping sweat.

"I really am doing okay," I tell him, undoing the Velcro on my gloves with my teeth. What I don't say is that one of the reasons I'm not thinking about Jayden very much is because I've been texting with Baxter Latcha . . . like, a lot. We'd graduated from DMs on the apps to sharing our numbers, and have been mutually blowing up each other's phone. I glance over at where mine rests on the bench, and I can see the red notification, bright against the green messaging app. Yep, he's texted me since I climbed into the ring. Probably at least five or six times, if the past couple days is any indication.

"What's that little smile about?" Rory asks, following my head movement when I try to duck his gaze.

"I maaaaaay have met someone," I say, drawing out the second word so that I at least sound hesitant, even though I'm not feeling that way. And technically, we haven't met yet. He was out of school today because he and his mom needed to get one more U-Haul truck of their stuff out of Chicago.

"Fast work," Rory says, his brow creasing slightly. "You're not giving one of your Instagram creepers a shot, are you?"

"Aw, hell no," I say, toying with the loose end of wrist wraps and looking back over at Dad, who gives me a thumbs-up when he sees I'm taking a breather. I'm under strict instruction to go easy on myself for the next couple of weeks. "Do you know Baxter Latcha?"

"The new kid?" Rory draws back in surprise. "He's regular as fuck."

"No, he's not!" I shoot back, yanking off my other glove. "He's interesting, and he's funny, and he's—"

"Oh, you mean his *personality*," Rory says, rolling his eyes. "I mean, I guess that could be fine. I've never talked to him. Passed him in the hallway a couple times and didn't strike me as anything special."

"What, not like Paul?" I ask, nodding toward the corner, where a lithe guy with a swimmer's body is taking out all his regrets on a punching bag. Every muscle is on display, right down to where his obliques meet his transverse abdominis.

"Nobody is special the way Paul is special," Rory says, his eyes glazing over a bit. "I can cancel my subscription to *Men's Fitness* now that he started coming to the gym."

"What, you don't read the articles?" I ask.

"I'd read his articles," Rory says.

"That's doesn't even make sense," I say, taking a pull on my water bottle. "And don't pretend like looks are the only thing Paul's got going on. You're constantly laughing when you talk to him, and you're not just looking at his ass. You love-lock eyes with him more than you do with yourself when you work out in front of the mirror."

"And that is saying a lot," Rory admits, flexing his bicep and admiring his reflection in the mirrored wall. "What about Baxter's ass, how's that? Can you give me a rating?"

"Haven't seen it," I admit. "I actually haven't talked to him face-to-face yet."

"So, you're, like, text flirting?" Rory asks, watching me closely. "And you're *blushing*? Oh my God, you're in fourth grade."

"I am definitely not having fourth-grade thoughts," I tell him.

"Like maybe climbing a tree, but that tree is his—"

"Stop!" I smack him, my palm sliding off his sweat-slicked arm.

"Wow, girl," Rory says, shaking his head. "I think you actually like this one."

"So far," I admit, but I can't add much else, or really explain why. Baxter is nothing like the other guys that have come at me. I can't even tell if he's flirting with me, where most dudes make it completely obvious that they would do just about anything to get a piece of this. Baxter has been playing it cool, asking about my day, what my favorite movie is, what kind of music I work out to, my thoughts about things in the news—which I started reading as soon as he shared his opinion about Ukraine.

"Just be careful, okay?" Rory says, eyes still on my face. "Seriously. You just got your ass handed to you in the hallway last week by someone you trusted."

"I can't rebound with someone I haven't even met," I say.

"I know you, Shelby Black," Rory says, ignoring my brush-off. "You talk tough and walk tall, but you're the marshmallow part of the s'more."

"Yep, warm and sticky on the inside," I tell him, and he gives me a shove, knocking me sideways.

"Don't domestic violence me!" I shout, rolling away from him. He tries to get me in a kimura, but I slip it and put him in a guillotine that he can't break. His skin tone is gray before he submits by tapping out, and we roll off each other.

"Whose ground game needs work now?" I ask him, and Rory sneaks a glance to see if Paul noticed him getting owned by a girl.

"Worried he'll think you're straight?" I tease, tightening my wrist wraps as I see Faith closing out the toddler class.

"Not. At. All," Rory says, winking at Paul. "He knows."

There is no world where aluminum folding chairs are classy.

But I guess the same is true of black eyes and burnt coffee, so I don't know why the setting is the first thing I have to critique when it comes to the Survivors of Domestic Violence support group I've been assigned to. It's a hodgepodge of women from around the county, which means that I don't actually recognize anybody, but some of them definitely know who I am. There was an audible gasp when I walked in, and the woman next to me had done a quick Google search, not tilting her phone far enough when she'd typed in "athlete blond girl teen boyfriend punch." I'd been the first result, but the ones after that went south real fast, causing her to close out the window when her kid climbed into her lap.

"If everybody is ready, I'd like to get started," our fearless leader announces. She's built like a praying mantis and looks like she should probably hit the doughnut table before she exerts much more effort.

"I'm Judy," she says, looking each of us in the eyes as if trying to form a soul connection through simple introduction. "If everyone would like to just share who you are as we go around the circle, that would be great."

Judy turns to the lady on her right, who has been holding a hand towel up to her lips the whole time. She opens her mouth to speak, and a trickle of blood runs out.

"Whoa," the mom next to me says, and the woman wipes it away, blushing.

"Thorry," she says, but it comes out fuzzy, and with a lisp. "I'm Bella."

"Hi, Bella," Judy says. "What's going on with you right now?"

Bella dabs at her lips preemptively before speaking, the towel coming away red. "Huthband pulled out my front toof wif a plierth."

"Seriously?" I ask, not sure I heard her correctly. *"Pliers?"*

Bella nods, looking at me over the blood-spotted towel. "Latht time it wath back teef. That wath bad."

She says this like the location of the tooth is what matters and not the fact that her husband used a hand tool to do it, but also—last time?

"Are you telling me you—"

Judy cuts me off before I can question Bella's decision to go back to him. "It looks like you need medical attention," she says. "Have you been to the dentist?"

Bella shakes her head. "No inthurance."

"There are programs that can help you out with that," Judy says. "Come and talk to me after class, okay? We'll get you taken care of."

I think the only thing that's going to get Bella taken care of is a backbone and a shotgun, but that sort of thinking probably won't fly here. Judy turns to the next woman, a young brunette with bruises circling her neck.

"Lindsay, I'm sorry to see you again," she says.

"*Again?*" I blurt out, and Lindsay ducks her head, her mouse-brown hair covering her face.

"I'm sorry, and you are?" Judy turns to me, pointedly.

"Completely shocked," I announce. "That's what I am."

"But not at a loss for words, apparently," she says, giving me a stern look.

I'm accustomed to those, and they've been thrown at me by people much more intimidating than Judy. I was thrown out of the Beech Street Box after only one CrossFit class, when the instructor informed me that their firm rules of no swearing and not going shirtless meant that I was—in her words—*not a good fit*. I'd informed her that no one there was all that fit, and that she needed to work on her snatch before I'd stormed out. Insulting a woman's snatch is always a low blow, and I'm usually more clever than that, but my comebacks aren't always at their best right after cardio.

"Lindsay." Judy returns to the bruised woman. "Would you like to tell us why you're here?"

"Got into a fight with Devon," she says into her lap, where her folded hands are twisting each other. "Found out he was . . ." Her voice fades out, and she glances up, her foggy eyes passing around the circle, seeking out each one of us in a desperate need for comfort, even from perfect strangers. "Found out he had another girl."

There's a collective groan, a commiserating breath escaping our chests, the deflation of trust and the death of something we'd never recapture mingling with the musty smell of the courthouse basement. I remember spooning with Jayden, his arm tightly around my waist, one finger circling my ear, as we watched something on Netflix. His phone lighting up with a text and a photo that was all flesh. Even hating him can't burn out that pain, the drop in my stomach and the missed beat of my heart that follows.

"Went in for my yearly at the doctor's, you know," Lindsay goes on, pointing at her crotch. "Got a call a couple days later, telling me I had gonorrhea." She shakes her head, tears falling as she says the last word. "He's the only man I've ever been with so . . ." Lindsay holds up one hand and shrugs, a simple gesture to illustrate the logical conclusion.

"I'm so sorry, Lindsay," Judy says, and Bella reaches over to pat her knee, one hand still holding the bloody rag to her mouth.

"Men are shit," a redhead with a splint on her wrist says as she bites off a fingernail. "All of them."

It had taken me a little longer to come to that conclusion. I couldn't ignore what I'd seen on Jayden's phone, but I had given him the benefit of the doubt, assuming that Savannah Halden was making her move—one that I could easily counter. But when I'd confronted her at school and she'd shown me her phone and the ongoing exchange of pictures between the two of them, I'd joined the infinitely long line of betrayed women, all of us undercut and at a loss, weak-kneed and internally shook.

"When I told Devon, he . . ." Lindsay stops again, words not fulfilling their duties. She points to her neck, the string of fingerprints on them like dark pearls, and I wonder where the bruises were last time and how familiar she is with the courthouse basement.

It goes on, the next lady explaining that the stitches on her arm are partially her own fault—she shouldn't have tried to stop her ex from storming out of the house, and it could have been an accident when he slammed the door in her face, the glass shattering, slicing through the air, opening her skin.

The mother next to me speaks carefully, using coded words so that her young daughter won't know what her father had done, leaving chunks of hair and drops of blood scattered across the kitchen linoleum when leftovers were not considered an acceptable offering for dinner. Then it's my turn, Judy giving me permission to speak, along with a look that lets me know I need to behave.

I'm not great at that.

"I'm Shelby," I say, and a few heads nod like they already knew that. "And my boyfriend broke my nose last week."

"I'm so sorry, Shelby," Judy says, reiterating what she'd said to Lindsay.

I wonder if there's a script and she's just inserting our names in the blank. The other women shake their heads, and Lindsay raises a hand to the raised bump on the bridge of her nose where bone had not healed correctly. My eyes follow her movement, the cold void of pity filling with something new—disgust.

"Ex-boyfriend," I say, correcting myself. "I'm not giving him the chance to do that again."

The heads stop nodding, a few women exchange glances as Judy's practiced mask of well-meaning kindness slips into something more wary.

"He didn't just hurt me," I go on, my voice quickening. "He *disrespected* me."

And no one disrespects Shelby Black. At the Breakout Corner Fightfest last year Amanda Clearcreek had refused to touch gloves with me pre-match. When I'd knocked her out in the second round, I'd raised her limp wrist and forced the fist bump, and the crowd lost their collective mind. That particular reel had gone viral and kicked off a period of "mandatory sportsmanship" videos.

"I won't allow it," I say, feeling my jaw muscles tighten, my back teeth coming together so that my next words come out in a growl. "He doesn't get a second chance."

Lindsay's head falls again, her hair covering her face as Bella pulls the towel away from her mouth, inspecting it for a clean spot to use. The toddler on her mother's lap looks at me, lips curled downward.

"You're mad," she says.

"Fuck yeah, I am," I burst out, temper flaring. "Why the hell isn't everybody else? You're all just sitting here like a bunch of—"

"Shelby," Judy cuts me off. "Perhaps you didn't read the brochure that was sent to you?"

"I read your damn brochure," I bite back. "'No swearing'—is that what you're going to ding me on? Or is it *outbursts of anger*?" I put the last phrase in air quotes, my voice mocking.

"I am angry," I shout. "I'm pissed off. And I don't know why the rest of you aren't!"

"You're done," Judy says, coming to her feet and crossing the circle to stand in front of me. "I want you to sit in the stairwell for the rest of the hour. I'll talk to you afterward about arranging alternative sessions."

I huff and get to my feet, taking the walk of shame with my head high. The stairwell is dark, the light of my phone screen glaringly bright when I pull it out. I've got eight texts from Baxter, and my smile grows as I read them.

Made it back. Mom drives like a peasant.

Although I guess peasants probably don't have cars.

Pedestrians are peasants, that makes more sense.

That wanted to auto-correct to pheasants.

I have more respect for pheasants than that.

Especially the ring-necked kind. Very regal.

How was your day?

I kind of picture it always being like this:

He's sent along a clip from one of my fights, where Gretchen Lafferty tapped out in round five, blood dripping to the mat from a cut over my eyebrow where she'd clipped me with a nasty combo right out of the gate. The fire of anger in my gut cools, settling into something different, the warm coals of validation.

Baxter has been watching my fights.

Rear naked choke is my specialty, I text back, rewatching the video as I deliver a technically perfect hold from behind Gretchen. The message is tagged as read immediately, and three dots pop up a second later.

Are we sexting now?

I laugh, the sound echoing in the stairwell. I start to explain that's the name of the move in the video, but he beats me to the punch.

Kidding, I read about it.

I read about you.

I tap the screen with my thumb, wondering how to respond to such a straightforward declaration. I finally settle on something, and send it.

You a big reader?

Only if the subject interests me.

"Oh, look at you, smooth operator," I say, before sending my reply.

So I have your attention?

His response comes in five short, rapid-fire texts.

You

Have

My

Full

Attention

I lean my head against the stair rail, enjoying the rush. Chairs scrape against the floor in the next room as the meeting finishes up. I put my phone away and come to my feet, not meeting the other women's eyes as they brush past, the toddler peering at me over her mother's shoulder, unsure what to think of my exile.

"Shelby, I'd like to speak with you," Judy says, motioning me back into the room as she puts the folding chairs away.

I don't respond, but I do help her with the chairs, lining them all neatly against the wall.

"If you'll come into my office," she says, nodding toward a cubicle near the stairwell. I follow her in as she turns on the desk lamp, the halo of light illuminating piles of manila folders and stacks of police reports. I sit down across from her, highly aware when I feel my phone buzz in my pocket, three, four, five times.

"Shelby, I am sorry for what you've been through, and I appreciate the strength and fortitude that you've shown by choosing to break up with your boyfriend. But you have to understand that many of the other women in the group don't have that option."

"Leaving is always an option," I say, crossing my arms.

"It might seem clear-cut to someone like you," Judy says. "You're young, you aren't legally bound to your abuser, you don't have children with him, you're not financially reliant upon him, and I'm guessing you also have a strong support system outside of him."

"Yes," I say slowly. "But that doesn't mean—"

"You're one of those women in the sense that you have been hurt," Judy says, a glint in her eye and a hardness in her voice that wasn't present in the circle. "But you've not been *beaten*. That's what has happened to many of them—not just by their husbands or boyfriends. Life has beaten them. They don't have power, and they aren't free to make choices. Many of them have children they could lose, homes they would never see again, if they left their abuser. They make hard decisions and stay in these relationships, not because they are weak but because they don't have alternatives. You shamed them for that."

She holds my gaze, and I'm the first one to look away, dropping my head.

"I can't have you back in this group," Judy goes on. "They need to feel safe here, and that's not possible if you are present."

A bright bloom of guilt unfolds in my gut, the knowledge that I had made women who were already broken feel more brittle.

"Sorry," I mutter, reaching into my back pocket to silence my phone, as it goes off with yet another text from Baxter.

Judy nods, and I don't clarify whether the apology is for my behavior, or for the interruption.

"On the other hand"—Judy sighs—"I still have a duty toward you."

"It's not . . . ," I begin, my hand moving through the air, searching for words. "It's not the same. I'm not the same as them."

Her brow furrows, the desk lamp throwing her wrinkles into high-definition. "How so?"

"Like you said, I've got options. I've got the freedom to leave, and I've got people to take care of me."

"There are some differences," she agrees. "But I'm worried that you're not acknowledging the severity of what happened to you."

"I get punched in the face all the time," I tell her.

"Not by people who are supposed to love you," she counters. "It has a different effect."

"It doesn't," I say, my muscles tensing. "A broken nose feels the same, no matter who did it."

"Physically, I'm sure that's true," Judy agrees. "It's the emotional damage that I'm worried about."

"I'm fine," I say stiffly. "I broke up with him. He's out of my life. I'm moving on. We got into a fight, I wouldn't get out of his face, and he lost his temper. Nobody is perfect, shit happens, end of story."

"Do you believe you're partially responsible for your own assault?" Judy asks.

I look away, run my hands through my hair.

"I've seen the video," she goes on. "And the commentary."

"Yeah, that," I say, ignoring the tears that have sprung into my eyes. "Everybody has an opinion. Including my stepmom, but she doesn't need an internet connection to share it."

Judy's eyes narrow. "What did your stepmom say?"

"Over the course of knowing her?" I ask. "A lot."

She's quiet for a moment, watching me. I don't elaborate, just stare down at my hands and the weightlifting calluses there. I'm the first one to break the silence.

"It's just not the same, okay? You're right, I don't belong here. I got hit once, one time, by someone who won't get a chance to do it again. I'm not like Bella, who had her teeth pulled out—"

"It's not that bad, by comparison," Judy interrupts me. "Is that what you're saying?"

"I mean, yeah," I say.

"Shelby, listen to me," she says, leaning forward, and for the first time, I feel like we're off script. "You were assaulted. The severity may be different from what you saw here tonight, but the harm remains. You trusted someone, and he hurt you, physically, mentally, and emotionally. You likely haven't felt all the repercussions yet—"

"I'm fine," I say again, my jaw setting.

Judy goes quiet, eyes still on mine. Finally, she leans back in her chair, shuffling through some papers.

"I have a friend who occasionally takes some of my clients on her caseload. Since we agree that the group setting is not helpful to you or the others, I can make arrangements for you to put in the rest of your hours with her, in a one-on-one setting. Is that amenable to you?"

"Sure." I shrug. "Whatever it takes to get this over with."

Judy hands me a business card, and I take it, glancing down to see that it's for a woman named Kathy Hildebrand, of Directions Recovery. In her picture she's wearing a bright blue shirt, her dark hair in a cut that's about five years out of style.

"I'll be sharing your contact information with Kathy as well," Judy says.

"In case I don't call her?" I ask, slipping the card into my pocket.

"Exactly," Judy says. "I have an obligation to the county to ensure that you are properly guided through your road to recovery."

I roll my eyes but don't respond. We stand up together and leave her office, taking the steps in an awkward silence. In the parking lot, she turns to me, a breeze sending eddies of snow in a whirlwind around our feet.

"Look," Judy says. "I know that you don't like me, okay?"

"Wow, intuitive," I tell her. "You are good at your job."

She ignores my jab, talks over me. "But that doesn't mean I'm wrong. You were assaulted, and it harmed you. It doesn't matter how tough you are, and it doesn't make you weak to seek help."

"Cool tip, thanks," I say, walking away from her. I get into my car and start it up, glancing at my phone. I have ten texts—eight from Baxter and two from Fallon, who sends me a third as I'm watching. I mute her, looking up as Judy drives past, giving me a little wave as she does. She doesn't seem bothered by my dismissal; she's not angry that I'm blowing her off.

I think she's actually worried about me.

A flare of panic erupts in my gut, slicing upward for my heart, which has suddenly started beating rapidly, a sheen of sweat breaking out on my face. I start the car, roll down the windows, and let the cool air in, let it take away the eruption of fear and evidence of panic as my skin dries.

Then I read Baxter's texts, and let his admiration comfort me.

CHAPTER EIGHT

Fallon

I am absolutely stupid. I am a total idiot. I am such a fool.

It's 3:00 a.m., and I have regrets. I'd felt like a soldier of fortune, a warrior for justice, a forward-thinking feminist in the fight against sexual confusion when I turned in the application at the rec center. I'd shouldered the door on my way in, handing the paper over to the employee at the front desk as if daring her to defy me in my march toward virtue.

A lot can change in twelve hours.

I've had time to think, time to picture the staff processing the application. I'd looked over the About Us page on their site, only to spot the former school librarian—Ms. Lauren—there. She'd left the school last year when the board tried to force her to take what Mal refers to as "the gay books," off the shelves. Ms. Lauren is young and quick-witted, and I can see her glancing over our application, furrowing her brow. In my imagination, she points at the name of the group and says, "Do the rest of you really not see it?"

In the anxiety reel spinning in my mind, some of the staff do, most don't, but Ms. Lauren helpfully explains and parents are called. Mine. Shelby's. Jobie's. I have no idea how an underground, off-campus, student-led sex ed group masquerading as a self-help class would go over at the other households, but I know what would happen in mine. My parents might be liberal enough to allow for the conversation that we had at the dinner table the other night, but my organizing a group with the intent of sexual revolution, and using public property to do it, would not go over well.

When Mom's phone rang at dinner, I froze.

At 9:03 p.m., I sent a string of celebratory texts to Jobie to distract myself, which she didn't answer.

At 11:19 p.m., I googled, "Can you get in trouble for putting misleading information on an application for reserving a public space?"

That didn't yield much in useful facts, so at 11:36, I googled, "Is the first person to sign a document more liable than the others?"

All that got me was a lot of stuff I already know about John Hancock.

After the internet failed me, I tried to watch *Pitch Perfect 2*, but mostly I just kept checking my phone to see if Jobie had answered me to say what a great idea she thinks SHAFT Class is, and that it's going to be super useful, and maybe stop girls from making really bad, uninformed decisions.

She never did.

So, now it's three in the morning, and I just googled something else. "Can you get in trouble for talking to a minor about sex?"

And yes, you really can.

And I can't get in trouble. I'm a fixer and a people pleaser. I am always trying to do the right thing at exactly the right time, and if I mess it up even a little bit, I analyze what I could have done different and promise myself I'll do better in the future. Like when I interrupted Mrs. Dalford's last lecture to point out that she was confusing Tolstoy with Dostoevsky. I'd laid in bed that night worrying that I'd hurt her feelings, or if she thought maybe I was mocking her, and ended up googling how early Crumbl opened on Monday so I could get her a half dozen before school, along with an apology.

Which I did.

Because I'm Fallon Holloway, and I need everyone to love me.

I'm standing inside the glass-walled yoga room, yelling at Jobie. She's on the outside, head cocked, watching my mouth move. She shoots me a text.

Can't hear you.

"How about NOW?" I shout, raising my voice.

She shakes her head.

"WHAT IF I YELL *PENIS*?"

Okay, that I heard.

Jobie opens the door and pops her head in. "But are we really going to be yelling the word *penis*?"

"Shhhh!!!" I hiss at her, glancing nervously through the glass. There is no one else on the second floor of the Presnick Recreational Center at the moment, and Jobie's voice is naturally quiet. But my nerves are on edge, and I can't shake the little cloud of dread that's been following me around since I woke up this morning.

"It's only the first meeting," Jobie says. "If you're going to freak out this badly every time, it might not be worth it."

I take a deep breath, practicing the breathing exercises a YouTube therapist said can help stave off a panic attack. "I'm not freaking out," I tell her—and myself. "I'm just aware of everything that could go wrong."

"And focusing on that, instead of what could go right," Jobie says, flopping down onto one of the yoga balls. "This is a good idea, Fal.

Just think about all the things you've had to explain to me over the years."

This is certainly true. Jobie had almost peed her pants in sixth grade on a trip to the zoo, because she was afraid she could get pregnant from a public toilet seat. When I explained to her that it was virtually impossible for sperm to live outside a human body for that long, she'd asked me what sperm was.

"You're right," I say, letting out a slow exhale with the words, just as Mal and Shelby come up the stairs, followed by two girls I'm pretty sure are sophomores.

"What the hell?" I wheeze, clutching my chest and motioning everyone inside the yoga room and shutting the door.

"What?" Shelby asks. "You said we could bring friends."

"I did?" I ask, looking to Jobie for confirmation, who nods. Apparently I'd made that call *before* I'd spiraled over possible repercussions. I close my eyes, centering myself. When I open them again, I realize I'm being extremely rude, and my people-pleasing urges kick in hardcore.

"Sorry," I say, locking eyes with one of the underclassmen. "I'm just a little on edge. I'm Fallon."

"I know," she says, nodding. She's a petite blonde with big blue eyes, and a cute little button nose with a tiny flash of a metal stud in it. "I'm January, and this is Amara."

"January is in marching band with me," Mal says. "I overheard her talking to Amara about taking genital warts off with WD-40, and I figured she should come to SHAFT Class."

"Okay, that's . . . no." I shake my head, reassured that what I'm trying to do here is necessary. "Please don't put abrasive chemicals on your vagina."

"I didn't," January reassures, taking a seat at the circular table. "I mean, I don't even have a wart, but I saw this TikTok where—"

"And don't get advice from TikTok," I add.

"There are actually some decent ones," Amara chimes in. "There's this chick that teaches self-defense moves, like how to get out of holds if someone grabs you, and stuff."

"Shoot me some links," I say, sliding my phone across to her. "I'll check them out."

"Cool," she says, texting herself from my phone, then handing it back to me.

"January, Amara, I'm really glad you're here," I tell them, as the other girls all take a spot on the mat, sitting crisscross applesauce. And I kind of mean it, now that my nerves are settling.

"Are we starting?" Jobie asks, glancing up from her phone.

"Do you need to bang a gavel or something?" Mal asks.

"Maybe it should be a dildo," Shelby says. "I can totally bring one if—"

"No," I say sternly. "No gavel. No dildo. I'm not banging anything."

"Yeah, we know," Mal says. "You already said you're a virgin."

"Wait," Amara says. "How are we going to get sex tips from you if you're a virgin?"

"First of all," I say, raising my voice enough to gain control of the room but hopefully not enough for it to be heard through the glass walls. "This isn't about sex tips. That is not the point at all. It's sex facts, sex education."

"Riiiiight, but . . ." January's eyes are on mine, light blue and apologetic. "How do you know stuff if you aren't, like, actually doing it?"

"I read," I say, to which Mal, Jobie, and Shelby all burst into laughter.

"Sorry, sorry," Mal says, holding out a hand. "Listen." She turns to the underclassmen. "Fallon formed this group, but she's not an instructor or anything like that. None of us are. We're all here to kind of pool knowledge, talk about things we've heard or stuff we have questions about."

"Okay, so, like, why does Cody Hughes's dick look funny?" January asks.

"He's not circumcised," Shelby says quickly.

"Confirmed." I nod.

"Oh, rock on, Fallon," Mal says, offering a fist to bump.

"I said I was a virgin; I didn't say I was chaste," I tell her, hitting her knuckles with mine.

"Wait, so we've all had our hands on Cody's dick?" January says.

"Count me out on that one," Jobie says.

"For the record, you can exclude me from any dick questions or considerations," Mal says. "Just in case you didn't already know. Really gay over here."

"Put that together on my own," January says, smiling.

"How did you know you were gay?" Amara asks Mal. "Like when did you figure that out?"

Mal shrugs. "Same way a straight person knows they're straight. You have a moment where you look at dudes and feel something. I feel that when I look at chicks. But not all chicks," she quickly amends.

"Seriously," Shelby jumps in. "I cannot get this girl into bed."

"I'm just not into you," Mal says.

"I'm straight, by the way," Shelby says to January and Amara. "I just like to flirt with Mal to raise her spirits."

"So, back to Cody's penis," I say, steering the conversation. "Any questions about circumcision?"

January has some—and isn't shy about asking—which prompts a few out of Amara as well. I can tell by Jobie's face that she's definitely learning a thing or two herself, although she does look away when I pull up a diagram on my phone. I glance at my watch, surprised to find that we've used up almost our whole hour of reserved time in the yoga room.

"We've got about ten minutes," I tell the group. "Any other burning questions before next week?"

"Uh . . ." January glances up, blushing. "It might be stupid . . ."

"There are no stupid questions," I reassure her.

"Is it true that the dye in Mountain Dew is a spermicide?" January says quickly, the words rushing out of her mouth.

"What?" I ask.

"She's about to retract the no-stupid-questions statement," Mal whispers to Shelby.

"I'm not," I snipe at them, leaning forward to address January. "No, Mountain Dew is not a spermicide."

"Did someone dip their dick in it and tell you they were good to go?" Shelby asks.

"No," January says, looking away. "I was dating Dan Taylor last year, and he told me that if he drank enough it would make him sterile, so we didn't need to use a condom."

"And you're somehow miraculously not pregnant?" Mal asks.

"I told him he had to pull out," January says.

"That's not an effective birth control method, either," I tell her. "Maybe next week we should focus on pregnancy?"

"Come play on my team," Mal says. "Girls don't get girls pregnant."

"Unless it's some weird Jurassic Park situation," Jobie adds.

"They didn't get each other pregnant," Mal corrects her. "They reproduced through—"

I hear footsteps on the stairs, and Ms. Lauren appears in the hallway outside. I slice my hand through the air, cutting Jobie off and say loudly, "It sounds like maybe we need to focus on the self-help aspect a little more?"

"For sure," Shelby says, catching on fast, even though her back is to the outer wall. "But wear comfortable clothing next time. I can't exactly instruct you all on self-defense when your jeans are so tight you're going to get a UTI."

She looks at Jobie, who is sitting next to her, and gives her a shove.

"Huh?" Jobie asks.

"Maybe some crafts next time, round out the self-help part?" Shelby continues, jerking her head toward where Ms. Lauren stands, watching us.

"Ohhh, absolutely." Jobie is instantly excited, but I can tell she has no idea what Shelby is trying to communicate. "How about potted plants? I've got this great Pinterest—"

"That sounds great," I practically shriek, aware that we are now committed to potted plants next Wednesday, like it or not.

I silently mouth *Thank you* to Shelby, as Ms. Lauren holds up her wrist, tapping on an imaginary watch. I give her a nod as the other girls come to their feet, the next group to use the room lining up outside. If I remember correctly, it's called Baby Weight, and it's for young mothers who want to shed their pregnancy weight, but you use your baby as the weight.

We file out, Jobie falling in next to me as Ms. Lauren pulls me aside.

"Pretty nice turnout," she says, eyes sliding over the other girls as they descend the stairs. "I'm impressed you could even bring anyone outside of your founding members on the first night. Getting teens to show up for programming is almost impossible."

"Self-care is important, and we all deserve some me-time," I tell her, reciting the canned response I'd concocted ahead of time.

January, Amara, Mal, and Shelby have all gone to their cars by the time Jobie and I reach the parking lot, where she dramatically throws herself across the hood of my car, the back of her wrist to her forehead in a fake swoon.

"Self-care is so important," she mocks. "I need me-time!"

"Shut up," I scold her, with a smile. "You didn't exactly have a great deflection, either."

"No, but maybe don't talk like something someone painted on their living room wall next time," Jobie says.

"Next time." I nod. "Also, pregnancy—do you think we should look up some common misconceptions, or just let everyone bring their questions?"

Jobie thinks about that for a second, making her way over to her own car, parked right next to mine. "What about inviting Mallory Bennington?"

"Seriously?" I say. "How would you word that? Hey, Mallory, you got pregnant freshman year, why don't you tell us what you did wrong so we don't end up like you?"

"I'd say that exactly," Jobie says, deadpanning.

I roll my eyes and open my door, but Jobie stops me at the last second, knocking on the passenger window.

"I'm not kidding about the potted plants," she says, when I put it down. "Mom went through this whole religious phase a few years ago, volunteered to be in charge of crafts at Vacation Bible School. The potted plant thing did *not* go over well, because—"

"Do you think Ms. Lauren thought it was weird we weren't doing anything?" I interrupt her, biting at my thumbnail.

"I don't know," she says, unaware that those three words are going to plague me for the rest of the night.

CHAPTER NINE

Jobie

@!Cute!_Amy is an absolute godsend.

After the humiliating fiasco that was my rb/HardLooksMaxxing first—and final—post, Amy's message about plenty of guys liking cute girls had grabbed my attention. I'd told her to send them my way, she'd responded, but I'd soured on Rock Bottom and hadn't revisited the site to see the notification. When I'd gone a few days without responding, the site had sent me an email to let me know Amy was still waiting on a response. I'd felt a weird flush of embarrassment, like I'd let down a friend, and take the time to respond to her in the parking lot of the rec center after SHAFT Class.

@!Cute!_Amy—There are plenty of guys out there who want cute.

@Jobster{Lobster}—send them my way, lol

@!Cute!_Amy—ha, ha, lol.

@!Cute!_Amy—but yeah I can tell you some things you can do, get a little boost

@!Cute!_Amy—I know it sucks to see all the hearts and fire emojis on everyone else's posts, but "hey there, cutie," still makes me feel pretty good.

@Jobster{Lobster}—Soooo sorry. I didn't see your messages until now

@Jobster{Lobster}—yeah sometimes I feel like guys would beg,

borrow, and steal to be with some of these girls, but for me they're like, "I mean I'd cross the road, maybe."

Amy's responses had come in while I drove home, the notifications sliding across my Pandora app since I'd reset my preferences so I wouldn't accidentally ignore her again. When I got home, Mom was at the kitchen table, laptop open, the expression on her face and the empty wineglass next to her letting me know that she was probably working, not dating. I gave her a quick wave, and she delivered a parental face scan. I must've looked relatively content, because she let me get away with a quick hug and a good night before disappearing into my room.

@!Cute!_Amy—nah, those guys are out there, and they'll do more than cross the road for you. I dated a guy once that whenever we were out together and a super hot chick walked by, he'd be like–she looks like work.

@!Cute!_Amy—and it was just nice, like, he wasn't going to lie to me and be like, you're prettier than her (I mean, duh, I'm obviously not). But he showed me that I was what he wanted.

@!Cute!_Amy—You just have to know how to put yourself out there so that they can see you as a girl that wants and deserves their attention.

I stare at that last message for a second, chewing my lip while I debate, which is going to put a hell of a hurting on the expensive gloss I bought after seeing it on *@Lipsa^licious*. I definitely want attention, and I'm not ashamed of that. Shelby wants attention, too. The only difference is that she doesn't have to do much of anything to get guys to go all in on her, and I have to pull out all the stops in order to get a second glance.

@Jobster{Lobster}—I want attention, for sure. I just don't want to appear desperate.

@Jobster{Lobster}—Or have to take off my clothes to get it.

There's a green dot next to Amy's avatar—the female bunny character from *Bambi*—so I'm not surprised when she responds immediately.

@!Cute!_Amy—Girl, no. You don't have to disrespect yourself.

@!Cute!_Amy—Check out my IG, you'll see what I mean.

She shoots me a link, and I click through. Her Instagram account is not that different from mine—an average teenage girl posting pics of herself doing very normal things. Just like me, there are shots of Amy at a football game, cuddling with her pets, sitting on a deck, watching a sunset, reading a book . . . but our likes and follows are a universe apart. Her most recent pic is of her—a cute but not overly attractive girl sitting on a dock, toes dipping into the water. She's not wearing a bikini; in fact, she's got on jean shorts, a ball cap, and a jacket. But the pic has over 600 likes and 225 comments. I scroll through, curious.

@HuntFish(Life)—You've got me. I'm yours

@Dylan/Tyler/Devon—Cute AF

@World[s]Away—Need you in my life

It goes on like that, nothing sexually aggressive or insinuating, just compliments and kindness. Do I want people to lose their minds if I post a pic of me in a sports bra hip-thrusting iron like a sex goddess? Yeah, I do. But I don't even own a sports bra, and I'd just end up in a pelvic cast if I tried to be Shelby Black. I'm never going to be the girl everyone wants to be with, but I can be the girl at least a certain portion of the population enjoys looking at. I flip back over to Rock Bottom and respond to Amy.

@Jobster{Lobster}—you've got a legit army of admirers!

@!Cute!_Amy—yep, and very few perverts, lol

@!Cute!_Amy—I'm not going to lie, I get the random weirdo in my DMs asking for feet pics, but I just ignore and block.

@!Cute!_Amy—You got an IG?

@!Cute!_Amy—By what I saw on HardLooksMaxx, trust me, you could have your own army pretty quick!

"Ha," I say aloud. It's one thing to read the comments on Amy's pics and feel some validation on behalf of all the fours and fives of the world, but believing that I myself could pull that kind of admiration is like the inspirational quotes board on Mrs. Dalford's wall—just because something looks good in cursive doesn't mean it's true. But I can't say I'm not interested in what Amy has to share. I know everything there is to know about lighting and angles, how to tilt my head and which filters to use. But all of that work has netted me a quarter of Amy's follows, and zero boys telling me they need me in their lives.

@Jobster{Lobster}—yeah, my IG is the same as here

@!Cute!_Amy—so are you an actual lobster or do you live on the shore or something?

@Jobster{Lobster}—lol, no

@Jobster{Lobster}—I have kind of a weird name so it's a nickname a friend gave me a long time ago when we were kids.

@Jobster{Lobster}—Jobie doesn't rhyme with anything

@Jobster{Lobster}—and no the only shore in Ohio is on Lake Erie and I'm not even close to that. Totally landlocked here. Can't get cute dock photos like you!

@!Cute!_Amy—Jobie is a totally awesome name.

@!Cute!_Amy—I can't think of anything nice to say about Ohio tho, lol

@!Cute!_Amy—And they aren't complimenting the dock!! Everyone in Oregon has dock pics.

@!Cute!_Amy—brb going to check out your insta

I feel a weird little lift in my stomach, a flutter of nervousness that Amy is going to see my extreme efforts that net meager reactions. I imagine her responses—*omg, get a better cat. Wtf is going on with your hair in this one?* And *Wow, seriously offensive high school mascot there.* I roll onto my stomach and click on my photo roll, pulling up the New You photo of the Jobie I could be if I had $75,000.

She's still there. Still perfect. Still unattainable.

The astronauts didn't just stare at the moon thinking about how cool it would be to get there but taking no steps to make it happen. I *can* look like this. I *can* be the girl that posts a selfie and every guy gets bricked. I *can* get hearts and fire emojis, and boys begging for attention in my DMs.

I just need a shit ton of money.

A notification pops up letting me know that Amy has messaged me on Rock Bottom. I flick back to the app, skipping over a message from *@Bras-Are-Boob-Prisons* to see what my new friend thinks of my Instagram.

@!Cute!_Amy—First of all, you are ADORABLE

@Jobster{Lobster}—omg stop

@!Cute!_Amy—not even kidding. You've got exactly what a lot of guys want

@!Cute!_Amy—you're attainable, but not low rent

@!Cute!_Amy—you're sweet and open looking

@Jobster{Lobster}—open looking?

@!Cute!_Amy—yeah, you look like someone could be like, hey let's go jump in the lake, and you'd be like, sure! I like to have fun!

@!Cute!_Amy—sorry, but your friend does not look like she would jump in a lake, lol

She sends along a screen cap of one of my recent posts, a picture of me and Fallon at the last home football game. Fallon's got her literal game face on—*PHS* painted under one eye. She has always adamantly refused to add our mascot (a caricature of a Native American, much to the dismay of at least five people in the district) to her other cheek. She's smiling, her perfectly aligned teeth shining brightly past her ChapStick-coated lips. There's nothing wrong with how Fallon looks, exactly, but I can see what Amy means. Her smile carries a little bit of duty in it; I'm sure she was thinking, *Great, another picture for Jobie's social media and one, two, three—smile!* And her eyes are missing the twinkle that mine have, that undeniable guarantee that I am actually having fun.

@Jobster{Lobster}—yeah, she's a pretty serious person

@Jobster{Lobster}—I mean, I absolutely love her, but no she would NOT jump in a lake.

@Jobster{Lobster}—well, maybe she would but she'd neatly fold all of her clothes first

@!Cute!_Amy—I've got a friend like that too. She's my bestie, for sure, but sometimes I'm like, omg can we do something other than organize your bookshelf by color? lol

@!Cute!_Amy—So, PHS? When you were in middle school did the cheerleaders have to shout P-M-S!

I snort, and Princess Tinyhead gives a small startle, rousing herself from a state of constant immobility. The cheerleaders did find themselves in a bit of a quandary in seventh grade, when they were faced with the question of what should be stitched on the front of their uniforms: a reference to menstruation or a culturally insensitive logo featuring a headdress. For once, I had not envied them.

A text from Fallon comes in—**Do you really think Ms. Lauren thought we were being weird?**

And seriously maybe asking Mallory to come next week is a good idea.

But definitely not the way we talked about in the parking lot!

The last text is followed by a crying smiley face, but I'm not fooled. Fallon is doing what she does best—worry. Worrying and planning are her specialties, and occasionally the two weave together into a panic attack tapestry. She typically sends me a series of texts that allude to what she's currently freaking out about, and it's my job to decode, then soothe.

A DM from Amy bumps Fallon's text, and I tap the Rock Bottom app.

@!Cute!_Amy—I've got some ideas for your IG, if you're open

Being open is what I just got complimented for, and finding out how I can up my game sounds way more interesting than taking care of Fallon right now. I swipe her texts out of the way, not accessing them. If she sees I read them and didn't respond right away, she'll just spiral further and I'll have more work to do tomorrow.

Right now, I'm going to work on me.

Fallon can go jump in a lake.

Or more likely . . . not.

PART TWO

The circle of mourners expands and contracts, everyone wanting a better view, a closer look, the right angle as the hearse arrives. It rolls into the cemetery, splashing dirty water onto clean clothes, leaving stains, muddy tear tracks tracing the naked legs of girls.

Some backpedal, others move closer. Some in the crowd shift, hiding their phones at their sides, capturing the moment under the guise of reverence, telling themselves it's out of respect for the dead, not proof of their own presence, evidence of their deep connection to the one who was lost.

Others pull blooms from flower wreaths, take them home to press, write her name underneath.

Someone twists a strand of her hair around their finger, plucked from her head during calling hours.

Another rereads the last text she sent them, screen-caps it to show others.

Everyone wants their piece, something to consume.

This is the fate of a girl.

CHAPTER TEN

Shelby

I do not believe in love at first sight.

In fact, a month ago I would've said I'm pretty sure I don't believe in love at all. I haven't exactly had the best models in my life; Mom and Dad split up when I was so little, I don't even remember them being together. Dad and Taylor have this kind of casual "we live together and occasionally smile, but don't really like each other that much" type of relationship. If I believe social media—and I don't—most of the girls I follow have found *the one* at least five times, and I've held enough ponytails while girls from the gym puked in the toilet after a hard post-breakup workout to know better than to let any boy cross the boundaries of my heart.

The boundaries of my body might be a little more penetrable, and I definitely run my mouth, but the truth is that while I've racked up heavy make-out sessions with most of the qualified options in Presnick, and the vast majority of anything worth touching in the fight circuits, I've only had actual sex with two guys.

Or, as Jobie calls it, "pee-pee in the hoo-hoo."

"That is definitely not the proper terminology, and I will not be referring to it that way," Fallon says, fingers tightening on a pen as she jots down notes for our next SHAFT Class meeting. The four of us have gathered at the coffee shop before school in order to discuss how we can continue to talk about sex at the rec center without anyone suspecting that we're talking about sex at the rec center.

"Shelby, you said the staff wanted some pics with you?"

"Yeah," I say quickly. "Ms. Lauren grabbed me after last week's meeting. I don't think she was actually checking in on us, or anything like that. She came up there for me, looking for ways to *broaden their messaging.*"

I make air quotes around the last phrase but don't add that Ms. Lauren had passed on pics that night when she saw my face and instead did a deep dive on my personal well-being. I'd assured her that I was fine, then made a big deal about how important our little group would be to my recovery.

"Self-defense, you know?" I'd said, taking a fake jab at her. She'd surprised me by dodging it, then asked some follow-up questions about why we were all sitting down instead of doing anything remotely connected to fitness. I explained about the lack of proper clothing but then pivoted and said, "But it's also a self-help group, right? So we're going to do some of that shit—sorry—some of that stuff, too. Like I think potted plants? Did you know if you talk to plants they grow faster? Everyone needs someone to talk to, right?"

I don't think that's exactly true, and I'm pretty sure that if I said everything I was thinking to a plant it would wither and die, but Ms. Lauren had seemed content enough with my responses.

"I doubled down on the plants thing," I inform the group. "So we're married to it now."

"Married to a plant," Mal sighs. "Just like the fortune teller warned me."

"Okay," Fallon says, making a note in her journal. "Jobie, you said your mom might be able to help us out with that?"

"Oh *yeah*," Jobie says, lighting up. "She got them from this overstock place, and Mom didn't check what the seeds were—"

"Did Ms. Lauren say anything else to you?" Fallon asks, interrupting Jobie, which is something I've noticed happens a lot.

Granted, Jobie's stories can get long—I have detailed information about how to push back my cuticles now, despite the fact that I explained to her that I just tear mine off with my teeth—and I'm sure Fallon has a lifetime of experience knowing when to hit the Jobie mute button. But if Fallon were a dude, I'd accuse her of sexism and then roll the tape on the number of times she shuts down Jobie in a day.

Jobie's phone goes off before I can answer Fallon, and she makes a grab for it, stopping herself just in time when Fallon gives her a look.

"You're not going to see how far you can stick that coffee stirrer in your ear, are you?" Fallon asks disapprovingly, referring to the latest social media challenge, which has ruptured a few eardrums of the less-than-intelligent types.

"Of course not," Jobie sniffs. "Why would anyone do that?"

"I don't know, why do you have a favorite flavor of Tide PODS?" Fallon asks, and Jobie colors a little, which tells me she's made some mistakes in the past.

"You're not the one who stole Mrs. Dalford's KIA, are you?" Mal asks.

"No," Jobie says. "I haven't done a challenge since . . ."

"The Dollar Store ran out of cinnamon?" Fallon provides.

"You filmed that," Jobie shoots back. "Which makes you a co-conspirator."

"Pretty sure it doesn't," Fallon says smoothly. "And once again, we're in a phone-free zone right now."

Jobie, Mal, and I had walked into Grind the Bean with our faces in our screens, and Fallon had promptly informed us that if she didn't have our full attention, she didn't want any of it at all. Normally I would've bristled, tossed my hair, and walked out, but her words were an echo of a DM from Baxter—**you have my full attention**. I do, and it feels good. I can't blame Fallon for asking for it as well.

"We should ask Ms. Lauren if we can put them in the big bay window in the back of the rec center," I say, bringing attention back to Jobie's potted plants. "Lots of light, right? Then when the seeds sprout, it's like our group contributed to the rec center. We'll look all helpful and giving."

"Helpful and giving . . . ," Fallon muses, jotting that down in her notebook. She stops midsentence, looking up at me. "Are you being facetious?"

"I don't know what that word means." I pause for a second, as if in thought. "Which is weird, because usually I have a pretty good handle on f-words."

"That's my girl," Mal says, fist-bumping me.

Jobie hides her mouth with a hand, and Fallon looks at me, trying hard not to crack her own smile. She ends up sighing and shaking her head.

"Anything else?" Fallon asks, as my phone goes off.

It's sitting face up next to hers on the table, and she instinctively glances at it.

"Sorry," she says. "I didn't mean to—"

"Oh my God, it's fine," I say. She hands my phone to me face down, and I feel an unexpected rush of affection. At the gym if someone is acting precious about an incoming text, we tend to take their phone and run around the mats screaming, "Who wants to see nudes?!" until someone tackles the thief and forcibly takes their personal property back. I've been on both the top and the bottom of that pile, and I thrive in that atmosphere.

But being around someone that has manners is kind of cool, too.

"I've been texting with Baxter Latcha," I admit, to which Jobie and Fallon lean in, eyes wide, eager for more.

"Not a fan," Mal says, and I shoot her a glance.

"You can do better," she adds.

"The new guy?" Fallon asks. "I don't think I've met him yet."

"Technically, I haven't, either," I tell her.

This is a big reason why I can claim I don't believe in love at first sight; I haven't actually *seen* Baxter yet.

"Wait, so you're texting, but you haven't actually met?" Jobie asks, confused.

"Yeah." I shrug. "Haven't you ever talked with someone you don't know in real life?"

"Uhhh . . ." Jobie's eyes cut to her phone, but Fallon has more questions.

"So are you texting, texting? Or is it more like, 'hi, how are you'? And also, seriously, how are you? We haven't really talked about . . ." She makes a vague gesture toward my face, which has mostly settled back into its previous shape, with only a tinge of yellow still lurking under the skin, the shadow of bruise.

"I'm fine," I say, repeating the mantra that I've used on Dad, Taylor, Rory, Coach Faith, and, most recently, Kathy Hildebrand, when I called to make my first appointment at Directions Recovery. "And I think we're texting, texting."

There's an *I think* thrown on there, because while Baxter is definitely flirting, he isn't coming all the way across. I'm used to perfect strangers flooding me with worship, asking for my hand in marriage, and offering to cut off an appendage—my choice of which one—to score a date. So, the bar might be set kind of high. Baxter has been operating in a way I'm not accustomed to; I've got a steady feed of contact, interest, and admiration, but no offers to subjugate himself yet.

Healthy people are weird.

"We are meeting up today at lunch," I tell the girls, to which Jobie and Fallon collectively inhale and clutch hands. "Oh my God, you guys," I say. "Get boyfriends."

"Pass," Mal says.

"Easier said than done," Jobie says, while Fallon rejects my statement with "I'm too busy."

"It is easy," I say, pointing at Jobie. "Males are desperate, pathetic creatures. They need us, not the other way around. Make them chase you, don't be picky, and you'll be fine."

"And if I've got time, you've got time." I switch my finger over to Fallon.

"I actually don't care a whole lot about it," she says, and I believe her.

"I care way too much," Jobie admits.

And I believe her, too.

Nerves are a bitch. So is my stepmom.

"No, Taylor," I say into my phone as I head out the double doors at lunchtime. "I'm not going to stop and get cat food after training just because you ask me to. Number one, it's your cat. Number two, there's no reason you can't do it yourself."

There's silence from the other end as I scan the grassy expanse behind the school, and the pine tree next to the exterior door of the boys' locker room.

"I've tried with you, Shelby, I really have," Taylor says, an old conversation coming up for fresh air. "It wouldn't hurt you to be a little—"

"Nicer," I finish for her.

"Just because you know what I'm going to say doesn't make it any less valid," she comes back. "I swear that the only thing that makes you happy is punching people and hurting my feelings."

"Let's combine the two sometime," I say blithely, but Taylor has been deflecting my one-liners for years, and the ability to shock her faded way back in sixth grade, when I explained to her that we could write off my Brazilian waxes as a business expense, since I fight in shortie shorts.

"Your boyfriend broke your nose, and you still haven't learned," Taylor says.

"Haven't learned what?" I ask.

"You're too much," she says. "Too much, too hard, too fast. A hundred miles an hour, twenty-four hours a day. Someday you're going to hit a brick wall, and you'll find out what happens next."

"Dad's got a great life insurance policy on me," I tell her. "What happens next is you'll buy yourself something nice."

I hang up, not wanting to give Taylor any more of my time when I spot someone sitting out by the Pee Pee Pine. My heart jumps into my throat, and I take a second to gather myself.

"Get your shit together, Black," I say.

But I can't deny that I'm nervous as I walk toward Baxter Latcha. I am accustomed to having the upper hand in most heterosexual interactions, and my competitive nature means that I'm usually calculating who has more power in any given relationship. Just about the only person I don't do this with is Rory; with everyone else, I'm pretty confident I'm the one in control. That isn't entirely the case with Baxter, so I'm extra breezy as I approach the boy sitting under the maples, head down in an issue of *National Geographic*. I glance at the cover.

"How's Zambia doing these days?" I ask.

"Oh, you know, lots of waterfalls," he says, looking up at me.

I didn't know Zambia had waterfalls, and couldn't even find it on a globe, but I nod while trying to look well informed about developing countries. Meanwhile, we're doing a very honest physical assessment of each other, eyes roving. Except, mine aren't traveling far. I'm captivated by Baxter's mouth, which has a little twist to it that makes me think he knows something I don't . . . and I have a very great desire to either prove him wrong, or find out what that thing is.

Except, of course, if it's Zambia facts, I'm going to have to admit defeat.

While I'm watching, his lips break out into a huge smile, revealing slightly crooked lower teeth that normally might make me keep scrolling, but for some reason on him it's endearing.

"Wow," he says, shaking his head as he comes to his feet. "Shelby Black."

Normally I'd respond with something like *Fuck yeah,* but all I can do is smile and say his name back at him, like we're children our mothers just introduced on the playground.

"Baxter Latcha," I say, and he takes a couple of steps forward, actually holding out his hand for me to shake.

It's oddly formal and weirdly comforting as he holds my gaze, his palm against mine. His hand is warm and soft, and for the first time in my life I'm insecure about my calluses. I look away, dropping my eyes as I feel the warmth of a blush rising, something that hasn't happened since I accidentally walked into the boys' locker room in fourth grade and got an early assessment of what my classmates were packing.

"Here, sit down," he says, motioning to the space next to him. There's about an inch of snow on the ground, but the pine has kept the area underneath it protected. The ground is frozen solid, I'm sure, but I'm not about to flinch at our first meeting.

"So . . . ," I begin, and quickly realize I have nothing to follow it up with. I'm socially comfortable, always sure of myself and able to make small talk with everyone, from the ref calling my fight to the girl whose face I'm about to beat in. I cast around, trying to remember what we last texted about, but the only thing I have in my head are Taylor's words.

Too much.

Too hard.

Too fast.

And while I generally think she's a useless person, I'm also aware that maybe my first face-to-face conversation with Baxter Latcha shouldn't be one-third concentrated on dick jokes, which is my usual icebreaker. So I go with my second icebreaker.

"You're not gay, right?" I ask.

To his credit, he only closes his eyes and shakes his head as if clearing it, then looks at me. "Coming out of the gate fast, huh?"

Too fast?

"Well, it's worth checking, because of the haircut," I say, and promptly regret it when his head jerks back, the twist of his smile disappearing.

Too hard?

"And the clothes," I add, my mouth barreling forward as I inwardly assess my performance, wondering if maybe it's not so much that I'm socially capable as that I just have no filters or regard for other people's feelings. "I mean, the clothes are nice they're just very . . ." I pause for the first time, aware that most of the words I was going to use to finish the sentence would get me canceled in any other county.

Too much?

"Trendy?" Baxter finishes for me, a tilt to his head that tells me maybe I haven't royally screwed this up within the first two minutes of our finally meeting.

"Yeah," I say, nodding quickly, agreeing fast. "We're just not used to men that actually groom themselves around here." A thought that immediately makes the word *manscaping* pop to the fore of my brain, which I wrestle with, extremely proud of myself when it doesn't make its way out through my mouth.

"I have eschewed the plaid and denim," Baxter says, the smile coming back. "It's cost me a bit, socially."

"You look fucking awesome," I tell him, letting that one slide out both because it's complimentary and because it's true.

I'd immediately done a height/weight calculation, plus a muscle-to-fat ratio as soon as Baxter came to his feet. Where I'd landed was that I could beat him up, but I didn't want to. He's taller than me by about an inch, his muscles wiry where mine are bulked, the outline under his Henley illustrating that there's a chest under there, but he's not going to be popping the buttons anytime soon. I'd made fun of his full head of hair straight out of 1973, but it's a shade of strawberry blond with highlights that girls pay hundreds of dollars for. As I'm watching, he tosses some out of his eyes, and the light catches it in all the right ways. Baxter Latcha might not be Instagram hot, but he is the first boy I've ever met that I would describe as being actually handsome.

And I like it.

"You look awesome, as well," he says, eyes meeting mine. They're a light blue, with a darker ring around the outside.

I catch myself staring and make a mental note that he doesn't swear, so maybe I shouldn't, either.

"Almost healed?" he asks, pointing to his own nose. It takes me a second to figure out what he's asking, because in order for me to recall that Jayden punched me in the face, I'd have to remember that Jayden exists, which has totally slipped my mind at the moment.

"Yeah," I say, looking away from him. "I'm fine."

It's the stock answer, the one that I've tossed out to everyone, letting it land on its feet and defy any response other than total agreement. But the seconds of silence that pass after I declare myself *fine* feel like an eternity with Baxter's eyes on me, and something extra spills out.

"He's coming back to school next week, so that's a little weird," I admit.

"Weird like the way trypophobia is weird, or weird like the way my *National Geographic* subscription gets me odd looks in the hallway?" Baxter asks.

"I don't know what trypophobia is, so I can't answer that," I tell him.

"Fear of circular patterns," he says. "Like honeycombs or lotus flower seeds."

"That's stupid," I say.

"It's actually not." He shakes his head. "It's attributed to the brain associating those patterns with danger, like the skin of a poisonous animal, or even the symptoms of infectious diseases, like smallpox or typhus."

"You had that answer ready," I say. "I'm going to assume you have trypophobia?"

"I mean . . ." He holds up a hand, and wiggles it back and forth. "I don't think it's entirely stupid."

I realize I'd just used that word to describe his phobia, and backtrack.

"Well, I don't have smallpox, so we should be good," I tell him.

"None of us have smallpox," he shoots back. "Everyone is vaccinated."

"Sorry, but I can't exactly guarantee you that everyone *here* is vaccinated," I tell him.

"A quick scan of the bumper stickers in the parking lot makes that quite clear," he says. "Although, I think we're likely safe from smallpox."

"Fingers crossed," I say, liking that he used the term *we*. "And I don't think subscribing to *National Geographic* is weird."

That's not exactly true, but I don't think I've ever known anyone that carried one around, so I hadn't really formed an opinion until about two minutes ago.

"Want to know a secret about *Nat Geo*?" Baxter asks, leaning in close.

"Yes," I say, meaning it.

He flips the magazine over, sharing a picture of some sort of gathering where no one is terribly concerned about nudity.

"Boobies," he says.

"So, not gay?" I ask. "Also, there are better ways to get your boobies."

"I grew up without a dad, so I couldn't exactly find anything lying around," he says.

"I grew up without a mom, but I had an internet connection," I hit back.

"Look at us, parentless and educating ourselves." Baxter smiles at me, and I find it impossible not to return it, my lips stretched impossibly thin, suddenly very aware of my own mouth and my teeth, as well as his. His eyes flick down to my mouth, and I know he's thinking the same thing.

"Just so we're on the same page, being gay is totally fine in my world," he says.

"Mine too," I say. "Actually, my best friend is gay."

Oh God, did I just do that?

"I have no friends yet, so I can't make any claims," Baxter says.

"Well, the electric car is not helping," I tell him.

"Maybe you'd like to form an opinion of it while sitting in the passenger seat?" he asks, and I have to take a second to review the question and make sure I didn't mishear it as "the back seat." But no, it appears that Baxter Latcha is not only handsome but also a gentleman.

A gentleman that just asked me out on a date. Or, at least, I think he did.

"Only if it's got a full charge," I say, which isn't all that clever, but Baxter has me scrambling in a way that's very new to me.

"Oh, I'm fully charged," he comes back, teeth showing again. "I'm just worried that my lack of conservative bumper stickers might put you off."

"As long as you're okay with me throwing empty beer cans out of your electric car, I think we can balance each other out," I say.

"Littering is a five-hundred-dollar fine," he says.

"Did you look that up as soon as you got here, or did you make sure you were registered to vote first?" I ask, and he bursts out laughing, holding his hands up in surrender.

"I was wondering if all your comebacks online took hours for you to put together or if you really were that quick," he says.

"Guess you learned something today, then," I say.

"A lot," he agrees, and we're smiling stupidly at each other again.

The bell that signals the end of lunch rings, echoing across the parking lot.

"Allow me an awkward fanboy moment before we go in?" Baxter says, and I nod. "Can I get a selfie?"

It's my turn to laugh, and I lean in as he snaps the picture, our smiles for each other, not the camera. We walk toward the school together, and he leans into me, our shoulders touching.

"Seriously, though, I'm in awe of the reality of you."

It's the most forward thing he's said yet, but unfortunately all it does is remind me of Fallon's comment about the reality of a penis, and I snort as he pulls open the double doors, our eyes meeting. For the first time, a shadow passes over his, a moment of indecision.

"What?" he asks.

"Nothing, it's just . . ." I shake my head, aware that I need to come up with something better than a brush-off in return for his compliment. I decide that the truth is the best route, even if it might be too much, too hard, too fast. "It made me think of something Fallon said, about the reality of a penis."

"Sounds like you have interesting conversations," he says. "Where do you land on that particular topic?"

I bite down very hard on my actual answer—which is *Past the tip*—

and come up with something slightly less aggressive.

"We agreed that it's something that needs to be dealt with," I say, which is actually pretty close to the whole reason why SHAFT Class exists in the first place.

The tardy bell rings, and he takes a couple of steps backward, still holding my gaze.

"To be continued," he says, pointing at me before turning away.

I slip into English class and my seat before Mrs. Dalford notices my lateness, only to feel my phone vibrating. I pull it out of my hoodie to see I've got an Instagram notification; I've been tagged in *@in*my*digitalopinion2025*'s newest post. I click over to see our selfie from outside, with his caption—**to a fortuitous first meeting**. If I'm going to be spending time with Fallon and Baxter, apparently, I'm going to need to brush up on my vocabulary.

Particularly, the f-words.

CHAPTER ELEVEN

Fallon

"You're being weird," Farrah accuses from the passenger seat, face buried in her phone.

"This isn't weird," I say, as I scan people leaving the McDonald's, especially the employees still wearing their visors. There's no response, so I look at Farrah and see her observing me skeptically over the edge of her phone.

"Okay, fine," I admit. "It's vaguely creepy. This is what happens when you ask me to pick you up from play practice."

"I find out my sister is a pervert?"

"I'm not—" My mouth tightens, and my hands curl on the steering wheel, just as a family of four are getting into their minivan. "Could you not say *pervert* so loud?"

"Per-vert, per-vert, per-vert," Farrah starts chanting, making me turn up the Rachmaninoff my Spotify playlist is currently offering, to which she completely changes her tactics, making a devil-horns symbol while headbanging.

"You're going to break your neck," I tell her, once she's finished.

"Maybe," she admits, eyes mildly unfocused. "But it's worth the rush. What's your excuse for your bad habits?"

"I don't have any," I say, watching the exit door.

“Except being a creeper,” she says breezily. “Seriously, who is he and why can’t you just be normal and stalk his Instagram instead?”

“It’s not a he,” I tell her, which she instantly latches on to.

“Wow, sis. I didn’t know, but it’s cool, and I support you.”

“Oh my God.” I finally give up, deciding the truth is going to be better than dealing with her half-cocked conclusions. “It’s not a dude, and it’s not a toxic thing. I need to talk to Mallory Bennington.”

“The pregnant girl?”

“She’s not pregnant anymore,” I tell Farrah. “Now she’s a mother.”

“Oh,” my little sister says, all humor gone from her voice. “That . . . I mean, is it bad to say that sucks?”

“I don’t know,” I admit. “That’s kind of why I’m here. I just need to ask her some questions.”

“About—”

But Farrah doesn’t get a chance to finish, because I see Mallory coming out of McDonald’s, head down, shirt untucked, barely picking her feet up as she walks.

“Be right back,” I say, throwing open my door and jumping out of the car.

“Uh-uh, no way,” Farrah says, and is on my heels before I can stop her.

“Are you serious?” I spin, hissing at my sister. “I need you to not be a total brat right now.”

“And I need to know why my sister suddenly has questions about pregnancy and being a teen mom,” Farrah shoots back, and I see the glimmer of worry in her eyes.

A matching flicker of guilt chases my irritation.

“Okay, listen . . .” I sigh. “You can come with, but no interrupting, and I’ll explain everything afterward. Also, I want you to know that

I'm giving in not because hounding someone until you get your way is the proper response, but because—"

"You know if you don't, I'll start screaming that you're trying to abduct me?"

I cross my arms and stare her down. "Literally everyone here knows that you're my little sister."

"Better get a move on," Farrah says, looking over my shoulder. "Your mark is getting away."

"Crapsticks," I mutter, turning to watch as Mallory climbs into a rusty Acura.

"Behave," I say sternly, poking a finger in Farrah's face before I approach the car. I bend down, knocking on the passenger window and giving Mallory a little wave. She's clearly confused, and I don't blame her. I know Mallory Bennington the way everyone knows everyone in Presnick, but we've never exactly hung out. She rolls down the window, eyebrows drawn together, and I hope she doesn't think I'm about to complain that my order was wrong.

"Hey, Mallory, it's Fallon," I say, to which the furrow over her nose deepens. Introducing yourself to people in Presnick is kind of like explaining that your dog is a dalmatian when it's clearly a black-and-white-spotted mammal.

"Would it be okay if I talk to you for a second?" I ask.

"I . . . guess?" Mallory says, her gaze shifting as Farrah comes up beside me, offering her own little wave.

"Can I?" I point at the door, and Mallory just kind of throws her hands up. I take it as an invitation and slide into the passenger seat, trying to hide my annoyance when Farrah includes herself by climbing into the back.

"Sorry," I say immediately. "I'm not trying to be weird, but—"

"No, everything about this is super normal," Farrah interrupts.

"I told you that you had to be quiet!" I say, turning to the back seat.

"I don't take instruction well," she says, shrugging.

"What the shit is going on?" Mallory asks. "I'm on my break, and I've only got fifteen minutes. So whatever you've got to say, make it fast."

"Sorry," I say again, turning to her, doing everything I can to make my body language open, my facial expression welcoming. Every people-pleasing tactic I have comes in full swing as I continue.

"Me and some other girls have been talking," I explain. "And it seems like many of our classmates have a lot of questions about sex."

"They put their dick in your—" Mallory begins.

"That's not exactly what I'm asking," I roll over her. "We've started a kind of . . . informal group," I continue, hoping that Farrah can keep a lid on herself for just a few more minutes. "After we met for the first time, it became clear that a lot of the underclassmen especially have misconceptions about how to prevent, uh . . ."

"Conception?" Farrah offers helpfully.

"Ohhhhh," Mallory says. "I get it. You want me to come in and be like a guest speaker on how they can not end up like me?"

I wince as she uses pretty much exactly the words I'd warned Jobie against. "No," I say, "not like that. It's more like . . ." I look out over the parking lot, trying to find words that won't be insulting.

"While you're figuring out how to be polite about this, I've got to pump," Mallory says, reaching into the back seat and dragging a duffel bag into her lap.

"Pump, as in—"

"Breast milk," she says, matter-of-factly pulling up her shirt and popping a boob out, then fitting it to a suction cup. She grabs a second cup and repeats the process, reaching into the bag and flipping a switch, causing a low hum to fill the car. Mallory leans back into her seat, head lolling against the headrest, clearly relieved.

"Lesson number one," she says. "Having a baby pretty much kills any modesty you had. I've been on my back with my legs in the air way more times over the past nine months than in my whole life before that."

"You are tits out in the McDonald's parking lot, so that's clear," Farrah says, making no attempt to hide her interest as Mallory's breasts empty, milk flowing through the tubes into collection bags. "We went to the McAllister dairy farm last year on a field trip—"

"Farrah!" I chide her, but Mallory only nods.

"Yeah, it's pretty much the same thing," she says, apparently not bothered by being compared to a cow.

"It's true," she goes on, when she notices the look on my face. "Your body becomes something different."

"What do you mean?" I ask.

"Like my vagina isn't just for sex, right? I gave birth to a whole other human being."

"So, it's like a passageway to another dimension . . . ," Farrah says, ignoring the warning glance I shoot her as she stares down in amazement at her own crotch.

"And my boobs, well . . ." Mallory indicates the electric breast pump in her lap. "They're not just for show anymore."

"What does that feel like?" Farrah asks, encouraged by Mallory's honesty.

"Uh . . ." Mallory glances down at her boobs, and the suction cups on them. "It's kind of like when you've got a really big zit, and you can feel it on your face all day and then once you get in front of a mirror to pop it, it hurts for a second and then it's just a release."

"Oh my God," Farrah says, almost crawling into the front seat in her enthusiasm. "I had one on my chin the other day. I swear, I'm surprised it didn't blow me across the bathroom when I popped that thing."

"It's like that." Mallory nods, the two of them apparently connecting. "Except it refills every three hours."

"Ugh." Farrah's hand goes to her chin and the scab there.

"But I don't think you want to know about the after part, do you?" Mallory asks, her eyes coming to mine.

"Not so much," I tell her. "Would you be able to come to the rec center Wednesday at seven?"

"I'm not working," she says, pulling up her schedule on her phone. "Can I bring Jesse?"

"Sure," I say, even though I have some trepidation about the group growing too quickly. "Does Jesse have questions about—"

"Jesse's my baby," Mallory says flatly.

"Oh," I say, talking fast to cover my flub. "Right. Of course. Sure. We'd love to have Jesse there." An alarm goes off on her phone, and Mallory begins to unhook herself from the breast pump.

"Thanks so much," I continue. "I'm sorry to bother you at work, and I'm sorry if we startled you, or offended you, or—"

"It's the most interesting conversation I've had all day," Mallory says. "Your sister is charming."

"Hell yeah, I am," Farrah says from the back seat, then raises her fist for Mallory to bump it. I crack open my door after giving Mallory my number, letting her know that she can get a hold of me if she has any questions before we meet.

"And hey," she says, just as I'm getting out. "I know everything I said probably makes being a mom sound like a shitshow." She fumbles with her phone, pulling up a picture and handing it to me. It's a selfie of her curled up in bed, Jesse cuddled against her, the baby's mouth hanging open in a deep sleep, one tiny hand resting on Mallory's cheek, fingers splayed.

"Would I change it if I could?" Mallory asks, taking the phone back. "Part of me says yes, because it's going to take everything I've got just to graduate from high school, try to make some money, and be a mom at the same time. But if I changed it, if I took it all back, then I wouldn't have my baby."

Not having a baby is definitely my preferred mode of life, but there's a glow about Mallory as she speaks, and a shine in her eyes that wasn't there before she looked at the picture of her and Jesse. Farrah is mercifully silent as we walk back to the car, and we're all the way to the one stoplight in town before she speaks up.

"So, Wednesday at seven?" she says. "I'm in."

"You're not," I say, as I take the turn. "And neither are any of your friends, acquaintances, or enemies. Talking to girls my age about this kind of stuff is way different than talking to a bunch of middle schoolers." The familiar rise of panic begins in my chest, billowing out to fill my throat. "There are some real risks involved—"

"No, I get it," Farrah says, agreeing so fast that I know there's more coming. "Is it okay if I take your line?" she asks, mouth curling into a mischievous smile.

"What's that?" I ask, shooting her a suspicious look.

"I've got an idea."

"Your ideas are bad," I say, half an hour later, facing Farrah across my bed.

"No, this could totally work," she says, pushing her phone toward me. "And you're the one that said sex ed was bullshit."

"Language," I say, cutting my eyes to the door. Mom and Dad are pretty chill, but swear words tend to carry farther than regular ones, and bringing our parents into this conversation is inadvisable to say the least.

"The school sex ed program is crap," I agree, whispering. "But that doesn't mean I can personally bear the responsibility of instructing every preteen in the district about the ins and outs—"

Farrah snorts at my choice of words, and I throw a pillow at her. "Seriously, dude," I say. "I don't want the group getting big. It'll draw attention we don't want."

"Which is why my idea is awesome," my little sister says confidently. "Start a social media account, and make some reels with highlights from your sex club meetings."

"SHAFT Class," I correct her.

"You don't want a big group at the rec center? Fine," Farrah says. "This way you can reach literally anybody. It might actually help a lot of people."

I can't deny the truth of that, and Farrah sees me wavering.

"Tell me one thing that's just totally ridiculous from your first meeting," she says.

"Mountain Dew can make you sterile," I say immediately.

"Why would anyone think that?" she asks.

"I looked it up. Yellow Dye 5 is what gives Mountain Dew it's color," I tell her, pulled into the conversation despite myself.

"The chemical name is tartrazine, and people got it into their heads that the mix of tartrazine and caffeine lowers sperm count. It doesn't," I make sure to add, giving her my serious face.

"I wonder how many Mountain Dew babies are out there running around," Farrah muses to herself, while tapping away on her phone.

"That would be difficult to answer," I tell her. "First, people would have to be willing to admit that was their method of birth control, plus you'd have to narrow your sample set—"

"Nobody really cares," Farrah says, cutting me off and handing me her phone. "Check this out."

She pushes play on a reel that she hasn't published yet, it's just a bright green background with Bill Hader dancing in a casually entertaining way to "Makeba" with the words *I was today years old when I found out Mountain Dew isn't a spermicide* splashed across it.

"Okay, that's actually pretty great," I admit. "But I can't just throw that out into the world on my socials. SHAFT Class is underground, remember?"

"Create an alt account," Farrah says.

I chew my lip for a second, staring down into my lap as Bill Hader tosses a saucy look over his shoulder. "But couldn't somebody figure out the location of the account?"

"Use a VPN to mask your IP address," Farrah says. "It spoofs your location, too."

"Do we need to talk?" I ask, raising my eyebrows at her.

"Apparently," she says. "How are you a teenager that doesn't know about VPNs?"

Farrah pulls up a new account on her phone. "Look, it's simple," Farrah says. "You probably shouldn't actually call it SHAFT Class, if you're trying to keep it on the down-low," she muses, typing in a few different alternatives to see if the account names are already taken. "How about this one?" She turns her screen to show me the name *@notyourmomssexed*.

I immediately downvote it. "Too easy to misread," I tell her. "Jennifer Ignatius found that out the hard way when she created a BookTok account with the name @girlwhoreads and ended up with a million subs in like two days, and not one of them interested in her book reviews."

"Fair," my sister says, thumbs flashing across the screen. "How about this?" She holds it up, showing me that she's added some punctuation for clarity.

@Not-Your-Moms-Sex-Ed

"I don't hate it," I admit. "Can you explain the VPN thing again?"

"Kids these days," Farrah mutters, rolling her eyes and holding her hand out for my phone. In a few minutes she's set me up on a VPN, created *@Not-Your-Moms-Sex-Ed* on Instagram, and used the Bill Hader / Mountain Dew reel as an initial post.

"Done," she says. "Just make sure you're signed into the right account when you post."

"Right," I say, glancing at my new online identity and gaining one sub in real time—*@not<that>farrah*. "Thanks for the follow."

"Are you kidding?" she says. "This is my new favorite thing on the internet. I can't wait to find out what Red Dye 40 can do for me."

"Or *can't* might be more accurate," I say, watching as *@Not-Your-Moms-Sex-Ed* gains two more followers, a repost, and three likes. "Seriously, good job with the name. I like it, and it's accurate. Mom's sex ed was probably better than what we have. At least they had bananas."

Farrah's eyes get a little wider. "I thought you said it was more like a plantain?"

"Depends on your luck," I tell her.

CHAPTER TWELVE

Jobie

We had to get more bouncy-ball seating for SHAFT Class, and Fallon is freaking out.

If *I have an idea* is what I hear out of her mouth the most, the second most common statement would be: *Is this a good idea?* She's asked me the same thing twice now, her voice dropping lower as attendance kept rising. We'd met Shelby on the second floor, holding her phone near a window and trying to get reception. Fallon shared the rec center Wi-Fi password with her, and literally fifteen texts from Baxter came in. I watched the notifications flood her screen, envy rushing in my veins.

Shelby had deserted us to respond to Baxter, disappearing into another room and then half-heartedly kicking a yoga ball down the hall while tapping out messages with the other hand. Mal had shown up with Amara close behind her, and January filtered in with three underclassmen in tow, which had prompted Fallon's first iteration of *Is this a good idea?* After that, my best friend's blood pressure continued to mount as the girls' basketball team showed up, followed by half the cheerleaders.

"We heard this was the place to be," Jacelyn Walters says as she walks in, teammates behind her. "Don't want a repeat of what happened over at Ridgeview. Pregnancy took out their varsity forward and point."

"I don't know what that means," Fallon says blankly.

"It means no more sports ball for mommies," Mal says, giving Jacelyn an upnod. "Probably cuts down on tumbling, too," she adds, turning to the cheerleaders.

The only good thing about Fallon's panic mode is that it also triggers her knack for delegation. "Jobie," she says. "We need potted plants, stat."

"Oh, wow, we're moving on to fetishes already?" Mal asks me, but I wave her off.

"Just do as you're told, it's much easier than resisting," I inform her.

Mal, Shelby, and I are sent out to the parking lot to get the planters and seed packets. I've got Fallon's keys dangling from my hand, along with strict instructions not to forget the three bags of Miracle-Gro in her trunk. Shelby's phone buzzes for the twentieth time as I pop open my own trunk and they get their first look at the planters.

"I'm triggered," Mal says.

From inside their box, a legion of ceramic circus clowns stare up at us with hideously massive smiles, arms opened wide on either side, a bowl emerging from the waistline of their pants.

"I'm weirdly not," Shelby says, cocking her head to the side as she takes in the ceramic clowns. Her phone goes off yet again, and she instinctively reaches for her back pocket.

"You've got to tell me the name of that vibrator app," Mal says. "Is it listed under Baxter or Latcha?"

"Oh my God," Shelby says, flipping Mal the bird but unable to hide the blush that rises in her cheeks, the red overtaking the last remnants of yellow bruising.

Amy chooses that particular moment to send me a string of DMs on Rock Bottom, causing my own phone to raise a ruckus in my back pocket.

"And what's yours listed under?" Mal asks.

"Cute Amy," I say, not able to come up with anything other than the truth.

"Nice," Mal hisses, nodding as Shelby motions for her to open her mouth, then promptly sticks ten seed packets in it.

"Better," Shelby says, patting her friend on the head.

"You guys go on," I tell them. "I'm on dirt duty."

I head over to Fallon's car and pop the trunk, pulling out my phone to see what Amy needs.

@!Cute!_Amy—totally stupid problem

@!Cute!_Amy—DM when you can

@!Cute!_Amy—god I'm so dumb

I rest against the back of Fallon's car, tapping out a response.

@Jobster{Lobster}—you ok?

@Jobster{Lobster}—what's up?

There's another message from *@Bras-Are-Boob-Prisons* in my message box, and I click over to it, having completely ignored her follow-up from our initial conversation.

@Bras-Are-Boob-Prisons—Rock Bottom can be a dangerous place for curious people. Just be careful out there, kid.

@Bras-Are-Boob-Prisons—Just checking in on you. Saw you haven't posted lately.

"Okay, creeper," I say, scrolling down to her most recent message.

@Bras-Are-Boob-Prisons—hey kid, just lmk that you didn't take that whole decapitation thing seriously, kay?

I debate answering her, then realize I can't even assume it's a *her*.

The mods at rb/HardLooksMaxxing had said they try their best to ensure members are female, or female-identifying, but can't make any promises. Her warning to be careful, following up with me when I don't interact, and checking my post history for activity has my warning bells going off. But I'm also a girl raised in the patriarchy, so cautiously polite is my default.

@Jobster{Lobster}—I'm fine. Just not really that into rb.

A rusty Acura pulls into the slot next to Fallon's car, the high wail of a baby emanating from it. Mallory Bennington gets out, gives me a nod, then pulls a diaper bag out of the car and fiddles with a complicated latch system on the baby seat, finally emerging with a baby, a bag, her phone, keys dangling from her mouth, and shutting the door with her hip.

"Single-mom skills," she says, words hissing around her keys, when she spots me watching. "You here for the sex thing?"

"Yeah," I tell her. "But definitely don't call it that. Fallon's on the second floor. I'm just getting the potting soil."

"Whatever," Mallory says, hoisting the baby seat and adjusting the diaper bag. "You people are weird."

I can't really argue with that, and begin my own complicated arrangement of trying to carry three potting soil bags in one trip so that I don't get in trouble with Fallon for *lollygagging*—and yes, she would call it that—when my phone goes off again.

@!Cute!_Amy—boy stuff, so dumb.

@!Cute!_Amy—I know I shouldn't let it get to me

A sympathetic noise comes out of my throat, and I drop the one bag I'd thrown over my shoulder, in a rush to commiserate. Amy had told me yesterday that she was going to take the leap and ask out the guy she was interested in, and I'd had my fingers crossed for her all day—something I'd illustrated by occasionally shooting her the crossed-fingers emoji while I waited for a report.

A text rolls in from Fallon:

Did you get hit by a car?

Followed by three from Mal:

Okay seriously get in here

She thinks you're dead

Like, actually

I mark Fallon's message as read so that she doesn't send out a search and rescue team, then throw a bag over each shoulder, carrying one in my arms and following Mallory's example by putting Fallon's keys in my mouth, something that will certainly result in her dipping them in antibacterial gel later. Ms. Lauren shoots me a look when I kick the handicapped button to open the door—something I'd also seen Mallory do—but rushes over to help when she sees how encumbered I am.

"Self-help project tonight?" she asks, holding out her arms to take a bag from me.

"Potted plants," I fumble for words, trying to find a way to reject her help without being rude. Unfortunately, I've still got Fallon's keys in my mouth, so it all comes out garbled and with jingles attached. Ms. Lauren is about to be forcibly helpful when a kid at the front desk starts hitting the bell repeatedly.

"This is not the county fair, and that is not Whac-a-Mole," she says to him, turning away from me. I make my escape up the stairs, grateful when Shelby meets me halfway, lifting both bags off my shoulders and draping them casually over her forearm. Her phone goes off three times before we can get inside the quiet room, and I see texts from Baxter lighting up her screen.

There are about twenty girls seated in a circle, each of them with a ceramic clown and a seed packet in front of them. Mallory's baby is also making the rounds, each girl handing her off to the next, some with marked enthusiasm, others taking a pass. To my surprise, Mal opens her arms when it's her turn, and Jesse dives for her face, cooing.

"Babies like me," Mal explains to the room. "Babies and animals. Jury is still out with humans over the age of five."

Mallory keeps an eye on the baby as Jesse makes a circuit, seeming not to know what to do with her arms when they aren't full. Fallon plunks a ceramic clown in front of her, to which Mallory gives my friend a glare.

"What is this?"

"Uh, are we in the wrong place?" one of the basketball players asks.

"No," Fallon says, clapping her hands to draw the room to attention, putting on a teacher voice she has perfected, even if it hasn't been earned yet. "If you're here to talk about sex—" She promptly claps her hand over her mouth, glances out of the glass walls, then drops her voice.

"You're in the right place," she goes on. "But the rec center thinks we're using this space for a self-help slash self-defense class, so we have to keep up that illusion."

"In other words," Mal says, pulling open a bag of potting soil. "You all just became very interested in gardening, okay?"

Everyone nods, and Fallon takes a seat next to Mallory, visibly wincing when Jacelyn upends the bag over her clown, dumping soil all over the mat.

"Mallory has offered to speak—"

"I don't have a speech or anything," Mallory says, taking Jesse back onto her lap.

"Why don't you just start by telling us your story?" Fallon offers, and I see Mal hide a quick smile.

I duck my own head and see a notification from Rock Bottom.

@!Cute!_Amy—it didn't go so hot

@!Cute!_Amy—he gave me the whole "you're nice and all . . ."

My heart sinks for Amy, having been told how nice I am more than once, quickly followed by a *See you around*, or *I'll follow you, though!* Not that I ever turn down a follow, even if it is motivated by guilt and I've probably been put on mute.

@Jobster{Lobster}—ugh.

@Jobster{Lobster}—did he also say he still wants to be friends?

@!Cute!_Amy—ya, like I have enough friends, dude.

@!Cute!_Amy—I'm good on friends.

@!Cute!_Amy—and get this, his follow-up was to ask me if my girl Cassie was seeing anybody.

@Jobster{Lobster}—Ouch. Sorry. That stings.

@!Cute!_Amy—Soooo much 😢

"I guess you all know me," Mallory says, shifting Jesse to her other arm. "I won't bother with the whole 'My name's Mallory, and I'm an alcoholic.'"

"Me too, bro," Mal says, raising a fist in solidarity, and getting some weak laughs. "I'm actually not," she says quickly. "Just for the record. Also, still gay."

"Noted," Amara says. "On both counts."

"I got pregnant last year," Mallory goes on. "Blake Carroll's the father, in case anybody is wondering. And he'd broken up with me about a week before I found out."

"How does that work?" One of the basketball players pipes up. "How did you know?"

"I'd missed my period, but that's always been spotty, so I wasn't too upset. I've been having sex since freshman year—always did the usual things, never had a scare," she says.

"Tell us what you mean by the usual things," Fallon encourages her.

"Condoms," Mallory says, ticking off her fingers. "Pulling out if we didn't have those."

"Is it true that you can't get pregnant your first time?" a freshman basketball player asks.

"Or when you're on your period?" another girl adds.

"You can definitely get pregnant on your period," Mallory says, pointing at Jesse. "Take my word for that."

"And losing your virginity can certainly gain you a family member," Mal adds. "There's no free pass for funsies on your first time."

"Not a lot of funsies, either," a cheerleader adds, rolling her eyes.

"Girl, same," another one says. "I was like, *Really? This is what I've been waiting for?*"

"Backtracking real quick," Fallon says, catching my eye and giving me a pointed look. I remember that I'm supposed to be managing the *@Not-Your-Moms-Sex-Ed* social media account. She'd told me to post pearls of pregnancy wisdom (her actual words), but to make sure to include other topics as well, so that the content isn't tied completely to what goes on at SHAFT Class. But I don't want to leave Amy sitting on read, so I'm left trying to decide which friend to disappoint.

"Pulling out isn't effective," Fallon says. "You can get pregnant your first time, and you can get pregnant if you're menstruating."

Fallon had given me a lot of explicit instructions about VPNs and masking my location, but Amy's updates had run my best friend's worry train right off the tracks of my attention span. I don't feel like making decisions based on paranoid delusions, so I throw together a post—**your first time might be a letdown, but you could still get knocked up**—on a yellow background, sticking with Bill Hader dancing, because honestly, it works everywhere.

I dutifully throw together two more posts based on Fallon's major talking points and then flip back over to Rock Bottom.

@Jobster{Lobster}—I'm sorry, really.

@Jobster{Lobster}—It just sucks.

I'm not eloquent like Fallon, and my emotions flow out of my eyes more than my mouth. My gaze wanders to Shelby, who is also surreptitiously texting instead of listening. A stab of jealousy hits my chest, making my breath hitch.

I wasn't exactly into Baxter, and there was no part of me that thought he was interested, but a new guy in school meant a fresh start for a girl like me. Baxter doesn't know about the time I accidentally said *Pubic War* instead of *Punic War* while reading aloud in history class, or that I wore glasses all throughout elementary school. I had something of a glow-up and changed my game in high school, but I'll always be just Jobie to everyone in Presnick. Baxter had been a chance to make a first impression, and he'd politely noticed, then given all his attention to the hot chick.

Because of course he did.

@Jobster{Lobster}—I know how it feels

@Jobster{Lobster}—been passed over too

@Jobster{Lobster}—can't say I blame him

@Jobster{Lobster}—she's a 10

I send along a link to Shelby's Instagram, and tune back in to SHAFT Class.

"I heard you can't get pregnant if you have sex standing up," January is saying.

"Gravity is a force of nature, not a form of birth control," Fallon says, which is actually pretty clever, and I immediately send it out over the social.

"What about douching immediately afterward?" a cheerleader pipes up. "My mom said—"

"And how many kids does your mom have?" Mal asks.

"Uh . . . five," she answers, to which Mal simply holds out her hands on either side, mimicking the posture of her ceramic clown.

"Sperm swim very fast," Fallon says.

"True athletes, every one of them," Jacelyn says.

"You wouldn't be able to douche quickly enough, plus douching can actually push them farther into your uterus," Fallon finishes.

@!Cute!_Amy—holy crap that's your friend?

@!Cute!_Amy—she's a 10, for sure

@!Cute!_Amy—but most guys don't want a girl who can bench press him

@Jobster{Lobster}—that one did

@Jobster{Lobster}—but whatever, I'm fine

@Jobster{Lobster}—you'll be fine too

@Jobster{Lobster}—guess we'll just keep being the "nice girls"

"Condoms, condoms, condoms," Fallon says, smacking her hands together each time.

I'm not sure what brought on that triple threat, but Jacelyn makes a face.

"I hate those things. I feel like I'm having sex with a guy trapped in a trash bag," she says.

"Honey, where are you buying your condoms?" Bethany, one of the cheerleaders asks. She whips out her phone and shoves it across the mat, nearly upending a couple of circus clowns on the way. "That's what you want. Can barely feel it, won't tear."

"And they'll protect you from STDs," Fallon adds. "*Both* of you."

"Right," Mal says. "So, if you ask him to wear a condom and all he's got is excuses, tell him you've got herpes."

"Maybe not that one," January says. "Herpes is forever."

"I thought only a thing of beauty was a joy forever," Mal fires back.

"That, and herpes," Amara says. "Nice Keats reference, though."

Mal makes finger guns at her.

"Wait—you can't get rid of herpes?" someone asks, which sets off some panicked googling. It's a good excuse for me to sneak another glance at my phone.

@Jobster{Lobster}—guess we'll just keep being the "nice girls"

@!Cute!_Amy—who has more fun than nice girls?

@!Cute!_Amy—good girls!

The last message is followed by a series of laughing emojis and fire, which makes me feel like there's a joke I'm not in on. I send her three question marks in response.

@!Cute!_Amy—crap, I forgot to tell you

I send the three questions marks again, dump some potting soil into my clown's pants while Fallon and January have a mild argument about whether the chlorine in hot tubs kills STDs. Hot tip—it doesn't. An ellipsis shows up next to *@!Cute!_Amy*'s avatar, and I keep one eye on it while opening a seed packet and jamming a couple of seeds down into the dirt.

@!Cute!_Amy—just scrolled back through

@!Cute!_Amy—I totally messed that up

@!Cute!_Amy—I forgot to tell you about the hashtag

Amy had coached me through a photo shoot the night before, with me sending her the pic that was going to be my offering for the current trend—things you do in bed other than sleep. The very obvious NSFW posts had flooded my feed, all of them blurred out because of my settings. Most people my age have seen more bodies doing more things than there were returned dogs at the pound post-COVID, but when it shows up sandwiched between reading recs and cat memes, it can send my day into a weird emotional trajectory.

The pic I'd sent Amy had been pretty cute, if I do say so myself. I'd curled up on my bed, adjusted my ring light, and popped off a few shots of me reading a book that I'd pulled off Mom's shelf, because the cover contrasted nicely with my throw pillows. Amy had complimented me right away, then followed up with some tips.

@!Cute!_Amy—open your lips a smidge, it's more natural

@!Cute!_Amy—showing just a little bit of teeth is good

@!Cute!_Amy—make those whitening sessions worth it, lol!

I'd tried what she said, taking a new pic, which she followed up with more suggestions—**curl your legs more, get your feet in the shot, tilt your hips one way, your shoulders the other, pull a couple of strands of hair in front of your ear, put your free hand on your torso, push your boobs together.**

@!Cute!_Amy—not that much, geez, this isn't OnlyFans

That response had come in when I'd taken her last bit of advice a little too far, and my cleavage was up in my chin. I was relieved at her response, since it was both out of my comfort zone and, quite frankly, painful.

@Jobster{Lobster}—no one would believe I'm reading the book anyway

@Jobster{Lobster}—I can't see it

I'd tweaked the photo twenty times, sending Amy the results for feedback until we hit on the perfect pose, the right lighting, and just enough of what Amy calls "cutesy teasey" without crossing the line into being purposefully sexy.

In other words, not like Shelby.

@!Cute!_Amy—that's money

@!Cute!_Amy—post it

I had, using bookish hashtags, as well as the trending *#whatbedsarefor*, to moderate success. With ninety-seven likes and twelve comments, I can't say it was a total bust, but me being cute while reading isn't pulling numbers the way Amy's posts do.

"Cold sores are a form of herpes," Fallon says, which elicits a shriek from a sophomore, who falls off her yoga ball and sends her circus clown flying.

"Great, I have herpes for the rest of my life now!" Her face is buried in her arms, her muffled voice barely audible.

Shelby reaches over, tapping her shoulder.

"It's not the same thing," she tells her. "It's—"

"It is the same *virus*, but it's a different *type*," Fallon clarifies.

"Maybe lead with that?" Shelby says, still trying to rouse the sophomore. "Seriously, it's not a big deal. One time I got a yeast infection on my back from the mats at the gym and I was all like, *oh my God, I've got a yeast infection!* But it wasn't in my vagina, you know? You've got herpes, but it's not in your vagina. It's not vagina herpes, it's mouth herpes."

The room has gone totally silent and Shelby finally notices, glancing up.

"What?"

"You can get a yeast infection on your back?" someone asks, and a new round of questions begins, just as Amy finishes a fresh string of messages.

@!Cute!_Amy—I forgot to tell you about the hashtag

@!Cute!_Amy—guys that are into cutesy girls follow #goodgirl

@!Cute!_Amy—throw that on there and you're gold

I do a quick search on the tag, and see that Amy's right. It's mostly pictures of girls like us—cute but not hot—doing non-sexy things like drinking coffee, having a picnic, or being otherwise casually adorable. A couple of dog owners had wandered onto the hashtag with their golden retrievers, and there are a few very obvious Only-Fans fishing posts, but for the most part *#goodgirl* looks like exactly what Amy says it is—a place where I can fit in . . . maybe even stand out. All the posts, minus the dogs—I mean they tried, but do your research—have thousands of likes, hundreds of comments, and most of the girls there are crushing it on followers.

I scroll through my photos, looking at some of the options I'd shot last night, after my conversation with Amy. I'd grabbed a few with Princess Tinyhead—for once, her immobility was a blessing; she proved to be posable—and a nice one with me looking out the window as gray storm clouds rolled in, the oversize neck on my shirt pulled slightly to one side, just showing my collarbone and the edge of the tank top underneath. There's a mug of coffee on the windowsill (I'd added the steam, I'm not above it), my messy bun looks perfect, and I'd been just the right mix of tired but hopeful at the time—and you can see it in my eyes. I look chronically sad but resilient, secure in the hope that someday, something will go my way.

Hell yeah, it will.

I post it, tagging the coffee company, the T-shirt brand, and use a few hashtags that throw a broad net and might pull in some randos. *#winter #stormyday #ohiosunset #cloudgazing*, and, finally, *#goodgirl.*

The hum of the other girls' voices had faded into a background noise, but when someone raps on the glass wall of the yoga room, everyone goes dead silent. I glance up from my phone to see a woman with a baby on her hip, pointing at her watch.

"We're being invaded!" Mal shouts.

"No, we went over our time," Fallon says, coming to her feet and shooting me a nasty look.

Normally I can brush those off, as they can appear at any moment: a side-eye from the passenger seat when I execute a rolling stop, or a full-on glare that accompanies anything from suggesting we go toilet papering to reminding her that her mom used to smoke.

But this time, I actually did screw up.

I was supposed to give her a high sign at five minutes to the hour, but instead I'd been creeping on my own Instagram. I make up for it by running past the baby-mom weightlifters while issuing a quick apology, finding a vacuum in a utility closet, and even using the attachments to get every last grain of potting soil off the mats before their class starts.

"You've certainly got good attendance," one of the moms says, watching as the girls filter out of the quiet room, ceramic clowns in hand. "What is it that you do?"

Jacelyn, January, and Amara revert to silent, wide-eyed panic without Fallon at the helm—she's delegating the process of returning yoga balls to their rightful places—so I try to make up for my lenient timekeeping skills by flashing my best *This is fine, everything is fine* smile.

"We're a self-help group," I say. "Just trying to find ways to unplug from our phones."

"The room's all yours," Fallon announces, coming out of the yoga room with red cheeks and rumpled hair. "I'm so sorry we went over our time. We can cut short next week if—"

All the girls holding ceramic clowns seem to also be holding their breath, until the mom who appears to be in charge shakes her head.

"No, no, just glad to see you guys doing something with each other, not sitting alone in your rooms. You take all the time you need."

A chorus of relieved thank-yous seem to please the moms, and we filter down the stairs, Shelby carrying what's left of the potting soil.

"So, that was great and all, but . . ." Jacelyn holds up her clown. "What am I supposed to do with this?"

Still in make-up-for-past-mistakes mode, I swoop in. "I asked Ms. Lauren if we can set them in the back bay window. I'll stop by and water them periodically."

By periodically I mean I'm going to forget and everything is going to die, but since no one seems emotionally attached to their potted plant, I don't think it will matter. Everyone leaves their clown in the window, twenty-two welcoming pairs of arms gesturing out over the expanse of the rec center's back lawn, soccer fields only holding snow. Fallon waits for me at the entrance, and we walk out together.

"Sorry about that," I say, well aware that I should address my faux pas. "I got caught up with sending out the sex tips on social media."

It's not technically true, but it's a good cover to hide why my face was buried in my phone for the last half of SHAFT Class.

"It's not sex tips," Fallon corrects me, and I just take that one on the chin because I probably deserve it. "Do you think any of those moms from the next class overheard us?"

"Uh, doubt it," I say, not able to offer a definitive no on that one, since I'd been admiring my own messy bun at the time.

"Do you remember what I said about posts from the Not Your Mom's Sex Ed account?" Fallon asks.

This is her version of *Pop quiz, hotshot,* but we're in my territory now. I was given explicit instructions on how to handle a social media account, and while I might have lost every game of tic-tac-toe that Fallon and I played as children, I know the ins and outs of all these x's and o's.

"I'm going to schedule posts for random days and times in between SHAFT classes, so that the account isn't only active during meetings. I'm going to post about different topics than come up in class, so that anybody who's showing up doesn't instantly know that it's us behind Not Your Mom's Sex Ed."

"It's blowing up fast," Fallon says, looking down at her phone and chewing her lip. "I have some control over how big class gets, but—"

"Blowing up is good, Fallon," I remind her. "You *want* to reach people, right?"

"Of course," she says hesitantly. "But—"

"Butt nut," I shoot back at her, resurrecting one of our childhood insults.

"Okay, fine," she says . . . because really there is no way to intelligently argue with *butt nut.* "I need to approve all posts, though."

She doesn't add *to be sure they're accurate*, but that's what's going on here, and we both know it.

"I will research everything," I promise, just as my phone goes off in my back pocket.

"I'll send you some articles," Fallon offers in return.

I decide not to argue when my phone vibrates again.

"I was thinking maybe we should do a series of posts about—"

"Ope, that's Mom," I say, reaching for my back pocket. But it's not, it's a message from Amy that begins, **girl, they love you. See what I mean about . . .**

I literally can't see what she means because the message is cut off by the character limit of the notification screen.

"Guess it was her night at home for dinner and I flubbed that, too," I say, giving Fallon a self-effacing shrug.

"Don't let me keep you," she says, immediately shifting into comfort mode. "Tell your mom I said hi!"

I nod that I will, get into my car, and have to stop myself from checking Instagram before driving away. Once I'm on the road, I end up putting my phone face down in the passenger seat so that I don't glance over whenever a notification comes in. But I can see the screen lighting up—a lot. I've barely got the car in park before I flip the phone over, scrolling through notifications in the dark as my hands get cold.

4 messages from Amy on Rock Bottom.

167 new followers on Instagram.

238 likes on my last post.

102 comments.

23 DMs.

I shoot a three-word response to Amy: **Hole. Lee. Shit.**

Then I meet my new admirers.

CHAPTER THIRTEEN

Shelby

"Jesus Christ, Black! You want that nose broken again just when it finished healing?"

I spit out my mouth guard so that I can enunciate when I tell Coach Faith to eat shit. She motions to me to get rid of the headgear, and I pop it off, ears ringing from Rory's last punch—a left hook that I had completely failed to slip.

"You here with us or not?" Faith asks, coming to the corner. "Because I'd say your head is somewhere else, except it's catching all Rory's punches."

I look at Rory, who only shrugs in response. He'll come to my defense if he thinks I'm right; but his mouth is firmly clamped shut.

"Shit," I say. "Sorry," I hold out a gloved hand for Faith to bump, which she does, but with a frown.

"Take five," she tells Rory, then climbs through the ropes and into the ring, draping her arms over my shoulders, forehead pressed against mine. It's intimate in a way that only athletes know; intimidating but vulnerable at the same time.

"Listen," she says, voice low. "I never asked, and you're not talking, but if you need some time off—"

I pull back, but her wrists are locked behind my neck, her eyes hard on mine.

"I'm f—" I begin, but she pulls me back in, cutting me off.

"You're not fine, Shelby," she says. "You haven't been ever since that shit stain of a boyfriend took a shot at you."

I snake my hands through her arms, bringing my elbows down hard on hers, breaking the grip. "I'm fine," I say. "Get Rory back in here."

But Coach Faith shakes me off, her mouth in a hard line. "I've been punched by people that hate me, and I've been hit by people I love. You and I both know it lands different. You're not fine, and I won't coach a liar."

I think about that for a second, my jaw locked, chin sticking out in what Taylor calls my *I'm right even when I'm wrong* look. Faith has always walked the tough-love line, both in and out of the ring, a coaching style that fits me well, even when it pisses me right the hell off.

Mostly because she tends to be right, even when she doesn't agree with me.

"Shit," I say, undoing my gloves with my teeth, the Velcro chafing my lips. "Fine," I tell her. "Fine as in, yeah, I'm not fine."

"Okay," she says, moving in a little closer. "That's a start. I can't help make things better until I know what's wrong." She's quiet for a second, waiting for me to answer.

But I don't have the response that she wants, the one I'm supposed to make about how Jayden broke more than just my nose, that my trust is forever trampled and punching isn't just for sports, now it's personal. Now it's *trauma*. That's what I'm supposed to say, but none of it is true, and Faith won't coach a liar, so I keep my mouth shut.

“Would it help to spar with a woman?” Faith asks. “I can gear up if—”

“No,” I say quickly.

Rory is the best partner I’ve ever had; he doesn’t hold back too much, and facing down a Mack Truck is easy compared to him. Every time I get into the ring and look at my opponent, the first thought is, *Well, at least it isn’t Rory.*

“Hang tight,” Coach Faith says, motioning Dad over from where he’s got three pregnant women on rowers.

“What, no!” I say, grabbing her wrist. “I don’t need—”

“Chill,” Faith says, twisting out of my grip. “I was waiting to tell you this until after training, but you need a foot in your ass.”

I’ve had Coach Faith’s foot in my ass plenty—Dad’s too—so I’m not exactly looking forward to it when he climbs into the ring, looking between us.

“You tell her?” Dad asks.

Faith shakes her head. “Thought I’d let you.”

“Oh my God, what already?” I ask. “Please say you’re leaving Taylor and marrying Coach?”

“Better,” Faith says, crossing her arms and smiling.

“Tara called this morning,” Dad says. “We landed Rebel.”

“We—” I look back and forth between the two of them, then down at Rory, who is resting in the corner, his smile all for me. “We got Rebel?!”

“*You* got Rebel,” Dad says. “Tara’s working on the contract, and Lee will let us know when you can make an official announcement, but you’re their new spokes—”

“WOOOO FUCKING HOOOOO!” I scream, and throw both of my gloves in the air, high enough that they hit the rafters and knock three years' worth of dust. It sprinkles down onto my braids, but more lands on Rory when he tackles me from the side in a hug, a cobweb attaching to his beard.

"Maybe less swearing?" One of the moms from the toddler class yells in my direction.

I spin, ready to tell her that I'm famous and she can fuck off, but Dad raises an eyebrow.

"Sorry," I say instead, cupping my hand in a Miss America wave, the other arm around Rory's shoulders.

"Such a professional," he whispers. "Maybe wax your pits before the photo shoot, though."

"I'm going to have to wax more than that," I tell him. "Did you see their summer line?"

"Not exactly what I follow on Instagram," he says, nudging me back toward Dad and Faith.

"Once Tara takes care of the fine print, we'll move forward," Dad says. "But Rory's not wrong—there's a photo shoot in your immediate future. I *do* follow Rebel, and as much as I support you, I will likely unfollow shortly."

"No hard feelings. I get it," I tell him.

Dad had to unfollow my socials after some of the comments made him have to spend a couple hours in the garage with a punching bag.

"I've got to get back to my mommies," Dad says. "But bring it in first."

I walk into his arms, smelling his aftershave, some of Taylor's perfume, and the absolute funk of the gym that always hangs over all of us.

"Proud of you, kid," he says, giving my chin a nudge before slipping out between the ropes.

I turn my back toward the mirror, glancing at Coach before looking over my shoulder. "I see my ass; there's no foot in it."

"Thought you might find it motivating," she says. "But seriously, what do you need from me, Black? You ask and you've got it, but I can't take care of you without any direction."

Direction.

"I've got therapy tonight," I say quickly. "Directions Recovery."

"I'm familiar with that practice," Faith says cautiously, which is not a surprise. The gym works with substance abuse recovery programs, trying to replace whatever their addiction is with exercise.

"Which counselor?" Faith pushes.

"Kathy Hildebrand," I say, and she uncrosses her arms.

"Kathy's good," Faith says. "She'll help you take care of your shit."

"Nice," I say, nodding. "So can you let me take that shit to her and deal with my other shit here?"

"Fair enough," Faith says, climbing back out through the ropes and motioning for Rory to rejoin us. "Because that's right on the money; what you're bringing on that mat is total shit."

"Suck my dick," I say, before putting in my mouthpiece.

But I can't deny that Coach Faith is right about one thing; I am distracted. It's not Jayden, or the bruises that still linger, or Ilsa Bunting reposting the video of me tapping out. What I'm distracted by is just as addicting as whatever brings in the shufflers who wander in for the 8:00 p.m. class, heads down, avoiding gazes.

I think I'm in love.

And I'm terrified.

"Shelby," Kathy Hildebrand gives me a smile from her wingback chair, which is set at an angle from the overstuffed couch she directed me to when I walked into her office. I'm not a smiler, and I don't like pastel colors, both of which this room seems to be geared to.

"I feel like I already know you, in a way," she goes on. "I've got notes from my constituent, of course—"

"Your what?"

"Judy, from the county program," she says, and I can't help but blanch.

"Do her notes mostly say that I'm a bitch? Because that didn't go so hot," I say.

"No." Kathy shakes her head, the smile still in place, although I think the twist at the edge of her lips is genuine now. "Clinicians don't really use that kind of language in our notes."

I think about that for a second, holding her gaze as we assess each other. "It's okay if I swear in here, right?" I ask.

"My main goal is your comfort," she says. "If swearing makes you happy, I don't want you to censor yourself."

Not censoring myself is something I excel at, but I have been making some adjustments lately.

"It doesn't make me happy, exactly," I explain. "It's just kind of my default mode. I have been trying to tone it down, though. I started seeing this guy, and he doesn't swear, so . . ."

I let the sentence trail off, hoping she'll pick up the crumbs. Baxter has filled my head so completely the past couple of weeks, his constant presence on my phone upgraded to an unceasing background hum in my brain. He's what I think about, and he's become what I talk about, fight stats and dick jokes taking a back seat while his name comes out every other sentence. Baxter said . . . Baxter thinks . . . Baxter is . . .

I'm self-aware enough to be mildly embarrassed by the fact that my boyfriend is currently my only topic of conversation, and I've tried to rein it in slightly by not directly bringing him up myself but leading others into asking, so that I can talk about him. Kathy walks right into it.

"You're seeing someone new?"

Kathy's good. She doesn't phrase it the way Taylor did—*That was fast.* Or Faith—*Dicks wobble the legs, let yours rest.* Or Rory—*You're not a basketball player, stop gaming the rebound stats.* Or even Fallon, whose initial enthusiasm for my new relationship had faded when she glimpsed my phone early one morning as we walked into school together and saw ten new texts waiting for me. *That's kind of a lot, isn't it?*

But kind of a lot is who I am and how I've always operated. Finding someone who meets my intensity is refreshing.

"Yeah, Baxter moved here from Chicago last month, but I actually met him online when he commented on that video of my boyfriend—ex-boyfriend—hitting me at school, and we got to talking, and then we met up and . . ."

I end the sentence with both hands in the air and a casual shrug, like I'm just a girl caught in the whirlwind of fate that put a boy in my path who is absolutely perfect.

"Let's talk about that video," Kathy says, smoothly ejecting Baxter from the conversation and bringing Jayden into it. "I said I feel like I already know you, but that's not just from Judy's notes. She sent me the link to that video, of course, but I admit that I was pulled into your social media. You're very charismatic. Magnetic, even. Your generation is accustomed to a level of exposure that mine never was, but you seem to have handled fame well."

"I'm not famous famous," I say, always quick to make the distinction. "In fight circles, sure, and I'm definitely recognized on the street within the state, but if you drop me out in, like, Colorado or something, nobody would know me from a ski bunny."

"I think that could change someday," Kathy says. "As shiny as it seems, fame takes its own toll, and I'm sure you know, the internet is forever. It's important that you deal with what happened between you and Jayden so that you can move forward in life prepared to confront any references to it as your career develops."

"Yeah, Ilsa Bunting threw that video up, too," I admit, shifting on the couch. On the end table, my phone vibrates in three quick successions.

"The girl I—" My teeth click together, not wanting to finish the sentence with *lost to*. I've never had to say that sentence before, never been anything but a winner. "The last person I fought," I explain.

"She's texting you?" Kathy asks, eyebrows coming together as my phone goes off yet again.

"Oh, no, that's Baxter," I say quickly. "My new boyfriend. Baxter Latcha."

Oh my God, I'm such a candy ass. But I like saying his name. I like stringing it together with the word *boyfriend*, and I like the way all the syllables come together, flowing off my tongue like an incantation that never fails to raise a smile. Every time.

Baxter Latcha.

"Tell me more about him," Kathy says, which at this point in my life is like offering a lit pipe to a tweaker.

Baxter is amazing. Baxter is funny. Baxter is smart. Baxter is sexy. Baxter is special.

"*Latcha* is one of the rarest last names in the country," I tell Kathy, sharing that particular tidbit, which had just elevated him further in my mind.

"Well, that's not a personal achievement—"

"It feels pretty special when your last name is Black," I tell her, laughing at my own joke. But the edges come out hard, scratching my throat. On the end table, my phone goes off again, four times, each buzz chasing the next.

"Is that him again?" Kathy asks.

"Just a reminder notification that I've got messages," I tell her, but I guarantee there are now seven texts waiting for me, all of them from Baxter. And I don't like the way Kathy phrased that question, or how she's looking at my phone.

"I can silence it," I offer, but she shakes her head, typing something on her laptop, adding to Judy's notes.

"How long have you been seeing each other?"

"Two weeks," I say promptly, something we'd determined after deciding that our first few DMs totally counted as a date, and our official fortuitous first meeting. Fortuitous means *happening by chance*. I'd looked up the word after seeing Baxter's post, and we'd agreed that his mom suddenly deciding she needed a change and randomly taking a job at the Honda plant was meant to be.

So that we would meet.

Because fortuitous also means *fortunate*, and that's how I feel—lucky.

So fucking lucky.

"That's early days," Kathy says, still typing on her computer. "I'm not dismissing your emotions; I remember what it's like to meet someone new. And at your age, emotions are always high."

"Yeah, Taylor said the same thing," I say. That particular conversation had come after my phone had gone off for the eighth time at dinner. And while I understand that I am acting like a total idiot, it also isn't my fault that Kathy and Taylor have never felt this way. This overwhelming, knee-buckling way.

They don't understand.

"Taylor is your stepmom?" Kathy asks, glancing at her laptop again.

"Yeah." I nod. "Did Judy, like, record our entire conversation?"

"No," Kathy says easily. "But she did mention that you and your stepmom don't always see eye to eye."

"We can't, because I respect myself," I say.

Kathy pauses, holding my gaze. "Do you think your stepmom doesn't respect you?"

"She always finds little ways to tear me down," I say. "Like, she tells me I'm too . . ." I wave my hand around, pretending that I don't remember her words exactly.

"Too what?" Kathy prompts.

"'Too much. Too hard. Too fast,'" I say, each word coming out clipped.

"You have a strong personality, it can't be denied—"

"Yeah," I interrupt. "Taylor would just say I'm a bitch."

"Has she called you a bitch?" Kathy asks.

"Nope," I say. "It's all implied. And I really don't want to talk about Taylor anymore."

"Okay." Kathy shifts in her chair, recrossing her legs. "What do you want to talk about?"

"Uh . . . what were you saying before? About falling in love?"

"Falling in love changes a little as you get older," Kathy goes on, now looking at me over her laptop. "You've got a better handle on your emotions, so there aren't the peaks and valleys of teenage years, but those first few weeks or months can still be quite intense."

Her voice fades out, and her eyes go a little glassy, and I think I might have to update my opinion that Kathy doesn't understand. But Baxter and I are all peaks, all the time, no valleys. If you can plateau at perfect, we've managed it.

"Yeah," I agree. "Intense is right."

Kathy snaps her laptop shut. "The chemical effect on your brain when starting a new relationship is similar to cocaine."

"Uh, what?" I'd been thinking about Baxter in terms of an addiction, but I hadn't meant it literally.

"It activates your reward system," Kathy goes on. "Oxytocin, vasopressin, dopamine—all the pleasure chemicals interact and flood your brain. It also reduces serotonin levels to the extent of someone who experiences obsessive compulsive disorder."

"Wait, no," I say, sitting up straighter. "This isn't like some weird obsession thing."

As I say that, my phone goes off twice.

"This isn't toxic," I say.

"That word gets thrown around a lot these days," Kathy says. "And I'm not implying that it is. I'm just letting you know that how you feel right now is not how you will feel forever. When you're falling in love, parts of your cortical regions linked to critical judgment have less activity, the result being that you can't find faults with your new person."

My mouth is in a flat line, and I can feel my chin beginning to jut out.

"Your cortical regions must be functioning just fine," I say. "You've got lot of judgment to pass around."

To my surprise, Kathy bursts out laughing.

"Being critical is my superpower," she says. "And sometimes I give it a little too much freedom. I hope we're not getting off on the wrong foot; I'm not saying that your new relationship is unhealthy—"

My phone goes off again.

"But I do want you to understand that these feelings aren't sustainable. After a few months, your brain chemicals will return to their former levels, and the ecstasy of early love will settle into something more foundational, more intimate. A lot of young people make the mistake of believing that once the magic is gone, there's a problem with the relationship. If there is something real between you and Baxter, it will take work eventually."

Work. I fight the urge to snort. Nothing with Baxter has been work. It's all been an effortless exchange, waking up to his texts and going to bed with his voice in my ear. I've never felt anything like it before, never had the little catch of fear or moment of indecision before I send my response, reading it twice, tweaking it so it's right, hoping it's perfect.

Like him.

"Have you two been intimate?"

"Uhhhh . . ."

"You don't have to share anything you don't want to, and everything you say to me is confidential. Unless I believe you pose a threat to yourself, or others, nothing you say to me leaves this office."

This office with its robin's-egg-blue walls, and a bookshelf full of stuffed animals for her younger clients. This office with a goldfish in a bowl and macramé plant holders hanging in the window.

"It ain't SHAFT Class," I say.

"What?" Kathy asks, truly bewildered.

"Nothing, just this feels like a weird place to talk about sex," I tell her.

"Believe me, a *lot* of people talk about sex in this room," she says.

And I do believe her, because even though Kathy might have gotten my back up by inferring that what Baxter and I share isn't going to last, she is super easy to talk to.

"No, we're not having sex," I tell her. "I'm all for it, to be clear, but Baxter said it was too early and we shouldn't rush things."

He'd shared that particular reservation with me when I'd had his zipper halfway down, and I'd been flooded with both disappointment and astonishment that a guy was actually passing up a chance to pound me. Not that I think he ever will, though. Baxter has been nothing but patient, and gentle, and kind . . . nothing like I've ever had before. Nothing I thought I would ever want.

"He also said we aren't going to be one of those couples that tells each other they're in love when they don't even really know each other. He said that words matter, and he doesn't say that one lightly."

"Baxter sounds wise beyond his years," Kathy says, just as my phone goes off again—twice.

"Oh, he is," I agree quickly. "At least two of those texts are Zambia facts."

"What?"

"*National Geographic*, you know what—never mind," I say. I clamp my lips together, not letting the rest of the sentence—*you wouldn't understand*—come out.

"Have you talked with Baxter about what happened with Jayden?"

"Yeah, for sure," I say. "It was actually a big part of our first conversation."

"Really? And what did he have to say about it?"

"Uh . . ." I think about that for a second, replaying our first meeting in my head for the thousandth time. It's been on a loop since it happened, the details only heightening as time passes. Except, now that I'm thinking about it, I realize Baxter didn't have anything to say about what happened between me and Jayden. I'd said that my ex coming back to school would be weird, and then the conversation had steered into trypophobia and *National Geographic*.

"I don't know," I say quickly. "It was our first time seeing each other face-to-face; we were both flustered, and it was just super intense."

"Okay," Kathy says, glancing at the clock that's on the wall over my shoulder. "We only have a few minutes left, and we haven't really talked about the reason why you're really here."

"Right," I say, my back stiffening. "Like I told Judy, it's really not a problem."

The same thing I'd told Dad, Rory, Faith, Fallon, even Taylor.

"I mean, I like talking to you, and I'll put in my hours or whatever, but shouldn't we talk about the things I'm actually worried about?" I ask.

Kathy cocks her head. "What are you worried about, Shelby?"

"*Thinking* about," I correct myself. "The things I'm thinking about."

"And what are you thinking about?"

"Baxter," I tell her honestly. "Like, all the time. It's honestly . . ." I take a deep breath, pulling in oxygen, letting it back out. "It's kind of scary."

"Do you think this is the first time you've been in love?"

"Well, I didn't say I was—" I try to roll my eyes, but they just won't go. "Oh shit, I *am* in love."

A frightened giggle comes out after the admission, and I cover my mouth with my hand, astonished that such a sound could come out of me.

"It can be scary," Kathy says, nodding. "Even when it's a healthy connection and a good relationship."

"Okay, so that's okay, then, right?" I ask, words tumbling out as my phone goes off yet again. "There isn't anything wrong, and me being worried or scared is totally normal and it doesn't mean that this is just, like, screwed up?"

"I wouldn't say *screwed up*, no," Kathy says. "But I would like to keep talking to you about Baxter, if you're willing."

Hell yeah, I'm willing. I have to *stop* myself from talking about Baxter most of the time. Kathy gets up from her chair, which must be my cue to go, so I come to my feet as well, picking up my phone and glancing at the screen.

Yep, all those texts were from Baxter. I feel the usual lift in my chest that's accompanied by a drop in my belly, the thrill of knowing that he's thinking about me mixed with the pressure of being able to match him over text.

"And, Shelby?" Kathy adds as I reach the door, hand on the knob.

"Yeah?" I say, turning back to her, even though my eyes are on my phone.

"I'd like for you to consider the possibility that there's another reason you're only thinking about Baxter."

"What's that?" I ask, raising my eyes.

"So that you don't have to think about Jayden."

CHAPTER FOURTEEN

Fallon

Buying twenty-five canisters of pepper spray should make a person feel safe, not vulnerable, but that's where I am right now. Specifically, staring at the back wall of a sporting goods store and wondering why some of them are packaged in pink, while Mom sucks on a Starbucks and lets me know how proud she is of me.

"I'm just glad to see you putting yourself out there more, making friends. I wish it would've happened before senior year, but some of us are late bloomers."

"Nice backhanded compliment, Mom," I say, debating over two different brands. One is slightly more expensive than the other, and I feel horrible that Mom had offered to pay for the equivalent of party favors for the next SHAFT Class. But I think I'd feel way worse if one of the girls was in a situation where she needed pepper spray, and it misfired because Fallon Holloway is a bargain hunter.

"Sorry, that wasn't supposed to come out that way," Mom says, flipping through some bracelets for female runners that have concealed knives in them. "I just mean that you and Jobie have been hip to hip since kindergarten. Sometimes I don't know if you make room for other people. This self-defense class seems like a good way to hang out with other girls. I just hate feeling like you put a checkmark next to the *friend* box and called it done after your first playdate with Jobie."

"What's wrong with having one really good friend and a lot of acquaintances?" I ask. The list of my "acquaintances" has gotten rather long . . . like I have a couple thousand. The DMs have been flooded on the *@Not-Your-Moms-Sex-Ed* account, from both Presnick girls and total strangers.

Farrah following the *@Not-Your-Moms-Sex-Ed* account meant that her friends had hopped on as well, whose older sisters had followed suit, reposted, and sent out ripples that ended up attracting most of the female population of Presnick, from middle schoolers to the middle-aged. After that it had just been a numbers game, each share bringing in more people, the ripples spreading outward.

But this trip isn't just about covering our asses by appearing to practice self-defense in SHAFT Class. I'd braced myself for some hate in my DMs, but the outright threats are what drove me to ask Mom about purchasing pepper spray in bulk.

@mon:key:see—keep posting about reporting rape and I'll make sure you get some firsthand experience at it

@red|right|hand—stop with the advice for gays, pedo-groomer. I find out who you are, you'll have hot lead some place you don't want it

@daltrydal!456—I've got something to shut you up, your choice

That last one had come with shots of a ball gag and a dick pic. It certainly wasn't the first time I'd gotten one of those, but the fact that the leather strap on the ball gag had a worn-out groove from repeated use had set my arm hairs prickling.

"You'll need to get over not liking people once you're in college," Mom says, biting the end of her straw. "And not just your roommate. Transitioning into—"

"Campus life from small-town life isn't easy," I finish for her, having had this conversation more than once before.

"It's different from when you went, Mom," I tell her. "I'm already connecting with incoming freshmen at Union. The college set up a whole Facebook group for us to connect. I mean, we moved it all over to Snapchat, because Facebook is for people that graduated in the nineties—"

"Brush up on your modern history," Mom says. "We used AOL Instant Messenger." She then starts making a static white noise, followed up by a "*Be-dee-boop*" and then a deadpan, robotic "*Welcome.*"

"Oh my God, stop," I say, looking around to make sure no one is watching us, but from the next aisle over, someone answers in a similar robot voice: "*You've got mail.*"

"Thank you! I'm teaching my daughter about the internet," Mom calls.

"Tell her about Netscape Navigator," comes the response.

"Could you please . . ." I've got my face buried in my hands, my pepper spray–filled basket hanging off my elbow.

"Oh, honey, and that was just the process of getting online," she tells me, as we leave the running area behind. "I need a new lanyard. You?"

"Probably not a bad idea," I tell her. "But please stop making AOL noises."

"Can I switch over to the Wii Fit lady?"

"No," I say sternly. "And if you could keep any cultural references to at least the last decade, I'd really appreciate it."

"Youths," Mom says, rolling her eyes, but she's smiling as we pick through dangling multicolored straps. I select a bright orange lanyard, trying to ignore how much it's shaking as I hold it; my phone had let me know I had another DM, and a quick glance told me it was from *@Trad!Dad/1996*. I slide my phone back in my pocket, hoping Mom doesn't notice the uptick in my breathing.

Even though other accounts have harassed and straight up threatened me, *@Trad!Dad/1996* is the one who bothers me the most. He's always polite—**excuse me, just curious who is taking my daughter's sex education into their own hands?** And occasionally helpful—**you misspelled coitus in that last post** (thanks, Jobie). It's his persistence that bothers me the most. All I had to do with the other accounts was block, report, or ignore, but this guy is careful; he hasn't said or done anything worth reporting, and he's genuinely tried to engage me in conversation more than once—**are you sure what you're doing is the right thing? Let's talk about this.** But his last DM that just rolled in carried with it the flat-out statement that baldly expressed my fears—**I am not going away and I will not stop.**

Will not stop until what? I can't help but wonder.

"The first thing I did when I got online was look up cheat codes for *Tomb Raider*," Mom goes on, sighing. "Things are a lot different for you kids. Apparently, Farrah is following this social media channel that answered any questions she had about sex. Why ask Mom when you can ask a stranger?"

I freeze, my hand suspended over an overpriced Hydro Flask. "What?"

"Yeah, something like the Your Mom's Sex Life channel?"

"It's not called a channel," I snipe at her, a bubble of anxiety rising up from my stomach and into my throat. But Mom's not listening; she's pulled out her phone and is tapping around.

"There it is: Not Your Mom's Sex Ed. I followed it."

"You—" I'm practically choking now, my words cut off. "Why would you do that?"

"Uh, because I'm a mother, if you weren't aware," she says. "My underage kid is getting sex tips from a stranger—"

"It's not sex tips," I snap.

"Oh, you know it?" she asks, glancing up from her phone.

"I'm aware of it," I say carefully.

"So far it seems fine," Mom says, heading out of the aisle.

I follow, not wanting to miss a word.

"I just thought I should monitor it, be aware of what my daughter is being exposed to. I told the other moms about it, too."

"Are they all following m—it?"

"Mostly, yeah. It's getting passed around. It's a brand-new channel—"

"It's not called a channel."

"But they've already got something like five thousand watchers."

"Subscribers."

And it's currently 5,692, but I keep that correction to myself. Mom puts her basket on the counter.

"I've got her, too," Mom tells the cashier, motioning for me to set my basket next to hers. I do, and the cashier gives a hard side-eye to my twenty-five containers of pepper spray.

"Anyway," she goes on. "I think it's all aboveboard, for now. But there are a lot of people asking questions in the comments, some of them pretty explicit."

She's not wrong about that. I've had to delete a few asking for blow job advice, but the comments are exploding, and I can't keep up.

"And I can't even imagine what their inbox—"

"DMs," I say.

"Look like, because even just the comments are pretty personal, and some of them are detailed to a degree that I'm not sure Farrah needs to be exposed to."

That's another point for Mom; I've had a few instances regarding comments where I had to balance my allegiance to the first amendment with the milligrams on my anxiety medication. I don't want *@Not-Your-Moms-Sex-Ed* getting into any trouble, or attracting the wrong kind of attention. But I also know *exactly* what is coming in over the DMs, and people have questions—very basic questions that someone should have provided the answers to a long time ago. Should that person be a random stranger on the internet? No, probably not.

But here we are.

"The account isn't responsible for what's posted in the comments," I say, as we layer up before going outside, buttoning our coats and adjusting our scarves.

"True, and whoever is running it seems fairly responsible," Mom admits, unlocking the car and tossing our bags in the back seat. "But I'm trying to be responsible, too." She turns over the engine, but her hand rests on the gear shift.

"Masey Altoll sent nudes last week," she confides, voice low. "Deborah just about lost her mind. She called me yesterday because Allison was coming over to hang out with Farrah, and I could hear something was wrong in her voice. I asked if everything was okay and . . . it's not."

"Whoa," I say. "Isn't Masey in, like, fourth grade?"

"Fifth," Mom says sternly. "When I was in fifth grade we were playing with My Little Pony toys, and doing hair on a big, fake Barbie head."

"That sounds super gender affirming," I say.

Mom puts the car into gear and pulls out of the parking lot, all willingness to joke having been left behind inside the store.

"Sure, there were some things that sucked about growing up then," Mom agrees. "But I also had Transformers and watched *G.I. Joe* on Saturday mornings. It wasn't all boys on one side, girls on the other. And we sure as hell weren't sending each other naked pictures."

I can't really argue against that.

"I don't know," Mom says, shaking her head at the light. "Sometimes I think the internet was a bad idea, and cell phones just make it worse. You all have the ability to produce child porn in your back pockets."

"Well, that's one way to look at it," I say. "We also can dial nine-one-one anytime we need to, and if I'm ten minutes late coming home, all you have to do is check Find My iPhone and you can see where I am."

I try to sound breezy as I say it, but Mom's casual drop of *child porn* has my blood pressure skyrocketing.

"Yeah, I guess so," Mom admits as we leave town, open field on one side of the road, trees on the other. She runs out of steam, eyebrows drawn together, clearly unsettled.

I tap my fingers against my knee, debating. Mom's reaction to sexual assault hasn't slipped my mind, but I have no idea how to talk to her about it—or even if I should. But how hypocritical is it of me to be supportive of perfect strangers while choosing ignorance when it comes to my mom's past?

"You know, I saw a post from Not Your Mom's Sex Ed that relayed rape statistics," I say. "It said that one in five women in America have been raped. So, feasibly, if you know more than five women—"

"I have my days where I just want to pack everything up and move us somewhere there's no signal and no Wi-Fi," Mom says, cutting me off and returning to the earlier topic. "I actually looked it up and—*shit!*"

Mom's not a swearer, and the peal of a car horn that follows makes my heart jackhammer as I look up from my phone just in time to see a deer dodge the front bumper, skittering off into the trees. Mom's arm is across my chest, holding me back in my seat, her foot still jammed on the brake.

"That was—"

"Wait for it," Mom says, and another deer runs out, spies us, changes its mind, and dashes back across the field.

"Okay." Mom eases her foot off the pedal. "If I may borrow my wise elder daughter's words—teachable moment. There's never only—"

"One deer," I finish for her. "I know, Mom. I live in Ohio, too. And you and Dad have been telling me to watch out for deer since I got my license."

"And we'll keep saying it every time you go out the door," Mom says, gently accelerating. "You can never be too careful—"

Mom's still talking about the dangers of white tails, but a notification pops up on my screen, distracting me. I've got thirty-six new DMs. Actually, *@Not-Your-Moms-Sex-Ed* has them. I don't think there's thirty-six people on the internet that know who I am.

And I have to make absolutely sure it stays that way.

"You are in deep trouble, missy," I say, barging into Farrah's bedroom and slamming the door behind me so hard she jumps, one of her earbuds falling out.

"What the hell?" she says, sitting up on her bed, sketch pad slipping sideways out of her lap. “What did I do now?”

“You told Mom about Not Your Mom’s Sex Ed,” I hiss, lowering my voice.

“Ohhhh . . .” Farrah’s eyes fall away from mine, her hand going to the stuffed bunny she still keeps around for comfort. “Yeah, I did do that.”

“Why?” I ask, flopping beside her on the bed, some of my anger dissipating since she isn’t trying to wiggle out of it. “Why would you do that?”

“I don’t know,” she says, shrugging. “I didn’t really want to talk to her and Dad about sex, so I was just like, hey, no worries, I’m covered.”

“Covered by the questionable social media account my sister is secretly running?”

“It’s not questionable,” Farrah shoots back. “And no one will ever find out you’re the one behind it. Not if you’re using the VPN like I told you.”

I sigh and roll over onto my back, throwing one arm over my eyes. “What I post might not be so bad, but I can’t keep up with the comments, and some of them are pretty coarse.”

“I’ll say,” Farrah snorts, flicking her screen. “Did you see this one?”

I take her phone and look at a response to the post Jobie had made about having sex standing up not being a method of birth control.

@Call^Me^Uncle—can’t get her pregnant if you turn her around and put it in her—

“That’s enough of that,” I say, tossing Farrah’s phone down. “See what I mean? I can’t defend what’s on the account if followers are being dirty dogs in the comments.”

“You don’t have to defend what other people are saying,” Farrah argues. "That's not your responsibility, it's out of your control, and you can delete it."

"Sure, I have the ability," I tell her. "But I've got a final in AP Calc coming up, and pages due for yearbook, and I'm supposed to be going through this list of one hundred novels to read before college."

I stop when I see that Farrah is making yapping gestures with her hands and throw a pillow at her.

"You already got into your first choice of colleges," Farrah says, swatting the pillow away. "You could just coast for the rest of high school and it wouldn't even matter."

"Nice life philosophy," I say. "Do your absolute best, then just quit."

"It's called pacing yourself."

"Tell Mom and Dad that when you're homeless. You were just pacing yourself," I say.

"Right." Farrah rolls her eyes. "Because anybody that stops for a breather ends up homeless. Let me write that down in my notebook of advice from my big sister."

"Next to it, add: *There's never only one deer, and make sure Mom knows her biggest secret.*"

"If an anon social media account is your biggest secret, we need to get some doozies in before you leave for Union. Too bad you already turned eighteen and we can't count on your record getting cleared of misdemeanors."

I close my eyes and press my palms against the lids, sending a kaleidoscope of colors across my vision.

"I think we need to kill the account," I say.

"What? Why?" Farrah asks, and I motion for her to lower her voice. "You're *helping* people, Fallon. Just look at all the DMs coming in."

It's true. This week I've explained to different people that you can't tell if your partner has an STD just by doing a visual scan, masturbation won't make you go blind, and that sex is not a good weight-loss program, since the average engagement time is three to seven minutes.

"Here's one you might want to look at," Farrah says, phone back in her hand. "From a woman who says she's a school nurse."

I take the phone from Farrah, propping my head up with her stuffed bunny. There are even more unread DMs in the *@Not-Your-Moms-Sex-Ed* account, but Farrah has highlighted one.

@boomers*brokethe*world—love what you're doing, need more info like this out in the world for teens (really, for everybody). Something you should mention is HPV—it's the most common STI and can lead to cancer. It's entirely preventable in females by getting the Gardasil vaccine. I'm a school nurse and sat in on the "sex ed" program the other day, where the presenter actually advised girls not to get the vaccine, because it "doesn't work anyway."

"Well, that's just flat-out unethical," I say to my phone.

"Uh-huh," Farrah says. "That's why you need to keep going."

@boomers*brokethe*world—It was hard to keep my mouth shut, but I need this job, single mom, kid headed to college next year (gee, wish I would've known the hot tub chlorine wouldn't kill sperm when I was seventeen!)

@boomers*brokethe*world—keep doing the good work

"If a school nurse thinks you're right, then you're probably right," Farrah says.

"I don't think I've ever seen that on a Pinterest board," I tell her. "And you can't just ignore that I also get DMs like this one."

I hand the phone back over, with the message in question highlighted.

@RedLocker<171>—teaching children how to do it and not get caught isn't something I'd want on my conscience. Check yourself before you post.

"Nothing you've posted does either of those things," Farrah says.

"They think it does," I tell her. "And that's one of the less aggressive messages."

"Yeah, I saw the one from Toad Runner. 'You should be shot,'" Farrah reads from the phone. "That's disconcerting."

"It *is*," I tell her. "Someone wants to shoot me. It's not a good feeling." I sit up and fiddle with the ears of Farrah's bunny. "And there's this other guy, Trad Dad."

"Yeah, I saw him," Farrah says, with no hint of worry. "He's the one that's 'concerned for the morality of all involved.'"

She's clearly mocking him, but I can't help but hear the echo of his earlier DM in my mind. **Are you sure what you're doing is the right thing?**

"What if I'm wrong?" I blurt out, and Farrah's smile fades. "Mom said today that a bunch of parents are following the account now, and a lot of the messages I'm getting are from adults who don't want an anonymous social media account being their kids' source of answers when it comes to sex. I can't argue against that."

"Then maybe they should try talking to them about it themselves?" Farrah says, shrugging.

"Right," I agree. "And now I'm offering up parenting advice."

"Without being a parent," Farrah says. "But, really, how is that any different from starting a sex ed class when you're a vir—"

I throw the rabbit at Farrah and it bounces off her nose, but she doesn't toss it back at me or start screaming that now she needs plastic surgery. She's still looking at my phone, and her face has gone gray.

"What?" I ask, all my alarms going off.

"This shit is exactly why you can't stop," Farrah says, for once deadly serious.

"What?" I ask again, my anxiety kicking up a notch.

Farrah wordlessly holds up the phone.

@Ko/Kreame/Krispies—my stepbrother rapes me every night. Please help.

CHAPTER FIFTEEN

Jobie

I don't know what it feels like to be an addict—unless you count that weird summer with Fun Dip—but I think I'm getting a taste of it. Ever since I used *#goodgirl*, my followers have grown, interactions have exploded, and my comments are a constant feed of validation and compliments. I scroll back to the post of me at my bedroom window, which has garnered more new likes and comments, even though it's a week old.

@hanks/on/third—aww, what's wrong baby?

@nowhere(nobody)noway!—bet I can cheer you up . . .

@thevoid$calling34—great pic, beautiful girl

@that$howyoudothat/19/—I would take care of you forever

Amy was right; there really is a large component of males who want exactly what I've got—average good looks with no pressure, zero intensity, and that quality she describes as *openness.*

@!Cute!_Amy—girl, you are on fire

@!Cute!_Amy—I see you blowing up over there

"Could you maybe not push the table away while others are using it?"

I look up to see Fallon, her lunch shoved to the side, an AP Calc book, notes, and a novel face down on the table. Everything is spread around her in a hodgepodge of being performatively busy and important. I've been lost in the lake of approbation that the *#goodgirl* tag has flooded me with, and had opted out of eating for chilling and liking the comments from what Amy calls the "safe sexies"—guys who are clearly into you but don't cross the line. But it appears that my method of chilling—knees tucked to my chest and pressing against the edge of the table—is making the wheeled lunch table scoot slowly away from us, taking all of Fallon's mountain of work (she probably considers it a security blanket) away from her.

"Sorry," I say, putting my knees down and pulling the table back toward us.

"It's fine," Fallon says, but her tone doesn't match her words, and I catch her gaze, seeing something more than the usual exhaustion that comes from attempting perfection every day. Maybe I should let her know that being perfect shouldn't be the goal; just being *good* has done wonders for me.

Or, maybe not. Fallon's never hidden her irritation at my needing a selfie every time we're doing anything even marginally fun, and I can't begin to imagine a conversation between Fallon and Amy.

@!Cute!_Amy—open your mouth slightly

@Its-Me-Fallon—mouth breathing can cause gum disease

@!Cute!_Amy—push your boobs together a little

@Its-Me-Fallon—mammary glands have a function, they are not for display

Even the thought makes me snort a laugh, and Fallon shoots me a look.

"Sorry," I say quickly, realizing it's the second time I've said it at lunch, and the only thing I've said to Fallon all day. She'd tossed her things on the lunch table and set to work with a *Don't bother me*, Fallon force field immediately going up around her in a three-foot radius. I'm used to her moods and had happily lost myself in my phone, only noticing later that Shelby had abandoned us to eat with Baxter (no surprise there), but Mal had also been repelled and was eating with January and Amara.

"What's going on with you?" I finally venture to ask. "You seem . . . off."

Bitchy is actually how she seems, but Fallon started a campaign against that word in seventh grade and will not allow females to refer to each other that way in her presence.

"I've got too much shit to do," Fallon says, which is certainly always true, but what is weird here is that she's swearing, a very un-Fallon thing to do. She's got her head bent over a calc quiz that she's—oh my God, is she correcting that? Did Fallon actually get a C and is having to grovel like the rest of us in the ditches of half-credit corrections?

My phone goes off with a notification from Instagram that I just gained a follower; the pleasant, near-constant hum of my phone spikes my happiness every time. I tap to see who my new admirer is, then slide over to the *@Not-Your-Moms-Sex-Ed* account—which now has almost eight thousand followers.

"Damn," I say, turning my phone so Fallon can see. "Look at you, lighting up the world."

I'd kill for that kind of growth, but Fallon only flinches. Her eyes meet mine, and I spot it again—a shadow of something behind her usual midlevels of freaking out. She picks her pencil back up, but her hand is shaking, and she jumps when her phone vibrates again.

I think something might actually be wrong. Not, like, *Fallon has thought-spiraled herself into imagining the worst-possible outcomes of every decision she's ever made* wrong, but rather like she's actually dealing with a real issue, not one that she's convinced herself is a problem. I tried asking, and she blew me off. So I go with a declaration instead.

"You're not okay, and I'm not stupid, so let's accept that both of those things are true and you just tell me what's going on."

Typically, now is when Fallon's resolve wobbles. It's not often, but every now and then she decides she actually needs other humans on an emotional level, not just to carry out small tasks that work toward a larger goal of her making. Every now and then, Fallon will actually accept help from other people.

But not this time.

"I'm fine," she snaps. "I didn't do so hot on this calc quiz, that's all."

But her attention isn't on the quiz; she's looking down at my phone, which is still showing the *@Not-Your-Moms-Sex-Ed* feed. She flips it over, clearly not wanting to look at it, which makes perfect sense. Because Fallon doesn't care about the same things I do; she cares about maintaining her GPA, not her social media presence.

"Why don't you let me handle the DMs on the Not Your Moms Sex Ed account," I tell her, dropping my voice and thumbing over to the app. "You worry about your—"

But I can't take care of her social media, because when I try to switch my account over to *@Not-Your-Moms-Sex-Ed*, I'm told that the autofill password is wrong. I frown, typing in the one we'd agreed upon—therealityofapenis—only to get the incorrect password notification again.

"Hey, did you change—"

"I've got it," Fallon says, and I glance up at her from my phone. Her eyes are hard and heavy on mine, her voice flinty in a way I haven't heard since Cody Hughes snapped her bra in fifth grade.

"Why did you change the password?" I ask, staring down at my phone. "I thought we were doing this together? I can't help you if—"

Fallon swallows and turns back to her quiz, head down. "Some of the stuff coming through on the DMs was pretty rough, people asking for advice about really personal situations. I thought it would be better if the answers are consistent, which means the same person should be responding to all of them. We don't want to be hit or miss."

"Right," I say, my former chill mode slipping down into frozen. "The implication being that me answering any questions is a miss."

"I didn't say that," Fallon says, not looking up from her paper.

"No, I worked it out all by myself," I snap. "You're being ridiculous. You're not going to be able to keep up with—"

"With what? Knowing when there's only five minutes left in the hour?"

I pull back, stung. I knew she was pissed about me flubbing the high sign at a meeting, but it's not like Fallon to let something stagnate, throwing it back out later. More than once in our friendship I'd asked her if she was mad at me only for her to say, "If I'm mad at you, I'll tell you."

"Whatever," I say, snagging my phone and flouncing off. I find a corner next to the vending machines and slide down the wall, my back against the bricks, pulling up the Rock Bottom app so I can see what Amy's up to.

But I can't.

Rock Bottom is down.

"Really?" I say, trying to access it through a browser instead, but getting nowhere other than the Rock Bottom icon—a rag doll with X's for eyes and stitches for a mouth—sitting slumped, with her head in her lap . . . literally. **Lost our minds temporarily—back soon!** is printed underneath the illustration, their way of letting users know the site has crashed.

The decapitated doll reminds me that *@Bras-Are-Boob-Prisons* had done another well-being check-in on me, but I can't respond to her—or anyone else—until the site is fixed. A bright flare of panic shoots from my gut up into my throat, leaving bile in its wake. Amy has coached me through my postings all week, leading to better and better results. I can't lose momentum, can't lose contact with her just when everything started to go right . . . everything other than Fallon turning into a withholding b-word, that is.

I switch over to Instagram and shoot Amy a DM there.

@Jobster{Lobster}—omg rb is down! I hope you answer DMs here!

Her answer is immediate, the green dot next to her profile pic lighting up.

@!Cute!_Amy—ikr? I was like gahhh!!! Can't talk to my Jobster!

@Jobster{Lobster}—thank god IG isn't down too!

I feel a lift in my stomach at Amy referring to me as *her* Jobster. I glance over to see Fallon still huddled with her calc quiz, brow furrowed. I don't think she even noticed I left. Over at their table, Shelby breaks out into a peal of laughter, Baxter clearly pleased with himself for causing it. And here I am sitting in the corner, talking to the only person who seems to care if I exist—and I'd almost lost contact with her.

@Jobster{Lobster}—what would we even do if IG crashed, lol!

It's a joke but it's also . . . not. The truth is that when I wake up in the morning, I check my DMs before my texts. I can always count on Amy to cheer me up, answer me right away, and overall just make me feel like I matter. Everyone else . . . not so much. Fallon has left me on read more than once this week, and Shelby clearly prioritizes Baxter's texts over anyone else's. I don't know Mal well enough to just shoot her random *I'm bored, keep me company* texts, and Mom has been lost in a maze of the new guy—it turns out his name is Jason and he's a cop. She even went so far as to ask me how I would feel about meeting him, to which I had said sure, whatever, while adding a little shine to my irises on a photo editing app.

@!Cute!_Amy—888-212-4612

@!Cute!_Amy—that's my number!

@!Cute!_Amy—in case some evil being crashes all the platforms

@!Cute!_Amy—we can't be separated!! Lol

The vending machine kicks into gear next to me, sending a low hum through the floor. It's calming and settles my nerves, along with the warm glow that filled my stomach when Amy sent me her number. I put it into my phone and shoot her a text.

No evil being can separate us!!!

This is Jobie, btw.

Lol

The bell rings, and I watch from my corner as Fallon gets up, throws everything into her bag, face buried in her phone, expression still set at *Do not approach* levels. She doesn't even look around to see where I am, just dumps her tray and walks out, probably assuming that I'm following somewhere in her wake, like I always have.

My phone buzzes in my hand.

Jobie!!! I'm putting you in my favorites, like right now!!

I smile, the warmth of affection blooming further as I put Amy in my favorites, too. Then I pop over to my photos and go to the New You perfected version of me—the one that will cost $75,000 to attain. I send it to Amy, along with a text.

You can put this as my profile pic in your phone, lol

#goals

She immediately sends me a series of fire emojis and hearts, followed by a text.

Girl, is that you?

In my vending machine corner, I let out a long sigh, which runs the length of the tardy bell. I need to get up, need to get my shit together.

In a perfect world, yeah

This is me if I had money

But it's not a perfect world, and I'm not that version of Jobie Vaughn. I'm a girl who lives in Presnick, Ohio, whose friends all seems to have better things to do than talk to her, who is going to walk into English late. My phone goes off, a series of comments and DMs from admirers coming in. I slip my phone into my pocket as I enter the classroom, ignoring the plastic tray Dalford uses to collect phones. It's not like me to break the rules, not like me to disrespect a teacher.

But there's more than one way to be a good girl.

CHAPTER SIXTEEN

Shelby

"Is this a *have to* kind of thing?"

"It is if you want to have more friends than just me," I tell Baxter, stripping off my sports bra while holding the phone to my ear, which takes real talent.

"I'm good with just you," he says. "Presnick doesn't exactly have a lot to offer."

While I can't disagree with his assessment, I feel a spike of annoyance at his words. Baxter might not fit in here, but he hasn't tried very hard, either. We've been going back and forth about whether to go to Cody Hughes's party all week, with the intensity of my ask amping up as it got closer to Friday, and his enthusiasm waning.

"Look," I tell him, hopping on one foot as I try to get out of my fighting shorts. "This isn't going to change your mind about Presnick. We don't have a big lake. We don't have the Sears Tower—"

"It's the Willis Tower now."

"We don't have *any* towers," I say. "But what we do have is beer and people that know how to party."

"Do I have to play beer pong?"

"Maybe," I admit, turning on the shower. "And you'll lose."

"Maybe," he comes back, but I finally hear a smile in his voice.

"Are you taking a shower?"

"Maybe," I say, then follow it up with something less coy. "I totally am, because I smell like ass right now."

"Why'd you have to take it there?" Baxter asks, but the teasing tone that accompanies most of our conversations is missing; he actually sounds annoyed with me.

"I'll pick you up in half an hour," I tell him, leaving no room for argument.

"Half an hour? That's fast." Okay, he found room for argument.

"I don't drive the speed limit," I tell him.

"No, like aren't you going to do your hair and makeup?"

"Uhhh . . ." I wipe away the fog that's gathered on the mirror, inspecting my reflection. There are still pressure marks on either side of my face from the headgear, and a small scratch runs across my cheek from where one of the jiujitsu beginners didn't get the memo about trimming her fingernails. Baxter has made it clear what he thinks of Presnick, and right now, I look about as Presnick as it gets.

The truth is that I only wear makeup if we're doing promo shoots for a fight, and the go-to for my hair if I'm not in the ring is a ponytail. If I'm going to wear it down I'll need to dry it, and if I'm going to wear makeup . . . I'll need to find some.

"Give me an hour," I tell him. Then I hang up, wrap a towel around myself, and open the bathroom door, yelling down the hall.

"Taylor! I need help!"

I have to admit that Taylor may have some skills worth learning.

I'm sure that her left hook is shit, and I could submit her within five seconds on the mat, but before I do, I need to make sure she puts together a tutorial for me on exactly how she managed this particular magic that is my face right now. I flip down my visor for another appreciative glance at myself, also noticing that my hair looks phenomenal. Taylor had clucked about broken hairs and split ends and the danger of constantly tearing out elastic bands, but she'd gone to work with a straightener and something in a spray can, and quite frankly, I look fucking fantastic. I've been idling on the curb for about five minutes, so I shoot Baxter a quick text—**I'm here!**

We've gone out a few times—in Presnick, *out* means that we've hit the coffee shop, the pizza place, and the state park. Baxter has insisted on driving every time, and I'd floated along in the silence of his electric car as if riding on a cloud. His experience in the passenger seat of my Honda Fit is going to be a little bit different. She's got over two hundred thousand miles on her, and the previous owner enjoyed smoking.

Out in a minute

Baxter's text is short and to the point, with no emojis, compliments, or a clever jab for me to counter. There's nothing here for me to respond to, and I scroll up, realizing that he hasn't texted me since this morning, which—for us—is odd. The front door opens, and he comes down the sidewalk, looking like a million dollars. He's wearing an honest-to-God scarf, but not like something his mom knitted. It looks like it might be silk. And that just figures, because my boyfriend is classy as fuck.

Unfortunately for him, his girlfriend is . . . not.

"Uh . . ." He opens the door, and eyes the passenger seat.

If the former owner of the Fit liked cigarettes, the current owner enjoys fast food and isn't picky about where she eats—after I work out, I pig out, and my car shows it. I bite my lip, surveying the wonderland of trash that I'd never really bothered to think about before.

My teeth come away sticky, the taste of makeup in my mouth when I realize I've eaten my lipstick.

"Sorry," I say, swiping my forearm across the seat and knocking a collection of paper bags, plastic cups, and aluminum cans of energy drinks into the footwell. Baxter gives the seat a dubious glance, then brushes it off a few times before getting in.

"Hey!" I say, trying to sound chipper, trying to recapture the typical magic of us.

But he doesn't make eye contact with me as I pull away.

"That's . . . a lot," he says, gesturing toward his feet and the trash I'd tossed there.

Too much?

"Yeah," I say, aiming for casual. "I have to grab food in between school and training, so there's lots of car eating in my life."

Baxter just kind of grunts in response, so I barrel forward, determined to be funny, to be charming, to display whatever quality I have that typically generates thirty to forty texts a day from him. Except . . . not today.

"And I've got preferences," I say. "A Whopper from Burger King, fries from McDonald's, a Frosty from Wendy's. That's my custom load-out. Doesn't really matter where you get your pop from, it all tastes the same."

"Soda," Baxter corrects me.

"Pop," I repeat. "You're in Ohio."

"How could I forget?" He sighs and twists in his seat, a Monster can crunching under his feet. "How long do we have to stay at this thing?"

"This thing is a party, and it's supposed to be fun," I tell him.

I've been looking forward to Cody's party since he'd tossed it out there on Snapchat when he learned his parents would be gone over the weekend. It's an open invite, which means anyone can show up—even the most resented quasi-famous blonde in the county. If everyone wants to ignore me because they're under the impression that I think I'm better than they are, they can cry into their beers while they consider the fact that maybe I am.

I've had constant Zooms with Tara, Lee, and the rep from Rebel as we iron out details for the photo shoot next week. Training takes up the rest of my time outside of school, and, while I would never bring it up, I'd missed a couple of sessions when Baxter had hinted that we weren't spending enough time together. Coach Faith hadn't been thrilled, but I'd floated the low-level lie that I had therapy, and she'd backed off.

And Baxter does feel like therapy. I'm happiest when I'm with him. Usually I'd say the same is true for him, too, but right now he looks very far from happy.

"Maybe it should be fun, but it feels like work," he says.

"Funny, I was just thinking the same thing," I say tightly.

"What's that supposed to mean?" he asks.

"Nothing," I say, regretting the bite in my words. "Never mind."

"That's textbook passive-aggressive," Baxter says, pulling out his phone and scrolling through Instagram. "One of my exes was like that."

I don't answer, very aware that the blush Taylor had spread across my cheekbones was entirely unnecessary; I've got a natural rosy glow born of pure anger right now. I want to tell Baxter that if I'm anything it's purely aggressive—there's nothing passive about me. And if his little footnote about one of his exes is supposed be some sort of warning, he needs to learn more about how to deliver a threat. I glance over and see that he's paused on Ilsa Bunting's repost of my fight with Jayden in the hallway.

Why the hell would he follow Ilsa, my opponent in the only fight I've ever lost?

And why would he be playing that video when he's sitting right next to me?

I look away, but I don't need the visual to see it. My finger in Jayden's face, following him down the hall, grabbing his shoulder . . .

She wants to fight.

The nature of the blood in my face shifts from anger to embarrassment. Why am I fucking things up with Baxter? Did I have to come at him with the implication that he's work? And yeah, he's being a douche about my car, but it *is* kind of gross, and who drives around advertising all their bad habits, anyway?

"You going to donate those to Locks of Love?" Baxter asks, pointing to the twenty or so elastic bands wrapped around my gear shift. They sprout hair in all directions, knots of blond mats wrapped around the colorful elastic, looser strands trailing to the sides. I flash back to Taylor, pinching one of them disdainfully between her fingers, nose wrinkled.

"This is hairy and gross," she'd said, tossing it in the trash, happy to assist me with my hair as long as she could get a dig in at the same time. I'd bitten my tongue, aware that if I threw out my comeback—*That's what Dad said about your vagina*—I would be left to my own devices when it came to hair and makeup.

Does Baxter think I'm gross? Is he getting a dig in, too? Or is he joking, trying to get us back to good? He did break the awkward silence, and maybe I could try *not* saying every shitty thing I think. I give him the benefit of the doubt and go for a laugh. It comes out hard and awkward, clawing its way past the self-doubt clogging my throat.

"I tried; they're not interested in broken hairs and split ends," I say, borrowing Taylor's words from before. "But they did say to let them know if my boyfriend ever decides to shave his head. They want dibs on fondling your follicles."

I wasn't kidding when I said I studied up on f-words, and my sudden turn into agreeableness and complimenting him works; Baxter smiles and closes out Instagram.

"Tell them there's a line, and you're in front," he says, leaning over the console to kiss my cheek. His elbow knocks an errant french fry into the back seat, but he either doesn't notice or is kind enough not to say anything. A warm rush of relief floods me when he loops his fingers with my free hand, turning into something else when he rubs his thumb along my wrist.

"Fondling sounds like a good plan for the evening," I say, as I pull onto Cody's road, gravel crunching under my tires.

"That's what I had in mind," Baxter says. "But the lady says there's a party we must attend."

"Have to take advantage of parental absences," I tell him, parking next to Rory's Jeep when I spot it in Cody's side yard. There are already at least twenty cars here, and the low thump of bass emanates from the backyard, along with a girl's high-pitched yelp.

"That's *also* what I had in mind," Baxter says, and my hand pauses on my seat belt.

"Your mom's not home?"

"Nope," he says, leaving an empty silence afterward.

I tap my fingers on the steering wheel, debating. Rory loves me and always will, but with the exception of Fallon, Jobie, and Mal, most of the girls in Presnick see me as competition in a game they're going to lose. Showing up at Cody's is a way for me to let everyone know that I might be hot shit, but I'm still small-town—and maybe a chance to show Baxter that Presnick isn't all MAGA hats and sweet-corn festivals.

"Two hours," I tell him. "Give me two hours of beer pong, and I'll give you . . ."

I want to finish the sentence with *whatever you want*, but based on past experience, what Baxter wants is for me to leave his zipper up and my bra on. The blush comes back, remembering how he'd pushed my hand aside.

God, does he think I'm a slut? Am I completely off base about his mom being gone?

"A gift subscription to *National Geographic*," I finish.

"I'm covered for the next two years," Baxter says, opening his door.

"Guess I'll have to come up with a different reward system," I say. "Now, come on. I'll show you how to do a keg stand."

CHAPTER SEVENTEEN

Fallon

Everyone is at Cody's party except me.

I'm sitting on my bed with every yearbook I've got sprawled across the covers, desperately trying to figure out who *@Ko/Kreame/Krispies* is. I'd responded to her initial DM with the best advice I had.

@Ko/Kreame/Krispies—my stepbrother rapes me every night. Please help.

@Not-Your-Moms-Sex-Ed—This is a crime and you do not have to live like this. Report your stepbrother by telling someone.

The response had come back immediately.

@Ko/Kreame/Krispies—I did. I told you.

"Okay, but let's consider that it might just be someone messing with you," Farrah says now. She's sitting across from me, her toes splayed out, a bottle of nail polish in one hand.

"Seriously," I say, looking up at her from my junior yearbook. "That's your knee-jerk reaction to someone reporting a rape? They probably made it up?"

"Ugh," Farrah says, her nose crinkling. "You're right, that's gross."

"Super gross," I tell her, going back to the glossy pages.

"But . . . ," Farrah keeps going. "Why would they tell someone on social media and not someone who can actually do something about it?"

"I don't know," I say, pinching the bridge of my nose. "But questioning their motives isn't the best reaction, and this is my responsibility now."

"Is it?" Farrah asks.

"Yes!" I snap at her, slamming the yearbook shut. "I opened this door, and that means anyone can walk through. People who have real questions, strangers who want to shoot me, and somebody suffering through repeated sexual assault."

"So this is the right response?" Farrah asks, motioning toward my yearbooks. "Doing the math on every family living situation in Presnick?"

"I don't know what else to do," I tell her.

Paging through each class since freshman year and making a list of whose parents I knew had gotten divorced, then remarried and combined households has been like trying to determine who used a filter—it's basically everybody. I'm all for found families and everyone living their best life, but the solution to this problem would be a lot simpler if the divorce rates were lower. I've currently got six options and would love to narrow it down further just based on my own personal opinions of the stepbrothers in question, but I know a rapist can wear polos and have an all-American-boy smile and still be a sack of shit.

"You don't even know it's someone from Presnick," Farrah says. "I mean, seriously, this could be someone in Broken Toe, Nebraska."

"Technically, yes," I tell her. "But I checked, and Ko Kreame Krispies was an early follower. She got on board along with a whole onslaught of Presnick people and not a lot of outsiders. Sure, she *could* be from anywhere, but given the data, it's not likely."

To make things worse, *@Ko/Kreame/Krispies*'s account has no posts, and no profile pics. They'd clearly created the account specifically to communicate with *@Not-Your-Moms-Sex-Ed*, which makes me feel worse, because that means I'm the only person they feel safe telling.

I roll my neck, and Farrah winces at the sound of vertebrae popping.

"Do you have to do that?" she asks.

"This is my only vice," I tell her.

"Sad," Farrah says, clicking her tongue.

"So, yes, I do think she's at least somewhat local, and that's all I have to go by," I say, bringing Farrah back to the topic at hand.

"Okay, but . . ." Farrah glances up at me, clearly uncomfortable.

"What? Just say it, whatever. I don't even care anymore," I tell her.

"Have you thought about the fact that if she's local, then maybe some of your haters are, too?"

"Yes," I admit. "Which is why it's critical that we keep the Not Your Mom's Sex Ed account and SHAFT Class separate."

What I don't tell Farrah is that both *@Trad!Dad/1996* and *@*Toad*Runner** were early adopters of *@Not-Your-Moms-Sex-Ed*, as well. I shake that thought off, not wanting to think about the fact that they could be sitting in the stands at a basketball game. Hell, one of them could be my dentist, for all I know. They both are just like *@Ko/Kreame/Krispies*—no profile, no followers, and only following *@Not-Your-Moms-Sex-Ed*. Although *@Trad!Dad/1996* had recently started following the Presnick Police Department account as well, which gave me a rash of goose bumps when I saw it.

“I’ve got it narrowed down to six girls,” I say.

There are two freshmen that I don’t know very well, a girl from marching band, a quiet girl who I’m pretty sure never leaves the library, two volleyball players, and—my current most likely—Bethany, the cheerleader who came to SHAFT Class. Farrah leans forward, but I flip my legal pad over with a warning glance.

“Whoever it is, they want privacy,” I tell her.

“Sorry,” she says. “And sorry to break this to you, but you are assuming a lot here. Not only that they are from Presnick, but also that it’s a girl.”

“I . . . well, crap,” I say, flipping the pad over and looking at the names I’d listed there. Farrah’s not wrong; I’d completely set aside the idea that *@Ko/Kreame/Krispies* could be male.

“Okay, fair point,” I acknowledge. “But ninety-one percent of reported rapes are female, so it’s not like I’m way off base here.”

“Wow, you had that stat, like, right now,” Farrah says, snapping her fingers.

“Yeah, I’ve had to google some really depressing things lately,” I tell her, feeling another headache blooming behind my eyes.

“Sorry, big sis,” Farrah says. “But I’ve got to drop another downer on you.”

“Hit me with it,” I say, digging my palms into my eye sockets.

“You’re just looking at high school yearbooks,” Farrah says quietly, waving at my bedspread. I consider that for a second, my stomach dropping. Farrah’s right again; *@Ko/Kreame/Krispies* doesn’t have to be in high school.

“It’s not like there’s an age limit on—”

“Yeah, I got it,” I snap, and look up to see Farrah’s mouth in a downturn.

"Sorry," I tell her. "This is just . . . it's all been a lot."

"And it's not all on you," Farrah insists. "Tell Mom and Dad, tell the guidance counselor."

"I can't," I tell her. "Everyone at school is a mandated reporter. As soon as I share this with them, they are legally required to take it to the police, which means there's an investigation, Not Your Mom's Sex Ed goes under a microscope, and I'm outed."

"So?" Farrah shrugs, not getting it at all. I have to explain.

"If you looked at my search history, you'd see that I've been trying to find out the specifics of corruption of a minor, lewd and lascivious behavior, pandering obscenity, and contributing to the delinquency of a minor," I tell her.

"Oh . . . ," Farrah says. "Can you actually be charged with that shit?"

"I don't know," I tell her, palming my face again. "But I'm over eighteen; so is Jobie. We're technically adults that gather minors in a public space for the specific purpose of discussing sexual acts."

"Yeah," Farrah says. "Probably don't put that on your résumé. Sounds skeevy."

"And possibly criminal," I say. "So, no, I don't feel like I can just tell an adult about Ko Kreame Krispies without bringing down a shitstorm on my own head."

"So the goal is to find her yourself?"

"While still trying to answer the hundreds of other legitimate questions that are pouring in," I tell her, flashing my screen at her, where 138 unanswered DMs are waiting for me.

"Have Jobie take those, or Shelby," Farrah says, but I shake my head.

"I changed the password for the account. If Ko Kreame Krispies is someone we know, they deserve privacy."

"Fair enough," Farrah says, returning to her toes. "What's on the backburner?"

I scroll past the messages from *@Ko/Kreame/Krispies* to the unreads. There's one from *@Iowa-Irish-Lass_2025.*

@Iowa-Irish-Lass_2025—my b/f says we can't use condoms b/c he has a latex allergy. Is that a thing?

@Not-Your-Moms-Sex-Ed—Latex allergies are a real thing, but whether or not he actually has one is a valid question. You can get condoms that are made out of polyurethane or polyisoprene. There are also condoms made out of animal tissue, like lambskin, but those aren't as effective when it comes to protection from STDs.

I follow up by letting *@Iowa-Irish-Lass_2025* know what brands to look for. I typically try to keep all of my responses fact-based and judgment-free, but I can't help adding my personal opinion on this particular matter.

@Not-Your-Moms-Sex-Ed—Only 6% of the population has a latex allergy. So there's a 94% chance that he's lying. Buy a safe alternative, present him with that, and if he still tries to wiggle out of practicing safe sex, find a boyfriend that will respect you and your boundaries.

"I'm rounding up on that ninety-four percent of the boyfriend being a liar," Farrah says, tongue sticking out as she applies the third coat.

@PHS/Pom!Mom78—is sexting cheating? Do I need to go to confession?

I sigh and bury my palms in my eye sockets. Heather Mower's mom needs to get a less obvious screenname. And when did *@Not-Your-Moms-Sex-Ed* turn into exactly that? I decide not to share this one with Farrah and try to compose an answer with a straight face.

@Not-Your-Moms-Sex-Ed—every couple will have a different definition of fidelity. Ask yourself how you would feel if your husband was engaging in similar behavior, and consider what is missing from your current relationship that is driving you to seek affirmation elsewhere.

I review my response, then change *husband* to *spouse*, since it's perfectly possible that *@PHS/Pom!Mom78* could be married to a woman. I totally know she's not. She's very married to a man, that man is the superintendent of our school, and I'm confident that Gary would not be happy about the situation. I'm also dying to know who exactly Mrs. Mower is sexting with, but I'm slowly becoming aware of the massive power I wield as the anonymous voice behind *@Not-Your-Moms-Sex-Ed.*

I answer a few more of the common questions—**can I get an STD from oral sex? (yes); does sex hurt? (depends, but it shouldn't); how do I know if I'm gay?** (I mark that one to include on the growing list to forward to Mal), and **is it normal that one of my boobs is bigger than the other? (yes, completely).**

The next one is quickly becoming one of my most asked questions . . . and it's making me realize that girls aren't the only ones who feel inadequate.

@plu$hvibe$overhere—do I have a little dick?

Plush Vibes has taken the liberty of sending along a visual aid, complete with a ruler, so I have a very accurate reckoning of the size of his dick.

As the follower growth of *@Not-Your-Moms-Sex-Ed* exploded, it brought along with it teens, adults, moms, daughters, girls, boys, and men. I'd quickly chided myself for being sexist by believing that only women had sex questions, or that we're the only ones who accept the responsibility for sex. Guys have flooded my DMs with worries about whether their girlfriend is faking it, how they can know if they're in love, and the best way to nicely, kindly, end a relationship. Sometimes I know the answers, sometimes I don't, but I've been doing my best . . . and gaining some respect for the opposite sex along the way.

But also—I get a lot of dick pics.

The vast majority of them are dudes that need reassurance; I've only had a few that sent along an invite to do more than just deliver an assessment, or ask for a reciprocal pic. The question is so common that I open up the Google Doc where I've saved my response, and copy-paste it into my DMs.

@plu$hvibe$overhere—do I have a little dick?

@Not-Your-Moms-Sex-Ed—it's very common for males to wonder where they land on this scale. In a recent study where men were offered custom-fit condoms for sharing their measurements, the average length is 5.57 inches, with an average circumference of 4.81 inches. Remember that this is an average, and—more importantly—the female G-spot is located only 2 to 3 inches inside the anterior wall of the vagina. In other words—size really doesn't matter. Also, since most males are exposed to porn, it's critical to remember that not only are the women's bodies greatly exaggerated and surgically enhanced, the same can be true for the male performers as well. No one should judge themselves against what they see on the screen.

I send the answer and Plush Vibes responds immediately with a happy face—and if the ruler is any indicator—it's earned. But while making this guy feel better about his dick does give me a weird little warm fuzzy, it also makes Mom's words from our shopping trip come to mind.

You all have the ability to produce child porn in your back pockets.

She's right, and just by the sheer number of pics that come into the *@Not-Your-Moms-Sex-Ed* account, I guarantee not all of them are over eighteen. I'm always careful to delete anything with pics, but everyone knows that the internet is forever, and the fact that I delete the message doesn't mean it's gone. The thought makes my hands shake, and a sheen of sweat breaks out on my upper lip. The next message doesn't help.

@Right/Side-Of-Life—I've reported this account. Your sexually coaching minors. Expect consequences.

I resist the urge to respond correcting *your* to *you're*. Instead, I block them but keep the message . . . just in case. This has been my approach ever since the attacks and threats started coming in. I block them but keep the message and move it into Priority, so that I've got the haters sorted. I tap over to Priority, scrolling over the 340 messages there.

Inappropriate . . . stupid bitch . . . loose morals . . . groomer . . . explicit content . . . encouraging sexual behavior . . . deviant . . . rape should be legal . . . coming for our children . . . suck my dick . . .

And now—**expect consequences.**

Glancing through those messages almost makes dealing with identifying *@Ko/Kreame/Krispies* seem much more appealing. I scroll back up my DMs and see that there's currently a green dot next to their profile pic—a generic gray outline. If I respond to them right now, they might fire back immediately, and I'll need to be ready for an exchange. Stalling, I scroll through my feed and see that Jobie is also online and just posted a pic of her cuddling with Princess Tinyhead. I guess I'm not the only person who isn't at Cody's party. I tap on her profile and try to think of something breezy to say . . . something to repair the damage I undoubtedly did today at lunch when she realized I'd locked her out of the *@Not-Your-Moms-Sex-Ed* account.

@Its-Me-Fallon—stop with the pussy pics already

It's immediately marked as read and then . . . nothing.

"Ooookaaaaaay," I say, shifting uncomfortably against my pillows. Looks like I'll need to do a little more work than I thought to get back into Jobie's good graces. Or, I could focus on someone like *@Ko/Kreame/Krispies*, who has very real problems and doesn't consider runny mascara one of them. As I'm watching, an ellipsis pops up in the DM, *@Ko/Kreame/Krispies* adding to the string of messages to *@Not-Your-Moms-Sex-Ed*.

@Ko/Kreame/Krispies—never mind. I shouldn't talk about it anyway. Deleting this account.

"Oh, honey . . . no," I say.

I think of Mom cutting me off in the car, avoiding the topic. Whoever *@Ko/Kreame/Krispies* is, someone needs to hear them out so that they don't have a panic attack at the dinner table in front of their kids in twenty years. I make a decision and start typing.

@Not-Your-Moms-Sex-Ed—Being sexually assaulted is never, ever your fault. Shame is a common reaction, but talking about it is important to eliminate the stigma associated with being a survivor.

@Ko/Kreame/Krispies—I can't talk about it. I tried once, with my mom, and couldn't even speak, I thought I was going to puke. I just froze up.

The ellipsis disappears, but the green dot stays on. Whoever *@Ko/Kreame/Krispies* is, at least they are listening.

@Not-Your-Moms-Sex-Ed—The physical symptoms you describe are trauma reactions.

The message is marked as read, but *@Ko/Kreame/Krispies* doesn't reply right away. I flip over to another thread with a different survivor of sexual assault who had also dismissed their own trauma reactions. I'd talked him through the biological responses, and there's no reason why I can't take the same approach here.

@Not-Your-Moms-Sex-Ed—there are four different trauma reactions—fight, flight, freeze, or fawn. Fight, flight, and freeze are self-explanatory. Fawn means that you try to appease or placate whatever the danger is.

@Not-Your-Moms-Sex-Ed—it sounds like you tend to freeze

@Ko/Kreame/Krispies—for sure. Like literally. I just lay still and pretend I'm somewhere else.

@Ko/Kreame/Krispies—he probably doesn't even think he's raping me

@Not-Your-Moms-Sex-Ed—he is, and you need to tell someone

@Ko/Kreame/Krispies—my stepdad says I'm a slut b/c I got an STD last year—from his son

@Ko/Kreame/Krispies—gotta go he's here

The green dot disappears, and I stare at my phone in disbelief.

"Shit, shit, shit," I say, bile rising in my throat.

"What?" Farrah asks, looking up from her toes.

"I think . . ." I stare at *@Ko/Kreame/Krispies* profile pic, willing them to come back online. "I think it might be happening right now."

Farrah takes my phone, reads through the messages, her face going pale. "What do we do?"

I flip over to Snapchat, then back to Instagram, riffling through the constant update posts from Cody's party.

"Whoever Ko Kreame Krispies is, they're home right now," I say, pulling my notebook toward me. I can eliminate a few of these names just based on who's at Cody's. Also, from what they said, it sounds like the family is made up of a mother and biological daughter, plus stepdad and his biological son. That will narrow down family units where the dad has the biological daughter and the mom has a son.

"And they said they had an STD last year," Farrah says, then rolls her eyes. "Not that that narrows the pool down much."

"Yes, but if she got it from her stepbrother, she wouldn't exactly tell people about it," I say, flipping through social media platforms and scratching names off my notepad when I spot them at Cody's party. Most of the girls are smiling and happy, flashing white teeth behind glossy lips. They're living their best life . . . while someone else is being raped in their own bed, by someone they live with and can't escape.

"And, Farrah," I say, glancing up at her. "Go get your junior high yearbooks."

CHAPTER EIGHTEEN

Jobie

Everyone is at Cody's party, except me.

I'm having dinner with my mom and Jason, who actually wore his cop uniform even though he's off duty. I don't know if he's trying to impress Mom or me, or if he thinks he's a stripper. The first option is clearly working, the second is not, and the third is outside the realm of possibility. Jason is . . . fine. He's got a dad bod (never understood the attraction), good table manners, and a haircut that I could use to scrub out the frying pan Mom used to make hot Nashville chicken, which Jason had taken one bite of, turned red, and downed most of his beer, all while trying to choke out a compliment.

Mom is smiling, laughing, actually happy. She made dinner instead of grabbing takeout. There's a man in the house for the first time since we had that one overly friendly UPS driver, and Princess Tinyhead is being social, abandoning her constant inert position on my windowsill to come downstairs, spot Jason's impeccable black uniform, and jump directly into his lap.

In other words, things are weird.

What's not weird is that there's a big social event going on that I'm not at. My feed is blowing up with pictures of people I know—can't call them friends since I'm not there, can I?—having a great time with each other. I spot January flipping a peace sign, her eyes artificially bright (*I know what filter you used*), Mal sprawled on a couch with Amara, the latter probably unaware of the look on her face as she gazes at Mal (*Don't think I haven't noticed*), and Cody passed out face down in a houseplant (*Clearly staged, try harder*).

My phone goes off yet again, vibrating as notifications from Rock Bottom illuminate my screen; the site must have come back up. Mom gives me a *Stop doing what you're doing* look, which consists of her eyes going very wide while her upper lip pulls back to show her canines. It's supposed to be both discreet and threatening, but it's very noticeable and super sexy, causing Jason to choke again, and triggering my *What? I'm just here* look, which actually is discreet but not threatening because I've certainly never been able to motivate someone else to do anything in my life.

Not even Princess Tinyhead, who has remained in Jason's lap throughout dinner after refusing to move, bringing on a barrage of apologies from Mom, assurances that it really was fine because he likes animals, and me doing nothing, letting the adults handle themselves while I looked at my phone.

Now Mom's face slides into *Please, I'm doing my best*, and I feel an actual stab of guilt. Jason has done nothing wrong, Mom is trying hard, and I'm clearly just waiting for an excuse to go to my room and be alone with my phone, which, yeah, is shitty.

"So . . ." Mom clears her throat, making eye contact with me. "How's school?"

It's a terrible conversation starter. I have nothing to say about school. But Mom's nervous, and it wouldn't hurt me to cut her some slack.

"It's fine," I say. "Fallon's really busy, and Shelby has a big photo shoot coming up."

Which isn't saying anything about me, but there isn't really anything *to* say about me. The only thing I'm doing these days is fielding compliments from strangers online, but I don't think saying that in front of Mom and a cop is smart. Mom might roll into another one of her looks-aren't-everything speeches—ironic, coming from the woman whose face is on the only billboard in Presnick—and Jason would probably give me a talk about stranger danger and make me feel like a villager in Safety Town.

"Shelby Black? The girl fighter?" Jason asks, then reddens. "I mean . . . just 'the fighter.' Not that I needed to add 'girl' to that. Am I doing this right?"

Mom's face collapses on itself as she tries not to laugh.

"Shelby Black, yeah," I say. "The fighter."

"Right, sorry," Jason says, still blushing. "I didn't mean—"

"You're fine," I tell him, and I think he might be, so I decide to put some effort into this. "Shelby just became Rebel Outfitter's new spokesperson, plus she's got a new boyfriend so she's got a lot going on. Fallon is . . . being Fallon."

"Always busy," Mom says, nodding. "If that girl can't find work, she makes it."

"Not a bad quality," Jason says.

"Kind of an annoying one sometimes, though," I tell him, quickly adding. "But she's my best friend, and I love her."

"How long have you been friends?" Jason asks.

"Oh, since forever," I say, not able to come up with numbers, and scrambling to sound like a nicer person than I probably just came across as, badmouthing my best friend. "When I was in third grade I decided I wanted to be a gymnast, but my dad said we couldn't afford the classes. Fallon bugged her dad until he came over and hung a trapeze up in our basement."

"Imagine coming home to hear two nine-year-olds screaming 'Skin the cat!' downstairs," Mom says. "The trapeze is still down there, if your gymnast phase gets a second wind."

"I'm good, thanks," I tell Mom, then turn back to Jason. "But yeah, Fallon and I do everything together, and also *don't* get to do everything together," I admit. "Like tonight, we're probably the only people not at this big par . . . tee . . ."

My words slow down, the last one coming out as two syllables when I realize I just told a cop about a huge party, where there's definitely some underage drinking going on.

"The one at the Cody Hughes' place?" Jason asks, and it's my turn to choke. "Don't think we don't know."

"I didn't . . . think anything," I finish lamely, setting down my water glass and eyeing Mom cautiously. My virtual life might be way more interesting than my real one, but my spot by the floor on the vending machine in the cafeteria is seriously low social real estate and could become my permanent mailing address if Cody gets busted because of me.

"We keep an eye out; that's about it," Jason says, all amusement gone from his tone now. "The Hughes kid is responsible enough to take everyone's keys when they come in the door, and I've never heard about anything more intense than some gummies being passed around."

"Which is still illegal if you're under twenty-one," Mom says quickly, giving me a hard look, as if she's worried I'm going to start blasting off upstairs, with the permission of stand-in cop-dad Jason.

"It is," he goes on. "But the truth is that kids will be kids; we'd rather know where you are and what you're doing and let it slide, than have everything appear fine when there's something shady going on."

Next to my plate, my phone goes off, and Mom heaves another sigh.

"Kids will be kids?" I try, one eyebrow raised as I use new-boyfriend's phrase for excusing illegal activities.

A smile twists one side of her mouth as she realizes that I've got her; I'm putting in family time and eating dinner with a cop while everyone else is getting wasted.

"Fine," she says, waving me away. "Go upstairs and spend time with your glass rectangle."

"I love my glass rectangle, thank you!" I practically squeal, jumping up from my chair. "Oh, and I love you, too," I add, planting a kiss on top of Mom's head.

"And . . . uh . . . you seem fine," I say, awkwardly giving Jason a pat on the shoulder.

"High praise," Mom deadpans.

"I'll take it," he says.

I dash up the stairs, phone in hand, and launch myself onto my bed to find three texts from Amy and a buttload of notifications from both Instagram and Rock Bottom. I've never had to prioritize who I respond to first, and I revel in the moment before landing on the person who I owe it all to in the first place. Amy's texts pick up where we'd left off as I skulked in the cafeteria.

Sorry! Real life needed me. College visit today!

Oh my god, this campus is amazing . . .

She follows this text up with a pic of a sidewalk lined with trees, twentysomethings with beanies and backpacks making their way to class. I react with a heart and scroll down to her last text.

Annnndddd. . . . Never mind. ☹

Underneath that is a pic of a screen in a classroom, the college logo in the corner, and the breakdown of tuition costs. Amy and I have shared enough with each other that I know she's living a life like mine—comfortable, but not enough to fork over fifty grand a semester. The fact that she went radio silent after this last pic makes me think she's probably in the same place I was earlier today—maybe not next to a vending machine, exactly, but with her feelings in the gutter. She pulled me up out of my funk this afternoon; I owe her the same.

But you've got good grades, right? There have got to be scholarships out there.

It's just about all I have to offer in the realm of financial wisdom, so I mentally run down the list of posters that I'd helped Fallon hang outside the guidance counselor's office.

What about FAFSA?

And work study?

A text bubble pops up, then disappears. Comes back, then winks out again. I reread my texts and roll my eyes, realizing that I just spouted college-saving TikTok tips and tricks like a champ. God, Amy just gave me her number today and I'm already being as mid as a lukewarm bath.

I click on the Rock Bottom app to find that *@Bras-Are-Boob-Prisons* has done another well-being check, which quite frankly is starting to send up red flags. I mark her message as read, then put her on mute, remembering the warning from the mods at rb/HardLooksMaxxing that they do their best to ensure their membership is all female but can't make any guarantees. I've got a friend request from *@Ask!Alice/Unchained!*, a name I recognize from the *#goodgirl* hashtag on IG. I click on it, and see she's sent along a message.

Hey! We've got a mutual friend in @!Cute!_Amy. I've seen you blowing it up on Insta. Good girls unite!

I decide to verify that with Amy before friending Alice, then I get cozy on my throw pillows, switch over to Instagram, and scroll through the compliments on my newest post. It's a straight-on selfie, no makeup, just a filter applied to plump my lips out and make my eyes shine. The teasing upturn on one side of my mouth and coy little head cock would've drawn a few likes before, but using the *#goodgirl* tag has unleashed a different world. That and the fact that I bought a pair of readers after I'd noticed that a lot of the girls who wore glasses did well.

@Mo$$y(Green)Man—natural beauty. No words.

@Nerdier^Herder—I'd like to take off more than those glasses . . .

@Back*yard*Boy_21—I'd make you smile the rest of the way if you let me

@James/Is/The!Name77—you're perfect.

I've got new follows from every one of the guys who commented, and DM follow-ups from a few that I left on read yesterday, most of which slid into my messages with **hey, cutie**, and **what's up?** But being a good girl doesn't mean that I'm naive; I haven't answered any of the strangers who messaged me, and the ones that started their conversations with dick pics got an immediate delete, report, and block.

A text from Amy comes in, sliding across the top of my screen.

Can I call you?

Oh, wow. We went from online friends to text buddies to talking in a single afternoon, which feels fast, but considering the fact that I just glad-handed her with TikTok self-help speak and she still wants to call me overrides the butterflies in my stomach.

Yes, of course! I shoot back, then scootch into my pillows and wait for my phone to ring, which it does in about thirty seconds, Cute Amy's name—with hearts on either side, how I saved her in my contacts—displaying.

"Hey," I say when I answer, trying to hit the right mix of *I owe my newfound self-worth to you* with *I make dozens of new friends every day and I'm totally not nervous.*

"Jobie, hey," Amy says back. "I'm sorry if this is like . . . weird, or whatever."

A small giggle follows that up, and I realize she might actually be nervous herself. The girl I've seen on her Insta is all smiles and self-assurance, but I bet that anyone who looked at my pics would also think that I can casually sail through a meetup conversation like a queen, not curled up in the fetal position and chewing on a lock of her hair for comfort.

"No," I say quickly. "It's fine. Totally, totally fine. Like, kinda cool, even."

I sound like an idiot, like the commenters on the *#goodgirl* hashtag that are actually pics of dogs because the original poster doesn't understand the internet.

"Okay, cool," Amy says. "I just didn't really know who else to talk to about this." Her voice is high and sweet, with just a touch of a Southern accent. It's adorable, and I make a mental note to advise her that a YouTube channel or a podcast should be in her future.

"What's up?" I ask, flicking the hair out of my mouth.

"So . . ." She sighs, and I hear a door close. "Sorry," she says. "Sometimes my parents can be creepers."

"Ugh, same," I say, even though that's totally not true. Beyond the monitoring app that she'd allowed to expire, Mom has always trusted me to make the right decisions, a thought that makes my stomach take an uncomfortable turn. I don't know how she'd feel about me talking to someone I met online, but it sounds like Amy needs me. I'd failed Fallon massively today—okay, she shut me out—but still, I'd like to step up for at least one friend in a twenty-four-hour period.

"Anyway, remember that pic I sent you today, the one about tuition?" Amy asks, and I hear bedsprings squeak as she throws herself across her own bed.

"Yeah, beg, borrow, and steal levels of money," I say.

"That's what I thought, too," Amy says. "Dad just got this real serious look on his face, and Mom poured herself some wine when we got home. I had pretty much resigned myself to life as a nail tech—not that I don't respect nail techs or . . . oh my God, is this the part where you tell me your mom is a nail tech?"

I burst out laughing. "No, she's a real estate agent. There's nothing wrong with wanting more for yourself," I tell her. "Didn't you say you wanted to be a physical therapist?"

"Yeah," she says, her voice suddenly eager. "My aunt has MS, and I've seen her go through so much. She says her PT is one of the only things that really helps, and I thought if I could do that for someone else . . ." She trails off, and Princess Tinyhead pushes my bedroom door open, the squeak of the hinges bringing me to my feet. I press the phone to my ear and shut the door, first poking my head out into the hallway to make sure I can still hear Mom's and Jason's voices downstairs.

"But it's eight years of school," Amy goes on. "After that, I'd have to get my master's—"

"That's insane," I say. "How is anybody supposed to be able to afford that?"

"That's exactly what Alice said," Amy sighs.

"Wait," I grab my laptop and scroll back through my Rock Bottom notifications. "Do you mean Ask Alice Unchained?"

"Oh, did she friend you?" Amy perks up.

"I told her she should, figured she might be able to give you even more tips than I can. She's the one that told me all about the *#goodgirl* hashtag. She is the *best*," Amy continues to gush. "She might even be able to help me figure out this tuition thing."

"What? How?" I ask, flicking Princess Tinyhead's nose as she pushes against my laptop, nudging it toward the edge of the bed.

"Well . . . that's why I wanted to talk to you." Amy's enthusiasm wanes again, trepidation creeping in. "Alice had some ideas that I'm just not really sure about."

"Do not make an OnlyFans," I say immediately.

"No, no, no, nothing like that." Amy laughs, and the weight that had begun to harden in my belly lifts.

"Then what?" I ask.

"Okay, so . . . oh my God, I feel so weird even talking about this," Amy sighs again. "So there's a *#goodgirl* sub-bottom."

"There is?" I ask, immediately navigating to rb/GoodGirl.

"Yeah, but it's—"

"Invite only," I say, frowning at my screen.

"Right," Amy says. "Alice is a member, and she got me in."

"Okaaaay," I say, drawing out the word, the danger warning of weight sinking in my belly again. "That doesn't sound good, Amy."

"I know, I know," she says. "I thought the same thing, but Alice sent me an invite, and I clicked around a bit. A lot of the guys that hang out on the hashtag on Instagram are there. You know, like, that Dylan Tyler guy and Backyard Boy." She reels off a few more of the screennames I recognize from the other platform, some of whom had

DM'd me, others hadn't, but all of them were decent enough and never pushed when I ignored them.

"And?" I ask. "What's the catch? What do they want?"

"That's what I thought, too," Amy says, and I can hear typing in the background as she clicks around on her own laptop. "But as soon as I joined, Alice posted me as a new member, and I got flooded with DMs, guys wanting—"

"Pics," I say, snapping my laptop shut.

"Yeah, but—get this," Amy says. "Not like boobs and butt stuff."

"Then what?" I ask, my eyes narrowing with suspicion.

"Well, I got the obvious request for feet pics," Amy says. "What is with that whole thing anyway?"

"I have no idea," I say, inspecting my own arches, which I have to admit, are fine. "What else?"

"A lot of guys wanting pics just like what we post on Insta," she goes on. "But they want their own, kinda, like, personalized? Not in a weird way, more like something that not just anybody on Instagram can get."

"Like, girlfriend stuff?"

"Yeah, exactly," Amy says. "Like . . . hold on." I hear her tapping away on her laptop, then she comes back on the line. "Okay, so like this guy, he said he'd like a good-morning video message, just like, 'I hope you have a good day,' kind of thing. I don't have to be naked or anything like that."

"Sounds lonely," I tell her.

"Yeah, and sure, kinda creepy, but . . . he said he'd pay me two hundred and fifty dollars for one week."

My hand tightens on my phone. "Seriously?"

"Uh-huh, and this other one, he just wants messages throughout the day, like 'What are you up to?' 'This is what I'm doing' kind of stuff. He offered me three hundred dollars for a month."

"Okay." I open my laptop again, returning to Rock Bottom. "That still feels weird."

"Yep," Amy agrees. "They basically want me to pretend I'm their girlfriend, like you said, but a *good* girlfriend. Not like some thot."

A message pops up on my DMs, another check-in from *@Bras-Are-Boob-Prisons*.

"Oh my God," I mutter.

"What?" Amy asks.

I tell her about the messages and she laughs. "Oh yeah, I got those. Total groomer shit. Perfect front, too. She—which I seriously doubt it's a she—swoops in on all the minors on HardMaxx and expresses concern about their well-being, then slips you compliments to butter you up. I don't know what her process is from there, because I blocked her after the account got booted from HardMaxx. Those mods can sniff out a perv."

"Ahhh . . . ," I say, scrolling through. "I didn't really get to the compliments part, but I spotted the red flags and put her on mute."

"Clever girl," Amy says. "Which, yeah, I realize I probably sound like a total hypocrite, blocking her but being cool with dudes who want videos, but at least they're totally up front, you know? They're like, 'This is what I want, and I'll pay for it.'"

"It doesn't make you uncomfortable?" I ask.

Amy's quiet for a second, and my finger hovers over the accept button on *@Ask!Alice/Unchained!*'s friend request.

"A little, yeah," she admits. "But I said I won't give them my phone number. Everything goes through Rock Bottom, and as soon as they push me for nudes, I'm out."

I accept Alice's request.

"I mean, if I'm making the rules, and guys are lonely and dumb enough to shell out for pics of my feet, why shouldn't I take advantage of that?"

I find myself nodding as I block *@Bras-Are-Boob-Prisons*, ignoring her last message.

"But that's why I wanted to talk to you about it," Amy goes on. "It gives me the ick, but there are obvious pros."

I minimize my browser, and the perfected image of me from New You that is now my desktop picture stares back at me.

"So, what do you think?" Amy asks.

I look at perfect Jobie, a version of me that could be real, could walk around outside in the world, no filters, no Photoshop, no shame. I look at what I could be if I had $75,000.

"I think this is where you ask yourself if you want to be a nail tech or a physical therapist," I tell her.

CHAPTER NINETEEN

Shelby

Cody's party is like if you crossed the Duluth Trading Company with a Budweiser commercial and then invited a bunch of underage Instagram models. In other words, everyone is drunk, there's a lot of plaid, and what isn't covered in flannel just . . . isn't covered.

I thread my way through the kitchen, fingers entwined with Baxter's as he follows in my wake. The crowd spreads for me easily, and I get us two beers before anybody can even mention the existence of things like lines. We make our way to a less crowded room, which unfortunately also seems to be the room where someone has decided to test the limits of eardrums with synth music.

"How's your beer?" I shout at Baxter, but he doesn't hear me. The look on his face after he takes a sip, then inspects the contents of his Solo cup makes an answer unnecessary, anyway.

"Is this all there is?" he yells back.

I just kind of shrug, rather than say what I'm thinking, which is a showdown between—*Well, we didn't BYOB because you waited too long to agree to come*, or *Yes, and also, you're welcome because I cut the line to get it for you.*

I drain the rest of mine, and Baxter wordlessly hands his off as well, to which I just offer another shrug and eliminate any qualms he might have about drinking bottom-shelf beer by finishing it for him.

"Do you want to—"

I'm about to see if I can get him to dance with me, when I'm hit by a wall of human muscle. Rory picks me up from behind and shakes me like a snow globe, spattering the entire room with what little was left of our drinks.

"Shelby Black's in the—"

I'm sure he was about to finish that sentence with *house*, but instead what he says when he spins me around is "What happened to your face?"

Rory has seen me with black eyes, split lips, and mat burn, so I know he's not reacting to any remnants of our earlier sparring session.

"It's makeup," I tell him.

"Why?" he asks, then his gaze drifts over my shoulder. "Oh," he says.

"Rory," I say, through a smile that could cut sheet metal. "This is Baxter. Baxter, this is Rory, my training partner."

"I'm gay, dude," Rory says immediately, which is his go-to introduction when he meets anybody I'm dating. "No threats here."

"Nope, nothing threatening about you at all," Baxter says with a lopsided grin, extended a hand. The knot in my gut unclenches a bit as Rory pulls Baxter in and then gives *him* the snow globe treatment, which my new boyfriend actually accepts with grace. When he's back on his feet, he's smiling, and I think it's the first true glimpse of happiness I've seen from him tonight. There's a stab at that, a hot tear in my gut that I wasn't the one to cause it, like maybe the *reality of me* that had so awed him at our first meeting might have just settled into . . . reality. The reality of fast-food trash and empty energy drinks.

"Gotta pee," I announce, chasing away the thought with a smile of my own, one that I don't entirely feel. The downstairs toilet is clogged, and by the time I've shouldered my way through to the upstairs bathroom, my bladder is in the kind of condition I would never try to do a heavy squat in. I'm trying to squeeze past a couple making out against the wall when I step on someone's foot.

"Sorry," I yell, tossing the word over my shoulder as I throw open the door to what I think is the bathroom.

It's not. It's a bedroom.

And I'm suddenly face-to-face with Jayden.

He's got his phone to his ear, one side of his face lit by the bedside table lamp, which is giving off what can only be described as mood lighting.

"I know, man," he's saying into the phone. "It's like—"

He looks up, freezing when he sees me. But unlike me, his only lasts for a moment. After that initial shock, something like happiness spreads over his face, a knee-jerk reaction to my presence that I can't deny used to be how my body behaved, as well. We've been on-again, off-again for years, but my brain always lit up like a Christmas tree during a power surge whenever we crossed paths, all anticipation and desire. That's not happening now, instead I'm locked up, all my muscles drawn tight like rubber bands that won't snap back.

"Gotta go," Jayden says gruffly to whoever is on the other end, stuffing his phone into his hoodie pocket. He stands up slowly, hands out like I'm a dog that might bite.

But I can't bite. I can't move. I'm not even sure I have teeth anymore.

"Hey, Shels," Jayden says, keeping his distance. I don't answer, because my tongue has gone wherever my teeth went, somewhere unattached to me, every piece of me removed and reassembled someplace else, leaving me here, a nothing shadow.

"You . . ." His eyes sweep my face. "You look really good."

My body may be gone, but my brain has kicked into overdrive, processing everything at a rapid speed. It's like this when I'm in the ring; colors are brighter, details sharp, every movement of the girl I'm fighting registering in high-def. Coach Faith says its biological instinct, that we don't have to beware of tigers anymore to stay alive, so most of humanity has slipped into a low level of awareness, on cruise control and walking around confident that nothing is hunting us. Those of us who fight move through the world always aware an attack could be coming any second, and we're always ready.

But you weren't.

"Seriously," Jayden says again, taking a cautious step closer. "You look good."

The last time he saw me my nose was in the wrong place, one of my eyes was already sealing up, and my top lip was split, blood leaking between my fingers.

"Are you wearing makeup?" he asks, pointing at his own face, and of course he isn't talking about disfiguring me in public, because that would be a weird way to start a conversation, wouldn't it? He's telling me I look pretty, and not like Rory did, and not like Baxter—

Except Baxter didn't.

He made a big deal about me getting done up to go to a party, and then we were late, and we didn't have our own beer, and he didn't like what was being offered, and he hated the trash in my car, and he never said a damn word about how I looked, or the effort I put in, and why am I thinking about any of these things at all, and why can't

I talk, why can't I move, why is my body frozen and my brain broken?

"Shels?" Jayden asks, hands still up, signaling that he's no danger. "You okay?"

I'm not. I'm not okay and I don't know why, and Jayden looks like he actually means it, like he wants to know if I'm okay, and cares if I'm not, and maybe will even try to make it better, like he used to, like the time in eighth grade when we got a pizza and it had banana peppers on it, and we didn't order that, and I hate banana peppers, and he picked every one off and ate all of them so that I wouldn't have to, and later he told me that he hates banana peppers, too, and that's what he tasted like when we kissed and—

Black spots form in my vision, floaters that mean either my blood pressure is bottoming out, or my brain doesn't have enough oxygen because I'm not breathing, haven't taken a breath since I saw him, because my body isn't here.

"Listen," Jayden says. "I'm so sorry, Shels. I can't—"

He stops, the black spots swimming around him, a tornado spiraling.

"I'm not allowed to talk to you, so I haven't been able to say . . . I mean—" He runs a hand through his hair, a stalling motion I know well, one he uses when he's about to cry. Like sophomore year when I told him we were done, because I didn't have time for a boyfriend.

"We probably shouldn't be talking *now*," Jayden goes on. "I don't know how this whole restraining order thing works."

Of course he doesn't, because he's never had anything like that happen to him before, and neither have I, and fuck, Judy from group was right, and Karen was right, and even Bella and Lindsay and all the women that got hit and went back to get hit some more were right, too. Because I've had broken noses and a beaten-in face a hundred times, but I've never frozen up when facing down an opponent, because he's not a sparring partner, and he's not a cage match, and he's not a stat on my record. He was my boyfriend, and he hit me, and that doesn't matter because I still just want to go to him and put my face in his neck and feel his arms around me and let him tell me that everything is going to be okay.

The black spots around Jayden converge, spilling in from the sides, so I force a breath, a deep, jagged one that expands my lungs, floods my blood with oxygen, draws strength back into my muscles. I've never frozen before, never been in a situation where my body didn't do what I wanted it to, didn't respond like the well-oiled machine I've trained it to be.

"Shels?" Jayden asks. "What's going on?"

The exhalation comes out, smelling like cheap beer and the last thing I ate—a Whopper Cheese, the wrapper crunching under Baxter's HEYDUDEs.

"Hey," Jayden says, concern edging his voice. "What do you—"

And I do something else I've never done before.

I run.

People bounce off me like Ping-Pong balls as I shove my way downstairs, gasping for air. I leave a trail of *Watch it*, *What the fuck?*, and *Told you she was a bitch*, in my wake, but nothing gets through, nothing matters other than getting away from Jayden, away from the fact that I wanted to hit him and hold him and fight and fuck, that I wanted everything at the same time but could do nothing.

I glance past Rory, who is chatting up a guy on the swim team, but Baxter's nowhere to be found. I find a spot on the wall and lean against it, pressing back, feeling the strength of my deltoids, the blood flowing again, my body coming back to itself.

You're Shelby fucking Black.

I am, but I'd forgotten that for a moment. I keep my eyes trained on the stairs, hoping Jayden is smart enough not to follow me, and my heart settles back in my chest, finding a normal rhythm, my brain reasserting itself.

You're Shelby fucking Black.

"Goddamn right, I am," I say, and a freshman sliding past shoots me an odd look, her gaze lingering.

"Seven out of ten. Your foundation is uneven," she tells me.

"Must've left some on your dad's pillowcase," I shoot back, and that's how I know I've returned in full force. I flip the girl double birds and push through the downstairs, searching for Baxter, but he's nowhere to be found. I pull out my phone, but there's no messages, no missed calls, no indication that my absence has been noted. My pulse picks up again, the beer in my stomach mixing with the cheeseburger I slammed, everything rolling into a warm knot. The air is close, somebody is wearing too much body spray, and I'm going to break the ulna of the next person who shoves their arm in my way because they're trying to get a selfie.

I push my way into the kitchen and spot the back door, where a beagle with a white muzzle is sitting expectantly, waiting for someone to let him out.

"You and me both, bro," I say, snatching a lead from the rack on the wall. I hook it to his collar, and he bolts through the door when I open it, jerking my arm as he barely makes it to what must be his favorite bush. He's clearly past his prime, and getting one leg up is too difficult, so he settles for a squat, looking up at me apologetically.

"It's okay, dude," I tell him. "I pee like a girl, too, but I still got balls."

A high, sweet laugh rings out, one that I recognize. I glance up to see January leaning against a car, vape pen dangling from her fingers, eyes bright, white teeth flashing in a smile. But she's not laughing at me; she's looking at Baxter. He's leaning next to her, one shoulder against the car, his body angled toward hers, his lopsided grin on full display, everything about him screaming a deep, abiding interest.

The beer-burger mix in my stomach takes another turn, and somebody in the backyard snaps a pic, their flash going off, a searing light, the bright slice of the message that was Savannah Halden's tits coming in hot on Jayden's phone while he cuddled with me on the couch. Everything inside me turns to liquid, except for my mouth, which is intensely dry, and it feels like I might not be able to spit, but I sure as hell might shit myself.

"Cute dog," January says, and I walk over to them. Baxter gives me an upnod, like he just passed his bro in the hallway.

"Not my dog," I tell January, then try to find something else to add to that, something clever and astounding, something that perfectly conveys the reality of me. "My dog is a German shepherd."

"You have a dog?" Baxter asks, clearly confused.

"Yeah, a German shepherd," I say again stupidly.

"Oh." He shrugs, shifting his gaze back to January. "You just never talk about him."

It feels like a failing, like somehow I should've slipped dog stories into our conversations, sliding it in there between Zambia and MAGA jokes, or whatever tons of other things that come up in the constant text exchange. The constant exchange that has fallen off.

"But yeah," January goes on, continuing the conversation that

I interrupted by stating that I have a German shepherd—twice. "I started sketching when I was a kid. Nothing amazing, just something to do, you know? But then Mrs. Jarelle told me about the scholarship, and I thought . . . *Could I, really? Is that actually something that could happen? I could go to art school?*"

Her eyes are big and wide, round, innocent and blue. The moon is flashing off her nose ring, and she looks like every white guy's manic pixie dream girl when she blows her vape out her nose like a snow dragon.

"You could definitely make it in art school," Baxter tells her. "That continuous line drawing you did last week was genius."

So January is a genius. She's a genius, and it sounds like this isn't the first conversation they've ever had, and apparently they're in the same art class, and now I'm trying to remember if Baxter lays his phone face up or face down when we're together, and if maybe one of the reasons our texting has dropped off is because he's spending that time on someone else.

The dog walks over and plops down squarely on my foot, looking up at me with an expression that says, *I really don't want to be at this party anymore.*

I don't, either, but I have options, and he lives here. I take him back inside, not saying anything to Baxter or January. The dog shoots straight for a mud closet, shelves lined with cleaning supplies and extra toilet paper, the floor covered in work shoes, some dog toys, and his bed. He curls up, makes eye contact, thumps the floor with his tail twice, then goes to sleep. I don't want to stay inside, where I could run into Jayden again, but I also don't really want to go outside and look like I'm uncomfortable with Baxter talking to January.

Except, I totally am.

"What the hell, Black?" I ask myself, and one of the beagle's eyes opens, apparently asking the same question.

"I don't know, man," I tell him. And it's true. I'm not a girl who locks up in fear, or has anything other than total disregard for someone who has disrespected me. I am not a girl who worries when her boyfriend talks to anyone else, because I'm confident that I'm his best option, at all times, and no one else can even compare.

"Because I'm Shelby fucking Black," I say, clenching my hands into fists.

I carry that with me as I walk back outside, ignoring the fact that my fists feel weak, my legs are unsteady, and that I don't really know what it means to be Shelby Black anymore.

"You don't look so good," January says, when I rejoin them.

Everyone has been telling me how fabulous I look all night—except for that one bitch with the foundation remark—and my first reaction to January is a deep urge to growl at her. But she doesn't say it to be shitty; she looks concerned. Baxter actually looks at me for the first time, and I must not look great at all, because I can see it on his face.

"I think I'm ready to go," I say.

"Oh, um, okay," he says, straightening up and giving January an apologetic look. "We'll finish this conversation another time?"

"Yeah, for sure," January says, but her eyes cut over to me. "I hope you feel better, Shelby."

"Thanks," I mutter, and head toward my car.

"I actually ended up having a good time," Baxter says brightly, as I pull away. "You should see some of the stuff January creates. It's amazing what she can produce with limited resources."

Which my mind translates as *Who is this astonishing creature and how is she thriving in a place like Presnick?* Then I get a visual of her and Baxter sitting next to a waterfall in Zambia, holding hands.

"I'm really glad you talked me into going," Baxter continues. "It was good to connect with more people."

More people = not just you.

More people = mostly January.

"You said your mom's not home?" I blurt out, as I pull onto his street. There is still that, a little bit of a promise that I've been holding on to all night. I've still got a chance to strip down and get his hands all over my body, erase Jayden's touch, wipe January from his mind.

"Oh . . . uh . . ." Baxter's already reaching for the door handle. "I mean . . . you said you weren't feeling good."

Actually, I didn't. January said I didn't look good. Baxter has made no comment at all on how I look, and I have made zero statements about how I feel.

"I feel fine," I tell him, forcing brightness, reaching for my own handle.

"No, when I was talking to January, and you came out with the dog," Baxter argues, "you said you didn't feel good."

Did I?

"I just don't know if we should . . ." Baxter trails off. "I don't want to get sick."

"Oh," I say, the one syllable coming out dead and heavy, bouncing off my steering wheel because I can't look at him.

"I had a good time, though," he says, hopping out, then pulling away a Whopper wrapper that's stuck to his shoe, tossing it back into the footwell. "I'll text you." And he turns around and walks away, showing me his back when I just offered to show him everything.

"What the fuck?" I say to the steering wheel, which apparently is my new conversational partner. I drive away, heading nowhere. Baxter probably thinks I'm some kind of slut now, a feverish, contagious girl who wants to dive into bed, even if I'm sick and he's healthy. I'm a girl who has bruises on her collarbone from barbells and carries around last week's trash in her car, while January creates masterpieces and is a quiet, adorable genius who is rotting away in Presnick.

My phone is face down on the passenger seat, but I see it light up. I pass a car wash, then turn around, digging in the console for quarters. I grab fistfuls of trash, and practically fill the bin next to the vacuum, which sucks up enough stray french fries to be its own meal. And yeah, that is gross, and I'm gross, and my nose is running and my stomach feels queasy, so Baxter was totally right to keep me at arm's length, and I probably *did* say I didn't feel good, because I sure as hell don't.

And I'm the one that told him he needed to meet people and make friends in the first place, so do I get to be mad about the fact that it's a cute blonde from his art class? I practically drug him to the party, and then once he started to have a good time I made him leave, so who should actually be the frustrated one right now? Probably Baxter, who isn't wrong that my car is dirty, and didn't do anything wrong by talking to January, and isn't wrong to not want to screw a girl who might puke.

God, I'm a bitch.

The vacuum craps out on me and refuses to restart even though I feed it quarters. It's probably jammed with leftover fast food and that one sock that I didn't grab in time that got sucked up. I use the rest of my quarters to get an air freshener so that the Fit doesn't smell like a locker room and a Dairy Queen at the same time, then I get back behind the wheel, my stomach still rolling, brain firing.

I should text Baxter. I should apologize.

So I pick up my phone, and I do exactly that.

CHAPTER TWENTY

Fallon

Here's the running list of people I can't currently make eye contact with: every girl at school who I think might be *@Ko/Kreame/Krispies*. My parents, who think I'm perfect and actually used me as an example of someone who doesn't need to keep secrets because they don't do anything shameful, when they caught Farrah with a vape last week. And my sister, who had looked at me expectantly, as if I was going to save her from being grounded by outing myself as the mastermind behind *@Not-Your-Moms-Sex-Ed*, which apparently has become a hot topic for adult conversation lately, based on screenshots that Mal had sent me from the county's Neighborhood Block Watch Facebook group.

The hamster wheel in my brain is spinning at a rate to make sparks fly as I try to figure out how to reengage *@Ko/Kreame/Krispies*, who hasn't DM'd again and is never online, while also trying to behave like I totally am a person that doesn't need to keep secrets, but who also has been entrusted with the big, bad, deep darks of just about everyone I know. Including quite a few of the adults who DM *@Not-Your-Moms-Sex-Ed* with their burning (sometimes literally) questions but then also post in the Block Watch about how the person behind the account is likely a groomer and a pervert, a dirty old man, or a recruiter for a sex trafficking ring. Mom and Dad actually got into something like a yelling match at dinner the other night about whether the account was doing more harm than good, which provided my anxiety hamster with some cocaine, and now I haven't slept for two days.

Apparently, somebody gave Jobie's hamster some freaking Xanax, because she cannot be bothered. My last DM to her has been sitting on read, and when I sent a text this morning reminding her to water the planters in the bay window at the rec center, she sent back a simple k. From a girl that had to get a new phone because her screen had a dead spot right where her smiley-face emoji appears, this is concerning.

So basically, I'm causing martial disharmony between my parents, my sister and best friend don't want to talk to me, but I've got hundreds of DMs from strangers waiting for a response. I'm spinning my phone in a circle on the mat in the yoga room, simply unable to continue answering questions about STDs, pregnancy, sexual assault, and whether being attracted to Bigfoot is a problem, when Ms. Lauren taps on the glass door. I glance up and motion her in.

"Hey, Fallon," she says, sitting down across from me. "I just wanted to touch base with you about the teen club."

"The self-defense class?" I ask.

"Sure, we'll call it that," she says, and I know that Ms. Lauren is nobody's idiot. I bet she's only twenty-five, and I'm sure she has TikTok and probably understands exactly what SHAFT stands for, and knows damn well what's going down on the second floor.

"It's going really great," I say, keeping my eyes wide, hoping that I look like a bunny rabbit and not a sly fox.

"It definitely is," Ms. Lauren agrees. "So well, in fact, that the rest of the staff is growing a little concerned about your group gathering in this room, because of fire code."

She locks eyes with me, and a couple of seconds of silence pass.

"Because . . . of . . . fire . . . code?" I ask, drawing out each word.

"Yes, *actually* because of fire code," she says, nodding. "There's been some discussion of whether it might be a good idea to move you to a larger, more open area."

A larger, more open, much less private area.

"I argued against it," Ms. Lauren says. "I said that you're teenagers, and I'm sure some conversations happen in here that might contain language not everyone would be comfortable with."

She'd be surprised, given the DM I got from one of the Baby Weight class attendees the other day about how to find other swingers, but I don't share that.

"But I certainly don't think a former librarian of all people should be asking you to practice censorship," Ms. Lauren goes on, eyes still on mine.

"I appreciate that," I say slowly, my tongue huge and dry in my mouth, trying to assess what's being said to me—and what isn't. "So . . . the only point of conversation regarding SHAFT Class has been in terms of attendance size?"

"Yes," she says, and a warm bloom of relief fills my stomach. "For the moment," she adds, and it drains back out. "I just thought you should know."

"Thank you," I tell her, and she nods, getting up to leave.

"Uh . . . ," I say, "is there any way you could, maybe keep me abreast of any further conversations?"

"Abreast?" Ms. Lauren asks, one corner of her mouth going up, so that it's quite clear that I know she knows, and I know that she knows exactly what we've been talking about here.

"Firmly abreast?" I ask, and she actually laughs, but there's a warning in her voice when she speaks again.

"To a point, yes," she says. "But if a line is crossed, I can't help you."

"Absolutely understood," I say, as she opens the door to leave, holding it for January and Amara as they arrive.

I just wish I had a better idea of where that line is.

Jobie didn't exactly come in clinch. With our ever-growing group, I wasn't sure that twenty-five canisters of pepper spray would be enough, so I'd asked her to stop at Walmart and grab more. Apparently, she'd read only the text preview and not my actual text, because she shows up with a yellow bag full of off-brand black pepper, which I just stare at for a few seconds before I'm able to identity what the miscommunication was.

"Are you serious?" I ask but don't bother waiting for an answer, because my attention is immediately drawn to something much more upsetting.

When Farrah walks in with her friends Kelsey and Allison, the room dies so fast that even Jobie notices, although it does take a couple seconds for her to look up from her phone.

"Uhhh . . . ," Jobie says, gaze cutting to me. It's the first time we've had any meaningful interaction in a while, but it's good to know that we can still read each other like a book. Not that either one of us is hard to decipher right now; she's advertising flummoxed, and I'm sure my face is broadcasting a mix of panic and rage that a Viking berserker would envy. I might be an anxiety-riddled people pleaser, but prioritizing has a calming effect, and I've got a significant problem directly in front of me.

"You can't be here," I say bluntly, to which Farrah gives Allison a *Told you so* look.

"Incorrect," Farrah says, whipping out her phone. "According to Article Four of the Presnick Recreational Center Patron Bill of Rights—and I'm quoting here—a person's right to use the center should not be denied or abridged because of origin, age, background, or views. The right to use public space includes free access to, and unrestricted use of, all the services, materials, and facilities the rec center has to offer."

Mal's mouth has a little twist to it when she turns to me. "Sorry, but when she said 'and I'm quoting here,' that was peak Fallon."

"You're not the only one of us who can do research," Farrah sniffs, flopping to the mat beside Jacelyn Walters, who had apparently brought along the JV basketball team as well as her starting lineup this time. Between the student-athlete arm and cheerleader contingent that's been added to SHAFT Class, January spreading the word through art classes, and a snare drummer bringing in most of the marching band, there are about thirty high schoolers in the room right now.

And three eighth graders.

"Okay, look," I say, taking a deep breath. "Far be it from me to question the Presnick Recreational Center Patron Bill of Rights, but—"

"What the shit?" Shelby says, and I break my staring contest with Farrah to see Cody Hughes and three other guys standing outside the door.

"No," I say, unable to come up with anything else. "No, no, no."

But apparently they need the consent talk, because they come on in.

"This is fine," I say to the pile of black pepper next to my feet.

"Is it?" Bethany asks, narrowing her eyes at Brandon Skye, a person she'd only referred to as her *bae* . . . until they broke up in spectacular fashion during lunch because he'd slipped some of his chew into her mashed potatoes. I'd always dismissed Bethany as a vapid blonde who probably doesn't know how to change a spare tire, but now that she's one of my best contenders to be *@Ko/Kreame/Krispies*, I've had to reconsider her.

"This the right place?" Cody asks, to which Brandon immediately tacks on, "That's what she said," which is all it takes to send me into administrator mode.

"This is what's going to happen," I announce, standing up. "We're going to continue with our meeting as regularly scheduled, including our—" I cut myself off, realizing I was just about to say *uninvited guests*, which would probably bring some sort of rebuff from Farrah via the Presnick Recreational Center Patron Bill of Rights.

"Our most recent additions," I finish.

"Right on," Cody says.

"Banger," Brandon agrees, and fist bumps make the round with the guys.

"This is what's *not* going to happen," I say sharply, bringing all eyes back to me. "'That's what she said' jokes," I say, holding up a finger. "Racist, sexist, homophobic, or intolerant language of any kind."

"Do you give this speech to every new person that comes in?" Cody asks. "Because if you don't, then you're the one being sexist."

"It's not sexism, it's lived experience," I shoot back, which gets a round of giggles from the girls.

"How about this," Shelby says, suddenly joining the conversation. "You say anything you wouldn't say about your mom, to your mom, or in front of your mom, I'll drag you to the parking lot and explain how fuck-around-and-find-out works."

"That might be intolerant language," Mal says. "But I'm here for it."

"Hey, seriously," one of the guys says. "I, like, actually want to be here."

He doesn't add anything, doesn't defend his buddies, or tack on any kind of rude rejoinder. Cody and Brandon go quiet, and I find myself wondering if the DM to the *@Not-Your-Moms-Sex-Ed* account from *@Brandon*g*dong* asking how to tell if his girlfriend is faking it was coming from inside the house.

"I want to be here, too," Farrah says, and Jobie looks at me again, then shrugs.

"My hands are tied," I tell her, and Cody's face immediately contorts as he tries to squash a *That's what she said.* To his credit, he manages, and the boys officially join us. There's some uncomfortable shuffling as we push even closer together, making room for them.

Mal looks around the room, taking mental attendance. She raises her eyebrows at January and mouths *Amara?*, which just gets a shrug from the freshman.

"Everyone take some pepper spray," Mal says authoritatively, and I give her a thankful glance as she distributes what we've got, then gives canisters of Great Value black pepper to those who come up short.

"What am I supposed to do with this?" Jacelyn asks, turning it in her hands.

"Improvise," Mal says, then turns to me. "What are we talking about tonight?"

"I don't have anything specifically planned," I admit. The truth is I've been so swamped running the social media account that I haven't given the actual, live group a lot of thought. "Let's just start with this—does anyone have any questions?"

Three hands shoot up, and I point at one of the basketball players. "This is just for the guys, and it's an honest question," she says. "Why do you send dick pics?"

"For real," a band member adds. "That's, like, how some of you say *hello*."

"I've never sent a dick pic," Cody says.

"Seriously," he adds, looking around the room.

"Taking a head count on that, no pun intended," Mal says. "Who here has ever had a dick pic from Cody?"

All the girls exchange glances, but amazingly, no one raises their hands, to which Cody crosses his arms and smiles smugly.

"My turn," Bethany hops in. "Who's had a dick pic from Brandon?"

Her own hand goes up, and then two of the basketball players, a woodwind, and—weirdly—Mal.

"I was super drunk," he says, pointing at her. "That was supposed to go to Mallory Bennington."

"The pregnant girl? Gross." Bethany huffs, then she goes quiet and broods, apparently unhappy with how well her experiment went.

Regardless, I can't have exes settling old scores, and I certainly don't need a line chart of who has whose nudes in Presnick. That might be wandering over the line that Ms. Lauren mentioned earlier.

"I really don't think we need to continue gathering stats on dick pics," I say, hoping to change the subject.

"But they never really answered the question," Jacelyn says. "Why do you send dick pics?"

Brandon glances at the other guys, then blows out his cheeks.

"Fine, I'll go. It just kind of depends, really. Sometimes it's meant as a compliment, like—look what you do to me. Sometimes I'm the one looking for a compliment, and *all* the time, I'm fishing for her to send me one back."

"You're fishing for her to send you a dick pic back?" Mal asks.

"You know what I mean," Brandon says.

"Titties," she says, and he gives her a double thumbs-up.

"How often does that actually work?" Jacelyn asks.

"Rarely," Brandon says.

"So, it's kind of like spam emails," Jacelyn says. "You send out a hundred, looking for that one sucker who will fall for it."

"I'm pretty sure that's predatory behavior," January says.

"What? No!" Brandon says, sitting up straighter. "It's not—"

"Okay, wait," I step in. "Technically and legally, if you send someone an unsolicited dick pic, it is sexual harassment."

"Wait, what?" Brandon asks, going pale.

"Yes," I tell him, trying to keep judgment out of my voice. "It's no different than walking around in a trench coat and exposing yourself to people on the street. It's flashing; you're just doing it digitally."

"And that works both ways," Mal says. "Chicks can't rando drop you boobs, either."

"For the record, you totally can," Cody says, addressing the entire room. "No charges filed from this end."

"Except, if they're under eighteen, they're sending you child porn," Allison says. It's the first comment from one of the junior high kids, and she blanches a little when everyone turns to her.

"What do you mean?" Cody asks, his voice tight.

"Okay, so . . ." Allison looks around the room, a blush rising. "My little sister, Masey, she sent nudes—"

"Wait, isn't she in like elementary school?" Jobie asks.

"Fifth grade." Allison nods. "She just thought everybody was doing it, and a classmate sent her a dick pic so she figured . . ." Allison just kind of shrugs to finish the sentence. "But apparently his mom has one of those parenting apps that tracks your kid. So she got a notification about his pic . . . and then Masey's came in. His mom lost her mind and called the cops.

"It turns out that even though she's sending her own pics, Masey can be charged with sending child porn, and the other kid can be charged with possession of it, and since the parents own the phones and the accounts, they can actually get into trouble, too, because it's on their tech."

"Holy shit, dude," Mal says, with a low whistle.

"That's awful," one of the guys says.

"It is awful," I agree, clearing my throat. "It's also worth noting that because Masey is in fifth grade, it seems appropriate to call it child porn. But if you're under eighteen, you are not a legal adult, and it is, in fact, child porn."

The room goes dead quiet, and I don't need to take a survey to ask who has sent or received nudes from anyone under eighteen; there's a lot of eye-contact avoidance going on right now.

"Even if you're both consenting and you're keeping it to yourselves, it's still illegal," I go on. "And that's best-case scenario."

"Worst-case, they share it with all their friends, or post it online as revenge porn if you break up," Jacelyn hops in. "Then anyone and their uncle can see you naked."

"Even your *actual* uncle can see you naked," a basketball player adds.

"Gross," one of the band members says.

"I just got the ick," a cheerleader adds, clutching her pepper spray a little tighter.

"It's gross, yes," I agree. "But Bethany has a good point; once you send nudes, you have no control over who sees them."

"I don't trust anyone enough to do that," Jacelyn says, shaking her head. "And even if I did, someone could steal their phone, or it could get hacked. It's just not worth it."

"So why would a girl do it at all?" Farrah's friend Kelsey asks, eyes wide.

"Uh . . ." A drummer from the band looks around, then sees that no one else is going to speak. "Okay, I'll take it," she says. "Do you remember what Jennifer Lawrence said when her nudes got hacked?"

"'Either your boyfriend is going to look at porn or he's going to look at you,'" Shelby says.

"Exactly," the drummer says.

"So even one of the most famous, most beautiful women in the world feels like she has to compete with porn," Jacelyn says. "How are regular girls supposed to feel?"

"You're not competing," Brandon pipes up. "It's not like that."

"Here we go," Bethany says under her breath, and I get the feeling this conversation has happened before, and tobacco in her potatoes was just the last straw in their relationship.

"Yes, we are," Jacelyn shoots back. "We're competing for your eyeballs, your sexual thoughts, all of it."

"And we literally can't," another girl says, putting down her pepper spray to hold up her phone. "You can get any girl, any body type, doing anything, with anyone, in an endless stream, anytime you want it." She puts her phone back down on the table and looks at it, sadly. "And we're just . . . us."

"It's cheating," Bethany says, sticking her chin out.

"It's not," Brandon fires back.

"You're jerking off to another woman," she says, her voice rising. "How is that not—"

"Okay, stop," I say, holding my hands up for peace. "Number one, we're getting loud. Number two, we're clearly getting personal."

Bethany and Brandon both lean back, pouting.

"What do you think, Fallon?" Farrah asks.

It's the first time we've spoken since she got grounded for being the bad sister, even though I'm possibly a felon, but there's no bite in her tone. She seems genuinely curious, but she had to pick a damn difficult topic.

"Well," I say slowly, as everyone's eyes turn to me. I give them the carefully curated answer I've handed out over DMs dozens of times. "Every relationship is different, and each couple sets their own boundaries. Porn is no different from anything else; if you've got expectations that your partner can't meet, you should find someone who can."

"Good luck," Brandon mutters. "We all do it."

"Not true." One of the other guys pops up, getting disbelieving stares from his buddies. "No shit," he says. "Peyton asked me not to, and I love her, so I stopped."

"You just became ten thousand times more attractive," Jacelyn says.

"Seriously," the drummer says. "If things don't work out with Peyton, let me know."

"It shouldn't even exist," Bethany says, still pouting.

"That's where things get sticky for me," I tell her. "Because that's censorship, and I am the last person who is going to advocate on behalf of that. I mean, this whole group exists because I don't think we talk about sex enough in school, but parents and groups have pushed to get sex ed out of schools, because they think it's pornographic. So . . ." I balance both hands in the air, like a scale, leaving them there, a question on my face.

"See, even Frosty Fallon is cool with porn," Brandon says to Bethany.

"Neat nickname," I bite back. "And, no, that's not what I said. There's currently an epidemic of ED in young men and much of the medical establishment believes porn is the cause. Like she said"—I nod at the girl who had held up her phone earlier—"you can get whatever you want, whenever you want it, in a much greater array and intensity than a regular, normal girl can give you when she's right in front of you."

"That explains a lot," Bethany says darkly, and Brandon goes bright red.

Farrah raises her hand. "ED? Porn gives guys eating disorders?"

"Erectile dysfunction," Mal says gently, and Farrah's eyes shoot to Brandon, now her turn to blush.

"Gonna jump in and save my dude here," Cody says. "Total subject change—do girls want guys to make the first move or not?"

"Yes," a lot of voices say in unison, but a few shake their heads.

"It's best when we both go for it at the same time," the drummer says.

"How do I know if she wants me to?" Cody comes back.

"We hold eye contact longer than necessary, or we look at your mouth a lot," the drummer says. "We tilt our heads toward you, we angle our hips, we drop one shoulder . . . I mean, we aren't that complicated. We broadcast across seventeen different channels and hope you're receiving on at least one."

"Right, but . . ." Cody loses a little steam, looks around the room. "With consent, and all that. It gets weird for us, sometimes. If I make a move and she just thinks she's *supposed* to go along . . ." He shrugs.

"You can just ask," a basketball player says quietly.

"Isn't that weird, though?" Cody asks. "Like if I just say, 'Can I kiss you?'"

"Actually, that's superhot," the drummer says. "Like, I just got goose bumps."

"Me too," says Jobie, and I look down to find that my skin isn't completely smooth at the moment, either.

"Oh." Cody leans back and smiles a little, looking at the drummer. "In that case, can I kiss you?"

She laughs, and flashes her pepper spray at him. "Maybe later. And if you don't ask, I can take this for a test run."

"Actually, we all need to wrap up," I say, glancing at the clock. "And if people could start trickling out a few at a time, that would be good. We may have exceeded fire code."

Everyone gives me blank looks as I gather the empty Walmart bags. "What? I'm serious."

"You have weird problems," January says.

"You have no idea," I say under my breath as people start to leave—Bethany and Brandon each waiting for the other to exit; Cody going over to the drummer, no doubt to get her number.

"Hey, Allison's mom dropped us off, but can I get a ride home?" Farrah asks, coming over to me.

"Yes," I tell her. "But you need to know I'm not happy with you right now."

"I'm not happy with you right now, either," she says. "Can we stop at McDonald's?"

"Oh my God, yes," I say, rolling my eyes.

"Hey, Jobie, burger run," Farrah yells across the room. "You in?"

"Umm . . ." She glances up from the black-pepper canisters no one took. "I'm not really hungry?"

Like all of Jobie's statements, it comes out more like a question, but she looks at me as if confirming that she's actually invited.

"You should come," I tell her.

"I can't," she says. "Mom's having Jason over for dinner again and wants me to be there. I think they're pretty serious."

"Okay," I say, my eyes lingering on hers. "Text me?"

"Yeah, sure," she says, breezing out the door that Shelby is holding open for us with one shoulder, eyes on her phone, Mal at her side.

We split up in the parking lot, and Farrah slides into my passenger seat, like we're all back to normal.

"I don't know how much longer they'll have the McRib," she says. "So I'm probably going to get two. Don't judge me, and I'll pay for your grilled chicken wrap or whatever girl dinner you're going to have."

"You know, that whole trend legitimizes restrictive eating and is problematic," I tell her.

"Really, big sister?" Farrah asks, resting her chin on her fist. "Tell me more."

"I'm going to tell you where to stick it, if you don't get off my case," I say, as we pull into the drive-through. "Also there's never only one deer."

"I think I've figured out where to stick it, thanks," she says. "SHAFT Class was super informative. And, yeah, I know the deer thing. Do Mom and Dad just have a scheduled text go out to you every time you leave the house telling you to watch out for deer?"

"It's the Midwest," I tell her. "We should all watch out for deer. And, you're still on my shit list for that Recreational Center Patron Bill of Rights thing you pulled," I tell her.

"Yeah, but you're also kind of proud of me, I can tell," she says. "And I want fries and a pie, too, thanks."

I order our food and then pull into the parking lot. We eat in silence for a minute, Farrah putting away one McRib and most of her fries before speaking.

"Seriously, though, that was awesome," she says, wiping her mouth on her sleeve.

"You're a monster," I say, handing her a napkin.

"Maybe, but that doesn't change my point. That whole thing was just cool. Like, we were talking about real stuff, and the guys were actually pretty chill, and, I don't know. It was just . . . it was nice."

"Yeah." I sigh. "You can make an impact statement on my behalf when I come up for parole."

"Still worried about that?"

"Yes," I say, resting my head against the window. "I am still worried about the legal and ethical repercussions of my choices, vape-breath."

Farrah's second McRib stops halfway to her mouth. "Like you really, really think you could legit go to jail?"

"I think I *could*," I say carefully. "It just depends on whether a judge takes it seriously or dismisses the charges, which would probably depend a lot on exactly how many parents are carrying pitchforks and screaming for my head on a pike. And, judging by the DMs I've been getting, that's a pretty powerful contingent."

"Oh," Farrah says, the mention of the social media account falling between us like a rock. "Any more luck with Ko Kreame Krispies?"

"No," I say, taking a deep breath as tears well up in my eyes. "And literally every night I go to bed thinking about what's probably happening to her at that moment, and I can't stop it."

"No, but you're the only person she's talking to," Farrah says. "You're still there for her, even if you can't stop it from happening."

"But . . ." My chest tightens, each breath becoming a spike. "Maybe I could, right? Like if I just came clean and went to Mom and Dad, or somebody at school, even the cops. They could probably do more, they could stop it, they could—"

"And throw yourself under the bus?" Farrah asks.

"Isn't that the right thing to do?" I say. "Shouldn't I be putting her welfare in front of mine?"

"Look," Farrah says, after swallowing the last bit of her second McRib. "I know you think it's shitty of me, and maybe it is, but I'm still not convinced Ko Kreame Krispies is a real person. What if it's one of your haters, trying to draw you out?"

"What if it's not?" I ask, my voice breaking as tears overflow, coursing down my cheeks in a hot flood.

"Shit, dude," Farrah says, coming over the center console to give me a hug.

I pull her in tight, smelling her curls and body spray and pickles and barbecue sauce.

"You're a good person, Fallon," she says into my hair. "But you don't have to be perfect."

"You're a good person, too," I tell her. "But you got McRib on me."

"Sorry," Farrah yelps, pulling back and handing me a napkin. We wipe our faces, and I toss her my trash, which she stuffs down in the bag.

"Well, if anybody comes after you, they'll have to deal with me," she says. "I don't care if it's Trad Dad or a court judge or somebody's angry aunt Tilly. I'll create a distraction and you can make a break for it. Just make sure your passport is valid."

"Thank you, but it's a real concern," I tell her, starting up the car as she digs out her phone. "I don't know how much longer I can keep it quiet. With the group getting so big, and the online account blowing up—"

"Uh . . . ," Farrah says, eyes wide, plastered on her phone.

"What?" I ask, pulling up to the stoplight.

"Have you looked at the news lately?"

"No, why?"

"You know how I put a Google Alert on my phone for Presnick schools after the bomb threat last year?"

"Yes," I say cautiously. "Please don't tell me there was another one."

"There's not," Farrah says, and turns her phone toward me, stabbing her finger at an article from a news station out of Columbus.

Online Sex Advice Account for Kids Has Presnick Parents Asking Questions

CHAPTER TWENTY-ONE

Jobie

When Fallon sent out a DEFCON 3 text telling me, Mal, and Shelby to meet at her place before school, the first thing I thought was that she must have been way less chill about dudes showing up at SHAFT Class than she let on. Actually, the first thing I thought was *What's DEFCON 3?* At which point I googled it and learned a lot more about nuclear war than I care to know. But it seems for once in her life, Fallon might have actually understated a threat, because Mal is acting like the bombs have already been loaded on the plane and radio communication has been cut.

"This is not good," she repeats, handing Fallon's phone back to her. "That article has over a hundred comments already."

"Most of them are not kind," Fallon agrees. "And all of them want to know who is behind the account."

"Right," I say carefully, watching Fallon.

Her eyes slide off mine; we never did have a talk about her locking me out of the account, and it seems like that's not going to happen anytime soon.

"And that reminds me, Mal," Fallon goes on. "I've been fielding a lot of questions from people who are questioning their—"

"Nope, no way, absolutely not," Mal says, not letting Fallon finish. "As soon as I start answering questions from gay minors I'm a groomer. The three of you might be able to get away with some sort of big-eyed, pretty-white-straight-girl innocence act if we get busted, but I'll be public enemy number one."

"Mal's right," Shelby says. "But how worried are we, really? I get that this article has your back up, but it's not linked to SHAFT Class. People can freak out about Not Your Moms Sex Ed all they want, be assholes in the comments, and send you shitty DMs—"

"They're not just shitty," Fallon says, sitting up from where she'd been resting against her pillows. "Some of them are threatening. You don't know; you haven't seen them."

Shelby straightens her spine, glaring at Fallon from her spot on the floor. "Honey, I've had death threats from fans of the girls I fight. Some of them get spicy and toss in rape jokes for fun. There isn't a damn thing you can tell me about what's in your DMs that I don't already know."

"Shit, dude," Mal says, tentatively reaching out to touch Shelby's shoulder. "Sorry about the assholes."

"World's full of them." Shelby shrugs, still giving Fallon the stink eye. "What you've got to know is that people will say shit online that they would never have the balls to say to you in person, let alone actually carry through on a threat."

I don't know about threats, but I can definitely agree that people say things online they wouldn't say in real life. For example, the three guys in my Rock Bottom inbox who I've told I hope they have a good day, and one of them who threw in an extra fifty bucks if I tell him I love him by the end of the week. I don't really care how their day goes, and I definitely don't love *@Jo-Rand-Band*Man*, but the new CashCrash account I set up already has almost $250 in it, and all I've had to do was type.

I'd been hit with the expected onslaught of dudes wanting nudes (there is an actual sub-bottom by that name, surprise, surprise) as soon as Alice and Amy ushered me into rb/GoodGirl. The boards themselves were pretty clean, but the DMs got naughty fast. I flagged and blocked everyone who came at me with boob and butt requests, but I left the four guys asking for feet pics on read, as I consider. I mean . . . it's my feet. I don't feel particularly dirty taking pics of my arches, something I'd discovered when I experimented with a few shots.

"Credible threats or not, they've got me freaked out," Fallon says, scrolling through her phone. "This guy says if he finds me, I'll die with dildoes sticking out of me like a porcupine."

It's alarming enough that I look up from the message I'm typing to *@Paul'sGho$t*, letting him know I hope his interview goes well.

"Damn," Shelby says. "Okay, that's pretty bad."

"Are you reporting any of these?" Mal asks.

"The worst ones," Fallon says. "And some of the accounts have been taken down, but they just create a new one and come right back at me, even more pissed off because I reported them."

"Welcome to the internet," Shelby mutters.

"I've been on the internet," Fallon tells her. "I've just never been the person everyone hates."

"You're far from hated," I chime in, pulling up the *@Not-Your-Moms-Sex-Ed* account. "You're at almost fifteen thousand followers after a few weeks. I'd kill to have those numbers."

That might have been true even a few days ago, but I've wandered away from my Instagram account, finding a lot more reward in the one-on-one of Rock Bottom DMs.

"Follows exploded after that article," Fallon says. "But I'm sure some of them are hate follows, and a lot of them are parents keeping an eye on me."

"So, kill it," Mal says, shrugging. "Take the account down and move on with your life."

All three of us look at Fallon, who is chewing her lip.

"There's a very real reason why I can't. Someone . . ." She takes a deep breath and taps her chest three times, an old centering trick I haven't seen her use in years. "There's someone in the DMs who's in an abusive relationship, and I'm the only person they're talking to."

"Abusive how?" Shelby asks.

"Physically," Fallon answers her. "But I've also got people asking me about emotional abuse. You know, things like gaslighting and bread crumbing—"

"What's that?" Shelby interrupts her.

"How do you not know this?" Mal asks. "Is your TikTok just squats and tricep curls?"

"And zit popping," Shelby adds. "But, yeah, that's about it."

I tap on a DM from *@BradChiefsFan*, one of the guys looking for feet pics, and send him my CashCrash handle and a price.

"But seriously," Mal says, turning back to Fallon. "An abusive relationship? That's above your pay grade. Whoever it is needs real help from people qualified to give it."

"Which is what I've been telling her," Fallon says. "But it'll blow up her whole world if she reports it. She's scared, and I don't blame her. I'm hoping that if I can keep her talking I can convince her."

"Set up a dummy email account and give her that, then shut down the account. This shit isn't worth it, Fallon," Mal says.

"Sure, but . . ." Fallon sighs, but it's a new kind of sound. Typically,

I hear a Fallon sigh when I've done something stupid or she's disappointed in humanity as a whole. This one is different; she sounds beaten.

"What does it say about me if I shut it down? I started something that I thought was necessary and important. It turns out I was right, but if I fold as soon as pressure is applied, I'm violating my own principles."

"Only you would use that phrase," I tell her.

"You're not folding as soon as pressure is applied," Mal argues, shaking her head. "You're being cautious after your enemies threatened to murder you with sex toys."

"Coach Faith says that enemies are the price of success," Shelby offers. "So, congrats, I guess."

"I don't think I've ever had an enemy in my life," Fallon says.

"That's not true," I tell her. "Remember the girl from Brookwood that you beat out for the regional spelling bee championship in sixth grade?"

"Oh yeah," Fallon says, eyes going wide. "She totally hates me."

"You're attracting crazies, Fallon," Mal says. "Shelby's right that a lot of it is just people shooting off at the mouth, but . . ." She lets the sentence trail off. "It only takes one of them being serious for some real shit to go down."

My phone vibrates, the CashCrash app letting me know that *@BradChiefsFan* just sent me twenty bucks. Damn, these feet people are serious. I flip over to my DMs, pick out one of the shots I took last night, and send it to Brad. Then I go ahead and let the other four guys know my CashCrash account, too.

"Sure, but let's be real here," Shelby says, looking down at her phone when it vibrates. "Can someone actually find you?"

I switch back to Instagram. "Not Your Mom's Sex Ed only posts words and Bill Hader dancing. It's not like either of us has ever posted any photos with identifying markers in them."

"And Farrah set me up with a VPN before I even started posting," Fallon says. "That'll hide my IP address, right?"

"I mean, I guess," Mal says. "I don't know about all that stuff."

"I think so?" Shelby offers. "And like I said, the social media account isn't connected to SHAFT Class. I guess someone could put it together if people at the meetings follow the account and notice that sometimes we talk about the same things—"

"Which isn't impossible," Mal warns. "The group at the rec center just keeps getting bigger, and word of mouth on Not Your Mom's Sex Ed went crazy locally even before it got viral."

"Speaking of the rec center," Fallon says. "Ms. Lauren is onto us."

"What do you mean?" Mal asks, eyes narrowing.

"I mean, like she totally knows what we're doing, and we had a coded conversation where she told me that I need to be careful to not cross any lines."

A text from Amy flashes across my screen.

Do you have any tattoos or piercings?

I drop out of the conversation, shooting her an answer.

Lol no why?

Got a guy who wants bare back shots, totally clean, no tats. I've got one on my shoulder blade so thought I'd pass him along to you?

I don't know about that one. I can get a shot of my back in the mirror easily enough, it's just a question of if I want to or not.

"But Ms. Lauren wasn't pissed off about it, or anything?" Shelby asks.

"No," Fallon says. "She actually seemed supportive. But I thought

I should let you guys know, since our names are on the paperwork for SHAFT Class. If we get burned—"

"Kill it," Mal says immediately. "Both of them, online and at the rec center. I know you guys think this is a nice, comfy small town, but I've had some real hate come at me, and I've walked to my car with my keys in between my knuckles more than once. This isn't worth it."

My phone vibrates as one of the feet guys pays up, including a tip. I send him the pic on Rock Bottom and shoot a text to Amy.

Just made fifty bucks off the same pic, lol

Wait—is it feet people? You don't want to do that. Sometimes they trade with each other, and they don't like it if they aren't getting personalized shots.

I didn't even think of that, and I don't want to lose somebody who is willing to pay. I send along a freebie from a different angle as well.

"Sorry, Fallon," Shelby says. "I know you're upset, and I'm not trying to be a bitch about this, but I just don't think it's that bad. I've had creepers and freaks in my DMs for years, and nobody ever showed up at my doorstep."

"There's also this," Fallon says, pulling a pillow across her lap. "My sister thinks the girl in my DMs claiming abuse is catfishing me."

"Why would she think that?" Mal asks.

My phone goes off, and I glance at it, see that Alice has sent me a DM on Rock Bottom.

"Because she never gives specifics," Fallon says. "She's hiding who she is—which only makes sense, given her situation. But Farrah thinks it could be one of my trolls, trying to get me to slip up in conversation, or reveal who I am somehow. What do you think?"

"With Ms. Lauren sniffing around and this person being weird, you need to watch your ass," Mal says. "Give that chick an email address and get the fuck off social media."

@Ask!Alice/Unchained!—did Amy get with you about the guy that wants the back shot?

@Jobster{Lobster}—yeah, I'm not sure about it.

Shelby looks up from her phone when Fallon clears her throat. "No offense, I think you're overreacting," she says. "If she's catfishing, then she's catfishing. Just be smarter than her, which shouldn't be difficult for you."

Fallon looks to me, but my phone vibrates with another notification from Rock Bottom.

@Ask!Alice/Unchained!—if you don't want it, I'll take it. He's offering good money.

I chew my lip, flipping back over to CashCrash and staring at my balance. I've made easy money so far, but I'm nowhere near $75,000, and that amount will take me years at this rate.

"Jobie, could you be present?" Fallon says, her voice slipping into mom-mode. "This is more important than your Instagram."

@Jobster{Lobster}—No, I'll take it.

I put down my phone and plaster on a smile when I look up. "Sorry," I say. "Mom wanted to know if I'm up for another bond-with-your-new-dad night."

"Oh," Fallon says, some of her superiority sliding away. "Sounds like she's serious about this one."

"I think so," I say. "He's pretty cool, so I'm good with it."

"What do you think?" Mal asks. "Should Fallon keep suffering emotionally, or is this not worth it?"

I think about it for a second and spot a way to get a jab in at Fallon, who is currently freaking out about social media, while also shaming me for using it.

"I don't think you should have to take care of all this on your own," I say to Fallon. "But I can't help you out with Not Your Mom's Sex Ed unless you give me the new password."

"Wait," Mal says, looking between us. "You kicked Jobie off the account? I thought you two were doing it together?"

"We *were*," Fallon says tightly. "When that girl showed up with some seriously intense personal stuff, I didn't think it should be aired to whoever was logged in at the time. And I can't get her to trust me if she's not getting continuity. A response from Jobie is going to be very different than a response from—"

"What she means is, when Fallon wants something done right, she does it herself," I say.

"Are we fighting now?" Shelby asks.

"No," Fallon says, and lets out a deep breath. "We are not fighting. Nobody is fighting, and nobody is mad at anybody."

"Vanilla," Shelby sniffs, and goes back to her phone.

"Okay," Fallon picks up her own phone and clicks around. "I'll give you the new password, but give me time to set up a throwaway email and share it with Ko—with this person, so that I can be in touch with them somewhere else."

I'm about to snap something sassy, when a new text comes in from Amy.

Alice said you want the back guy. All yours. He'll get with you through RB.

And . . . weird question—how do you feel about food stuff?

"Sure. Whatever. Take all the time you need," I tell Fallon, as I type out a text to Amy.

Food stuff?

A screen cap comes in from Fallon, with the login for the *@Not-Your-Moms-Sex-Ed* account, the password visible.

"That was fast," I say, still looking at my screen when Amy's response comes in.

Yeah, I caught a weirdo who wants a video of me eating an entire container of cottage cheese.

"You're not serious," I say aloud, which Fallon thinks is a reaction to the new password—*nomoredickpics*.

"I needed an outlet," she says, and my phone vibrates. "She was online and responded right away when I gave her an email to reach me at. I deleted her messages, so you can log in whenever."

But I'm lactose intolerant. Bummer.

I shoot back my answer—**how much?**—then log in to *@Not-Your-Moms-Sex-Ed*, and immediately regret winning that particular power struggle. There are over two hundred messages waiting for a reply, and the one at the top is apparently from our government teacher, who seems to use her staff photo everywhere online.

"We really need to talk to adults about online privacy and better screen names," I say. "Because I don't think I can look at History Is Cool 1776 in the face tomorrow morning after answering this question about nipple hair."

"Yeah," Fallon says. "And you're still using a VPN, right?"

My phone goes off in my hand, Amy's response coming in.

He offered $75.

But he says if you send him the receipt, he'll pay for the cottage cheese, too.

"Jobie?" Fallon asks.

"Yep," I say, waving her off as I text Mom to ask if she needs anything from the grocery store.

Because I'm making a stop after school.

The guy who likes backs is waiting in my DMs when I get home, as well as the weirdo who has a thing for cottage cheese. I get a nice shot in the bathroom for *@DaveDoes*Stuff** after clarifying what he wants—hair loose, over the shoulder, no profile necessary, just the bare back. I take care of Dave, shoot a couple of check-in messages to *@Jo-Rand-Band*Man* and *@Paul'sGho$t*, then set up my ring light and grab a spoon. Eating an entire container of a dairy product isn't easy, but I choke it down, smiling the whole time, and send the video to *@Croc<Lock>25*.

Princess Tinyhead crawls into my lap as I lie back, tromping her way up to my face to push her nose against mine. She's not typically this affectionate, so I give her a scratch as my phone goes off, my CashCrash app letting me know that payments have come in, and there's a response to my pic from *@DaveDoes*Stuff** on Rock Bottom.

@DaveDoes*Stuff*—nice, payment sent

@DaveDoes*Stuff*—you eighteen?

The cottage cheese in my belly turns into a hard lump, my fingers hovering.

@Jobster{Lobster}—yes

His response comes in fast, the bubble popping up immediately.

@DaveDoes*Stuff*—$250 if you turn around

I exit the app, pushing Princess Tinyhead aside. Amy said this might happen, that a couple of guys had raised the stakes on her. She'd reported them to the rb/GoodGirl mods and blocked them.

Which is exactly what I should do.

Instead, I pull up the New You version of me, and look at her for a few minutes.

Then I go into the bathroom, and I take another picture.

PART THREE

People are crying, most because they can't help it, some because they are supposed to, a few because they know people are shooting videos and turn their good side to the camera. But all of the tears taste slightly of fear.

Eyes bounce off eyes, none able to hold the gaze of another for long.

Wondering who knows, who shared, who repeated, who told.

At the bottom of the grave, two inches of water wait, the final resting place of a three-thousand-dollar casket.

And one girl.

CHAPTER TWENTY-TWO

Shelby

"That's a textbook trauma reaction."

I snort, my eyes cutting away from Kathy's to focus on something else in her office, settling on an overstuffed sequined pillow that other girls probably clutch to their midsections while they cry about whatever made-up drama they're currently suffering through.

"I don't have *trauma*," I tell her, crossing my arms. "I'm a tough motherfucker, and I told you—my boyfriend hit me, I broke up with him, end of story. If I never see him again, that's a happily ever after for me."

"Except you did see him again," Kathy says, moving her laptop off her knees, where she'd been typing away when I told her about Cody's party. "And when you did, you froze. It's one of the four trauma reactions—"

"Yeah, I know," I interrupt her. "Fallon brought all those up when we talked about sexual assault at—" I cut myself off, then finish lamely. "At a slumber party. But there was a whole lot going on at Cody's," I continue. "I think I was starting to get sick, I drank a couple of beers too fast, I'd just had a serious training session. I overreacted when I ran into Jayden. It's not like I have PTSD or anything.

I haven't been in a war, or been raped, or witnessed somebody being murdered."

"No," Kathy says carefully, "but all the things you're mentioning are what we call 'big-*T* traumas.' There is such a thing as 'little-*t* traumas.' They can still profoundly affect you, cause trauma reactions, interfere with normal functioning, and have specific triggers."

"Like my uncle who was in Desert Storm and can't go to Fourth of July parties because fireworks make him freak out?"

"Kind of like that," Kathy says. "But on a smaller scale. You said there was a lot going on the night of the party. Why don't you walk me through it?"

"Okay." I sigh, leaning back on the couch and checking the clock, wishing this was over already. "I had a pretty intense training session. Tara wanted me fighting-fit for the photo shoot with Rebel, which went really well."

It certainly had; Dad was ready to choke out half the cameramen, especially the one who came in for a closeup and asked if I was eighteen under his breath.

"That's a lot of pressure," Kathy says.

"I like pressure," I tell her. "And Baxter had kind of blown me off about the party all week," I admit, hating that I'm saying something bad about him. "And when I called him he made a comment about—actually, you know what, never mind. Just things weren't totally awesome between us when I picked him up, that's all."

"What do you mean?" she asks.

"I don't know." I shrug. "Just normal shit."

"What's normal shit, for you?" Kathy presses.

"Uh, like, he thought I should put a little more effort into my appearance for the party, but then didn't tell me I looked nice, or anything like that. And when I picked him up, he was clearly grossed out by my car—which was a total trash heap, by the way, he's not wrong about that—and he was just kind of shutting me out all night, and he was kind of crappy about the beer at the party, and then he said this weird thing about my dog . . ."

I trail off. "I sound like an idiot, just never mind."

"What did he say about your dog?"

"He—ugh." I shake my head. "This is really stupid. Like, I'm stupid for talking about this."

"Did it bother you?" Kathy asks.

I take a deep breath, remember Baxter's dismissive tone, the seemingly deep disappointment of me never talking about having a dog before.

"Yes," I say.

"Then it's not stupid," Kathy says. "What did he say?"

"It was just . . . so Cody's dog needed to go outside, and nobody else was going to do it, so I took him out to take a piss and Baxter was talking to January, and I said my dog was a German shepherd, and he basically made it seem like I was some kind of bad pet owner or something, because I've never mentioned that I have a dog."

"Did you talk to him about it?"

"No," I huff. "Because it's stupid."

Kathy is quiet for a second, eyes on me. "So, did you join in this conversation with January?"

"I mean, I tried," I say, picking at a corner of my thumbnail. "But they were talking about art, and shit I don't know anything about, and he was telling her how fucking great and talented she is, and I was just kind of standing there like an idiot, and he hadn't texted me all day, and it was like all the nice things he used to say to me now he's saying to her, and—"

I break off, my throat closing up. The ends of my mouth are turning down, and words can't find their way out; my eyes are filling up, and holy shit I'm about to start crying because my boyfriend didn't text me and talked to another girl.

"Dammit," I say, grabbing for a tissue. I pluck three out and swipe at my eyes, mascara coming away, stark black against the white.

"Sorry," I say immediately. "This isn't like me. I don't cry. I'm so fucking basic right now; this is stupid."

"You keep saying that," Kathy says. "Why?"

"*Because it is stupid!*" I yell, then clamp a hand over my mouth. "Sorry, I didn't mean to shout at you."

"It's okay." Kathy smiles easily. "I'm pretty used to being shouted at."

"And I'm used to being hit," I come back at her. "So I should be able to just move the hell on and forget about it."

"Maybe." She shrugs. "But a client yelling at me and my husband yelling at me are two different things. One is my work life, and one is my personal life."

"Yeah, I guess so," I say, twisting the tissue in my hand.

"I want to go back to Baxter," Kathy says. "It sounds like him talking to another girl upset you."

"Yeah, and that's stu—"

Kathy raises a finger, and I cut myself off.

"Yeah, it bothered me," I admit.

"But I'm sure he talks to other girls at school, just as part of his day. What was it about this that got to you? Did something else happen?"

"Well, Jayden happened," I say. "And then when I went outside, somebody was taking a selfie and their flash went off, and for whatever reason it made me think about that bitch that sent him titty pics—

"Sorry," I say again. "The girl Jayden traded nudes with when we were together."

"This is making more sense," Kathy says, leaning forward. "You were retraumatized when you saw Jayden, which brought back not only the feelings you experienced when he hit you but also the betrayal that caused that fight. Then you immediately find your current boyfriend talking to another girl, and you draw the worst conclusions."

"Right," I say, but without much conviction.

"Shelby?" Kathy asks. "Is there more?"

"I don't know," I say, another sigh escaping. "Things with Baxter have been . . . weird."

"Weird how?"

"It's just . . ." Another tear escapes, and I wipe at it angrily. "When we first met, it was like constant compliments. I was perfect, I was amazing, I was special. He texted me all the time, told me he was thinking about me, and then it just kind of . . . stopped."

"That can be normal," Kathy says. "Like we talked about, the beginning of relationships can be intense. When that magic fades, it can feel like something has gone wrong."

"Yeah, but . . ." I shift uncomfortably. "I know that feeling, right? Jayden and I were on and off for years. I've had shit start with other guys and fizzle out. This just . . ." I look up at the ceiling, trying to use physics to stop the tears from falling. "I feel like I'm chasing him now. Like I was the most perfect girl on the planet, and now he's finding little things wrong with me."

"I notice you're wearing makeup today," Kathy says.

"Yeah," I say. "I'm going over to his place after this. I just wanted to look nice."

"Because he'd made a comment earlier about you not trying hard enough with your appearance?"

I don't answer that, just stare down at the tissue and remind myself to make sure that I throw it away in Kathy's office and don't take it down to my pristine, newly vacuumed, trash-free car.

"Are you familiar with the term *love-bombing*?" Kathy asks.

"No," I say, wiping my nose.

"It's an emotional manipulation tactic that typically occurs at the beginning of a relationship. The bomber will flood their partner with compliments, make them feel like the center of the universe, attempt to create a situation where all of the victim's positive feelings about themselves come from the relationship."

"That's not what's going on," I tell her.

"The next step is devaluation, where the manipulator pulls back on the compliments and starts to make small, negative comments about the other person, effectively taking away the pedestal they'd put them on. It makes their partner feel as if they've done something wrong, because they are no longer treated like they are special, or perfect."

Kathy is quiet again, and I twist the tissue harder, shredding it.

"The partner then starts to make small changes, catering to the manipulator to try to recapture the initial feeling—"

"That's not what's going on," I say again, interrupting her. "It's not like that."

Kathy sits back in her chair, eyeing me. "You're the one who knows the inner workings of your relationship," she says calmly. "But, based on what I'm hearing here, I would just ask that you do a little reading about love-bombing and emotional manipulation before we meet again."

"I can try," I say grudgingly. "I don't really need homework."

"Fair enough," Kathy says. "Please consider it."

"Sure," I say, getting to my feet and checking the mirror by her door for mascara streaks. "But it's not going to do any good. Baxter's not like that. Jayden is a piece of shit, like *actually* abusive."

"Emotional abuse isn't like physical abuse," Kathy warns, following me to the door. "It's much more difficult to identify, but the damage is real."

"'Kay," I say, pulling open the door. "But that's not it."

And it's not, so I must still be kind of sick, and that's why I feel a little queasy when I check my phone and see he hasn't texted me. And it's not, so it's probably just nerves about SHAFT Class that has my hands shaking as I start the car. And it's not, so it's probably talking about Jayden that has me crying before I even pull away.

It's not the fact that everything Kathy just said fits our relationship.

It's not trauma, and I'm not triggered, and I'm not some little bitch.

I'm Shelby fucking Black.

And I'm perfectly fine.

I get to Baxter's house and ring the bell five times before I have to acknowledge that he must not be home. I go back to the curb, settling in behind the wheel and shooting him a text.

I'm here???

I look at it for a second, wondering if those three question marks might be a little too aggressive.

Too much?

I consider editing the message, tap my fingers against the phone for a second, realize that I'm overthinking, and flip over to Instagram. January just posted a pic of her latest piece of art, and it's got quite a few likes . . . including one from Baxter. My stomach tightens up, and I scroll through the comments.

@in*my*digitalopinion2025—remember I can get you some Chi town art school hookups!

It posted seconds ago. Seconds ago, like when I sent my text that hasn't been read. Seconds ago, when he was talking to January on Instagram while ignoring my message. I click on his profile, see the green dot. He's online. He's using his phone. He's ignoring me.

I go back to January's feed, scrolling through pics of her art, selfies with friends. It's a very regular-girl photo spread, pics with her cat, her little sister, at a football game, then a coffee shop. There's a stab in my gut when I land on a selfie of her from last summer, lying in the grass, smiling up at the camera. She's so pretty, in a clean, classic way. She doesn't look like she's ever been too much, or too loud, or been kicked out of a basketball game because she told the ref he needed to dig around in his asshole for his glasses.

Baxter liked that pic, too.

"What the hell?" I mutter, then scroll back up. He's gone through her shots, liking everything. I get to the most recent one, stare at his comment.

@in*my*digitalopinion2025—remember I can get you some Chi town art school hookups!

Remember . . . like it's something that he's said to her before. Like they've been talking.

Heat flushes my whole body, like I just slammed a triple dose of pre-workout. Sweat breaks out across my face, and my hands start shaking. I grab the steering wheel, squeezing it with all my strength.

"What the hell?" I say again, but this one is directed at myself.

"Get your shit together, Black," I say through clenched teeth.

I go back to my texts. Baxter's left my text unread, just like I've ignored a text from Coach Faith asking when we're going to make up the session I missed today. Technically, I had time after therapy, but Baxter had made a comment about having not seen me much since the party, so I'd told a little fib and ducked Coach Faith when Baxter said his mom wouldn't be around again tonight.

Except, apparently Baxter isn't, either, and I should probably be in the ring right now, not wearing makeup and waiting on a boy who is talking to another girl on Instagram rather than answering me. A series of texts from Baxter flash across my screen, the sight of his name sending my heart into my throat.

Sorry sorry sorry!!

I was getting my new driver's license.

The DMV is like the seventh level of hell.

I'm escaping now!

The texts flood in, like they used to, chasing each other across the screen, my phone vibrating madly, my smile getting wider with each one, my stomach settling back into the warm rush that I've come to associate with Baxter as I respond.

It's okay! Ready to see you!

I close out the app as Baxter pulls into the driveway, tooting his horn at me. I meet him by his car, and he envelops me in a hug as he gets out, burying his face in my neck.

"You smell amazing," he says, giving me an extra squeeze before he lets go.

"I took a shower," I tell him, which sounds dumb, but is totally true. I also put on makeup, and may have paid more attention than usual to below-the-belt shaving, and took some DayQuil just in case, so that my nose wouldn't be running.

"Personal hygiene is hot," he says, taking my hand as we head to the door.

"So are you," I say, tracing a finger along the back of his neck, watching as goose bumps rise in its wake.

"Speaking of hot," I say, pulling up my phone. "Lee sent me some of the early proofs from the Rebel shoot."

I scroll through my recent photos, tapping on one of the shots that both Tara and Lee had tagged as a great option. I'm leaning against a rig, abs tight and on display—along with the rest of me. Rebel's summer line isn't for people who don't want to show off their bodies, and while it's first and foremost an athletic line, the sports bra I'm wearing in this shot also has a liner that pushes my tits up to my ears. Add in the stars-and-stripes theme and—like one of the crew had told me when Dad was out of earshot—every red-blooded American male is going to want a piece.

"Check it out," I say, handing my phone over to Baxter.

He glances down, his eyes widening. "Uh . . ."

"That's your girlfriend," I tell him. "How's that feel?"

"I thought this was a clothing line?" he says, handing my phone back.

"It is," I say, ignoring the fact that I didn't get a compliment.

"You're not wearing any clothes," Baxter says.

"Well, yeah, but, I mean, Rebel Outfitters makes workout

clothes for women," I say, floundering. "Like, they really support female athletes."

"Looks like they support patriarchy and capitalism," he says. "Kind of a turnoff."

A turnoff? I just showed my boyfriend a pic of my oiled-up, bared-down body, and he's turned off?

"I . . ."

"Look, it's just kind of . . . you know what, never mind," he says, looking away from me.

"No, wait," I say, catching his arm. "I want to know what you think."

And I do, and I tell myself it's not just so I can claim to think the same thing.

"It's like this," he says, leaning back against the kitchen counter. "Mom's been asking about you, and—"

"Really?" I ask, a rush of adrenaline surging. Because if I meet his mom, then this is real. If I meet his mom, it's one step closer to . . . to . . .

"Yeah, and I can't exactly show her your Instagram," he says.

"Why not?" I ask, gut sinking.

"Seriously?" he asks, one brow raising as he pulls his phone out. "Should I show her the reel where you're sliding a plate back and forth on the end of a barbell and making sex noises?"

Too much.

"Or the one where you fart really loud on a squat?"

"Hey, that happens," I say, going for a laugh.

"Sure, but how am I supposed to show that to my mom and say, 'This is my girlfriend,' and expect her to be anything other than horrified?"

Horrified. I'm horrifying.

Of course, I am. *I'm too loud, too much, too fast.*

I'm Shelby Black.

My Instagram isn't continuous line drawings and coffee shops and selfies lying down in the grass. He could show January's pics to his mom, and she wouldn't be horrified. He could say that's his girlfriend, and nobody has to be uncomfortable because she doesn't promote the patriarchy and capitalism and make money off her body because she's a genius and can use her amazing talents and skills to do that, instead.

"Just pump the brakes a little, is all I'm saying," Baxter adds, reaching out to touch my shoulder. "I'm not trying to make you feel bad. You know I think you're beautiful, right?"

I do, but I haven't heard him say it in a while. Now that he has, I revel in it. His voice. My compliment.

"You do?" I ask, raising my eyes to his, but unable to stop myself from getting a quick jab in. "But what would your mom think?"

"I'm home alone with Shelby Black," Baxter says, pulling me in close. "I've got something very different on my mind than what my mom thinks."

I shiver as he kisses me, loving how he used my full name, like I'm larger than life. I bet he doesn't even know January's last name. I lean into his kiss at the thought, pressing him against the counter, our waists locked tightly together, when it becomes blatantly obvious exactly what is on his mind. I pull away, breaking the kiss.

"I'm sorry," he says, cupping my face in his hands. "I just . . . sometimes it's hard knowing that every guy out there gets to look at my girlfriend's body, you know? Like, what part's just for me?"

"Let me show you," I whisper, thrilling at the phrase *my girlfriend*, the fact that he said it, the fact that it's me.

"Where's your room?" I ask, and he leads me to the stairs. The hallway is dark, and I squint as he shoves open a door, the hinges squeaking as he turns on the light.

There's pressure in my throat, even though I'm certain I cried more tears in Kathy's office today than I have in an entire year. I can't have any left, can't cry in front of Baxter—especially right now, when we're about to seal the deal. I tear off my shirt, suddenly desperate to bring him close, give myself over to him, make him stay. I waste no time, lying down on the bed and easing out of my leggings, while Baxter does the same, sliding under the covers next to me in his boxers.

We're both in our underwear, and soon, not even that. He rolls on top of me, his weight somehow more than I expected, my chest pressing against his. Baxter looks down at me, brushes hair away from my face.

"This is okay, right?"

No boy has ever asked me if it was okay. They either assumed it was or that I would stop them if it wasn't. The girls at SHAFT Class were right—asking permission is sexy.

I lock eyes with him, grab his hips, and pull him in.

"Yes," I say.

Kathy is wrong, and January doesn't matter.

Because this is perfect.

CHAPTER TWENTY-THREE

Fallon

I'm sitting on the mats in the second-floor yoga room, with five different things I should be doing but only one thing on my mind; Jobie's voice, on repeat—*when Fallon wants something done right, she does it herself.* Then Shelby asking, *Are we fighting now?*

We're not. We are definitely not fighting. If there's one thing I don't need in my life right now it's friend drama. Is there static between me and Jobie? Yes, for sure. Has that been the case a million times before and everything turned out fine? One hundred percent. Part of me knows that I should do a vibe check with her, clear the air, or just flat out ask what's wrong. But the truth is that what's wrong is probably that Princess Tinyhead had to have her anal glands expressed again, or she just found out that Essie stopped making her favorite nail polish color and she only has twelve bottles stockpiled.

Meanwhile, I've got an essay on *King Lear* due, the shortlist of contenders who I think might be *@Ko/Kreame/Krispies* to narrow down, a reminder from Farrah to get tampons on the way home, plus a fresh DM from my favorite hater.

@Trad!Dad/1996—just taking the temperature of the room.

@Trad!Dad/1996—because it's getting warmer.

Under that is a screen cap of the county Block Watch page on

Facebook, which is where old people go to post their personal beefs and illustrate how well they know how to use stickers and inspirational GIFs. On any given day the Block Watch can be counted on for thoughts and prayers, threats and recriminations, vaguebooking, and an update on who is letting their dog run loose and eat other people's chickens. If you would've told me that an Instagram account would make all of these people join together in a shared opinion, I would've guessed that account would be run by a golden retriever puppy and only post Bible verses.

But no, the Block Watch page has definitely united—against me.

Someone had posted the article about the *@Not-Your-Moms-Sex-Ed* account, which had brought it to the attention of anyone who didn't already know about it. There are a ton of comments, a lot of tagging, a thousand guesses about who might be running it, and at least one helpful explanation of who Bill Hader is.

I back out of the conversation with *@Trad!Dad!1996* when I see his green dot light up; he's online. Even though I've got privacy on the *@Not-Your-Moms-Sex-Ed* account set to not alert people of my status, I still don't like the idea of sharing a space with him, even if that space is the vast mesa of the internet. I flip over to my personal account instead and notice that my last DM to Jobie is still sitting on read, with no response. Jobie isn't online, which, come to think of it, I haven't seen her on Instagram hardly at all lately. I pull up my texts and see that she never responded to my last one there, either.

"Hey, fearless leader," Mal says as she waltzes in, flopping onto the mat next to me.

"Hardly," I snort.

"To the fearless part, or the leader part?" she asks.

"Do you think Jobie has been acting weird?" I ask her, ignoring her question and scanning the hall outside in case someone else shows up early.

"If you want to worry about somebody, worry about Shelby," Mal says, popping a breath mint and cracking it loudly between her teeth.

"What? Why?"

"Have you not noticed? When's the last time she made a dick joke?"

"I . . ." I mentally scroll through the last SHAFT Class meeting and realize that Shelby hadn't said much. I'd been worried I'd have to corral her to keep things aboveboard, but that hasn't been a problem.

"She's been quiet," I admit. "But I don't know her all that well, so I can't—"

"Well, I do, and quiet isn't her thing," Mal says. "Even if she did say something, it'd be muffled by Baxter's rectal lining, her head is so far up his ass."

Both Jobie and Shelby are driven right out of my mind when an email comes in from *@KoIKreameIKrispies*. She hadn't responded after I'd sent her the contact info for the new email account I'd created, and the hard lump of concern that had been forming in my stomach suddenly leaps up, knocking my heart into a higher gear.

Bethany was definitely not at Cody's party the night I was DM'ing with *@KoIKreameIKrispies*, which struck me as odd because she's the kind of girl that is at *all* the parties. Her stepbrother is a fellow senior—Grady Henshaw—who I wouldn't trust to take care of a rat carcass, and *he* wasn't at Cody's, either. I can't really put a lot of weight on that piece of evidence, though, because Grady is more likely to be at parties where the drugs are injected rather than smoked.

I know for a fact that Bethany did have an STD last year, and there was a period of time when she really "let herself go," as the other cheerleaders had put it. Bethany had put on weight, not washed her hair on a regular basis, and definitely let the skin care routine take a back seat—which could all be signs that she was trying to make herself less attractive to her new stepbrother, as their parents had just gotten married a month earlier. Or, maybe it was a bout of hardcore depression after she and Brandon broke up.

The email from *@Ko/Kreame/Krispies* is brief and to the point—**are you there?** She's online, so I switch over to Google Chat and shoot her a DM.

@Not-Your-Moms-Sex-Ed—yes, are you okay?

@Ko/Kreame/Krispies—I mean, no. lol.

"What?" Mal asks, her attention shifting away from Shelby to me. My fingers are flying across the screen, and she glances down at my phone.

"Is that—?"

"Yes," I say tersely, tipping it away from her so she can't see.

"Fallon," Mal says sternly. "You need to stop."

I shake my head, still typing. "I can't just leave her hanging, and we've talked about this. I've taken all the necessary precautions—"

But I don't get to finish my sentence, because Mal slaps the phone out of my hands. I yelp and come to my feet. "What the hell, Mal?"

"Your sister is right," Mal says. "You don't know who this is, and even if she is for real, you are not the person she should be talking to. You're going to get in some real fucking trouble here. Have you seen the Block Watch page lately?"

"Yes," I tell her, retrieving my phone. "One of my trolls sent me a screen cap."

"The Karens are mobilizing," Mal warns. "Don't fuck with Karens. It's not smart."

"No, it's not," I have to agree. "But I also have a duty to—"

"You *don't*, Fallon!" Mal practically yells at me. "You are not responsible for everyone, and you don't have to fix the world's problems."

When Fallon wants something done right . . .

"Sorry," Mal says, when I go quiet. "I didn't mean to yell."

"It's okay," I say, taking a shaky breath as voices can be heard coming down the hallway. "Can we talk about this later?"

"Sure." Mal nods. "But don't expect me to change my mind. Somebody's going to get hurt before this is all over."

"Somebody already is," I tell her, and try to not think about *@Ko/Kreame/Krispies* as Jacelyn walks in along with her cohort of athletes and a few girls sporting varsity jackets from Riverview. January and Amara show up, all smiles. Brandon, Cody, and Will—the guy who gave up porn for his girlfriend—and the cheerleader contingent arrive. I'd warned Farrah off, so I don't have to worry about an onslaught of junior high students. At five minutes after the hour, Jobie and Shelby both show up, each of them with their noses buried in their phones.

Bethany, however, does not show up. And the green light next to *@Ko/Kreame/Krispies*'s email account stays on.

"Some new faces tonight," I say, looking at the Riverview girls.

A few weeks ago, the idea that word about SHAFT Class had spread to other schools might have sent me into orbit, but my universe has shrunken to the size of a phone screen, and the words of a simple message.

@Ko/Kreame/Krispies—I mean, no. lol.

"I don't really have anything specific for tonight," I admit, glancing down at my copy of *King Lear*, which remains closed, and the journal with my notes about *@Ko/Kreame/Krispies*, which is, luckily, also closed.

"I'm kind of scattered at the moment," I say, a jagged laugh escaping. "So, I guess we'll just open up the floor to questions."

Glances move across the crowd, and one of the girls from Riverview speaks up.

"Are UTIs an STD? Because I had one and my boyfriend lost his shit."

"No," I say firmly. "UTIs are definitely not an STD, and you can't pass one on to your boyfriend if you have one."

"But also, totally don't bang while you have one," Jacelyn says. "I mean, ouch."

"What's a UTI?" Brandon asks.

"Urinary tract infection," I explain. "Girls can get them pretty easily."

"Pee after you have sex," a band member offers. "That helps."

"But, like, in the bathroom," Cody tacks on. "Not—"

"Great insight, Cody, thank you," I say, cutting him off. "Anybody else?"

"Wait, so is a UTI the same thing as a kidney infection?" Will asks. "Because my little sister was peeing blood this one time, and we had to take her to the emergency room, and my dad was all pissed off because he thought someone hurt her—"

"Uh, back up," Mal says. "Why would he think that?"

"Because she was bleeding out of her . . . you know?" Will says, big, round eyes pleading with Mal to not make him say the word *vagina*. But that isn't exactly the problem here.

"We don't urinate out of our vaginas," I inform him, forcing my face to stay straight.

"You don't?"

"No." I shake my head. "We—"

"Look, buddy," Shelby says, standing up. "It's like this. Piss, baby, shit." She points to each part of her crotch in illustration.

"I wouldn't put it like—"

"Wait." One of the band members raises her hand, cheeks bright red. "We've got . . . are you saying we've got *three* . . . ?"

"Dude, even I know that," Brandon says. "Who says porn isn't educational?"

"Stop, stop, stop," I say, putting my hands in the air. "How many of us are unaware of what . . ." I struggle, looking for words and hoping to find better ones than Shelby had. "Of how girls are made? No judgment."

Quite a few hands go up.

"For real?" a Riverview girl says. "None of your mommas set you up with a hand mirror?"

"A hand mirror?" Amara asks.

"Let me take this," Mal says, nudging me. "I'm sure that Fallon will find an appropriate medical reference chart."

I glance up from my phone, a little miffed that she'd guessed exactly what I was doing.

"But if you want to know your own body—and we all look a little different—you can take a hand mirror and, uh . . ." It's Mal's turn to color a little, so Shelby slips into the gap once more.

"Like this," she says, standing up and propping a foot on Cody's shoulder. "Put one foot on the bathtub or the toilet, then stick a mirror down there and take a peek. Or your phone, just make sure you have the flash on, otherwise it's really hard to—"

"Okay, we're good," I say, waving Shelby off. "Thank you."

"And if you'd like a rating," Brandon offers. "My number is—"

"You're done talking," I inform him. "Does anybody want to add anything?"

"Yeah," Jacelyn says, "this is why we can't 'just hold it' when we're bleeding. It's two completely different body parts."

"Speaking of, has anybody tried those period panties?" a band member asks, and I reach behind me for my phone, hoping *@KolKreamelKrispies* is still online.

CHAPTER TWENTY-FOUR

Jobie

The whole conversation about UTIs has me crossing my legs and wondering if I should be holding my pee in this long, but I don't want to risk the wrath of Fallon by getting up and leaving while people are talking. Or while we're "in session," as I'm sure she would say. I pull up the *@Not-Your-Moms-Sex-Ed* account and start flipping through DMs, answering the easier ones first.

Yes, you can have sex while you're pregnant, and no, it won't get you double pregnant. No, nobody can tell if you're a virgin just by looking at you, and likewise, you can't tell if someone has an STD just by looking at them, either. Yes, blue balls are a thing, but it won't kill him, and it's not your responsibility to take care of that. No, if you really loved him you wouldn't sleep with him, you'd ask him to respect your feelings. No, masturbation doesn't mean you're a lonely pervert. No, not everyone is having sex.

"Definitely not," I say to myself, shifting in my chair, and accidentally bumping elbows with one of the Riverview girls.

"Sorry," I tell her, then put together a couple of posts for the account about UTIs, and dive back into the DMs.

@Viola[Mae]2028—is pee stored in a guy's ball sack?

Oh, wow. I thought I'd heard some real bangers during the

meetings, but this one sets me back. My fingers hover as I try to find an answer that won't be condescending.

@Not-Your-Moms-Sex-Ed—no, they have bladders just like us.

An ellipsis pops up immediately, so Viola must be online.

@Viola[Mae]2028—god I'm an idiot.

I know exactly what it feels like to believe you're the dumbest person in the room, so I respond.

@Not-Your-Moms-Sex-Ed—you're not an idiot, you just didn't know.

I look at my answer, consider what Fallon would say, and keep typing.

@Not-Your-Moms-Sex-Ed—you asked a question, and you learned something. Keep asking!

I doubt Fallon would use the exclamation mark; the only things she gets excited about are report cards coming out and new seasons of *The Great British Bake Off*.

A notification from Rock Bottom pops up, letting me know I've got a DM from *@DaveDoes*Stuff**. I tap on it, looking at his latest message.

@DaveDoes*Stuff*—you don't have to, sorry I asked

My stomach bottoms out at the idea of $250 getting away from me. I'd taken a nude in the mirror after he'd asked, but didn't send it because I didn't want to be impulsive. Both my guys that asked for flirty messages throughout the day haven't gotten back to me, which makes me wonder if I was doing it right. The cottage cheese weirdo sent a thumbs-up, but didn't recontact, and I've got to get fresh foot shots if I want to make any more money off the people sitting in my inbox.

@Jobster{Lobster}—I took a pic . . . just deciding

@DaveDoes*Stuff*—how can I make up your mind?

Viola messages the *@Not-Your-Moms-Sex-Ed* account again,

and I flip back over to Instagram.

@Viola[Mae]2028—okay I've got another one

@Viola[Mae]2028—what's a good boob size?

I can answer that one quickly enough without googling.

@Not-Your-Moms-Sex-Ed—pretty sure dudes would say all boobs are good boobs

It's not a very Fallon-like answer, so I look at it for a second, leaving the cursor blinking as I think of a better follow-up. While I'm thinking, Dave DMs me again on Rock Bottom.

@DaveDoes*Stuff*—pay in advance?

Is this guy seriously offering $250 for nothing? I could take the money and run.

@Jobster{Lobster}—how do you know I'll send it?

@DaveDoes*Stuff*—trusting you

My CashCrash app lights up, letting me know $250 just landed there. I flip over to it, looking at my balance.

@Jobster{Lobster}—okay, full disclosure. I've never done this before.

It only feels fair. The pic is not spicy, it's literally just me with no shirt on, looking down at my phone and facing the mirror. I'd tried a few different pouty looks, but I hadn't looked sexy—I'd looked like a girl who was trying to be sexy. If I wasn't doing the messaging thing right with the other guys, who knows how badly I could screw up nudes. I don't want to lose Dave because he's expecting something different. Something better than just actual me.

@DaveDoes*Stuff*—first time?

@DaveDoes*Stuff*—that's hot.

The CashCrash app pings me again; another $250 came in, but this deposit is waiting to be released upon confirmation of receipt of "goods or services."

@DaveDoes*Stuff*—just doubled my offer. You've got half up front.

"Holy shit," I say to myself.

"What?" the Riverview girl asks.

"Nothing, don't worry about it," I tell her.

@DaveDoes*Stuff*—take your time, think about it.

@DaveDoes*Stuff*—no pressure over here.

I send him a thumbs-up, then move back over to Instagram. The posts I'd just put up about UTIs on the *@Not-Your-Moms-Sex-Ed* account already have a few thousand likes and about thirty comments, most of them from women recommending their favorite over-the-counter remedies, or at-home treatments.

I would love nothing more than to post a reel of Shelby explaining girl parts in graphic shorthand—it would go viral in two seconds—but that's obviously not an option, so instead I find a color-coded medical chart and throw that up . . . but it disappears two seconds later.

"What the hell?" I whisper, looking up. Across the circle, Fallon catches my gaze. Her mouth is in a straight line and she's shaking her head.

What??? I text her.

No pictures, no graphics. We can't give them a reason to shut us down.

I roll my eyes so that she's got a visual on the tone I'm implying with my response—**that was from a health encyclopedia.**

Doesn't matter. It's a representation of genitalia. It'll be reported as pornography.

By who? Someone who's never seen actual porn? I shoot back.

Across the circle, Fallon only shrugs, and an ellipsis pops up on my screen.

I'm not saying it's wrong, I'm just saying don't do it.

"Riiiiight . . . ," I say under my breath. But Fallon doesn't have to say I'm wrong in order to make me feel like I am. I log off Instagram and switch over to Rock Bottom.

Where the people who actually appreciate me are.

CHAPTER TWENTY-FIVE

Shelby

I haven't really talked to Baxter since we hooked up. He'd hustled me out of his house when his mom called and said she was on her way home and given me a quick peck before shutting the door. I'd walked to my car feeling a weird mixture of elated and rejected, then spent a stupid amount of time trying to figure out what the appropriate text follow-up would be. When I saw that I was the last person to text, and thought maybe I should stop being so pathetic, I decided the follow-up text should be on him, and then I tried to watch a UFC fight and not pick up my phone every thirty seconds to check for a message that never came.

The day after, I sent him a text before leaving the house—**good morning! I love you!**—which had gotten a thumbs-up reply but nothing else. It had sent a wave of pins and needles all through my body, but not in a good way. When he didn't show up at school, I sent a follow-up text—**you sick?**—to which he had responded with a simple *yes*. I'd shot back—**shit, hope that's not my fault!**—and waited for a response that said something about how maybe it was but the risk was totally worth the reward.

That text didn't come, either, and I was so distracted during my sparring session with Rory that Coach Faith told me to get out of the ring before I got hurt. I'd dragged my sorry ass home and taken a shower, thinking that surely Baxter would have responded by the time I got out. When he didn't, I went to get coffee, expecting to see a message once I got to Grind the Bean. There was a text from Rory telling me to call him but nothing from Baxter.

I don't want to talk to Rory; I want to talk to Baxter.

And tonight, I finally get to. After four days of not showing up at school and sending brushoff responses over text, I've finally got a date, and my gut is churning as I turn over conversational topics in my head while I comb out my hair. Obviously, anything I'd mentioned over text—ice cream, how much I miss him, gerrymandering, and not-so-veiled references to our one night together—had all failed to elicit any interest. I'd tried food, sex, emotions, and politics, which had all worked in the past, only to get a few thumbs-up and one smiley face.

I breath out hard, fogging up the mirror while I lean in to put on makeup. I'm pondering the depths of the oldest question known to women—why do our mouths fall open when we put on mascara?—when my phone goes off. It's Lee, my publicist. I debate, letting it ring a few times before hitting speaker. I've got to be on point tonight for this date if I'm going to recapture the original forest fire that burned between me and Baxter. I can't have my phone going off the whole time, and this is the third time today I've ignored Lee.

"Hey," I say. "What's up?"

"Heeeeyyy," Lee says. "How's it going?"

"Fine," I say as I get out a brow pen.

"What's up?" I ask again, even though I know exactly what's up, and why she's calling me for the fourth time.

"Do you have a sec?" Lee asks, still bright and perky. "I'd like to talk about the messaging on your Instagram account."

"What about it?" I ask.

"Well," she takes a deep breath, and dives in. "I couldn't help but notice that you took down a lot of your earlier posts."

"I took down tits and ass shots, yeah," I tell her. "I guess I was just tired of catering to the patriarchy." And also holding on to the hope that Baxter would now find the content appropriate for sharing with his mom after identifying me as his girlfriend.

"Perfectly understandable," Lee says, not missing a beat. "And I'm all for taking that angle, but you need to talk to me before you pivot."

"'Kay," I say, as I dig through Taylor's blush brushes.

"Also, I can't help but ask, what's with all the dog pics?"

"That's my dog, Brutus," I tell Lee.

I'm sure the sudden onslaught of pics with me and my German shepherd—riding shotgun in my car, sitting in my corner while Rory and I duke it out, and chilling with me on the couch while we watch a compilation of the best women's knockouts in history—had thrown Lee for a bit of a loop. It certainly had done a number on my followers. I've had a lot of people ask for less canine, more pussy this week.

"Okay, but . . ." There's a hesitation from Lee, confusion building. "Why?"

"Because I love my dog," I tell her simply, which is the truth, but not all of it. The truth is that I'm trying to show Baxter what a great dog owner I am. The truth is that he's already liked four of January's posts this week, one of which she had crunched up her face to match the expression of her pug, tiny nose stud glittering. Baxter had not only liked the post but also commented.

Love you both.

My stomach flips upside down, remembering his words. Sure,

he'd put a little blue heart next to the words, not a red one, but I've spent four days in a text desert, while he apparently scrolled through January's Instagram and ignored all of my equally adorable posts with Brutus.

"It's fine," I say aloud, and Lee must think I'm talking to her, because she responds.

"It's more than fine," she reassures me. "People love pet pics! But we should have a talk sometime about staying on brand—"

"Yeah, let's do that," I say, giving my face one last look-over in the mirror. "Maybe next week, gotta run!"

"Okay, but, Shelby—"

I hang up on Lee, double tapping the text that had just came in from Baxter—**I'm here.**

There's no follow-up saying he can't wait to see me, that he's been looking forward to it. There's not even an exclamation point at the end. It's just a statement of fact regarding his geographic location.

Be right there! I text back. **Been waiting all week for this!**

My texts are immediately marked as read, but there's no response, and no ellipsis. But that's okay, because we're going out tonight, and I look hot as fuck, and—good Lord. I might look hot as fuck, but it's cold as shit outside. I grab a hoodie from the rack by the door and pull it over my head on the way to Baxter's car.

"Hey," Baxter says, still looking down at his phone when I climb into the passenger seat.

"Hey!" I say, echoing his words but not his tone. I sound excited to see my boyfriend; he sounds like an Uber driver.

"I thought we'd go to that new sub place," he says, putting his phone on the console in between us.

I can't help but notice it's face down.

"Cool," I say . . . and promptly run out of anything to add. Baxter drives to the end of my street, takes a left turn, then a right, all without speaking.

"How's your mom?" I ask loudly.

"What?" Baxter asks, not looking over at me. On the console, his phone vibrates.

"How's your mom?" I ask again.

He doesn't answer, just looks over and makes eye contact with me for the first time. "Why are you being weird?"

"What?" I laugh, making it a joke. "I'm not—"

"I love this song," Baxter says suddenly turning up the music.

"January told me about this band," he yells over a mix of synth and cymbals that makes me want to jump out of his smoothly running electric car. "She's got great taste in music. Aren't they awesome?"

"Yeah, it's like getting twenty-five COVID shots right in the asshole," I say, but he can't hear me because he's rocking out to music that his new favorite person turned him onto.

On the console, his phone goes off again. In my lap, mine remains silent and unmoving.

We leave Presnick and head to Delton, the closest place that has enough of a population to be considered a city, not a village. Baxter finally turns down the volume on January's favorite band, and I reach for his hand as we cross the parking lot toward the restaurant. He takes it, gives me a squeeze, and then promptly lets go. He'd told me a while ago that he's not into public displays of affection, so I try to focus on the squeeze and not the release.

When we walk into the sub restaurant, the guy behind the counter does a double take. Pretty girls are used to this; as a semi-famous girl, I've learned how to tell the difference between being checked out and being recognized—and this guy definitely recognizes me. He does the full-on head tilt, plus elbows his buddy standing next to him.

"Hey," I say, approaching the counter with a sense of confidence I haven't felt for a while.

"Hey," says the blond one, whose name tag identifies him as Ricky. "So, I'm going to be that guy. You're Shelby Black, aren't you?"

I used to respond with things like "In the flesh," or "Fuck yeah I am." But I quickly discovered using words like *flesh* and *fuck* either encouraged dudes in a way I wasn't looking to or embarrassed them unnecessarily. Luckily, I've got a good publicist in Lee, who has given me some pointers over the years.

"I am," I tell him, using the smile that Rebel signed me for. "And you must be Ricky?"

"Actually, no," he deadpans, nodding toward his friend. "I'm wearing his name tag."

Mostly when I confirm my identity guys either get flustered or flirty, so I'm not ready for the quick comeback. I snort and lean over the counter for a fist bump, reaching past the plastic divider displaying all our meat and vegetable options.

"Nice one, but you definitely look like a Ricky," I tell him.

He fist-bumps me, then pulls away like I broke his knuckles. I laugh, then feel pressure on my other elbow. Baxter has a hold of my hoodie and is pulling me back. I glance over my shoulder and see that his mouth is in a thin line, his jaw muscles flickering.

Is he actually jealous?

I step away from the counter, checking myself. I don't think I've done anything wrong, but I also vowed to make this date the great comeback where the heat of our fortuitous first meeting was restored. I stand beside Baxter, leaning against him. He pulls away, putting some distance between us while he orders. Ricky and his buddy take the hint and shut down, making our food without any more small talk. I give them a little wave as we go to our table, then sit down across from Baxter, who still looks like someone with IBS took a shit in his coffee.

Determined to ignore his mood, I reach for my sub and start unwrapping it. "So, I was thinking—"

"Are you really going to keep that on?" Baxter asks, interrupting me.

"What? This?" I tug on the front of my hoodie, confused. "Yeah, I'm cold, and it's not exactly—"

"You are covered in dog hair," Baxter says tightly. "Absolutely covered. It's going to get into your food, it's going to get into *my* food, and when you leaned over the counter you probably got it in everyone else's food, too. Did you not notice? Those guys were disgusted."

"Uh . . ." I definitely didn't think Ricky and his friend were disgusted by me, but apparently, I'm reading everyone wrong today, because Baxter wasn't pulling me away from them because he was jealous but because of deep concerns for public health and food safety.

"I've just been spending a lot of time with Brutus lately," I tell him, not adding *because that's what I thought you wanted me to do.*

"That doesn't mean everyone else has to," Baxter says. "Seriously, I had to change my sheets the other night."

"I think you would've had to do that anyway," I tease, nudging his foot under the table.

"Don't be gross," he says, and I pull away.

Gross. That's what I am. *Gross* and *disgusting* are the two words that my boyfriend used to describe me today. I look down at my sub, suddenly aware that I got a triple-meat sandwich with extra mayonnaise and hardly any vegetables. Plus, it's a foot-long. Baxter got a six-inch vegetarian flat wrap with sugar-free vinaigrette, which sounds horrible but probably won't clog his arteries—or the toilet tomorrow morning. When I look back up from my food, Baxter has his phone on the table and the Ilsa Bunting fight is playing again.

"Why do you keep watching that?" I snap.

"What?" He glances up. "Are you going to start telling me what I can look at now? That's controlling. I had an ex like that."

That's the second time he's compared my behavior to one of his exes, the emphasis always landing hard on *ex*. A text from January flashes across his screen, and my stomach balls into a hard little knot, but if I question it, I'll *definitely* be controlling. He flicks it out of the way, watching intently as Bunting puts pressure on my carotid artery. My face is pressed into the mat, cheeks purpling, blood running down the open cut above my eye. I look away before I tap out.

"The better question is, why don't you watch it *more*?" Baxter says.

"Because I lost," I hiss. "For the first time, ever."

"Right, so why wouldn't you watch it and figure out what you did wrong? Don't you want to improve?"

"So that's why you've got it on replay?" I ask, trying to keep the acid out of my voice. "You got some tips for me?"

"Actually, yeah," Baxter says, leaning forward. "I think if you . . . What?"

For the first time in the history of our relationship, I'm the one moving away from him, pressing myself against the back of the booth.

"Oh, I see," he says. "You only take advice from overpaid professionals. What could your boyfriend possibly know?"

Anger is welling up in me, reinflating my stomach after it collapsed when I saw the text from January. I tamp it down, try to readjust. He's being a world-class dick right now, for sure, but he's still referring to himself as my boyfriend. And I can't expect him to be perfect, right? And I did get that little hand squeeze in the parking lot, and yeah, I am totally covered in dog hair in a place where people eat, so there is every possibility that I am being a bitch right now.

I take a deep breath and attempt something that I've never really done in a relationship before. Instead of snappy comebacks and the occasional headlock, I try being honest.

"It just hurts my feelings that's the only fight of mine you watch," I say. God, I sound so stupid. This is why people don't talk about their feelings; when feelings make it out of their hearts and into their mouths, it sounds weak.

Baxter looks back at me, unblinking. "Well, yeah," he says, a hint of a scoff in his voice. "This one is a real fight."

"A real fight?" I repeat, staring back.

"C'mon, Shelby, let's be real," he says, pushing his phone aside as another text moves across the screen. "Becca St. James and Nova Renly are half your size—"

"We're in the same weight class," I say flatly.

"Then I question the scales they used."

"We use the same scale at weigh-in."

"Never mind," Baxter says, pushing away from the table. "I'll stop taking an interest in your career."

"I'm going to the bathroom," I say, getting up quickly. In the stall I google "Is it okay if another girl is texting my boyfriend?"

At the sink, I double-check Becca St. James's and Nova Renly's last official weigh-ins. In the mirror, I fix my mascara with the tube I've started carrying around with me. At the door, I take off my hoodie. I walk out just as the door to the kitchen opens, Ricky's head poking out.

"Hey," he says.

"Hey." I turn to face him, ready for the selfie request, or maybe an autograph.

But instead he says, "You okay?"

"Huh?" I flounder, suddenly unsure what to do with my hands. "Yeah, I'm fine."

"All right, well"—he comes out into the hallway, a step closer to me—"it's okay if you're not okay."

"Did you seriously just 'it's okay to not be okay' me?" I ask, a smile tugging on the side of my mouth.

"I did," he confirms, smiling back. "Keep talking to me and I promise to find more interesting things to say."

Keep talking to me . . .

My smile widens, my eyes go back to his name tag, which now identifies him as Jackson.

"So, you're really not Ricky?" I ask.

"Nah." He shakes his head. "Ricky's an asshole."

I laugh, the sound bouncing off the walls of the tiled hallway.

"And hey, for the record," Jackson adds. "So's your boyfriend."

My laughter dies; our eyes lock. From the kitchen someone yells, "Jackson! Some help in here!"

"Take care of yourself, Shelby Black," he says.

Baxter is quiet while we eat, but his phone is not. Texts keep coming in, and he takes time to answer each one, not speaking to me. Maybe Baxter is an asshole sometimes, but Jackson only knows the Instagram version of me, doesn't know what Baxter puts up with. If Jackson dated me, he'd see my filthy car, and my dirty jokes would get old; he'd hate that I fight in clothes that make other men gawk at me, and he probably wouldn't hug me before he left for work, because I'd get dog hair all over him. He'd see that I'm gross, that I'm disgusting.

Suddenly nervous, I reach across the table, my fingers interlocking with Baxter's.

"Sorry," I tell him.

And I am. I'm sorry that I look like such a great package at first, but the shine wears off real fast once you get to know me. I'm sorry that every single thing I've said and done on this date was defensive or bitchy, and I'm sorry that I flirted with another guy outside the bathroom when my boyfriend was right there. I mean, who does that?

A shitty person, that's who.

A shitty girl that's lucky to have what she's got.

"Sorry," I say again, and Baxter pats my hand as he taps out a text with the other.

CHAPTER TWENTY-SIX

Fallon

The kitchen countertop is covered with all the things I should be doing: tabulating the results from a student council poll, correcting a lab from AP Chemistry, and sorting through photographer bids that the prom committee offered as options. Plus, I've got to come up with some sort of plan for SHAFT Class tonight, which should probably include some actual self-defense, in case someone walks past the yoga room. But instead, I'm scrolling through my ongoing chats with *@Ko/Kreame/Krispies* and cross-referencing them with the list of possibilities on my yellow legal pad—which is getting shorter. There is a very big part of me that just wants to type, **Bethany?**

But if it is her, it could scare her off.

If it's not her, it could scare her off.

Either way, the person on the other end will know I've been trying to figure out who they are, which breaks some of the unspoken trust I've tried to build between us. Mom walks into the kitchen, and I quickly flip my phone over, face down, followed by my notebook.

"What's up?" she asks, her eyes going toward the movement, brow furrowing.

"Nothing," I say. "Just trying to balance all this stuff and thinking about how much harder undergrad will probably be than high school." Which isn't totally untrue—it's one of the many swirling thoughts that have threatened to pull me down into the Charybdis of my own spiral.

"Eh." Mom shrugs, pouring herself some coffee and leaning against the counter. "It's not that much different. There's an adjustment period, but for someone who worked so hard in high school like you have, it won't be that bad."

"Right," I say, my eyes skirting over my laptop screen, willing *@Ko/Kreame/Krispies* to respond to my last message, which had been another plea to tell an adult.

"What's going on, Fallon?" Mom asks. I'm so taken by surprise that when I look up, I've got no mask on, the trusty *I'm Fallon, and I'm fine* look falling away.

"It's . . ."

On the island, my phone hums.

"Nothing."

"Uh-huh, well"—Mom sets her mug on the counter and crosses her arms—"I know you've heard this phrase from me a hundred times, but get ready for one hundred and one. I'm your mother and—"

"I can tell when something's wrong," I finish for her, a smile pulling on the corner of my lips.

"Winner, winner, chicken dinner," Mom says, nodding. "Seriously, what's going on?"

My phone buzzes again. Both our gazes go to it, and her eyes narrow.

"You know I have always respected your privacy," Mom says carefully. "But that ends right now if you won't tell me—"

"It's Jobie," I blurt. "We're kind of . . . not getting along."

A weight lifts in my belly with the words, and I have to acknowledge that maybe there's more truth to them than I thought.

"Oh," Mom says. "That's totally normal. You're nearing the end of senior year; you'll be going separate ways. I'm sure you're both feeling that, and it's probably making you act a little differently toward each other."

"Yeah," I say. "That makes sense."

Mom walks over, joins me at the island. "I know I've told you this before, but it's true every time—the friends you have in high school might not be your friends for the rest of your life. You're going to leave Presnick and meet so many—"

My phone goes off again, this time with a call.

"Sorry," I tell Mom. "I'll let it go to voicemail."

It does, then immediately starts ringing again, Mom's face falling back into the worried zone. "Fallon, are you sure—"

"I better get it," I say in a rush. "It could be about . . . the FAFSA."

I grab my phone and laptop, then head upstairs, really wishing I was better at lying on my feet. Mom knows nobody is calling me about the FAFSA, and I just dug myself into a longer conversation for the next time, but right now I'm operating out of the belief that what Mom doesn't know won't hurt her. Like how she doesn't know that my friends for the rest of my life might not be the ones I meet in college but the ones I meet in jail. My phone is vibrating again by the time I make it to my room and shut the door behind me.

"Mal, what the hell?" I say, when I answer.

"Dude, big fucking problems," she says, as I toss my open laptop on the bed. Mal is out of breath. Her last two texts read—**call me right now**. Followed by—**never mind I'm calling you**.

"What—"

"Amara sent me a pussy pic," Mal says.

"Whoa!" I almost drop the phone when it vibrates in my hand again, this time with a notification that *@Ko/Kreame/Krispies* sent me a message on Google Chat. I crash onto the mattress next to my laptop, navigating to the message.

"Yeah," Mal says, her voice dropping. "I have no idea what the actual fuck to do right now.

@Not-Your-Moms-Sex-Ed—You really, really need to tell someone about this. Someone who can actually do something.

@Ko/Kreame/Krispies—You can do something.

"Okay," I say to Mal. "When did this happen?"

"Like, just now," she says. "We've been texting. She's . . ."

"Gay?" I supply.

"I did not say that," Mal says. "I am not outing her."

"*No*," I agree, as an ellipsis pops up next to *@Ko/Kreame/Krispies*'s avatar. "You didn't out her."

"She just had some questions," Mal says. "I was answering them the best I could without it . . . you know, it getting weird, or whatever."

@Ko/Kreame/Krispies—You can help me.

There it is, what I've been hoping for, an opening I can walk through.

@Not-Your-Moms-Sex-Ed—I can't help you if I don't know who you are.

@Not-Your-Moms-Sex-Ed—or where you are.

"What do you mean, weird?" I ask Mal.

"I mean weird like personal. For the record, I didn't think she was flirting with me, and I definitely was not flirting with her."

"And then she sent you a nude, and weird went out the window."

"Kind of?" Mal says. "Remember how we talked about girls not knowing what we look like down there?"

"Yeah?" I say, my eyes still on *@Ko/Kreame/Krispies*'s chat box.

"I guess she took a pic and uh . . . she was a little surprised. She thought something was wrong, like it looked funny to her."

@Ko/Kreame/Krispies—Can I trust you?

@Not-Your-Moms-Sex-Ed—Absolutely.

"Are you trying to tell me that Amara has some kind of abnormal—"

"No," Mal says, cutting me off. "She looks perfectly fine. She's just never seen one before, I guess. Or you know, we *do* all look different and hers wasn't what she expected. I don't know, okay? Just, the point is, she sent it to me asking me what I thought, and I don't know what the fuck to do."

"Delete the photo, right now," I tell her.

"I already did," she says. "But you know how that shit works. She sent it. I received it. I can delete all I want, but it was on my phone and—"

"It's child porn," I finish for her. "And you're a legal adult."

"Yeah, which translates as totally fucked if anyone finds out."

@Ko/Kreame/Krispies—If I wanted to go to the cops, can you help?

My heart ramps up, fingers shaking as I type a response.

@Not-Your-Moms-Sex-Ed—Yes. What do you need?

@Ko/Kreame/Krispies—Will you come with me?

I stare at the blinking cursor, torn. *@Ko/Kreame/Krispies* can't possibly know that I'm close by, that it's even feasible for me to go with her to the police station. Unless, like Farrah said, she's been in SHAFT Class and noticed that posts to the *@Not-Your-Moms-Sex-Ed* account synced up with what we talked about at early meetings, before we got smarter. Unless, it's Bethany, whose personal hygiene took a hit right after Grady Henshaw moved in with her.

"Fallon?" Mal asks. "What do I do?"

What I want to say—*I don't know*—is on the tip of my tongue. But Mal is in this position because I put her here, and to some extent, so is *@KolKreamelKrispies*. I made a decision, and I followed through on it, because I'm Fallon Holloway. And now there are consequences.

So I make another one.

"This is some fucking stupid, batshit-crazy stuff, right here," Mal says.

She's sitting in my passenger seat, holding a steaming take-out cup of coffee that she definitely does not need, judging by the way her left leg is tapping out a staccato rhythm in the footwell. She'd clearly been crying when I met her in the parking lot at the rec center, and when I announced what we were going to do, it had not calmed her nerves at all.

"At least you're not going by yourself, I guess," she acknowledges now. "Now we can be murder sisters."

"That's not—" I was going to say *statistically likely*, but I hadn't googled death stats on people that meet up with random strangers on the internet before I left the house. Mal had just about jumped out of the car when I told her where we were going—the state park—but when I'd come clean about the nature of *@KolKreamelKrispies*'s situation, and the fact that I thought it was Bethany, she'd reluctantly agreed.

"I am ninety-nine percent sure it's her," I say again, as I turn onto the highway.

"Or, your little sister's right and it's someone catfishing you, and you've got a big-ass hook right through your cheek right now," Mal says. "In that case, we're driving toward a person that has a grudge against you, and maybe a gun."

"One percent chance," I agree. "Which is why I didn't come alone."

"But you'll risk the lesbian?"

"That's *not* what I meant," I say.

"Maybe not, but if this was a horror movie, you know I'm going down."

"We're doing this right before SHAFT Class for a reason," I remind her. "If we don't show up, people will know something is wrong."

"But you didn't tell anyone where we're going," Mal argues. "That's, like, Basic Safety 101."

"No, I didn't," I say carefully. "Because the park closes after dark—"

"Welp, it's after dark," Mal says, gesturing toward her window. "Too bad, guess we can't go, after all."

"They don't close the gates," I tell her. "And if I told Jobie or Shelby where we were going, they'd know something was up and want to come along, and a group might scare Bethany—"

"Or a murderer—"

"Away. If I told *any* adult what I was doing they'd want to know why, which is very much off the table. If it helps, I'll drop a pin to my sister when we get there."

"For real?"

"Yes," I reassure her. "I'm not going to be entirely stupid about this. Now, tell me more about Amara."

"It's not pretty," Mal says. "Her family is super conservative, and she's just been keeping her head down. I swear to you, Fallon, there was nothing going on—"

"I believe you," I tell her, as we approach the turnoff for the park.

"I mean, she's cool and all, but I'm not messing around with a minor. What I told you is true; we get busted for any reason, and the gay one is going to be the one burned at the stake."

"I won't let that happen," I tell her, dimming my lights as I turn into the park.

"I did everything I could for her," Mal says. "And I was careful. Then she sent me *that*, and I haven't even responded, and she's probably freaking out, and I don't even know what the hell I'm going to say to her at SHAFT Class—"

"We'll talk to her together," I tell Mal, as we slide past the nature center, closed up for the winter, then down the hill toward the lake, the naked limbs of trees gathered over us. There's a dusting of snow across the access road . . . and one fresh pair of tire tracks ahead of us.

"They're here," Mal says quietly.

"Yeah," I say, my tongue clicking, mouth dry. We take a sharp turn to the right, following the road down to the lake. There's a parking lot down there, long and thin, stretching alongside the lake.

"How are you so fucking calm?" Mal whispers.

"I'm not, I'm dying right now," I tell her. "But this is the right thing to do."

"And you always do the right thing, don't you?" Mal says, as I creep forward. The tracks from the earlier vehicle fade into the distance, toward the end of the lot, where I can just see the outline of a car parked under a tree.

"Drop that pin right fucking now," Mal says, and I do. "Why did they go all the way to the end of the lot? Did you tell them to?"

"No," I say, after dropping a pin to Farrah and sending along a text that says—**I'm fine, this is just an FYI.** Then I flip over to my chat with *@Ko/Kreame/Krispies*.

@Not-Your-Moms-Sex-Ed—I'm here.

The green dot next to *@Ko/Kreame/Krispies* lights up, but there's no response. I squint into the distance. "What kind of car does Bethany drive?"

"I don't know," Mal says. "Fallon, I don't like this."

In my hand, my phone vibrates.

@Ko/Kreame/Krispies—I see you.

I turn the phone so Mal can see the screen. Her eyes meet mine. "This is not good, Fallon."

I take a deep breath, then flick my headlights at the car at the far end of the lot. My brights flash for a second, and their lights come on in response. Mal reaches over, squeezes my wrist.

@Ko/Kreame/Krispies—I'm scared.

"Me fucking too, honey," Mal says.

I pop my car door, and the overheard light comes on. Mal immediately reaches up and covers it with her hand.

"What are you doing?"

"I'm going to walk over there," I tell her, swallowing the lump in my throat as I reach for my phone. "If anything happens—"

"Not by yourself," Mal says, unlatching her seat belt. "If anything happens, I'm not just *watching* it happen. Murder sisters, remember?"

"Maybe stop saying that?" I ask.

We get out of the car together, our shadows are black and elongated, reaching for the other car.

@Ko/Kreame/Krispies—Who is with you?

I look down at my phone, realizing I never clarified that I might not be alone.

"What?" Mal asks, watching as I type out a response.

"She wants to know—"

My phone vibrates with a call coming in from an unknown number. I hold it up to show to Mal, who shakes her head.

"It's local," she whispers. "Maybe—"

"Hello?" I answer, my voice unsteady.

"Fallon? It's Lauren from the rec center," a voice says, and my stomach bottoms out.

"Yeah?" I say, holding the phone out so that Mal can hear as well, while I also type out a response to *@Ko/Kreame/Krispies.*

@Not-Your-Moms-Sex-Ed—It's a friend who wants to help.

@Not-Your-Moms-Sex-Ed—I should've told you there would be two of us, I'm sorry.

@Not-Your-Moms-Sex-Ed—Is this still okay?

"I got your number from your application to use the space," Ms. Lauren goes on. "I hope it's okay to call you, and I'm sorry to be the one to tell you this—"

"What?" I ask sharply, interrupting her.

"We don't allow food in the exercise rooms. Given our last conversation, I assumed you don't want any unnecessary attention drawn to yourselves, so I thought I'd give you the heads-up."

@Ko/Kreame/Krispies—Yeah, it's okay.

"Food?" I ask, my eyes going to Mal's.

"Yeah, sorry," Ms. Lauren says. "One of your girls wanted to surprise everyone with food, but she walked in with like fifteen bags of Chipotle, and I had to tell her—"

"Geez, Jobie," I say, rolling my eyes.

"Oh, no. It's not Jobie," Ms. Lauren says. "It's Bethany Morrell."

I freeze, my breath stopping in my chest. Mal reaches out, hangs up the phone, her eyes wide.

"Fucking. Run," she says.

We break for the car at the same time, snow sliding out from under my shoes as I wrench open the driver-side door. Mal throws herself into the passenger seat just as I hear the other car roar to life. I throw the car into reverse, tires sending up a haze of white as I whip it around, then gun it, rear tires sliding.

"Oh shit, oh shit, oh shit," Mal is saying over and over, trying to put her seat belt on.

The tires finally get purchase, and we shoot forward, the headlights of the other car bright in my rearview mirror. I spin around the steep turn, gravel flying as we approach the gate. We break out onto the highway, and Mal twists in her seat, eyes behind us.

"They're following," she says calmly. "Drive straight to the police station and fuck the speed limit."

I nod in wholehearted agreement, stepping on the gas. In the cup holder, my phone goes off with an alert. I've got a message from *@Ko/Kreame/Krispies.*

"What's it say?" I ask Mal, who grabs my phone.

"'Where are you going? What are you doing? Please come back. I need help.' You know, all the shit someone says when they're trying to fucking lure you in, Fallon."

"Right," I say, my eyes going back to the rearview mirror, where it looks like the headlights are falling back. "I don't think they're following us anymore."

"Maybe not so closely, but that doesn't mean they're not following," Mal warns me. "Police station."

I comply, weighing my options. Just because Bethany is at the rec center doesn't mean that whoever was in that car had bad intentions.

"It could still be legit," I tell Mal. "It could be any of the other girls I had it narrowed down to."

"Yeah, it could be," Mal says. "And we were all going to go to the police station together, so really you didn't break your word to her. We're just going to get there before them and with higher blood pressure."

We pass the Presnick town limits, and we both heave sighs of relief when we're back under streetlamps. Mal swivels, looking out the back.

"There's still headlights," she says. "But I don't know if it's them or not. Also, your sister texted you."

"Okay." I nod, making a series of random turns. "What did Farrah say?"

"Uh . . ." Mal glances at my phone. "'Why you at the park at night, brah? Drugs or sex?'"

I groan and pull into a parking space at the post office. Two cars pass behind us, a blue four-door and a yellow hatchback. I hold out my hand, and Mal passes off the phone.

Not drugs or sex. Not at park anymore. I'm fine.

"Are you fine?" Mal asks, watching me send the text. "Am I fine? Are you sure we're fine?"

"I don't know," I admit. "Did you recognize either of those cars that went past us?"

"No," Mal says. "And I'd like to point out that the post office and the police station are two different things."

"They are," I admit. "But I don't really see the point of going to the police now."

"After being chased?" Mal asks incredulously.

"Were we chased?" I ask. "Or did they just bolt because they got scared when we freaked out? And what do you want me to do, waltz into the police station and let them know that we were in the park after dark, meeting a stranger who found us online through our divisive, sex-centric social media account?"

Mal stares at the dashboard, considering. "No," she finally says. "I guess not."

"It's almost time for class, anyway," I tell her, starting the car again. "We'll see if Ko Kreame Krispies recontacts and then go from there."

"Okay," Mal says. "But don't drive right to the rec center, okay? Whoever was at the park could have followed us into town."

"Right," I say, pulling out of the post office. I drive down Main Street and take a few random turns, once indicating with my blinker that I was going to turn left, then turning right at the last second.

"Oh, fancy," Mal says, still twisted in her seat to watch behind us.

"We okay?" I ask.

"I mean, this gay teenager with no experience whatsoever in shaking a tail says yes."

"That'll do," I say, and head for the rec center, where we find Bethany standing next to her car and pouting.

"What the hell am I supposed to do with all these damn chips?" she asks. "This is why I don't ever try to be nice."

CHAPTER TWENTY-SEVEN

Jobie

Fallon, Mal, and Bethany are absolutely destroying some Chipotle in the parking lot when I pull up. Fallon has some queso on the tip of her nose, but I decide not to tell her. I couldn't even if I wanted to, because she keeps talking to Bethany, asking questions about things like what a "switch kick double-twist basket" is, which I guarantee she googled, because Fallon definitely does not give a crap about anything connected to cheerleading. Except, now Bethany must be her new best friend, because she's touched her arm twice while talking to her, and even ate some guac, even though she gave me a lecture last year about how American consumption of avocados contributes to deforestation in Mexico.

My phone goes off with a text from Amy. **Did the food guy follow up?**

No. Paid in advance for the cottage cheese thing. Never asked for more.

Shelby pulls up and gets out of the car, picking dog hair off her shirt as she joins the group and the extravaganza laid out across Bethany's hood. The queso makes the rounds, and I wonder if I could take a quick video of the four of them going to town on chips and dip and send it to him as a freebie, as well as a reason for recontacting.

K. I wondered. He showed up in my DMs and I wanted to make sure he pays up.

I frown at Amy's message. I didn't exactly know what to do with his request; there weren't any specific instructions, and he'd sent me a thumbs-up on the video. I hadn't done anything wrong, but I clearly hadn't done everything quite *right*, either, because he's shopping around to see what Amy has to offer.

Thought you were lactose intolerant? I shoot back.

I am, she says. **He wants me to dump a can of pork and beans over my head while wearing a tube top.**

"Oh my God," I say aloud, and Fallon glances up.

"What?"

"Nothing," I tell her. "You've got queso on your nose."

All yours, I tell Amy. **I don't own a tube top.**

"We should head inside," Fallon says. "Ten minutes to class. And hey, Shelby, do you think you could illustrate some actual self-defense moves tonight?"

"Sure," she says, shrugging as she crumples a Chipotle bag and tosses it into the back of Bethany's car without asking.

lol I'm sure he'd buy you one, Amy responds.

He offered to reimburse me for the can of beans

What a gentleman pervert

I smile and text her back, telling her he'd done the same for me with the cottage cheese. And yeah, it's definitely a weird kink, but he does pay up front, and he's never asked for any nudes or sent them unsolicited, himself. A few guys had pulled that in the rb/GoodGirl sub-bottom and I'd immediately reported them to the mods, who had them blocked. It's not a huge group; with barely two thousand members, the mods try to keep it small, quiet, and congenial. At first, I'd appreciated that. But now, with some of my paying contacts seeking out other girls on the sub, I'm wondering how many of those members are dudes buying and how many are girls selling.

I'm also wondering if I had an initial onslaught of interest because I was the new girl. Like Amy said, they talk to each other and even share pics. If word got out in the sub that *@Jobster{Lobster}* won't do nudes and reports dick pics, it could mean losing some payouts that might otherwise come my way. Amy has very specifically stated to me on more than one occasion that she does not, never has, and will not ever send nudes, but she'd also sent me a screen cap of her CashCrash app, which made it very clear that she's doing something way more lucrative than interacting in bad taste with canned food.

We move as a group toward the entrance of the rec center. I've got my face buried in my phone, and I collide with Mal. She's in front of me, backpedaling and scanning the parking lot.

"Sorry," she says, bending down to pick up my phone when I drop it. "It didn't crack, did it?" She instinctively glances at the screen, her mouth pulling into a frown.

"Thanks, it's fine," I say, snatching it back from her. "I'm fine."

"Rock Bottom?" she asks, as the sliding doors open, a wave of heat hitting us. "That's not the nicest place on the internet."

"You recognized it pretty fast," I say, closing out the app.

"There are some safe spaces for marginalized people there," she says.

Fallon hangs back at the front desk, apparently apologizing to Ms. Lauren about something.

"But it's also really popular with fringe groups," Mal goes on, her eyes still on me as we climb the stairs together. "You can stumble onto some real—"

"Intense stuff?" I finish for her. "Yeah, for sure. I've accidentally gone down a few rabbit holes, but I'm mostly just there for the My Little Pony fanfic."

"Ah, got it," Mal says, her face relaxing. "That makes a lot more sense."

I pause at the door to the yoga room, letting the other girls file past us. "A lot more sense?" I ask.

"Yeah," she says, looking back toward the stairs, clearly watching for someone. "I just don't really think of Rock Bottom as a place for girls like you."

"Girls like me?" I repeat again as January comes up the steps.

"Yeah, good girls," Mal says, offhandedly, then turns her attention to January. "Hey, is Amara with you? Do you know if she's coming?"

January shakes her head, and they fall into a conversation as I follow Bethany into SHAFT Class. Jacelyn shows up with her cohort of athletes, and some girls from Riverview trickle in, along with the band contingent. Will tries to back out when he sees he's the only dude, but the drummer convinces him to stay. I find a spot in the corner and lean back against the wall, reopening the Rock Bottom app.

I've got two new messages from guys I don't know, but who are rb/GoodGirl members. One is a simple **hey**, while the other is a casual **what's up?** I sigh and type out appropriate responses—friendly and open—but in my experience the ones who are serious come right in with their ask and split if you're not into what they want. The conversational ones tend to just be lonely, which is too bad for them, but I'm not here to make friends. A DM from Alice comes in.

@Ask!Alice/Unchained!—I thought this guy was one of yours?

She sends along a screen cap of her DMs with *@Jo-Rand-Band*Man*, who apparently isn't satisfied with my fake-girlfriend chatting skills, because he's real-life breaking up with me and moving on to Alice.

A text from Amy slides across my screen.

Welp, caught a weirdo!

It's followed by a screen cap of her Rock Bottom DMs, where it seems *@DaveDoes*Stuff** has been sniffing around. Their conversation is much like how mine with him went—direct and to the point. He likes barely legals, and will take as much of them as they're willing to give, but he's never pushy or rude. His last message to Amy reads—**no pressure, if you're not game it's cool. I should probably be cruising the rb/badgirl sub instead.**

I flip over to my DMs, where my last message from *@DaveDoes*Stuff** is still resting on read. He'd said the same thing to me—*no pressure*—and the fact that he hasn't recontacted in a week proves that he means it. The boob shot that I'd taken is still sitting in my hidden photos, waiting for me to make a decision. I text Amy back.

Lol rb/badgirl?

She responds immediately.

Uh, yeah do NOT go over there.

Stay on the side of the light!

I tap back a thumbs-up just as Fallon walks in, her gaze set on IRS levels of intensity. She and Mal exchange a look that I don't quite understand as Fallon shuts the door behind her.

"All right," Fallon says, clapping her hands together like we're at kindergarten roundup. "Tonight we're going to do something a little different. I'd like to put more effort into pretending that we're doing self-defense in here, so I'm going to give the floor to Shelby."

Shelby gets up somewhat reluctantly and scans the room, then tells everyone to find a partner. The awkward dance of everyone figuring out the pecking order of their friendships plays out, leaving Shelby standing at the front of the room, and me still sitting in the corner holding my phone. Fallon paired off with Mal, who is apparently her new best friend. She makes eye contact with me and raises her brows.

"Uh." I glance around the room, looking for an out. "We've got uneven numbers, so maybe I'll just . . ." I point down at my phone, indicating to Fallon that I'm focused on operating the *@Not-Your-Moms-Sex-Ed* Instagram. Then I open it up and pretend that's what I've been doing all along.

"Right, sure," she says quickly. "I mean, you've got asthma anyway."

I give her a shrug and return to my phone as Shelby starts instructing. Hundreds of unread messages are waiting in the DMs, so I start plowing through them. *@Viola[Mae]2028* is back, asking if doing it doggy-style means you'll get pregnant with puppies (I'm starting to think she's messing with me), along with a question from *@Bar+Bell+Boy* asking if slipping some tongue in on a first kiss is moving too fast.

Shelby rattles off the names of some of the self-defense moves she's teaching. Fallon has been on me hardcore about making sure that *@Not-Your-Moms-Sex-Ed* isn't always reflecting what we talk about in SHAFT Class. So as much as I'd love to quickly find accounts that have reels illustrating Shelby's moves and repost them, instead I throw up some stats from the CDC about herpes. I add the appropriate hashtags, having to stop myself as I automatically tap out *#goodgirl*, catching it just in time before I post.

"Sorry," one of the Riverview girls says, when she accidentally steps on my foot. Her partner had successfully clipped her on the chin with an elbow strike, knocking her back into me.

"Maybe less actual contact?" Fallon says.

"Yeah, stay on the side of the light," I echo Amy's words to the Riverview girl, rolling my eyes when I look up at her. She snorts and goes back into the fray as I flip over to Amy's last text. I'm not stupid, and I'm definitely going to follow her advice about not wandering over to rb/BadGirl. I've stayed very safely within the mold of a good girl, both on- and offline.

A DM to the *@Not-Your-Moms-Sex-Ed* account comes in from *@Trad!Dad/1996.*

Herpes? Did your lifestyle finally catch up to you?

I scroll back through his messages, remembering Fallon's comments where she said he's antagonistic but never outright threatening. It looks like she's never responded to him, strictly adhering to her policy of not feeding trolls. But I'm not Fallon, and I'm tired of doing exactly what he's angling at—being safe, being such a good girl that Mal was surprised I was on Rock Bottom at all.

How bored are you, even? I shoot back. I consider adding a link to rb/BadGirl, and telling him that should take some free time off his hands, but I stop there, reminding myself that Fallon took down an encyclopedia diagram of a vagina last week. Linking to real ones probably won't get me back in her good graces.

A notification pops up from CashCrash, reminding me that there's $250 waiting for me from *@DaveDoes*Stuff**, upon receipt of goods and services. I glance around the room, but everyone is deeply invested in either putting their partners in a side headlock or escaping from one. My lock screen stares back at me, the perfected ridges of my sculpted New You face practically daring me. I pull up my photo roll, unlock my hidden album, and look at the single photo there.

She looks nothing like the perfected version of Jobie.

She just looks like me.

I send the pic.

CHAPTER TWENTY-EIGHT

Shelby

If I had to estimate, I'd say I've spent approximately one-third of my life trying really hard not to be a bitch. The slice on that pie chart is currently expanding, as I try not to tell Kathy Hildebrand that she doesn't know what she's talking about. I don't care about the fancy office and all the capital letters after her name. She doesn't know me, and she doesn't know Baxter, and she doesn't know a damn thing about our relationship.

"That's not—"

"Shelby," she interrupts me, her mouth movement catching up with the audio a second later. We're on Zoom, which makes everything even more annoying than usual.

"I want you to think about what you just told me," Kathy says. "You made a change in your behavior—spending more time with your dog—because you perceived that Baxter found some sort of fault in you. Then, he took issue with the result, which was having dog hair on your clothing."

"Which is disgusting," I say back to her.

"Did you hear what you just said?" she asks. "You're using Baxter's words to describe yourself."

"He's not wrong," I say, sticking my chin out.

"Would you have ever called yourself disgusting before?"

I cross my arms and look away from my laptop, but the defiant movement changes, slipping more into a hug, the grasp of a desperate person. Baxter and I haven't talked much all week, despite the fact that I tried to salvage our date by apologizing. Afterward, I'd come home and looked at old screen caps of texts he'd sent me in the past.

You are the best thing that's ever happened to me

You're not like anyone I've ever met before

You're what I think about as I fall asleep, you're my first thought when I wake up

Except now I'm not. Now I get **k** back in a response, if he even answers me at all. How does that change so quickly? How did I go from filling his mind to being an afterthought? What did I do wrong?

"Shelby?" Kathy asks. "Can you hear me?"

"Yeah," I say, rousing myself. "No, I wouldn't have called myself disgusting before, but I also didn't really think bad things about myself, like ever. I probably needed a reality check."

"After our session will you humor me about something?" Kathy asks. "Will you look up narcissistic personality disorder?"

"Is that what you think is wrong with me?"

"No. I don't think there's anything wrong with you," Kathy says firmly. "I'm not Baxter's therapist, so I'm not able to diagnose him but—"

"Baxter is not a narcissist," I say.

Kathy's face smooths out into her listening mode, but I don't continue.

"Consider his reaction when the boys at the restaurant recognized you," Kathy finally says. "You were the center of attention. He was reminded that you're somewhat famous; he's not. It made him feel small, so instead of being proud of you, he found ways to drag you down."

"That's not it," I tell her. "I can be wrong about things without him being some sort of monster. I used to drive around in a car filled with actual trash. I used to walk around dressed like a gym rat and not brush my hair. I used to post skin pics for attention. I ignored my dog and had shit taste in music. Baxter is actually making me a *better* person, so why is that bad?"

"And what does Baxter do wrong?" Kathy asks.

"I . . . What?" I sputter.

"What are some things that you've asked Baxter to change?"

I look away from the camera again, feel my jaw muscles flickering.

"Shelby," Kathy says gently, like she's coaxing a wounded animal out of its hiding place. "Please read about it. I can recommend some good resources—"

"Yeah, sure. I will," I say. "I've gotta go. I've got a thing."

"We still have fifteen—"

"I gotta drive to the rec center, and it's snowing," I tell her. "I need to leave early."

"Okay." She nods. "I will email you some links to articles that I'd like for you to take a look at. Some of them are also about emotional abuse—"

"'Kay," I say, and close the window, revealing some of the screen caps I'd been looking at earlier, Baxter's text messages from back when everything was amazing, and I was the center of his universe.

You're perfect.

I look at the date on the text, trying to figure out how I could go from perfect to perfectly disgusting so quickly. It's from the week of Cody's party, a few days before it. A few days before he started talking to January.

Baxter isn't what's wrong with my relationship.

January is.

I wasn't exactly thrilled when Fallon put me in charge of SHAFT Class; I don't care about this right now. I don't care about anything other than getting out of here and calling Baxter, asking him what he wants, what I can do to save this, what needs to happen in order for me to be perfect again. I've got the aftertaste of queso in my mouth, and no one here has any idea how to get out of a half nelson. I've demonstrated more than once and some of the athletes are getting it. The one guy is doing everything he can to not obliterate his partner, who is a tiny thing that plays the flute. But the others are lost causes that need to rely on running and screaming instead of fighting back.

I call a break when Bethany dramatically declares that her partner has broken one of her ribs, and we all go for our phones, which are scattered around the edges of the mat. I've got no texts, no messages. January is all up in her phone, actively tapping away. I open up Instagram and see that Baxter is online. So is January.

"What the fuck?" I ask no one, and the Riverview girl sitting next to me glances over.

"Does anybody have any questions, since we're taking a break?" Fallon asks.

"Yeah, uh . . ." One of the sophomores raises her hand. "I know this is supposed to be about sex or whatever, but can I ask something kind of related?"

"Sure," Fallon says. "If you've got FAFSA questions, I'm a pro at that."

There's a scattering of giggles, one of which comes from January, but she's not listening to Fallon—she's looking at her phone.

"Yeah, no," the girl says. "But, how do you know if you're in love?"

A quiet pall settles over the group, an awkwardness that wasn't there when we talked about porn, dicks, body hair, or STDs. Even Fallon's professional face has gone a little frozen.

"What's the question?" January asks, the silence making her look up.

"How do you know if you're in love?" Mal repeats.

"Oh!" January lights up. "It's like you're always vibing because you have the same interests, and when you look at each other, you feel this internal warmth."

"Yeah," Will says, his eyes going dreamy. "And I hope this isn't offensive, or whatever, but when I see a hot chick, it makes me start thinking sexy thoughts, but then immediately my brain is like, *I wonder what Peyton is doing?* Like it's not just sex that I want, it's sex with *her*."

"And you want to be in touch with them—*a lot*." January holds up her phone.

My heart kicks up a notch, blood gaining speed. It's like she pointed a gun at me.

Fallon's glance moves to the hallway, where someone just walked past. "Let's get back to it," she says, coming to her feet. "Shelby?"

"Let's practice takedowns," I say, tossing my phone aside and watching as January finishes tapping out a message.

"Takedowns?" Mal asks, eyebrows coming together. "That's not self-defense."

"Maybe not," I admit. "But any fight in the real world ends up on the ground. Do you want to be on the bottom when you get there, or the top?"

“I call top,” Jacelyn says, which gets a laugh.

I tell everyone to form a circle around me, then motion for January to join me in the middle. She glances around nervously, then stands across from me, wariness in her eyes.

“Please don’t kill me,” she says, with a weak laugh.

“Why would I kill you?” I ask.

She laughs again, but her eyes are unsure; she knows it’s a serious question. Across the circle, Mal’s frown has deepened. The room is quiet except for Jobie tapping away at her phone. Someone walks past in the hall, and Fallon cranes her head, following their movement.

“This is called a basic double-leg takedown,” I say. And then I grab January around her waist, ducking under her arm and lifting her bodily off the ground. There’s nothing to her; she’s light as a feather, her bones easily felt through her skin, muscles slack as she puts no effort whatsoever into stopping me from doing whatever I want. She’s tiny and feminine; she’s everything I’m not.

So I throw her down.

January hits the mat on her back, all the wind rushing out of her in a gasp.

“Whoa,” one of the Riverview girls says. “I don’t think—”

January’s face is all confusion and fear, the look of a person who has never been hurt before in their entire life.

“That’s real,” I tell the class. “You all think you’ll be fine because you carry around pepper spray and take turns slapping at each other in here. But if someone actually comes at you, I guarantee you’re going down. And once that happens—”

I sprawl on top of January, giving her no warning. She yelps and tries to crawl away from me, but I pin her easily, flipping her onto her belly and wrapping my arm around her neck.

"What the fuck?" someone yells as I start to squeeze.

"Who are you talking to?" I whisper into January's ear.

"What?" she gasps. It's a flicker of breath barely brushing the inside of my elbow.

Someone grabs at me from behind, arms fully locked around my waist. I don't let go of January, so she comes up with us when I'm thrown backward, all three of us going down into a pile. I come to my feet and spin on Will, who immediately holds up his hands. I turn back to January, who is still on the ground. Jacelyn is trying to help her up, but she's crying, pulling wet hair out of her face, completely and utterly shocked that the world can change so quickly.

That things can fall apart.

There's blood coming from her nose, and Jacelyn immediately pinches it shut, January's eyes tracking the flow as the red slips down the other girl's wrist; something that's supposed to stay inside her body has been let out.

"Shit," I say, looking down at my own hands, where there's a smear of blood across one knuckle. "I didn't mean to—"

I move toward Jacelyn and January, but suddenly there's a wall of Riverview varsity jackets in front of me, Mal trying to elbow her way through them. Fallon is pressed against the glass, blocking as much of the view from outside as possible. Jobie is on her feet, mouth hanging open, staring at January, who is looking up at the ceiling while Jacelyn holds her nose closed.

"I'm fine," January says, the sound clogged by tears and blood. "I get bloody noses really easily, it's not a big—"

"You're not fine," Jacelyn says, shooting me a look. "And neither are you. That was unhinged."

"Get her to the bathroom," Fallon orders Jacelyn, her eyes scanning the hall. "And everybody else, get out. This class is very much over." Everybody files out, no one meeting my eye as I wipe the back of my hand across my hoodie.

"What the fuck?" Mal says, coming over to me. "Why did you go after January?"

"She's trying to steal Baxter," I say. Hearing the words spoken aloud hits all the harder; my heart starts to jackhammer, black spots chase each other across my vision.

"That's . . ." Jobie joins Mal, looking at me skeptically. "Are you sure?"

"Pretty fucking sure," I bite back.

On the floor, my phone vibrates. Fallon picks it up, hands it over to me. It's the text I've been waiting for all day, the one where Baxter opens up and shares his feelings with me, like he used to. The one where everything gets fixed and we can go back to good. The one where he finally answers me with more than one word.

But only the last part is true.

What the fuck is wrong with you?

CHAPTER TWENTY-NINE

Fallon

"She's either going to die or kill somebody," Mal says.

We're standing in the parking lot, watching as Shelby tears away, horn blaring as she cuts someone off, her middle finger flashing out.

"Do you think she's okay?" January joins us, the rim of one nostril red-flecked with dried blood, her gaze following Shelby's taillights as she slams on the brakes at the stoplight, then slides through the intersection and keeps going.

"I don't care if she's okay," Jacelyn says, following close behind. "That was bullshit, and you should press charges."

My heart goes up into my throat at Jacelyn's suggestion, fully aware that anything like that will bring a spotlight onto SHAFT Class in a way that we don't need. But January only shakes her head.

"No, I'm fine. Seriously, I get a bloody nose if I sit up too quickly. I just don't understand why—"

"She thinks you're going after her boyfriend," Mal says.

"What?" January's eyes go wide. "Baxter? No way, I mean he's nice and all, but honestly, I think she could do better."

"She can," Mal says. "And everyone knows that but her."

"There's nothing we can do right now," I say, my voice suddenly losing power when I spot a yellow hatchback in the parking lot.

Mal follows my gaze, and I hear her intake of breath.

"Everybody just get home safe, okay?" I say, trying to recapture a normal tone.

"I'll call Shelby, once I think she's done losing her mind," Mal says.

"Right," Jobie says doubtfully, wincing when we hear the screech of brakes and another horn blare in the distance. "Whenever that might be."

Mal and I both stall as we wait for Jobie and Jacelyn to take off, then for January's mom to pick her up. Once they're gone, she leans against the side of my car, joining me.

"You think that's the one that followed us?" she asks.

"I don't know," I tell her. "I didn't get a plate."

I do now, though, taking a quick pic just in case. There's no one inside, and when I glance back at the rec center I don't see anyone watching us from the lobby.

"I think we're fine, but you leave first. I'll wait and keep an eye out. I'll leave after—"

"Aw, shit," Mal says, when her phone goes off. She lifts it to show me that Amara's calling. "This is a conversation I'd really rather have face-to-face."

She lets it go to voicemail, but it rings again seconds later. "Apparently not an option," she says, sighing as she walks to her car. I wait until she pulls away, then get into my own car. I turn the defrost on full blast and flip on the windshield wipers, sending drops of sleet flying off into the night. I lean back in my seat, press my skull against the headrest, my palms against my eyes, and take a deep breath.

I'm the opposite of Shelby as I pull out, driving cautiously, using my signal in the lot, and even waving someone else ahead of me at the three-way stop, like building good karma now might pay off later. I'm outside town, flipping between brights and low beams once the rain picks up, not sure which one is providing better visibility, when headlights appear in my rearview mirror—coming on fast. I instinctively slow down and turn on my hazards, encouraging whoever wants to drive fast in this weather to go ahead and pass me.

But they don't.

They get right up on my ass and slow down.

I'm reaching for my phone just as a call from Mal comes in. If I hit the brakes, whoever is behind me will ram me, possibly run me off the road, and then do God knows what to me. The rain is pounding down hard now, drumming against the hood, splashing back upward, falling again, my pulse threading with it, hands shaking as I answer the phone.

"Fallon, we're in big fucking trouble." Mal is talking low and fast, as breathless as I am. "Amara didn't know it, but her whole family's phones are hooked up to the same cloud. Her dad saw that pic and went apeshit. She took her phone and ran off. She's sitting on the floor in the post office soaking wet and crying, I don't—"

"Mal," I say evenly, cutting her off. "They're behind me right now."

"What?" She shrieks. "Get the fuck out of there!"

"I can't," I tell her, my voice rising in pitch as I yell over the pounding rain. "I can't see anything, I can't go any faster and I can't—"

My phone lights up with a DM for the *@Not-Your-Moms-Sex-Ed*

Instagram, the preview filling my screen.

@Trad!Dad/1996—Is this Fallon, Jobie, or Shelby?

I stare at it dully, all my fears condensed into a backlit rectangle.

"I've gotta go, Mal," I tell her. "I'm headed west on Old Plank Road. Call nine-one-one."

I hang up, breath coming fast, panic building, every nerve in my body singing. My phone vibrates in my hand with another message from *@Trad!Dad/1996*.

"How?!?!" I shriek at the screen. "How the hell did you—"

The answer is in his response, a link to an article that walks the reader through how to capture the IP address of an Instagram account through DMs, using Command Prompt and an IP address lookup while you're both online.

"No, that wouldn't work," I say to the screen, denial taking over. "I used a VPN."

Except, I wasn't running the account tonight—Jobie was. Jobie, who hasn't actually been listening to anything I've said lately. Jobie, who blows off everything that isn't a follow or a like, or whatever it is that matters to her so much more than—

Trad Dad sends me another message, a screenshot of the IP database that offered up the latitude and longitude of the Presnick rec center. It's immediately bumped by another screenshot, this one of the calendar of events for today, SHAFT Class circled in red highlighter.

"And our names are listed as class leaders on the site," I say, sorting out the ending for myself. "And now—"

@Trad!Dad/1996—you're fucked

He finishes the sentence for me, followed by one last screenshot—

of the county Block Watch page.

"NO!" I scream, slamming the gas in spite of the rain. Behind me, the other car accelerates, matching my speed. My back tires slide, and gravel spins out from under them, the rain a pure sheet now, pounding against the glass in a constant thrum, one that matches my unending litany.

"No, no, no, please don't, please don't, please don't."

I have to get home. I have to get home right now, I have to tell Mom and Dad before they find out from Facebook, I have to explain that I'm a terrible person and I've made a huge mistake and I'm so sorry and I love them very much and I'll do whatever it takes to fix this and I'm so sorry and I'm so sorry and—

My phone goes off.

Mom is calling.

Farrah is calling.

Mal is calling.

Dad is calling.

Jobie is calling.

I answer, and her voice comes through my car speakers, soft and weak.

"Fa-Fallon?" she stutters, she's crying. "I'm in trouble—"

"YOU'RE GODDAMN RIGHT YOU ARE!" I shriek, words tearing at my throat, my voice like lightning. "HOW FUCKING STUPID ARE YOU?"

And that's when I see the stop sign, a flash of red cutting through the storm.

I slam the brakes and swerve as the other car sails past me, horn blaring. The world spins, spare change flies through the air, my phone hits me in the face. I'm rolling, I'm flying, I'm screaming.

And then it's water.

Water and Jobie crying.

Then there's not even that.

CHAPTER THIRTY

Jobie

Mom's not home when I pull in, but I've got a text saying she went over to Jason's and would I be comfortable staying by myself tonight?

I text back—**I'm an actual adult**. Followed by—**have fun!** 😉

Princess Tinyhead is sprawled across one of my pillows, and I have to nudge her aside to lie down.

"You would not believe the drama at SHAFT Class tonight," I tell her, brushing her tail aside as it whips my face. Shelby losing her damn mind had almost made me forget about the fact that I just sent my first nude.

I open my CashCrash app, but *@DaveDoes*Stuff** hasn't released the next $250, which sends a butterfly shooting across my stomach. I flip over to the Rock Bottom app, but get an endless spinning circle, which is no surprise because the app is trash. Unsettled, I reach for my laptop, navigating straight to my DMs on Rock Bottom.

The pic shows up as delivered, but Dave's messages are gone, replaced with **message deleted by user**. His username is gone as well, now reading only as **account deleted**. My stomach rolls over, and I shove Princess Tinyhead away as she tries to crawl in my lap. Next to me, my phone vibrates and—thank God—it's Amy calling. I'll tell her what happened, and she'll know what to do, or Alice will.

Someone, somebody, somewhere will know what to do and this can get fixed. I grab the phone, breathless.

"Amy, I did something stupid—"

"Gotcha," a man's voice says, and everything stops.

My breath.

My heart.

My blood.

"Amy?" I ask again. "Or is this Amy's dad?" My voice shoots up at the end of the question, high and hopeful, Jobie endlessly asking someone else for an answer.

"Noooo," he says slowly. "You were right the first time. This is Amy."

My hand clenches the phone, the case cutting into my fingers. "You're not funny," I whisper, my breath barely passing between clenched teeth. I grab my laptop, type out a frantic message to Amy on Rock Bottom.

@Jobster{Lobster}—I think someone stole your phone

"No one stole my phone, Jobie," the voice in my ear says, and a sob escapes me.

"I *talked* to her," I say.

"Did she sound like this?" Amy's voice asks, bright and chipper, the slight Southern twang trickling out of my phone.

"It's AI, dumbass," the man comes back.

"No," I say, shaking my head, tears flying. "That's not—"

"Possible?" He interrupts me. "Listen, I've got to go through this with every single one of you dumb bitches, so let me just make it clear—this is happening. I've got your titty pic, and you're going to do exactly what—"

"Wait—you're Dave?" I whisper, the phone shaking against my cheek.

The man sighs, sounds almost bored. "Yeah, I'm Dave. And Amy. Alice, too."

My room gets smaller, the walls closing in as my skin does the same thing, all my organs moving closer together, fighting for space.

"I've got money," I blurt out. "Give me the pic back, I'll give you—"

"Five hundred and twenty dollars?" He cuts me off, naming the exact amount in my CashCrash account.

"How do you—"

"Because that's all *my* money, sweetheart," he says. "Every dime you've got was from me, or one of my partners. I actually made a little on a side bet about the cottage cheese thing, my buddy said you wouldn't do it. I said you would."

Princess Tinyhead walks across my stomach, the tiny indentations from her paws not dissipating, because I've stopped breathing.

"I said you'd do it," the man goes on. "Because you want money, because you want to be *prettier*."

He whispers the last word, drawing it out, raising a blush in my cheeks.

"I'll give it back," I say. "I'll give all your money back, just please—"

"Nah, you can keep it," he says. "You earned it. The sad part is, you don't need to be prettier, Jobie. Amy wasn't lying when she said there's a lot of men out there who want what you've got—no tats, no piercings, just clean, tight skin that's never . . . been . . . touched."

Everything in my stomach shifts, threatening to come up, but it can't because my throat is closed, bile squeaking up halfway, then slipping back down, burning a path.

"People pay money for that, Jobie. I've got a particular customer who is very interested in spending a lot of money on *you*, because he likes to watch good girls get wrecked."

"I'm hanging up," I say, tearing the phone away from my face.

"I know where you live," he says, his voice floating up, my finger hovering over the red button to end the call.

"No, you don't," I say.

"1382 Quince Lane," he rattles off. "It's a nice little two-story, brick—"

"HOW?!" I shout, dropping the phone, screaming at it as Princess Tinyhead runs for the door, her tail flicking in distress.

"Because you are very, very, stupid, Jobie," the man says, as I put the phone back to my ear. "You told me you live in Ohio. You had PHS painted on your face in football game pics, so your high school name starts with a *P*. That narrowed it down to about seventy-five towns. There was a license plate in one of your pics—and you thought you were smart, because you smudged the plate number out—but you missed the last three letters of the county at the bottom of the plate. It was easy enough to figure out the county from that, then look for a town that starts with a *P*, and guess what the only one is?"

"Presnick," I say dully, the phone loose in my hand, all of my muscles gone slack.

"Yep," the man continues. "You're dumb enough to tell me your actual name, so all I had to do was google *Jobie* and *Presnick* and I get a nice article from the *Presnick Hometown Press* of you and Fallon presenting the donations you raised for the dog pound, so I got your last name from the newspaper. That was really nice of you, by the way."

"You son of a—"

"You also told me your mom's a Realtor, so once I knew your last name it was easy to find her, and once I knew *her* name, all I had to do was look at the county auditor's site, and that's how I know where you live."

"You can't—"

"I *can*, Jobie, that's what you're not understanding. I know your name, and I know where you live, and I've got your cute little titty pic. I can do whatever I want, and you will do whatever I say, and we are going to have a lot of fun together. Or, at least, I will."

"I'm not doing a goddamn thing," I say, anger finally stirring. "My mom is dating a cop, and—"

"Yeah, your mom's hot," he says. "I'm looking forward to meeting her."

"What?" I ask, hot slipping back into cold, rage into fear.

"I just set up a showing," he says, and I hear keys clicking in the background. "Tomorrow, eight a.m. You know that townhouse that's been sitting on the market for a couple of years? It would take a motivated buyer to move that piece of shit, but I am motivated, Jobie. I'm very much looking forward to it."

"If you hurt her—"

"I *will* hurt her, Jobie," he says, his voice sliding over into a growl. "I've got all kinds of buyers with all kinds of interests, and there's just as much money in her skin as yours."

There's silence for a moment, a few seconds where I get to believe that he's gone, that this isn't happening, that Amy is real, and I am not an utter fool.

“So which one do I get?” he asks. “Mommy or daughter?”

“I’ll text her,” I say, voice shaking with tears. “I’ll tell her not to go to the showing, I’ll tell her—”

“Tell her what, Jobie?” he says. “That you’re a fucking idiot who has fake friends? That you’ll do whatever anyone asks you to for a little bit of money? That you’re a whore who sends her boobies to any stranger with cash? That’s what you are, Jobie. You’re a whore. A stupid, fucking whore who will do anything so that she can be pretty like her mommy.”

I have no words, just a sob, an echoing cry in my throat.

“It’s embarrassing, Jobie. I’m embarrassed for you.”

“I’m sorry,” I say, the words stumbling out of my mouth. “I’m so sorry.”

“It’s okay, Jobie,” he says, his voice sliding back down into a smooth baritone, a low lull that throbs against my cheek. “She doesn’t have to know. You mom doesn’t have to be disappointed in you, and she doesn’t have to get hurt.”

“Please, don’t hurt her,” I say, nodding now, swiping at tears, clutching onto his last words. “She’s finally happy. She’s finally—”

“I won’t,” he reassures me, and my phone goes off against my ear. Once, twice, three times. Four. “You just have to do this one thing for me, okay?”

“Just once?” I ask, my voice squeaking.

“Just once,” he says. “You know the motel out by the freeway?”

“Yeah?” I say shakily.

“I’ll meet you there in an hour and a half. I’ll text you the room number.”

“I thought you lived in Oregon?” I ask.

"Oh my God, how fucking stupid are you, Jobie?" he asks, anger spiking again. "*Amy* lives in Oregon, and Amy isn't real. I am, and I'm not very far from you. Pretty soon I'll be closer. Much closer."

"I don't know if I can—"

"You can," he says. "See you soon."

There's a click and he's gone, but my phone is still buzzing, there's a missed call from Mal, texts from January and Amara, and a notification that *@!Cute!_Amy* has responded to my DM on Rock Bottom. I stab at it, hope rising, like maybe she's an awful person and this was all some horrible prank, but I won't have to—

It's a dick pic, with the caption **can't wait.**

The vomit comes up all the way this time, and I run to the bathroom with one hand clamped to my mouth, hot bile slipping between my fingers. I make it to the toilet, where I lose everything that I have inside me, the tiles cold on my face as I lie on the ground, heart pounding, body throbbing with the movement. I stare at my phone where I dropped it, my recent calls backlit, Cute Amy's name with hearts on either side of it at the top.

Farther down is a different name, of my best friend. Someone who always has the answers. Someone who can fix anything. I touch her name, and hear the connection, a dull, thudding noise and rushing air.

"Fallon?" I say. "I'm in trouble—"

"YOU'RE GODDAMN RIGHT YOU ARE!" she screams at me, the phone rattling against the tiles. "HOW FUCKING STUPID ARE YOU?"

And then she's gone, and I'm left with her words and the deep, resounding knowledge that they are true.

I wash my face, and drive to the motel.
I text him for the room number.
I knock on the door.
There are three of them.
And I am a very good girl.

CHAPTER THIRTY-ONE

Shelby

What the fuck is wrong with you?

This can't be a text from Baxter, can't be his name floating above those words, can't be what the boy who is amazed at the reality of me said. Because it wasn't that long ago that he texted me every morning to tell me to have a good day, and called me every night so that his voice would be the last thing I heard before I went to bed. It wasn't that long ago that I was his everything and nothing I did was ever wrong, so it's not possible that he hates me now. It's not possible that he's not answering his phone. It's not possible that he's dismissed my call the ten times I've tried to contact him, because he wouldn't do that, because we had a fortuitous first meeting, and this is fixable.

If I can put myself in front of him, I can explain myself. I can be the girl he met outside the locker room, the one that is quick and funny, the one whose car is clean and who wears makeup. The girl who stopped swearing and pays more attention to her dog, and won't try to kiss him if she's sick. The girl who doesn't work out in her sports bra anymore and doesn't make sexy reels. I can be the girl he wants me to be, because that's a better version of me anyway, and who doesn't want to be better?

I'll be better. I'll be better for him. I'll start right now.

"Please let me," I whisper, my words barely audible over the rain slashing against the car. The lights are on at his house when I pull into the drive, my front bumper scraping against the curb because I'm going too fast. I jump out of the car, pull my hoodie tight around my face against the rain, and run to the front door. I ring the bell, once, twice. When there's no response I knock, my first coming down too hard.

Too much.

Too hard.

Too fast.

Too *Shelby*.

But I have to see him, have to explain myself, have to tell him that I'll stop being me as long as I can have him. The door opens halfway and he's there, phone in one hand.

"Hey!" I say. Too loud. Too bright. Trying too hard.

"Shelby, what the fuck?" he says. "Why are you here?"

"I wanted to talk to you," I tell him, trying on a smile that I'm sure is all teeth, no lips, desperate as hell. "Some things went down tonight, and I want to explain—"

"You wanted to explain attacking January?" he says tightly.

"I didn't *attack* her," I scoff. "I was showing the class how to do a takedown. Why? Did she text you?"

"No," he says, mouth a grim line. "But Jacelyn did."

"Okay," I say, trying to sound like that's totally fine. Like it doesn't bother me, because it's not a problem, because I didn't lose my mind and go full monster in public without a good reason. "Can I tell you my side?"

Baxter pauses for moment, eyes cold on mine. "I guess so," he says. "But it's not going to change anything."

His words send a spike of fear through my blood, my heart picking up a staccato beat, my breath catching. But he doesn't know what I'm going to say, doesn't know that I can explain, and I can fix this, and everything is going to be fine, if I just find the perfect words, and go back to being the girl from before, the one he couldn't get enough of.

I take a step forward, but he doesn't open the door any wider.

"I can hear you from there," he says. "You don't need to come inside."

"You didn't have a problem with me being inside before," I try.

"Things were different then," he says, no emotion on his face.

"*That was last week!*" I scream, and he closes the door a little further, the slice of his face that I can see getting smaller, our connection being cut.

"No, wait!" I cry, holding my hands out. "I'm sorry, I'm so sorry. Just, please, listen."

The door doesn't close any more, but he doesn't say anything, his expression not changing.

"Please," I try one more time. "Please, can I come inside?"

If I can see him, if he can see me, if I can be fully in front of him and show him all my beauty and all my pain at the same time, maybe it can go back, maybe it can be like it was.

"It's raining!" I plead, as a gust hits me from the side, soaking me to the skin.

"Say what you have to say," Baxter tells me.

"*Please!*" I beg, crying now, hot tears mixing on my face with cold rain.

"I don't feel safe right now," he says, eyes on mine, chilly and unresponsive, cut off.

"You don't feel *safe*?" I repeat, incredulous.

He doesn't respond, just stares at me.

"I messed up, okay?" I admit. "Things haven't been the same lately between us, and you've been distant, and I've been trying to fix it, but I didn't know how. And when I saw you talking to January at Cody's party I didn't like it—"

"That's ridiculous," he says.

"It's *not*—" I take a deep breath, let my anger simmer for a moment, try to show him that I can be calm, that I can be rational. "I'm trying to tell you how I feel."

"How you feel is ridiculous," he repeats.

I take a step to the side as the wind pushes me, trying to keep my balance. "That's not fair."

"Fair?" Baxter asks. "What's fair to January, who just had an older, much bigger girl lose her mind and go apeshit on her for no good reason?"

Apeshit. That's what I am to him, a huge, crazy simian with no logic that attacks smaller, prettier girls.

"That's not true," I come back, shaking my head. "I'm trying to explain—"

"There's nothing to explain, Shelby," he says, practically sneering my name. "You're a crazy person. I should've known, it was right there in front of me."

"What do you mean?" I ask, trying to encourage conversation, at least keep him talking so that door won't shut, won't cut me off from him and any chance I have of saving this.

"How did we meet in the first place?" Baxter asks, holding up his phone. "I commented on a video of you running down your boyfriend at school."

"HE HIT ME!" I scream, anger flushing my face. "You said so yourself—men shouldn't hit women, there are no extenuating circumstances," I say, quoting his comment on the video.

"Yeah, well, I guess I didn't know you then," he says.

The words hit hard, pushing me like the wind, colder than the rain.

"You—*what*?" I ask. "You . . . do you think I *deserved* it?"

Baxter actually rolls his eyes. "Don't make it like that."

"Like what?" I ask, stepping forward. "Like my boyfriend broke my nose, and that's somehow my fault?"

"This is pointless," Baxter says, edging the door nearer to closed. "I'm not debating with you about Jayden, or January, or anything. This conversation is over. We're done."

"Wait, no!" I yell, hurtling forward, jamming my foot in the opening, ignoring the pain as he tries to shut it.

"Shelby, Jesus Christ!" he yells. "What the fuck is wrong with you?"

There it is again, something is wrong with me. Something dark, buried deep. Something that comes out in fists and fucks, yelling and fighting, being too much, too hard, too fast.

Being me.

Something is wrong with being me.

Words didn't work, so I just stare, begging with my eyes, trying to maintain some form of contact with him. He stares back, finally shaking his head.

"You're just like my exes, you know that?" he says. "Every time I think I've found a girl who can meet me at my level, I get to know her and—"

"Fuck you," I snarl, the words coming out before I can stop them.

"So now you're swearing at me?" he asks, apparently ignoring the fact that he's been swearing at me, too. "That's considered assault, Shelby. Now get out of here, or I'll call the cops."

He waves his phone at me, the phone that he texted me from, telling me how amazing I was. The phone that my voice came through for hours and hours, conversations that went on into the night. The phone he's going to use to call the cops, so they can haul his crazy ex-girlfriend away, the one who can't make it to his level.

I pull my foot out of the door, and it shuts the rest of the way, my last glimpse of his blue eyes, the shock of hair falling over his forehead. I turn around and walk to my car, limping a little, my toes bruised. I fall into the driver's seat, water dripping from my hands as I start the car. I'm driving for about a mile before I realize my lights aren't on, an oncoming driver blaring their horn at me, flashing their headlights.

I flick them on, glance over when my phone goes off. Mal is calling, probably wants to tell me the same things Baxter did, that I'm a crazy person, that I lost my mind and went gonzo on January and no one should ever talk to me again or be my friend because I am a piece of shit that exists on a lower plane of existence than everyone else.

I trudge inside when I get home, leaving wet prints on the living room carpet, something Taylor will yell at me for later. I flop onto my bed, pull up Baxter's number, and try to call one more time, because maybe if he's calmed down now, I can try again. It rings once and goes straight to voicemail. I shoot him a text—**can we talk, please?**—but it sits on my screen, not registering as delivered.

He blocked me.

"No, come on," I say, pulling up Instagram. He's unfollowed me there, and made his account private. I send a friend request, knowing it's pointless.

I see his eyes again, framed by the door, that lock of hair constantly falling over his forehead, no matter how many times he—or I—pushed it back. That can't be the last time I see him. The last words between us can't be about calling the cops.

I can't talk to him online. I can't call. I can't text.

The only thing I can do, is go back over there—which would make me look even crazier.

"Don't do it," I tell myself. Then I think about the perfect words, think about him coming to the door, think about what I'll say, think about the smile I used to be able to cause, what I can do to make it happen again. How I'll be better. How I'll fix this. How I'll change.

It's intoxicating, and I'm putting my wet shoes back on before I know it, just as another call from Mal comes in. I'm hopping on one foot when I turn my head, hoping it's him, hoping he's changed his mind. I lose my balance and fall to the ground, crashing onto my shoulder, my head hitting the floor, bright light shooting across my vision. I shake my head, waiting for it to clear.

"Get your shit together, Black," I growl at myself, sitting up. I tear the one shoe off my foot. "Don't be a fucking crazy person. Don't go back over there."

I should listen to myself, because I'm right about this. But I don't know if I can stop myself, don't know if I can resist the urge to be with him, in front of him, to do whatever it takes to get back to five texts waiting for me and the feeling that I am the most important thing in someone else's life.

That I was a winner.

I need to go to bed, and let everything calm down and try again in the morning. But I know I'll never sleep; I'll just stare at my ceiling fan and run through every possible scenario of what could go right and what could go wrong, my emotions riding the roller coaster of each one.

I'm telling myself I need sleep when I go into Taylor's bathroom and find her Vicodin.

I'm telling myself I'm being responsible when I take the first one.

I'm telling myself I'm making sure I don't do anything stupid when I take the second.

I'm telling myself that I won't have to think about it anymore when I take the third.

I'm telling myself that Baxter will be sorry with the fourth.

I'm telling myself that it'll be over soon with the fifth, sixth, and seventh.

And after the rest of the bottle, I'm not telling anyone anything.

CHAPTER THIRTY-TWO

Fallon

There is a darkness, a crack of light, and a shadow passes through.

"Mom?" I ask, but it doesn't come out right. It's not a word, just a grating sound, an animal in pain.

"Fallon? Are you awake?" a woman asks, but it's not Mom.

I make another noise, and the light comes on. I'm in a hospital room, there's something up my nose. IV lines snake from my arm, and my eyelids are like stones.

"Mom?" I ask again, hoping.

The woman comes closer, a nurse, wearing Snoopy scrubs and a name tag that identifies her as Sharon.

"Fallon," she says again, calmly and slowly. "You're in the emergency room, you were in a bad car accident. Your leg is broken. You're going into surgery soon."

I let the stones fall, let my eyes close, try to go back to the darkness.

Because I remember now. I remember Mal calling and the DM to *@Not-Your-Moms-Sex-Ed*. I remember the car behind me and screaming at Jobie.

"You were lucky. Your friend had already called nine-one-one . . . you thought you were being chased?" Sharon looks at me, but I don't elaborate, not willing to say anything until I know more, myself. "Your car flipped and went upside down into a drainage ditch," she goes on. "They were able to pull you out before it went entirely underwater."

Water, rising. Jobie, crying.

"Where's Jobie?" I ask, a question that makes no sense to anyone but me, a question that swells from the haze of my brain, a thought trying to form even though they must have me on some serious pain-killers, because it's so hard to think.

"You had your ID in your wristlet, so we were able to call your parents," Sharon goes on, skipping over my question. "Your mom will be here when you come out of surgery."

This should be a relief, what I had wanted as soon as I was conscious. But dread follows quickly, chasing any comfort with the dull, throbbing certainty, that everything has changed and nothing will ever be the same again.

"Mom?" I swim up from the darkness again, the stones falling from my eyes to let in the light. This time she's here, sitting next to my bed, her eyes red and swollen, tears running down her cheeks, a shredded tissue in her hands.

"Fallon," she says. "Can you hear me?"

I nod, tears rising instantly, the only words that matter falling from my lips the second I see her face.

"I'm sorry," I say, and I can't stop saying it. "I'm sorry, I'm sorry, I'm sorry." It pushes through my swollen throat, barely escapes my lips as a sob, evolves into a blurred series of sounds as she comes to me, wrapping her arms around me. My air tube comes out of my nose, slick with snot as I cry, my tears soaking into her hair.

She finally pulls back, fixes my air tube, wipes my face, holds my chin.

"Fallon, we need to talk."

I nod viciously. This is what I want, is to talk. To find the right words to make everything better.

"You already know?" I ask, saving her the explanation. "Somebody posted it to Facebook, didn't they?"

"Yes," Mom says. "A lot of people are very upset right now."

But I don't care about a lot of people, I only care about the people I hurt the most, the ones who trusted me and believed I was being responsible, doing the right thing.

"Farrah told me some," she says, then goes quiet.

In her silence I see anger, I see disappointment, I see all the things that I've been trying to avoid for my whole life by always stepping up, always being good, always achieving and climbing, pushing higher . . . until I fell.

"Mom, I'm sure people are saying shameful, dirty things, but it wasn't like that. I swear. I was trying to—"

"Stop," Mom says, holding one hand up in the air. "Just please, stop."

I fall silent, watching her.

"Farrah and your dad are at home," she says. "We were all here together last night, but—"

"Last night?" I ask. "How long have I been out?"

"A while, honey," Mom says patiently. "They had to put pins in your leg. It was a long surgery, and I told your dad and Farrah to go home, get some sleep."

"What time is it?" I ask, instinctively reaching for my phone, then realizing it's probably at the bottom of the ditch, along with my car.

"It's a little after noon," Mom says. My heart sinks. I'm sure approximately zero people said they should wait until I'm conscious and able to defend myself before cranking the handle on the gossip mill.

"What's going to happen?" I ask, a thousand scenarios spinning into a million constellations, each meeting I've conducted a crime, every message I've answered a felony.

"Fallon," Mom says, her voice calm and low. "You need to listen to me."

She takes a deep breath and there is fear in her eyes, and if my mom is scared then something has gone horribly, horribly wrong. I am still, dread blooming.

"Honey." She takes my hand, and another breath, my own stopping in my chest.

"Jobie is dead."

CHAPTER THIRTY-THREE

Shelby

"Dad?"

My brain is broken, an animal with no legs rolling around inside my head.

"Dad?" I ask again, but it's a scratch in my throat, a word with no meaning.

"Shelby?"

I force my eyes open and see Taylor.

"You've got to be fucking kidding me," I say, and that makes it all the way out.

"Can we not do that right now?" she asks, and I'm surprised to see that her eyes are red. She's not crying, but she was at one point, which sets me back.

"Sorry," I mutter, a word that I don't know I've ever said to her before.

"You're in the ER. Your dad is talking to someone from mental health—"

"I want Kathy—" I say immediately, the hard *k* of her name catching, making me cough, which feels like lightning slicing through the thin tissues of my throat. I gag and there's blood in my mouth, something gritty in my teeth. I spit into my hand, where black specks swim in red-tinged bile.

"They pumped your stomach," Taylor says. "Then they dumped charcoal in there to soak up any—" She stops, takes a breath. "Any of my Vicodin they didn't get."

There's guilt in her voice, which makes no sense, but I'm not interested in making Taylor feel better right now, because I remember why I'm here.

"I need my phone," I say.

"No," Dad says from the doorway. "Not yet. We've got to talk first."

My eyes flick to his, and whatever shame Taylor feels, it is nothing compared to mine, as my bloody trachea contracts, tears swelling in my eyes.

"I'm sorry," I say, the sides of my mouth slipping downward, face collapsing. Dad comes to the bed, wraps his arms around me, and I fall forward, leaning into him, smelling aftershave and the faint aroma of the gym that perpetually hangs around both of us. And I want this to fix everything, want it to be the right ending, the one where a hug from my dad is all it takes to heal me.

But it's not, because the first thing I say when I pull away is, "Where's Baxter?"

"It doesn't matter," Dad says firmly. "You're never talking to him again."

Which is exactly what I don't want to hear, because it's my worst fear, and the panic I'd been trying to escape tears upward, ripping a new path in my throat.

"I have to see him," I say. "I need to tell him—"

"Shelby," Taylor says, coming to the side of the bed. "There are more important things we need to cover first."

But there can't be, because Baxter is what makes me happy, and Baxter is the most important thing. Nothing else has my attention, and nothing else matters.

"I want my phone," I say, my chin jutting out.

Dad and Taylor share a look, a communication I can't follow.

"Shelby," Dad says, taking my hand. "Your friend Jobie is dead."

"What?" I ask, then repeat it. "What?" Because there is no other response to those words in that order, something that makes no sense and shouldn't be said.

"And Fallon was in a bad accident," Taylor goes on, pressing me back down onto the bed when I try to sit up. "She's okay, she's here in the hospital, actually."

"What?" I ask again, because I have no bearings in this world where Jobie is dead and Fallon and I are both in the hospital and everything is fucked.

"Where's Mal? Where's Rory?" I ask, suddenly needing to know that everyone I care about is okay, and that not all is lost.

"I'm sure they're fine," Dad says. "But—"

"You tried to kill yourself, Shelby," Taylor says, cutting right to it.

"No, I didn't," I spit at her. "I just wanted to . . ."

I stop, and they're both quiet, watching me.

"Baby girl," Dad says. "What?"

"I just wanted to not feel this way anymore," I say, face crumpling again, a cry that starts deep in my gut crawling forward, escaping through my teeth as my mouth opens, a deep swell of pain that seeps from every dark corner inside me. Corners filled with failure and fear, with not being enough and being way too much at the same time.

"I can't," I say, my eyes searching for Dad's, not knowing what I mean, just knowing that it's true.

“I can’t,” I say again, and he pulls me into him, his strength the only thing holding me together.

“It’s okay, baby girl, it’s okay,” he says, rocking me.

“I want to go home,” I cry into his neck.

Taylor’s hand is on my shoulder, her voice weirdly calm. “They want to keep you for seventy-two hours. It’s what they do when—”

“*I want to go home*,” I say again, the words tasting like blood and charcoal.

But even when I get there, I know nothing will ever be the same again.

CHAPTER THIRTY-FOUR

Fallon

A lot of people are pissed at me, and for once in my life, I don't care.

Mom hasn't let me have my phone back, partly to protect me and partly because my lawyer said it might have to be turned over to law enforcement. The phrase *my lawyer* is a new one to me, and I don't particularly care for it, or how often I've had to use it in the past twenty-four hours.

"I can Sharpie some tears onto your cheeks, if you want," Farrah says. "That means you killed somebody. Could keep you safe in prison. Don't wash your face, though. Your skin care routine is about to take a serious dive."

"You are not helping," I say, glaring at her as she whips out another colored Sharpie and continues to decorate my full leg cast.

"I'm doing the only thing I know how," she says quietly, and colors in the mane of a unicorn, which also appears to be a Pegasus.

"Do you know anything more about—"

"No," I say flatly, interrupting her. Because that's the answer, no matter what her question was. I told the cops everything about SHAFT Class, *@KoIKreameIKrispies*, the state park, how I thought someone was chasing me after I left the rec center, about Jobie and Shelby and January . . . but not Mal. And not Amara.

But I didn't have to; they already knew.

Amara's father is very, very angry.

"Fallon?" Mom says, appearing in the living room doorway. "You have a visitor."

This is a surprise. Not only has Mom turned away everyone that tried to come and see me—Mal, January, Jacelyn, and Bethany, even Ms. Lauren. The only people I've seen in the past three days are my family and my lawyer. But the person who follows her into the room is neither one of those—it's Jobie's mom. Her face is a swollen mess, her eyes red-rimmed, her voice hoarse when she says my name.

I thought I didn't have any more tears inside of me, that all the pain and fear of the past two days had leaked out. But I'm learning that there's always more, and it hurts just as much every time.

"Come on, Farrah," Mom says. "Let's leave them alone."

My sister puts one last touch on the unicorn—adding a third eye so that it's now a unicorn-Pegasus-cyclops—and gets up to leave, giving my hand a squeeze before she goes. Jobie's mom takes her place on the footstool beside the couch, the pain in her eyes matching mine.

"Are you hurting?" she asks, and all I can do is nod, but it has nothing to do with my leg, or the bruises on my face, or the splint on my wrist.

"Mom didn't tell me . . . wouldn't tell me," I try, searching for words to explain how my best friend could be dead, and I don't know how or why. Don't know the details about a girl whose outfits were planned out for the rest of the week, and I always knew what she would be wearing, and what body spray she'd paired with it.

Except, that hadn't been true lately.

"Mom said you found her—" I try again.

"She was in the basement," Jobie's mom says. "I had a no-show for the townhouse in the morning, went straight there from Jason's. When I got home she wasn't in her room, but her car was in the garage. I went through the whole house, calling for her, but she wasn't there, and I went back up to her room—"

I imagine her, yelling Jobie's name, the call becoming higher, more panicked, going back to Jobie's room because maybe this time, she'd be there.

"But she wasn't," her mom goes on. "And there's no reason for her to be down in the basement, but it was the only place I hadn't looked, and—"

She stops, takes a breath, her body failing her as her mind won't stop wondering what happened to her daughter.

"We don't know what happened," her mom says. "We think . . . it's so stupid, Fallon. It's so goddamn stupid . . ."

She pulls Jobie's phone out of her pocket, hands it to me.

"She was filming herself," she goes on. "I guess there's this online challenge, something like, how long can you hang upside down? She got on the trapeze, and she must have lost consciousness, or fallen, or . . . I don't know. Her . . . her neck was—"

Jobie's mom stops talking, her words choked off.

"But we don't really know," she says again. "The coroner is doing an—"

Her face contorts; she can't say it.

"An autopsy?" I ask, and she nods, tears slipping out from under her lids.

She opens her eyes again, irises bright blue against inflamed red. "Her battery was dead by the time I found her. I charged it, but I don't know her passcode. I thought you might, I thought . . ."

"I know it," I say carefully, squeezing Jobie's phone. "But I don't know if you should—"

"I don't want to watch it," she says quickly. "I don't think I could. I just, I wanted . . . I called her that night, and I left a voicemail. I felt bad about not being home, and I just wanted to touch base. I . . . I told her how much I loved her, and that I felt like things were going so well in my life now, but I wanted her to know that she's always the most important thing, the one thing—"

She stops again, voice catching.

"I need to know if she heard it."

"Okay," I say, my own chest tight. "I can look."

"Not now," she says, hand grabbing mine. "I'm going home. You don't have to do this right now, it's whenever you're ready. I know it's a lot, I know it's a huge thing to put on you, but I—"

"I can do it," I say. What I don't tell her is that the last thing I said to my best friend before she died was to tell her she was a fucking idiot. That she called me crying, and I screamed at her, that I never asked what was wrong. That I hadn't asked what was wrong in a very long time, even though I knew something was. I was worried about someone else, a stranger, not my best friend, right in front of me. Someone asked me for help, and I gave it, but it was the wrong person.

It wasn't Jobie. And now she's dead.

"I can do it," I say again, before she leaves. But it's a long time before I can, a long time while the sun moves across the living room floor, shadows changing places, heat leaving the room, like it's gone from Jobie's body, in a morgue somewhere, on a table in a room with knives and bone saws.

I swipe my finger across her phone, but it's not our prom picture

I see, the background that both of us put on our phones last year. It's Jobie, but . . . not. A perfected version of my friend stares back at me, cheekbones higher, eyes wider, lips fuller. She is beautiful and frightening at the same time, a skewed version of a person I know, fantasy meeting reality and daring each to deny the other.

Confused, I type in her passcode and go to her voicemails. One from her mom is there, unplayed. I tap on it, listen, hear the love in her voice, the happiness, the relief that finally, maybe, the two of them were going to be okay. I close it out, pick up my own phone, text Jobie's mom.

She listened to it.

She heard you.

It's a lie, but I'm getting pretty good at those.

My fingers shake, hovering over Jobie's phone, very aware that I am trespassing, but also that I have committed worse sins. I tap on her photos, and see the last one is a video that's nearly an hour long—the time it took for her battery to drain. The preview thumbnail is a close-up of Jobie's face as she set up the camera, but there's something off about it, something as wrong as the perfected wallpaper version of herself. I hesitate, a well of unease opening in my gut as I click on the video.

It opens with Jobie crouching in front of the phone, making sure it's set up. Her eyes are swollen and red, the whites bloodshot from crying.

"Okay," she says under her breath, words meant only for herself, a low mumble that slides each word into the next. "Back to doing this, just this, this and nothing else."

She backs away from the camera, and the trapeze comes into view, the chains shortened so that the bar is up near the rafters. There's a pause while Jobie takes a second, readies herself, assumes a pose, cocking her hip and checking her hair, adjusting her shoulders and lifting her chin until she likes the angle. I've seen it a thousand times, stood bored to death, holding her phone while she prepared herself to do the next great thing, hoping that people would care.

"I guess it's my turn!" she says brightly, her smile awkward and forced, her eyes flat, not matching her tone. "Let's see how long I can hang upside down!"

Jobie jumps and grabs the trapeze, hooking her ankles first and then pulling forward until the crooks of her knees are on the bar. Then she slowly lets go, easing herself downward. Her hair is loose, falling toward the concrete floor, tips swaying with the momentum, arms extended downward, fingers still at least two feet from the ground.

Her cheeks go red after a few minutes and she twitches her legs, readjusting them, the slick fabric of her tights making it hard for her to hang on with her knees. Jobie was never physically strong, and her pain tolerance was so low that she went to bed for an entire weekend after tearing off a particularly nasty hangnail in seventh grade.

"I'm okay," Jobie says to herself, closing her eyes.

She didn't silence her phone, and when the message notification goes off her eyes pop open, gaze going to the screen, bloodshot eyes wide, trying to read it upside down. Her eyes focus, and when recognition hits, she twists, trying to get free of the trapeze, trying to get to the phone, stressed muscles failing her.

It's not the height of the fall; it's the angle of her neck.

Jobie hits the concrete while twisting, eyes still on the phone as her temple connects with the floor, the weight of her body popping vertebrae in her neck.

I hear them crack, a series of snaps. I watch them go, a ripple of bumps rising from the side of her throat, her spine somewhere it should not be.

"Jesus God, no," I say, tears swimming to my eyes, unable to look away as Jobie continues to stare at the phone, one hand reaching. The light in her eyes dies, and soon they begin to dry, losing their sheen. I can't speak, don't have words, watch as her life leaves her, as she dies on camera.

"I'm so sorry, Jobie," I say. My finger slips, advancing the reel, scrolling forward through nearly an hour, until I lift it, toward the end.

"Jobie?" Her mom's voice is soft, faraway, echoing through the house. Footsteps thud above as she moves through the first floor, still calling, her voice fading as she moves upstairs, then comes back down again.

"Jobie!" she says her daughter's name again, higher now, and panicked. The steps sound closer, the voice louder, more clear. The creak of the basement door, and a question, softly asked.

"Jobie?"

The next sound is not soft, and it's not a question. It's a scream, bright and piercing, as Jobie's mom runs onto the screen, grabbing her body, Jobie's neck rocking unnaturally to one side, rolling wildly, as her mom keeps screaming. She calls 911. She rocks her, she cries, but I can see in her face that she knows. The battery dies before the medics show up, the screen suddenly going black as her mom says, "I'm here, baby. I wasn't here, but now I am. I'm here."

I back out, tears streaming, heart broken, but with a lingering question. I tap on Jobie's messages, looking to see what text had come in that made her panic.

There's a text from January, asking if they can talk, one from Bethany asking what the hell is going on, and one from Mal telling her to call ASAP, all of them unread. At the top, is a text from someone called Cute Amy, with hearts on either side of their name.

The message says **thought you'd want something to remember me by.**

There's a video attached. I tap it.

I watched my best friend cry when her parents got a divorce.

I watched my best friend cry when she failed an algebra exam.

I watched my best friend cry when she got a speeding ticket.

Now I watch my best friend cry as she is gang-raped.

CHAPTER THIRTY-FIVE

Shelby

"Where do you want to start?" Kathy asks.

It's such a ridiculous question, all I can do is sputter, spit dripping off my lower lip. I wipe it away with a tissue, something I carry with me constantly now.

"Well, Dad finally stopped sleeping on my floor—there's that," I say.

"Your dad loves you very much," Kathy says, with a smile.

"Yeah, that's one person, at least," I say, trying for my own. It fails, twisting into a grimace. It's quiet for a minute, just the sound of my tears dripping off my cheeks, hitting the backs of my hands.

"What the fuck is wrong with me?" I ask, raising my eyes to Kathy's. "I can't stop crying."

"You have a lot to cry about," Kathy says easily.

But I shake my head, sending tears flying. "This isn't right, this isn't how I behave, this isn't normal, this . . ." I raise one finger, pointing it back at myself, accusing. "This is not me."

I hang my head again, shame creeping back in.

"Shelby, it's perfectly normal to cry when so much has—"

"*It's weak!*" I scream, throwing one of the pillows off the couch, the words tearing at my swollen throat. "I'm Shelby fucking Black!"

My chest heaves, my finger returns to point at myself, at the swollen eyes, the falling tears, the mouth already threatening to turn upside down again, to sob.

"This isn't me."

"Shelby Black is a human, correct?" Kathy asks, but I only glare at her, swiping at tears. "Shelby is a human, and humans have emotions, and it's normal for you to feel all of them. You don't have to be ashamed."

"But I am," I say, eyes darting to the side, to the pillow I threw. "Sorry," I say, looking back to Kathy.

"I have a lot of pillows," she says, shrugging.

It's quiet again for a moment, all of my words dead inside my chest, the sad ones, the angry ones, the begging ones, the pleading ones that I poured onto Baxter in the rain—and it didn't matter.

"Do you want to talk about your friend?" Kathy finally asks.

"Jobie?" I look up, shake my head. "No. We weren't close. I'm not going to cry and make TikToks and talk about how much I'll miss her, like everybody else who suddenly wants to say how close they were, for the clicks."

#ForJobie had trended for a week, and she'd suddenly gained the tens of thousands of followers she'd always hoped for, as they dove into her reels and posts, telling her how beautiful she was, how loved she was, how tragic it all was. *#HalfmastForJobie* had also trended, pictures of flags only half raised soon overridden by dick pics, the worst parts of the internet crawling out to take their stabs at a dead girl.

"I read that the men who harmed her have been taken into custody, and that many of their other victims have come forward," Kathy says. "Is there some comfort in that?"

"No," I growl, twisting the tissue until it tears, fibers flying up into the air.

"Can we talk about the Vicodin?"

I sigh, shift my eyes to the ceiling. "I didn't try to kill myself."

"Shelby," Kathy says my name.

Says it again. Waits until I look at her.

"Yes, you did."

"That's—"

"Stupid?" Kathy finishes for me, the word I've said the most in this office.

"What do you want me to say?" I screech. "That I'd rather be dead than be what I am right now?"

"What are you?" Kathy asks.

"A f-f-f—" It stutters, not wanting to get out. "A fucking loser," I finally spit. "I lost a fight, and I lost my boyfriend, and then I lost *that* fight, and then I lost another boyfriend, and then I lost . . ." I stop to breathe, pull in air, hot and tight in my lungs. "I lost my goddamn mind."

"And that's okay," Kathy says, closer now, sitting next to me on the couch, her hand resting on my wrist.

"It's not," I hiss back. "I thought Baxter was cheating on me, but he wasn't. January texted me, showed me some screen caps, her messages with this guy from Brookwood she's been seeing. And she *was* messaging Baxter, but she sent me those screen caps, too, and it was just art school stuff and it was perfectly innocent, but I made up this whole thing in my head because I'm ridiculous just like Baxter says, I'm crazy and I'm—"

"You're not crazy," Kathy says. "Have you ever heard of hypervigilance?"

"No," I say, wiping my nose.

"It's a symptom of PTSD—"

"Stop with that shit," I say. "I don't have trauma. I'm not fucking traumatized."

"Do you remember what I said about little-*t* traumas?" she asks.

"Yeah," I say grudgingly. "You also said Baxter was a narcissist and emotionally abusing me, but I'm the one who showed up on his doorstep and tried to force my way into—"

"We'll get back to that," she says smoothly. "Little-*t* traumas are still very painful, like going through a breakup, your pet dying, even being in a car crash. Repetitive stress, and living in a high-stress environment, suffering through little-*t* traumas, can accumulate into something called complex PTSD."

"Sounds awful," I say. "Also like something I don't have."

"It is awful," Kathy says. "And if you don't mind, I'd like to walk you through some things without interruption."

She's quiet again, and I raise my eyes to hers.

"Yeah, okay."

"You're a girl who grew up winning," she begins. "You've always known what to do, always had the upper hand. I'm guessing you'd never been through a breakup where you weren't the one doing the dumping, am I right?"

"Damn straight," I say, sucking in some snot.

"Suddenly, that changed," she says. "You lost a fight."

I flinch but don't interrupt her.

"Your boyfriend, someone you trusted, cheated on you."

I close my eyes, see Jayden's phone light up.

"Then he hit you."

My hand goes to my lip, the tiny scar there where my teeth split the skin.

"You'd always been able to brush off your stepmother's criticism, but suddenly it became louder, harder to ignore, because you were starting to believe it was true."

A hand goes to my earlobe, twisting it as I hear Taylor's words. *Too much. Too hard. Too fast. Too Shelby.*

"Then you met Baxter, and he told you everything you needed to hear. You were perfect. You were beautiful. You were exceptional. You were different. It felt good. Finally, something felt good."

My hand goes to my heart, which skipped a beat at his name.

"He gave you all your confidence back, built you up, set you on a pedestal. Then he started chipping away at it, taking away small things, making criticisms, forcing you to work to get it back, get back that feeling that only *he* could give you."

"Yeah," I say, a croak. "But I still went flipping apeshit—"

"Hypervigilance," Kathy goes on, "is a symptom of PTSD and C-PTSD where a person is in a constant state of high alert, always looking for dangers, always trying to protect themselves. Your brain wants to keep you safe, Shelby. Your lifestyle has taught you to always be on guard. Jayden taught you that you can't trust. Baxter taught you that the only good thing you had was him. And so, when there was the barest evidence of a threat to your happiness, you saw it as real, and you acted, to protect yourself from being hurt again."

I suck in a breath. Let it out. Pull in another. This one comes out more easily, the knot of muscles in my gut loosening enough for me to try again, take a breath, let this one go deeper.

"So, I'm not crazy?"

"I don't use that word, and neither should you," Kathy says. "But no, if that's what you need to hear—you're not crazy. You're a person who has suffered, and your suffering has caused damage, and you have reacted to that damage."

I test air again, let it go in, actually feeling it this time, slipping past tears and the swollen tissues of my throat.

"Everyone is the way they are for a reason," Kathy goes on, then falls silent, waiting for me to talk.

My hand slips inside my hoodie, clasping on to my phone when it vibrates. I know it's not Baxter; he'd maintained a strict no-contact policy even after I'd come home from the hospital. But it might be Mal, checking in on me. Or it might be Rory, asking if we're still on to spar tonight. Or it might be my agent, letting me know that the first payment from Rebel came in.

"Everyone is the way they are for a reason," I repeat, wiping my nose again. "What if I want to be something else?"

"Then we do the work," Kathy says, squeezing my wrist. "We do the work, and we build you back up, not basing your worth on a boy, or a relationship, or the outcome of a fight, or your social media, or what people say or think about you. We build you up and make you strong, using your own words and your own beliefs about yourself. We build you up, using things that no one can ever take away from you again."

I look down at my hands, at the busted knuckles and the calluses, at the tear streaks and the indent on my wrist where the hospital bracelet was too tight.

"Okay," I say. "Let's fucking go."

CHAPTER THIRTY-SIX

Fallon

One Year Later

Christmas in a town where people haven't forgiven you isn't fun.

Getting out of Presnick for college is, and will continue to be, the best thing I ever did. Not because Presnick lacks opportunity, or it's close-minded, or it's as white as sliced bread, but because most people here won't look me in the eye anymore. It doesn't matter that the judge dismissed the case against me and the other founders of SHAFT Class. It doesn't matter that the cops were never able to find who ran me off the road, or that *@Ko/Kreame/Krispies* disappeared, maybe never existing in the first place. It doesn't matter that I never breathed a word to anyone about a single DM that came in to the *@Not-Your-Moms-Sex-Ed* account. I know a lot of things about a lot of people that they wish they'd never shared, and seeing me seems to open up a well of shame in the hearts and minds of the good people of Presnick.

That's not on me, and I've become comfortable with walking into the coffee shop, grabbing gas, or popping into the café and everything going silent. A year ago, this wouldn't have been possible. A year ago, I would've broken out in hives at the thought that I'd upset everyone. Then, all the shit that has ever been shat hit the biggest fan in the world, and that kind of put everything in perspective.

The one place I haven't gone back to is the rec center.

I'm sitting here now, running the heater in my car, and listening to the voicemail from Ms. Lauren again.

Hey, Fallon . . . it's Lauren, from the rec center. I heard you were home for the holiday break and, uh . . . well, there's something I thought you should see. I think Mal and Shelby should, too, if you're still in contact with them. Just give me a call back, or text me, okay?

I had called her back, and she'd told me to meet her in the parking lot. Mal and Shelby pull in at the same time, Mal glancing around as she gets out, beanie pulled down to her eyebrows. As she'd predicted, she'd taken the brunt of the public pushback, the more conservative people in town associating her sexuality with bad behavior, and—as she'd known it would—the word *groomer* was tossed around. Even with Rory offering to bash the skull in of every person who said it, Mal's family had decided to take her out of school, and she'd finished her classes online, not showing up to graduation.

"Hey," I say, waving at her as I get out of my car.

"Hey," she says back. "How's college? Still a virgin?"

"Why is that the follow-up question?" I ask, stepping in for a hug.

"I'm still *not* a virgin," Shelby announces, getting out of her car. "That shit doesn't just grow back, you know."

Shelby encircles both of us with her arms, giving a solid squeeze.

"Especially not with a new man in the mix," Mal says, stepping back from both of us.

"Oh, really?" I ask, raising an eyebrow at Shelby.

"Yeah, this guy I met a while back. Jackson," she says, actually blushing a little.

"Hey, girls!" Ms. Lauren walks out of the rec center, pulling her coat around her, tying the belt as the wind tries to snatch it away. "I guess I should say *women*," she corrects herself as she joins us. "You're all adults."

"Full-ass adults," Shelby agrees.

"Yeah, I saw the Rebel ad," Mal says. "Full ass is right."

"Those are called compression shorts," Shelby shoots back. "The rest is up to your imagination."

"What did you need?" I ask, turning to Lauren before the conversation goes too far.

"Well." She smiles, some new lines crinkling around her eyes. "It's a lot easier if I just show you. Follow me?"

She motions around the corner of the rec center, and the three of us exchange glances. I shrug and follow Lauren, shooting a dirty look back at Mal when she asks, "Is this another shot at being murder sisters?"

"I'll protect you," Shelby says. "Just get behind me."

"Nice view," Mal says, and I hear Shelby shove her.

"Guys," I hiss, turning back to them. "Could you not be so—"

"Holy shit the bed," Mal says, her eyes popping.

Shelby for once, has no words, her mouth hanging open.

"What?" I ask, spinning around to where Ms. Lauren stands next to the bay window, the one where we'd placed all of our ceramic clown planters almost a year ago. I'd forgotten about them, assumed Jobie had, too, that whatever we'd planted had died, and someone had tossed the clowns in the dumpster.

Except, that's not what happened.

What we planted took root and grew. Grew while no one paid attention, dust gathering on the deep bay window, in a place few people went, and apparently no one cleaned. Twenty-two ceramic clowns face me, arms to the side, huge smiles on their faces, a thick, single cactus jutting out of the front of each of their pants.

"Talk about a prick," Shelby says, and erupts into laughter.

"Oh my . . . ," Mal says, one gloved hand covering her mouth. "Oh my Lord."

"We didn't know," I say quickly, turning to Lauren. "I swear we didn't—" But I can't quite finish, because I don't actually feel like apologizing, and there's something coming up from my gut, from a place I didn't think I could feel anymore, making a sound I didn't think I still had in me—laughter.

"Jobie knew," I say, realizing it's true, remembering when she told us she could handle the first self-help element of class. How she'd smiled, back when she was still doing that.

"I believe you," Lauren says. "Obviously, once one of our patrons noticed . . ." She sighs and sweeps her arm toward the window. "They have to go, but I thought you might want a picture."

"Damn right," Shelby says, digging in her pocket and handing her phone to Lauren. "Get over here, Fallon."

I come to her side, her arm across my shoulder, heavy with the weight of her strength. Mal scoots under my other arm, resting her head against mine.

"SHAFT Class reunion," Mal says under her breath.

"Fuck 'em all," Shelby says, head high.

But I can't say anything, and in the picture, I'm crying.

ACKNOWLEDGMENTS

A writer's life is a solitary one, but it takes a team to put a book together. This one was no exception. Thanks as always, to both editors who helped me bring this one into proper shape and form, Ben Rosenthal and Erica Sussman. Thanks as well to my agent, John Cusick, who at this point has probably accepted that none of my emails will ever be confined to a single topic or project.

A big thank-you to my friends Amanda, Mel, Debbie, Ashley, Holly, and Morgan, who dutifully tell me I'm funny when I text them a random line I just wrote and really, really need reassurance. To Marlo and Marnie, who have illustrated to me the difference between my "thinking face" and "mad face." It's subtle, so I appreciate their ability to distinguish between the two.

Lastly, greatest thanks, respect, and support to all the educators, librarians, and booksellers operating on the front lines during the current onslaught of book banning. They take the brunt of the charge, and books like this one are available to read because of the personal and professional risks that they take.

Solidarity, my friends.

Mindy